D0938339

The Pickwick Murders

A Dickens of a Crime Mystery Series

By Heather Redmond

A Tale of Two Murders

Grave Expectations

A Christmas Carol Murder

The Pickwick Murders

The Pickwick Murders

Heather Redmond

KENSINGTON
PUBLISHING CORP.

www.kensingtonbooks.com

KENSINGTON BOOKS are published by

Kensington Publishing Corp.
119 West 40th Street
New York, NY 10018

All Kensington titles, imprints, and distributed lines are available at special quantity discounts for bulk purchases for sales promotion, premiums, fund-raising, educational, or institutional use. Special book excerpts or customized printings can also be created to fit specific needs. For details, write or phone the office of the Kensington Special Sales Manager: Attn. Special Sales Department. Kensington Publishing Corp., 119 West 40th Street, New York, NY 10018. Phone: 1-800-221-2647.

Library of Congress Card Catalogue Number: 2021938940

The K logo is a trademark of Kensington Publishing Corp.

ISBN-13: 978-1-4967-3428-0
ISBN-10: 1-4967-3428-9
First Kensington Hardcover Edition: November 2021

ISBN-13: 978-1-4967-3429-7 (ebook)
ISBN-10: 1-4967-3429-7 (ebook)

10 9 8 7 6 5 4 3 2 1

Printed in the United States of America

For Dorothy Grant with great affection

Cast of Characters

*Real historical figures

"And to this day the stone remains, an illegible monument of Mr. Pickwick's greatness, and a lasting trophy to the littleness of his enemies."

—Charles Dickens, *The Pickwick Papers*

"But if I were at my liberty and might choose, I ensure you, Master Secretary, for my little time, I have spied so much honesty to be in him that I had rather beg my bread with him than to be the greatest queen christened."

—Mary Boleyn Carey Stafford, Letter to Thomas Cromwell, 1534

"I've lingered near thee night and day
When thou hast thought me far away;"

—Joanna Baillie, *Fugitive Verses*

Chapter 1

Eatanswill, somewhere in Essex, January 5, 1836

A bugle blared in Charles Dickens's ear, coming from a raggedy band of marchers passing him on the way to the hustings set up in Eatanswill's market square. Yellow-brown cockades pinned to the lapels of old-fashioned tailcoats and ladies' capes demonstrated that these were the followers of the local Brown party, allied to the Whigs. Charles tipped his hat at a particularly pretty daughter of the voters. She went pink and put her hand in front of her mouth, then dashed to her mother's side. Behind her straggled a couple of young boys, beating drums out of time.

To the right, another group marched between a coal distributer and a cloth merchant's place of business, also routed to the hustings. A streaky royal purple banner attached to a bakery's awning flapped in the bitter January wind. The cloth already shone white at the top, where a light rain had loosened the dye. This must be the Purples, allied to the Tories.

He surveyed the scene from a two-foot rock embedded next to a public house door. It gave him enough height to see across the Election Day crowd. Would the vote be for Sir Augustus Smirke, the favorite son of the Purples, or go to Vernon Cecil, the darling of the Browns? One or the other would become a member of Parliament for the first time.

Charles, parliamentary reporter for the liberal *Morning Chronicle* newspaper, hoped Cecil would carry the day. With any luck, a clear majority would offer its voice and the local sheriff could call the election instead of having to schedule a poll some few days in the future, in which case Charles would not be able to go back to London that night. He'd have to write his story and send it on the express mail coach back to the *Chronicle* offices in London.

Resounding "huzzahs" blazed into the air as another phalanx of men appeared between the buildings. He recognized William Whitaker Maitland, the new High Sheriff of Essex, leading the parliamentary candidates, who were followed by their most prominent supporters. Sir Augustus towered over Sheriff Maitland, a man well above average height, with a majestic belly to match. Mr. Cecil did not have the height, though the profusion of gray-streaked reddish curls poofing out from underneath his top hat gave him at least one measure of distinction. Charles knew him to be the son of an important local landowner, but felt unease for his prospects as age and experience were not on the Brown candidate's side.

Shouts came from the left, displaying real alarm this time, instead of pride. A small group of horsemen galloped into the square, coattails fanned out behind them. The first man had a shotgun across his arm and the other half dozen held rakes or hoes as if they were jousters of old, ready to go head to head in battle with other knights. In their work-worn attire, they looked like they belonged to the logging or hunting trades in Epping Forest, rather than professions here in town.

The horsemen pressed forward through the crowd of locals.

People jumped back or fell in their wake, moving like the wind-blown brown and purple banners that hung on posts jutting from some of the houses. A horse and rider knocked over a boy. The boy clutched at his foot and screamed. A man hurried to his side, grabbed him, and hoisted him into the air, settling him on his shoulders.

While Charles had been watching the intruders, the high sheriff and candidates climbed onto the hustings. The tempo-rary stage had bunting in the parties' colors decorating the wooden railing. A lectern, probably borrowed from St. Mary's, a venerable medieval church on the edge of the square, was set up for speeches.

Sheriff Maitland pointed his finger at the gunman as he thun-dered up to the very edge of the hustings. "I see you, Wilfred Poor. You and your men are welcome to vote, but not until you hand over that shotgun."

Wilfred Poor lifted the gun and for a moment Charles stiff-ened, afraid he would fire at the high sheriff. Instead, Poor fired into the air. The crowd ducked instinctively, including Charles. Initially, pandemonium reigned. But just as quickly as the crowd reacted with screams, they subsided, until the only nearby sound was a dog barking in one of the houses near the church.

Poor lowered the muzzle of his gun until it was pointing into the belly of that giant, Sir Augustus. "Where is my Amy, my daughter?" he screamed.

Sir Augustus's lips curled, but he said nothing. A trio of his men pushed forward, as if to provoke a reaction, but Sir Au-gustus's long arms spread out, holding them back.

Poor repeated his anguished query, the tendons of his neck in high relief.

"What's wrong, Wilfred?" Sir Augustus mocked. "Can't keep control of your own womenfolk?"

One of the horsemen chuckled and glanced at the man next

to him, his expression changing at the anger in his neighbor's face.

"You aren't much of a man," Sir Augustus said in a teasing lilt.

"Come now, Sir Augustus," one of the horsemen said in a rough country drawl. "Amy's been missing these past three days."

"No one's forgotten she's your maid," added another.

The shotgun, which Charles had not taken his glance from, shook in Poor's hand. The horseman closest to the upset father patted Poor's arm.

"We know you've hidden her away," another horseman said to Sir Augustus. "Just give her back and we can get about this business of the election."

"Speech," called a brave soul in the crowd.

The horseman closest to the speaker threw his hoe in that direction. A man fell. Charles craned his neck, looking for blood spill. No one screamed this time. The high sheriff called for his men, a few local constables hovering around the edges of the bunting, to arrest the rider, but he wheeled his horse around and galloped off before they gathered their wits. One of the constables broke away for crowd control, pushing a couple of women who were attempting to climb the hustings to escape the horsemen. Another knelt next to the fallen man. The last constable raced out of the square in pursuit of the villain on the horse.

Charles whipped his head around when he heard the sheriff call out an order. Charles's brand-new hat caught in a gust, which sent it flying past the window of the public house and down the shadowy street. He leapt off the rock to chase the expensive felted beaver cut in the Regent style. He loathed having to replace it so soon, and in a crowd like this, some light-fingered thief would grab it if he took his eyes off it for even a moment.

He reached out, his fingers just touching the brim before the hat flew again. Stumbling, he put on a burst of speed in front of the open door of a tobacconist and snatched his hat before it tumbled off the pavement and into the dirt road in front of the square.

He glanced up, grinning with his success, and saw a young man, hat lowered over his brows. The lean form and rather worn clothing caught Charles's eye with a note of familiarity. The youth jerked. He straightened, then vanished around the side of the tobacconist's shop, black curls fluttering around his neck.

Charles's thoughts flew back to last summer, and a vegetable plot not far from London's Eaton Square. Curls like that had spilled out from a straw hat worn by the young farmer, Prince Moss, so enamored of the cold, beautiful, and amoral Evelina Jaggers, the foster daughter of Charles's deceased neighbor.

Charles followed the pavement to an alley passing behind the shop. He stepped in, figuring this was a small town and violent criminals were unlikely to be lurking in alleyways in daylight. The young man had vanished.

Charles surveyed the collection of barrels and rubbish. He heard the crackling of a fire, probably coming from the smithy that backed up against the alley. A couple of warehouses boxed in the smithy. The youth could have gone anywhere.

He turned away. His job was to follow the election, not chase men who had a clear right to go wherever they wanted. If it had been Prince Moss, he had reason not to greet Charles after the events of last summer. Charles and his friends had hoped that Miss Jaggers and her swain had left England entirely, but they were not wanted for any crimes.

He returned to his stone perch. Two local voters were carrying the fallen man from the crowd into one of the houses on the left side of the square, probably a doctor's office. The constables were standing next to the horsemen who had remained in the square, keeping a vigilant eye on them.

Wilfred Poor had surrendered his gun into the high sheriff's hand. He gave an anguished cry, that of a wounded animal, then swayed in his saddle, shaking.

"Why don't you go home, Wilfred?" said Sheriff Maitland, not unkindly.

"I'll stay for the vote," the broken man said. "I want to make sure that blackguard doesn't win."

"Speech!" called a man from the crowd.

"Let's get on to business!" cried another.

The high sheriff cleared his throat and introduced the Brown candidate. Charles took rapid notes in his best-in-class shorthand, but the speech was nothing out of the ordinary. Protect the working man, keep trade free, expand the franchise. All the usual sort of things, customized to the town's interests.

The less-than-enthusiastic reception made Charles concerned for Mr. Cecil's success. Then Sir Augustus was introduced as the Purple candidate. He spoke about protecting the town and the country from liberal encroachment, calling out several men in a humiliating singsong, such as a local schoolteacher he called a trumped-up peasant, and similar insults. The better dressed men in the crowd shouted "Hear! Hear!" several times and Charles had the impression of a vicar speaking to his faithful, despite the insults.

His gaze drifted to Wilfred Poor, but overall, his temperament seemed far more even than that of Sir Augustus, who, as he came to the end of his speech, was red in the face, spittle flying. He finished with his fists in the air, the crowd shouting "Protect Eatanswill!" along with him.

The mayor walked to the center of the hustings and called for a vote. The back of Charles's neck prickled as Mr. Cecil's name was called. He glanced around, feeling like he was being watched by unseen eyes, but saw no one.

As expected, Mr. Cecil only received a faint round of applause. Mr. Poor wheeled his horse around, the dark circles under his eyes deepening as he saw how limited the support was for the liberal candidate. One of the other horsemen still present took his arm. Mr. Poor stared at his shotgun, but obviously decided he'd never have it returned now. The horsemen left the square at a sedate walk while the high sheriff called Sir Augustus's name.

Charles winced in disgust as the crowd of men surrounding the platform called their support. No need for this election to move to the polls. Sir Augustus had won easily, returning a Tory to Parliament for 1836.

Charles walked into the tobacconist's shop to buy a cigar as soon as the proprietor entered from the square. He asked the man for a brief history of Wilfred Poor, and soon had an earful of his family's mistreatment by the Smirkes. Dead wife, missing daughter, hand-wringing old mother who had quite lost her senses in despair.

Not twenty minutes later, Charles walked to the coaching inn at the edge of the main road, so he could catch the stage back to London to file his report. His editors would be pleased by his article, if not by the election's outcome.

"Well done. It's so pretty, Kate," said Mary Hogarth, admiring the blond lace decorating the neckline of her sister's new evening gown the next evening. "I can't believe this silk was secondhand."

Kate spread out the skirt made of spotless, unsnagged silk. "It's lucky we visited Reuben Solomon's stall that day. I'll bet you this dress was only worn once. A wine stain down the front and havers, off it goes to the old clothes man."

"It must be pleasant to be so wealthy." Mary pinched her cheeks to bring color into them.

Kate followed suit. "Wealth comes with its own burdens. I shall like keeping our little suite of rooms with just you to help me." Charles had agreed they would add Mary to his household after they wed, assuming Mother could spare her, which would make up a foursome then, since his brother Fred lived with him, too.

"It will be a treat," Mary agreed.

The sisters talked about their neighbors while they dressed for the party. It wasn't often they were invited to an evening at a titled lady's home. In fact, they had only become acquainted with their neighbor at Lugoson House across the orchard one year before, when they had heard screams during their Epiphany Night party.

That had been the night Kate met Charles, then a new parliamentary reporter working for John Black and her father at the *Morning* and *Evening Chronicle* respectively. Little had she realized as they stood vigil in the room of dying Christiana Lugoson that she would fall so deeply in love with him less than two months later.

Both of Kate's parents and their parents before them had travelled in distinguished literary circles, first in Edinburgh and now in London, but with someone like Charles joining the family, they had acquired new status and important friends. Charles had a brilliant future ahead of him and Kate could scarcely believe she was the wife he had chosen. He had promised they would wed in the spring. In a few weeks, they would ask for the banns to be called at St. Luke's down the street. Soon, she would be his and he, hers.

The door rattled, then opened. Georgina, eight years old and bursting with self-importance, announced, "Charles is downstairs and everyone is ready to leave." They followed Georgina out of the room the sisters shared, excepting little Helen, and went down to the dining room where the family always gathered.

When Kate walked into the dining room and saw the thick dark locks, bright hazel eyes, and full lips of her fiancé, her face went so hot that her cheeks reddened of their own accord. She drank in the sight of him.

He spotted her and sketched a bow. She curtsied with a laugh, and then he touched her hand. A tremor went through her at the press of his flesh to hers. She could scarcely wait for spring.

Her mother sorted the older from the younger children with a no-nonsense air, then her father led the way to the front door and down to the street. Kate held Charles's arm on the pavement, even though she was in no danger of slipping. The rain had held off, though the air was bitter cold. Conveyances rolled by on the street, out of sight, holding other revelers.

Mary, on the other hand, stayed close to her mother. Kate knew her sister feared giving Fred, a year younger, too much attention. Fred had tender feelings for her, but Mary considered the young man a child, even though he had a position at a law firm now.

A liveried footman had the door of the renovated Elizabethan mansion open when they came up the steps, as another party was ahead of them. Kate recognized Lord and Lady Holland, quite the grandest personages she had had occasion to know.

The Hogarth and Dickens party passed through the doors behind the Hollands. The old-fashioned front hallway still had wood paneling, though Lady Lugoson was slowly modernizing the premises now that she'd committed to staying in England. Any visitor's eye went immediately to a double staircase directly ahead of them, but Lady Lugoson did much of her entertaining in the long drawing room that looked out over her formal garden.

After they left cloaks behind and the ladies changed shoes,

the footman took them to the room's entrance and Panch, the venerable butler, announced each party in turn. Few paid attention as the room held quite a crush of people.

Still, Lord Lugoson, just sixteen and home from school, dashed up to greet them, and seemed happy to meet Fred Dickens for the first time. He took the lad off to meet other youths.

Kate spotted Charles's fellow reporter, William Aga, standing next to the closer of the two fireplaces heating the room. Charles tilted his head at Kate and they disengaged from her family to greet the Agas.

Kate's father did not like Julie Aga, William's wife, who had once trod the boards and tended to create complications. But Kate and Julie were often thrown into each other's company and had come to terms.

"Excellent reporting," William exclaimed, thumping Charles on the back as soon as he was close. William, tall and athletic, had a ready smile that everyone responded to. His reporting focused on crime for the *Chronicle*. Julie, red-haired and lovely, scarcely showing her pregnancy yet, took Kate's hand and squeezed, her eyes dancing merrily as she took in the new gown.

"Part of your trousseau?"

"No," Kate said, blushing. "But I am working on that."

Lady Lugoson, an ethereal blonde, approached them on the arm of her baronet fiancé, the coroner Sir Silas Laurie. Her gown was cut much lower on the bosom than Kate's, and had few decorations. The beauty lay in the perfection of the best black silk, with a white silk and lace underskirt. Kate saw Charles's gaze dart over the gown, then he inclined his head.

"I read your latest article, Charles," Sir Silas said. "Very dynamic. I wonder that your Mr. Poor did not assassinate Sir Augustus right at the hustings, given the fervor of your descriptions."

"Sir Augustus is dreadful," Lady Lugoson interjected with a toss of her head. She had been a political hostess while her first husband had been alive. "How unfortunate it is that he won the election."

"Do you know him well?" Charles asked. "He is a conservative."

"Sadly, he was a friend of my late husband." Lady Lugoson's soft mouth turned down. "They were at school together and remained close."

Kate winced. Everyone knew the late Lord Lugoson had been an evil seducer, with just enough charisma to charm the families of his victims. The future sounded bleak for that Mr. Poor's daughter. The shotgun-wielding assailant might be correct in his assumption that Sir Augustus had taken her. "Such dangers you find yourself in," she murmured to Charles.

"Have done," Charles said with a chuckle. "There were hundreds of men in the square, and not a few women and children. I was nowhere near the gun."

As her father came alongside Kate, William said, "I should report on the missing girl for the newspaper. Maybe I can find her."

Her father cleared his throat. "We couldnae print the story. We may be a liberal paper, but that is reaching too far, even for us."

Julie frowned. "What can be done to help the unfortunate girl?"

"Nothing until she is located," Kate rejoined. "I wonder if Sir Augustus will bring her to London?"

Charles's head felt a bit dim the next morning, the possible consequence of too much cigar smoke and rum punch at the Epiphany party. It had been a jolly night however, and unlike the previous year, no one had died.

He arrived at the *Morning Chronicle* newsroom at 332

Strand almost on time the next morning. After greeting his fellow reporters, he found a messy pile of correspondence on his desk. The letters included an offer of work at an inferior newspaper, a letter from a member of Parliament thanking Charles for quoting his speech properly, and a note from William Harrison Ainsworth, inviting him around for dinner that night.

He ignored the rest of the pile and dipped his pen into his ink pot to scrawl a note at the bottom of the note, expressing his regret that he could not attend dinner with the popular novelist. He suggested he reschedule for some time next week. That night, he and Kate were promised to a member of Parliament's dinner party.

Charles blotted the note and sealed it up, then set it aside for one of the office boys to send. Tom Beard, who had helped him procure this job two autumns ago, winked at Charles as he passed by. Charles watched his friend until he was half turned around.

"Hate mail," William Aga remarked, tossing down a letter and pushing his chair backward until it bumped against Charles's chair.

"From who?" Charles asked, extricating his legs from the position they'd become tangled in.

"Newgate Prison," William said with a shake of his head. "You would think a prisoner would better spend his money on lawyers than complaining to members of the press."

"I have nothing so exciting," Charles said, reorienting his chair before flipping through the rest of his pile. He spotted a very fine piece of linen notepaper, addressed to Charles Dickens, Esq. The seal was so large it might have covered a gold guinea, as some people did to send funds to relatives. "I may have spoken too quickly."

William leaned over the letter, exposing Charles's olfactory senses to the pomade separating his friend's tawny curls. He poked his ink-stained finger on an emblem centered on the seal. "This is from the Lightning Club."

Charles sat back, then bent forward again. He didn't know what to do with his hands. His fingers danced nervously on his thighs. "The Lightning Club? You don't think I'm being offered a membership, do you?"

Chapter 2

"Why would you be offered a membership in such an exclusive organization?" William quizzed, lifting his finger from the letter. "Surely they have writers in their distinguished collection of followers."

Charles shrugged. John Black, the *Morning Chronicle*'s editor, walked by, but didn't stop at his desk. "Then what else could it be? An invitation to speak?"

"An invitation to report on a meeting?" William suggested. Always fastidious, he wiped his finger with a handkerchief and tucked it neatly away.

"I wouldn't be asked to do that. They aren't political. Their members are prominent in the sciences. And in poetics, sportsmanship, art."

"Hmmm," William mused. "Maybe they don't have any great parliamentary reporters."

Charles poked his elbow into William's ribs. As his friend pretended to gag, he slid his letter opener under the seal and opened the trifolded note. He stared at the contents, his body filling with prideful warmth.

"Well?" William prompted.

"Unlike you, they see my greatness." Charles grinned at his friend, feeling a boyish degree of excitement. "I'm invited to join the exclusive Lightning Club."

"I wonder why," William said in a wry tone.

Charles shrugged with an insouciant air. "With my first book of sketches about to release, I'm getting noticed and rising in the world."

William's upper lip curled up. "Excellent."

Charles glanced at the note again. He was supposed to attend an initiation ceremony that evening at eleven p.m. How very upper-crust. No workingman would keep those kinds of hours. He'd have to ask Fred to escort Kate back to Brompton so that he could attend. He wouldn't miss this for the world.

"What's that?" John Black said. He'd made it to Charles's desk without him noticing.

"Charles has been offered membership in the Lightning Club," William explained.

"You don't say." Black nodded thoughtfully. "A prestigious organization. I've always believed in you. It's good to know others have the same high opinion."

Charles puffed out his chest. "Yes, sir."

"That Eatanswill election article has created a considerable amount of interest," the editor said. "Word is out that the famed Boz wrote the piece. A great number of strongly worded letters in the post this morning."

"I was faithful to the experience," Charles said, wondering how the Lightning Club had tied his literary nickname to his real name.

John Black stared off toward the door out of the newsroom. "I appreciated the vivid language. However, I was disappointed the Tory candidate won."

"We'll get the next one, sir," Charles said.

"Back to work, back to work now." The editor waved his hand and moved to the next desk.

"I don't think Mr. Black really noticed I was still here," William said thoughtfully. "Perhaps I had better try my hand at a novel."

"Any ideas?" Charles asked.

"Something about a dastardly member of Parliament," William said. "Murder in a gloomy old country seat?"

"I can't wait to read it," Charles enthused. "But set it in the past since historical novels are all the rage."

"Less likely to anger people," William agreed. "Why, no, Sir Nonsensical, I did not base that character on you. Did you not notice George the Fourth covering the throne like a great pudding in my volume?"

Charles laughed. "Exactly. You'll make your fortune."

That evening, Kate exited a carriage in Queen Square, Charles's arm firm under hers. The warmth of his flesh under his glove soothed her chilled skin, battered by the January ride in an open cab. They were attending a political dinner down the street from St. George the Martyr church. Kate always enjoyed being his companion for these events and longed for the day when she'd be introduced as Mrs. Dickens, instead of merely Miss Hogarth.

A middle-aged man in a fur-collared coat lifted his cane as he hurried into the street. He held a doctor's bag in the other hand. "Hold, please."

Charles nodded at him, then the doctor climbed into the carriage. While Charles paid the driver, Kate glanced around. She hadn't been in this part of Bloomsbury before. While the buildings around them seemed plain, she understood the views from the square were exceptional, if it were daylight and not winter. She supposed that helped the invalids housed on the square to recover their health and wits. King George III had been treated in one of the houses here, so they must have very fine medical men. She watched the doctor in the carriage speculatively as the driver called to his horses. His powers of intellect were not evident, unlike those of Charles's, whose quicksilver wit shone in his bright, ever-moving eyes and restless body.

"It is not so very foggy tonight," she remarked, drawing her cape around her. Underneath, she wore the same beautiful new gown she'd worn to the Epiphany Night party. Such finery would grace any room in London, though most women who wore it would not have had the skill or interest in making the gown herself. She hoped Charles appreciated the evidence of her industry. He had the tendencies of a dandy and her skills as a needlewoman would be challenged by the requirements of his wardrobe.

"No. I can see the footman at the door," Charles said, directing her to the steps.

"Do you know the host?" she asked.

"Yes, I've met Edward Baines a number of times," he assured her. "He is a newspaperman and an author from Leeds."

"Father must know him," Kate said. "From the newspaper world."

The footman greeted them at the top of the stairs. She noted his gloves glowed white. The scrupulous cleanliness of the servants said a great deal about how a house was run. He took their things and directed them to a high-ceilinged drawing room with navy draperies swathing the windows and political prints framed on the walls in trios.

Kate ran her hands down her skirts to straighten them then pasted a smile on her face. "Do you recognize anyone?"

He murmured in her ear, the intimacy making her shiver. "A fair number of the guests, members of Parliament like Mr. Baines."

A man turned, pushing spectacles up his nose, as Charles said, "Let's go toward the fireplace to warm you."

"Oh," Kate said, as the man beamed at Charles. He recognized her fiancé.

Charles smiled back. "Why, it's Dr. Manette. How do you do, sir? You look very well."

The man patted his rounded belly. "Charles Dickens," he exclaimed. "I have not seen you in months."

He had a French accent but an air of ease that told her he had been in London for quite some time.

"It has been too long. What brings you to Queen Square?" Charles asked. He introduced Kate and the doctor to each other.

"Many of my fellow countrymen settled in this area," the doctor said. "I have a number of friendships and patients here. How is your young friend Ollie doing?"

"He is working hard in school," Charles said. "We continue to be grateful to you for your excellent medical care after his accident. Despite the loss of his hand, I think he'll be a successful clerk in a few years."

The doctor nodded. "I am glad to hear the amputation has healed well. We live in a world full of clerks."

"My brother Robert is one," Kate added. "Though Charles is attempting to teach him shorthand. As is Charles's brother Fred."

"A charming point." Dr. Manette glanced at a man, taller than average, walking toward them. "Do you know our host's son, Edward Baines, Jr.?"

"I know of him," Charles said agreeably. "He's running the *Leeds Mercury* now, one of the better Yorkshire newspapers."

"Mr. Baines," Dr. Manette said as the man stopped. "May I make Charles Dickens and Miss Hogarth known to you?"

"Ah, t'*Morning Chronicle*," the man said in a pleasant Yorkshire accent. In his mid-thirties, his dark locks flowed over a strong brow and piercing eyes. "What a lot of trouble you are bringing upon yourself."

"Why is that?" Kate asked, wondering if the man had them confused with someone else. Charles stiffened next to her.

"Well, Miss Hogarth," the newspaperman said, "Sir Augustus Smirke is thoroughly evil."

Kate shivered. Mr. Baines spoke of Charles's excellent, if tempestuous, article about the election. "I have been afraid of that. Charles heard an altercation about a girl Sir Augustus is supposed to have kidnapped."

Mr. Baines nodded, his mouth a thin line of sincerity. "Your fiancé should avoid reportin' on him further, lest he bring t'man's wrath down on him. It's a sad day that such a man was elected to Parliament."

"I reported the truth," Charles said, his voice flat. "Nothing more than the events of the day."

"Ah, but Mr. Dickens, you have a knack for making t'most mundane things memorable," Mr. Baines said.

Kate smiled at his praise. Her fiancé instantly relaxed.

"I am the best in the business," Charles boasted. "And I'll not stop reporting out of fear, nor would my editors allow it."

Kate hoped her father would never put Charles into danger, but he was only one of the editors at the *Chronicle* newspapers. She had worried about Charles bribing coach drivers and stable boys to drive faster, give him wilder horses, all in an effort to get his reports to London in time. It hadn't occurred to her to worry about risk from the actual news reports themselves.

"I appreciate your attitude," Mr. Baines said. "If you ever want to come up to Leeds, I'd hire you."

Kate's eyes went wide. She liked London. What if someone offered Charles a great deal more money to work elsewhere?

Charles inclined his head. "Thank you, but I plan to remain in London."

She let out a tiny sigh of relief. While she knew her brother Robert was in training to go abroad to work, and her parents planned to send her younger brothers to school in Germany soon, for now, all her family was in London and she didn't want to leave them.

"I can see, with such an inducement." Mr. Baines smiled at Kate. "When is the wedding?"

"Very soon," she said quickly. "Charles is waiting for suitable rooms to open up at Furnival's Inn, and then we can call the banns."

"A home is t'thing," Mr. Baines agreed. "I wish you both all t'best, but beware of Sir Augustus. He is an enemy to t'workin' man. A thorough villain." He glanced up as his father approached.

Charles greeted Mr. Baines, who steered the conversation away from the newly elected member from Eatanswill. Kate smiled politely, but no one engaged her further, and she looked forward to her opportunity to be introduced to one of the small knots of women, so she'd have someone to talk to in an appropriate circle.

"Ah, there he is." Charles pointed at a slender shape detaching itself from the shadow of a carriage. Kate huddled close to him at the base of the stairs, protecting herself from a stiff breeze. "Fred will see you safely home while I attend to my initiation."

"It's so strange, Charles. Are you sure this is really the Lightning Club and not some elaborate prank?" Kate asked.

"No one would go to the trouble of creating a false letterhead," Charles said. "And the seal? Quite elaborate."

"You didn't show it to me," Kate said.

Fred stepped into the glow cast by a streetlight, fog swirling around his feet. His gloved fist covered a yawn.

"Take good care of our Kate," Charles admonished. He pulled out his invitation and held it under the streetlight for Kate and Fred to admire.

"It does look real," Kate agreed. "I hope they don't keep you up all night."

Fred stifled another yawn. "Charles will be fine, as will we. Good luck tonight."

Charles tucked the letter away. "I'm sure it will be fascinating. I've never been initiated into a club before."

"Don't let them do anything atrocious," Kate warned. "Like dunk you in a pool or something. You catch the most dreadful colds."

"I'll be fine, darling," Charles said, kissing her cheek. "Don't let Fred keep the hot bricks to himself. I don't want you to catch a chill, either."

Fred helped Kate into the carriage, then climbed in himself and waved. Charles handed up coins to the driver, then Fred closed the window, and Charles patted the side of the carriage. It moved into the road.

Charles let his own yawn loose. He'd been holding it back, so Kate wouldn't fret that he was too tired for adventures this evening. Now he needed to go to a house on Finsbury Square, some two miles distant, across from the Bunhill Fields Burial Ground, where his hero Daniel Defoe, author of his beloved *Robinson Crusoe*, was interred.

He heard bells ring across London and counted ten. An hour before his initiation began, plenty of time to walk. He knew this area pretty well, even though it stretched into Islington. Given the surprising absence of fog, he enjoyed the stroll, and thought about what the Lightning Club had to offer. He considered the new experiences that might open to him as one foot fell in front of the other. Lectures, dinners, intimate conversations with important men? Possibly some good clubs might open their doors to him.

As he closed in on the square, he wanted to avoid whatever mischief might be present in the burying ground at this time of night. He came across a number of solitary men, then small groups that seemed to be chatting quite intimately. He remembered the rumors that called the south side "Sodomites Walk" long ago.

"Charles! What brings you here?"

The familiar voice pulled Charles out of his contemplation. He heard the hiss of a lucifer striking. When the dark shape lifted it up, he recognized his friend, Breese Gadfly. The flame glinted off the brass handle of his walking stick.

"Isn't it a bit cold for you to be out-of-doors?" he asked, knowing perfectly well why Breese would be in this particular part of London late at night.

"Just stepped out of my carriage," Breese said easily. He tucked a cigar into the side of his mouth and used the lucifer to fire the end. His dark, leonine facial hair illuminated. "There's a tavern nearby where a lot of us songwriters like to tell lies to each other about our successes. Besides, I have a new hat to keep me warm."

"Indeed. You always have a new hat." Charles didn't believe him.

"You should come," Breese exclaimed, dropping his lucifer and stepping on it. "You haven't been writing with me since the holiday season. Maybe you need another writing partner?"

Charles had a second to admire Breese's new fine leather shoes. He was the best dressed man Charles knew outside of Parliament. "No," he said, relaxing. "I'm going to a private museum of curiosities."

"*Oy vey.* At this time of night?" Breese took the cigar from his mouth and waved it in the air.

"I'm being initiated into the Lightning Club." Charles couldn't hide the pride in his voice.

"I knew someone who was a member," Breese said. He knocked ash to the street. "I think his name was Peter Snodgrass. Had quite a successful turn as a songwriter a couple of years ago. Turned to drink after that, or was it opium? I can't remember."

"The membership is very elite," Charles snapped.

"I'm not saying Snodgrass wasn't a talent, just that he fell into less distinguished pursuits," Breese said carelessly. "Leaves more room for us young fellows to rise, no? How is your comic opera going?"

"Still unfinished, I'm afraid. I had quite a lot to do. Maybe next month we can get it done. John Hullah has not finished the music, either."

Breese chuckled. "A lot to do. Modesty doesn't suit you, Charles. Uncovering a fiendish murderer, editing your first book? I'd say you did a lot in December."

A man walked by, whistling, another man close at his side. Charles saw their gloved hands were close together, maybe even touching. Fingers of fear crept up his spine on their behalf, his senses poised to hear the rattle of a constable, ready to arrest them. The cold air felt suddenly oppressive, laden with the fear of these men who, nonetheless, could not help themselves from risking the necessary exposure it took to find like-minded companions.

He shuddered. "You shouldn't stay on the street, Breese. Find a hot drink at that tavern of yours, shelter indoors. It's going to get colder tonight."

Breese regarded him, his curly black hair catching blue fire in the gaslight from the lamp above. "I can take care of myself, Charles. I'm not the one poking at Sir Augustus Smirke and his ilk. You took a risk, naming him as an accused seducer of young village girls."

"How do you know he's dangerous?"

Breese shrugged. "I know the enemies to my kind."

"Sir Augustus is an enemy to the Hebrew people, or to—" Charles wouldn't risk saying the other out loud, for Breese's sake.

"Anyone who isn't Church of England, married to some plump vicar's daughter," Breese said derisively. "He hates the Catholics, the Irish, anyone he sees as lesser than himself. We have to fight, you know, against people like that."

"That's why I won't shy away from reporting about him when he's accused of dastardly deeds," Charles said, tipping his top hat to a more rakish angle. "Having the opportunity to join the Lightning Club will only enhance the power of my words. I must go now. But please, Breese, take care of yourself."

Breese coughed and put his cigar back into the corner of his mouth. "Don't plotz, Charles. With friends like you, I'm in no danger." He turned away, disappearing into the night stealing light from the few gas lamps.

Charles sighed and crossed the square, looking for the museum. If Breese had visited the prisons like he had, he might not be so casual about his proclivities.

The museum's entrance was on the corner, illuminated by a streetlamp. A standard house of a newer generation, it had four stories and a set of green-painted iron railings leading up to the front door. Each story had three windows, except the first, which had a door in place of the far-right window.

He had memorized his letter of invitation. It said nothing but that he was to arrive at the appointed hour. At loose ends, he paced in front of the steps, watching his cold breath mist into the air until he heard church bells marking the hour, then went up to the door, his half-frozen feet stumbling.

He rapped the knocker three times, then waited, counting down seconds. No one came to the door, so he tried again. Frustrated, he stamped his feet to keep his toes warm and thought to try the door. This was a museum, not a private house.

The door opened. It had been unlocked. He mentally cursed himself and passed indoors. If the door had been a test, he had failed it. His breath immediately ceased being visible, indicating a rise in temperature of some fifteen degrees or more.

Inside the door he found a small mahogany table. On it was a portable lantern and a box of white and dirty yellow shells. Other than that, the entry had no distinguishing marks. A narrow flight of stairs led up. He expected only one door to the right, and a blank wall on the left, but instead saw doors on both sides. The proprietors must have knocked two houses into one or built behind two façades from the start. Often the building behind the façade in these London squares had been constructed out of tune with what faced into the park.

Instead of opening either closed door, he decided to walk the passage alongside the staircase because he could see a faint glow in that direction.

Picking up the lantern, he moved that way and soon decided he'd made the right choice. The walls were flanked with portraits of the board of directors of the Lightning Club. He knew this because each oil painting had a brass plaque screwed into the bottom of the frame. Examining the first face, that of Samuel Pickwick, president of the board, he noted a kindly, spectacled visage, rounded and late middle-aged. Next on display was a much younger man, one balding, long-faced Tracy Yupman, Esq., vice president of the board.

The glow burned brighter at the end of the passage, so he didn't take the time to closely examine the other three or four portraits. As he came to the end of the gallery, he found an open door on the left, with a matching table and another box, this one of palm-sized rocks. When he held his lantern over it, the shape of a mollusk embedded in the top rock appeared. A fossil.

"Come, Mr. Dickens."

Charles, startled by the invitation, set down his lantern and stepped through the open door. The chamber contained a long table with room to seat some dozen guests, abundantly lit by candles above. The walls came alive with animal portraits and not a few heads of exotic African beasts, their false eyes glittering in the candelabra's light, sharp tusks threatening the coats of anyone broader who passed them.

A man stood from a seat at the end. Charles recognized Tracy Yupman from his portrait, though he was taller than expected.

Charles walked the length of the table and shook the vice president's hand. "Very good of you to invite me," he said.

Mr. Yupman inclined his head. His eyes half closed, and his mouth opened slowly, then shut again. He turned his head from side to side, as if checking with the heads of the beasts. Only then, he spoke. "You are among great men, Mr. Dickens."

Charles swiveled around, thinking that others might come through one of the doors, but they seemed to be alone. "I did see the portraits, sir."

"The six men of the board," Mr. Yupman said in that same sleepy way.

"Distinguished," Charles praised. "I have heard the name of Pickwick, that famed man of science. Did he collect the fossils?"

"Oh yes," said the vice president languorously, "in concert with Mr. Twinkle. They made a collecting trip to Wootton Bassett last year. The mud spring is famous, you know."

"Lovely," Charles said. "I'm afraid I haven't heard of Mr. Twinkle. I am acquainted with the work of Mr. Snodgrass."

"A sad story," Mr. Yupman said. "Well, all men cannot remain great." His teeth clenched on the final *t* as if closing the unfortunate Mr. Snodgrass into his coffin.

"What is expected of me tonight?" Charles asked. While he had faced many challenges during his short but adventurous career, this new experience had him ruffled, not that he'd admit it to anyone.

Mr. Yupman checked the time on the ornate watch that hung from a chain across his waistcoat. "The ordeal of initiation, Mr. Dickens. As we were founded by that famed naturalist, Mr. Pickwick, we have taken for ourselves the emblem of a nautilus shell."

"You don't say. How interesting," Charles exclaimed. "I didn't see that emblem on the letter you sent."

"It is a clue, given to you now," the vice president said, checking his watch again.

"Is the time of evening of significance?" Charles asked.

"No, but I have an, err, lady to see tonight." He rubbed his hands together and his eyelids lifted. "Now, on to business."

Charles pulled his fingers into his palms. Leather rubbed against leather as he shifted onto the balls of his feet. He noted the clue. "I'm ready."

"You must prove your intelligence, Mr. Dickens, your worthiness to be included in this august group of men," said Mr. Yupman. "A lightning bolt of insight is required. All your senses must be fired. An active man is never tired. To fail the maze would be dire."

A maze? Something clattered above as Charles registered that Mr. Yupman's words sounded like directions of a sort. Charles glanced up, catching the barest glimpse of a metal tray coming down over the candelabra before the room went dark, leaving only the faint glow of his lantern on the table outside the door to illuminate into the space. Footsteps went in that direction. Mr. Yupman, departing? Before Charles could follow, the door closed, and the room went instantly dark.

Charles stayed in place, breathing in the cooling beeswax and a faint undertone of plaster. His eyes grew accustomed to the velvety darkness as the darting lights in his vision, caused by the quick snuffing of the candles, melted away. He considered the poetic instructions of the vice president. If he understood properly, he needed to figure out something using his senses. He would need stamina to traverse this maze, probably in the shape of a nautilus shell, so a spiral of some kind.

Lastly, he couldn't allow himself to fail. This distinguished club was meant to include him. He considered the layout of the room. No furnishings present except the table and chairs, but he'd noted two doors, the one he'd entered and one leading toward the front of the house, where room existed for another chamber larger than this one.

He stepped carefully toward the door he'd entered, staying toward the table, so he wouldn't be stabbed by a tusk or long tooth. When he reached the door, he found it had been locked.

He hadn't even heard the key rasp against the metal. What else was he missing?

Chapter 3

Charles closed his eyes and attempted to map out the room. After he thought he had the location of the most protuberant tusks fixed in his mind, he returned to the central table and tried the other door. To find it also locked. He suppressed the groan that threatened to break free from his throat.

The entry to the maze was disguised. Charles was no stranger to a game of this kind. He'd found a hiding place in a chimney last summer. "You think you're swell, do you?" he muttered.

He walked back to the ornate armchair at the head of the table. A pop sounded, a fire in another room, perhaps, or some settling in a wall. No footsteps, no voices. Where had Mr. Yupman gone? Would there be a party with all the members when Charles triumphed over the maze? Were they gathering somewhere silently, ready to welcome him?

Before he concerned himself with the future celebration, however, he had to outsmart them. As luck would have it, he was up to the task.

The maze would be in the shape of a nautilus shell. He drew one in his mind. Where would the entrance be? He considered, turning in a circle. The center of the shell would be the center of the maze. That told him the entrance to the maze would most likely be along an external wall, to give the shell shape. Ultimately, the entrance would be exactly across from the center. He'd have to count his steps. Returning to the inner wall he'd entered from, he committed the number of paces to the outside wall to his memory.

When he opened his eyes, he hoped shapes would be visible to him, but no, pitch black reigned over his recalcitrant vision. He stepped back to the door, then walked along that wall to the outside of the building, counting. This wall ran along the street and would be the easiest place for workmen to access. Outside, he had noticed the main external staircase to the basement. It ran alongside the room he hadn't been in. That might be where he would exit the maze. But he would have to worry about that later.

He ran his hand carefully along the wall at waist height, making light taps with his knuckles to listen for a hollow space that might reveal a hidden door. "Reveal yourself to me," he ordered. But he couldn't hear a variation in the wall's thickness.

The entire long length of plaster, interrupted by game trophies, gave him no useful information. When he reached the far wall, he lifted his hand to shoulder level to try again. Pain sizzled through his hand and up his arm.

"Bloody—" He stuck his forefinger knuckle in his mouth. One of the tusks had bit into his flesh. When he'd stopped the bleeding, he pulled savagely at the offending animal part, but nothing shifted. He remembered two animals had tusks or horns on this wall. He found all four of them and tugged, but nothing.

Charles wasn't a tall man, but they knew that, so the lever to open the secret entrance wouldn't be higher than his head. He also stubbornly refused to believe the entrance was anywhere but on this wall because of the shape of the shell. Trusting in his own intelligence had always served him well.

Dropping to his hands and knees, hoping the floor was well swept for the sake of his trousers, he ran his hand along the baseboards. They were some six inches high and perhaps a foot in length before the next baseboard lined up in turn. With a lack of success there, he turned back, running his fingers along the smooth wall just above the baseboard. A floorboard creaked underneath his right knee.

Since that was the first sign of any shift, he stopped immediately and felt along the board. It was short, only a couple of feet long. Why hadn't he noted the flooring in the room before now? Berating himself, he investigated the area. The boards were shorter here. In fact, the floor had been patched with a rectangle of shorter boards.

"Got you," he crooned.

This must be the door to the maze, in the floor. Nothing could be more obvious. How could he open it? No notches or grooves gave the secret away. He poked around, hoping to dislodge something, then tried his penknife in the grooves around the rectangle, trying to pry it up. No success.

Finally, he paused, and thought hard about the room when he came in. What had struck him as odd at the time? He remembered Mr. Yupman had been sitting at a chair next to the head of the table. It hadn't truly seemed off-putting to him, because he wasn't the president. Mr. Pickwick was.

Still, it might be a clue. Avoiding tusks, he returned to the table and sat in the vice president's chair. He felt around it. The chair moved along the floorboards when he kicked back. It seemed unlikely to be attached to the trapdoor. The unmoving features of the room were the paintings and animals.

Then he realized the table, gargantuan as it was, might also fit that category. He felt the table and the leg next to the chair. Nothing. The understructure seemed unadorned. He could smell ground-in cigar ash. Frustrated, Charles pushed the chair back an inch to rise again. His foot slid and bumped a slight disparity in the floorboards.

Grinning, he lifted his foot and pushed down. He heard a creak across the room. Success! He'd found the entrance.

Too elated to move carefully, he darted around the chairs and knelt at the edge of the open rectangle. He would be some eight feet or so above the maze. Expecting stairs, alarm swept him when he felt only air beneath his reaching hand. Now what?

More methodically this time, he swept his arm through the rectangle, feeling the tingle of colder air on his fingers. It smelled musty, tinged with the faintest hint of metal. When he still felt nothing, he thought about dropping down, taking the plunge as it were, but that didn't seem a wise reaction to what was effectively an intelligence test. Instead, he felt around the underside of the trapdoor, crawling around the outside to reach every inch.

Finally. His fingers touched the rough weave of thick rope, and it didn't seem to be part of the door mechanism. Still, he moved slowly, not wanting to snap the trap on his arm. He tugged the rope. More and more coiled up at his side as he pulled.

The rope seemed to be threaded through a metal ring that rasped along the length. He heard a snap, then a light flared to life. He blinked hard, wondering if he'd triggered the light somehow or if another person waited underneath in the shadows. Below him, he could see words, perhaps painted onto the floor, swimming into his vision.

He peered down, squinting, and read aloud, " 'It is pitch black inside. Find the center of the maze to demonstrate you are worthy. In the maze's center, locate a lantern and light it to prove you have won your way through.' "

No instructions on how to safely descend. He decided to keep pulling the rope toward him.

When he finally found the end of it, he'd pulled some six feet into the room. How had the rotund form of Samuel Pickwick swung down on a rope to be initiated? Perhaps he had established the fiendish process after he had formed his club.

Charles was pretty sure this entire situation was some kind of philosophical puzzle made reality, but he didn't take the time to consider which philosopher. Instead, he dropped the rope straight down, free of its metal loop, then swiveled and sent his legs over the lip of the trapdoor. The light went out abruptly. Spots flared again until his eyes adjusted. After he wrapped his legs around the rope, he let it take his weight, praying he'd made the right decision.

He shimmied down, cursing the damage the fresh rope was probably doing to the wool of his trouser legs. His feet touched ground before his arms had run out of rope, just as he'd predicted.

Well done. Now, he had achieved the maze. All he had to do was follow the maze into the center.

He calculated where he was, based on his step mathematics. The center would be directly across from him, but he would have to circle the room. Still, he ought to be roughly aware of where he was as long as he counted his steps.

Reaching out his arms, he tried to see if he could touch the inner edge of the maze with his fingertips. But like a shell, the mouth of the maze was wide. He started walking, keeping contact with the outer wall. After only a few steps, his feet left the flagged stone flooring and encountered dirt. The space smelled increasingly dank, still with that faint taste of metal that caught on the back of his tongue.

He stumbled on something and crouched down. The edges were rounded and cold. It seemed to just be a rock that no one had cleared.

He heard footsteps. Pausing, he put his hands behind both of his ears, focusing his hearing. The footsteps vanished. Was that a grunt? Quickly, he put one hand against the wall. He didn't want to lose contact. They were trying to disorient him.

Despite this knowledge, he wanted to flee when a high-pitched squeak came from somewhere to the left. In the center of the maze, perhaps? Were there rats?

His fingers encountered plaster instead of stone. The wall turned in. He was entering a tighter spiral. When he reached out his other hand, he felt plaster instead of air. Holding both sides made him aware of how his chest was exposed. He dropped one hand and put it over his heart.

The walls closed in around him. His senses swam as his body scraped against the wall. He smelled something like fresh meat and heard more footsteps, some heavy breathing, a rattle. His own breath rang in his ears.

Finally, he couldn't go forward with the present alignment of his body. He turned sideways as the plaster walls narrowed, wondering if he'd have to solve another puzzle. But just then, his questing hand touched air. He'd found an open space.

"Success!" he whispered exultantly. He'd reached the center of the maze. The scent of raw meat was stronger here. Were they going to cook it after he passed the initiation?

He remembered the instructions he'd seen under the trapdoor and felt around for some kind of table or niche. Shuffling his feet, he moved slowly, not wanting to kick the lantern over if it was on the floor.

When his first pass accomplished nothing, he went back to the start and anchored one hand to the wall. He took another twelve paces before his thigh brushed against a hard edge. The table at last. He slid his fingers down the wall, stopping when something sticky coated his fingers. After he rubbed his hand dry against the wall, he felt over the table. He came into contact with a metal box, then a bit of sandpaper next to it. Opening the box, he smelled phosphorus matches. He took one out and ran it along the sandpaper. A tiny flame flared to life. A lantern appeared out of the darkness, on the table. He lit it, then lifted it to eye level.

It took a moment for his eyes to become accustomed to light again. Spots danced in front of his sphere of vision, dampening the rest of his senses. He closed his eyes to listen. All the strange sounds that had confounded him earlier had subsided. But the smell of meat and metal did not.

Foreboding swept him. The arm holding the lantern gave a convulsive shake, quite involuntarily. He gathered himself together, then opened his eyes again.

He'd been on one side of a circle. The table had been opposite. If he drew a triangle, he'd find a third point in the center of the maze. He swiveled to check the point.

Right there rested a sprawled body, faceup, the once-white cravat covered in dark blood.

Chapter 4

His heart pounding, Charles dropped the lantern to his side. Fighting the instinctive revulsion of the living for the dead, he stepped forward, arcing the lantern over the body. Aspects of it emerged in turn, the rest descending into shadow.

He recognized the face, which was quite undamaged. Such a pity. He'd wanted to meet the Lightning Club's president, Samuel Pickwick, in life, not death. When he crouched down, he discovered the man's throat was slit. Charles's lower lip tremored so he pressed his lips together, then thought better of it, not wanting to breathe through his nose just then.

He dearly wished he had William at his side at this moment, like he had been when they saw Jacob Harley die. Someone else to record the facts. The nice suit, a clean cravat, except for the shower of blood. Polished shoes. Everything a gentleman should be, in death or life. He touched the hand gingerly. Cold flesh met his.

In wishing for William's presence, Charles realized he was alone. In a maze. Also, that metallic odor that he had first smelled when peering into the trapdoor had probably been blood. This man had been dead before he'd ever gone through the opening, and probably for quite some time before that, though given the coldness of the underground space, he had no idea how long.

He stilled as horrifying thoughts struck him. What if those footsteps and other noises had been real? What if the killer was still here? His heart rate picked up. He had to get out.

Standing, he crept against the wall as if it might shelter him, and raised the lantern. The light beam slipped past his free hand. It was splotchy. He brought it closer to his eyes. Blood. That sticky substance had been blood, on the other side of the maze's center. What terrible events had happened here? Had the body been moved after the murder?

His gaze darted around the space, in and out of the light. He couldn't remember how to get out of the maze. He'd never known how to get out. Was there a ladder somewhere? Another door? Should he go back to the start and climb up the rope? Was that trapdoor still open? What if Mr. Yupman had planned to leave him down here? Did he know there was a dead man in the maze?

"Get hold of yourself, man," he whispered fiercely. No reason existed to hold him in this maze. While he couldn't convince himself that this death had been an accident, it could be a suicide. Though the specific mortal injury made it unlikely.

He searched the space, hunting for the deadly knife. It didn't appear in the lantern's beam. Could it have fallen under the body? He shuddered and couldn't bring himself to look.

He only saw one exit to the central space, which was also the entrance. Speeding into a trot, he went in that direction and reversed himself through the maze. What had he expected to happen? Not this. It made no sense to enter the maze and then return the way he'd come.

Although he did have the lantern. It proved he'd been in the center. Surely there were men upstairs, ready to celebrate his initiation. As the president likely had been, before he met his death.

The lantern also proved something else. It proved he'd been near the body. And he had blood on his hands. He swore at himself.

It only took him a fraction of his previous time to return to the rope. It still waited for him, and all was darkness above. He'd seen no doors in the plaster walls, or the outer wall, as he'd trotted back to the nautilus's exit. When he paused, he heard no noises, but he could still smell the blood.

Grimly, he set the lantern down a couple of feet away from the rope and grabbed for it, using his upper body strength to pull himself up the rope. He needed to get back to civilization. He needed to find help.

If the club members had fled in the horror . . . but no, the man was dead before he went in. That didn't mean that Mr. Yupman had known President Pickwick was there, however. But someone close to him, someone who had access to the club, did.

His bloodstained fingers adhered to the coarse rope with each handhold. He knew he was getting the sticky substance on the rest of his clothes as he pulled himself up. Being disheveled, however, was the least of his problems.

When he reached the top of the rope, he swung one arm over the lip of the trapdoor, then released it and hauled himself onto the floor. He left the door open and lay gasping, winded from the exertion.

After half a minute, he heard his own breath slow. He pushed himself to his feet and found the edge of the large table with his hand, then walked around it and found the door he'd entered through, what seemed like hours before. Still locked.

The late hour pressed in on him. He often walked at this time, but tonight his exhaustion was acute. With what felt like the last of his strength, he pounded at the door.

To his surprise, he heard voices in the passage outside. He couldn't make out actual words, but then he heard the rasp of a key on the other side.

The door opened. He jumped aside so as not to be hit in the face.

Multiple lanterns glowed, making Charles blink hard. Shadowy figures didn't coalesce into people, thanks to his tortured vision.

"What is on your hand, sir?" one of them asked.

Charles held it up in front of his eyes. In the light, he could see where the blood had dug in around his fingernails, and ground into the creases in his palm, but not a great deal was left. He was hardly dripping life's blood onto the floor.

"A man is dead," he said succinctly. "In the center of the maze. Throat slit."

A hand came out of the shadows. An index finger pointed at him.

"He is a murderer!" said a man's voice.

Charles peered into the darkness. He thought he recognized Mr. Yupman, just as the body of his accuser collapsed in a faint.

Charles realized suddenly the other shapes were three men, and all were uniformed constables.

He'd been set up. Not to become a member of this august organization, but its scapegoat.

Cold wind sneaking through the inch of open window made gooseflesh on Kate's arms, even through her quilted wrapper. She had heard the grandfather clock downstairs chime once. Charles should be done with his initiation by now. Even in the fog it would only take him an hour to walk from there.

She heard a soft murmur, then rustling as Mary turned over.

"Are you still awake?" Mary asked sleepily. "Return to bed, dear."

"Charles said he'd come. I don't want to miss the pebbles against the window."

"He's the persistent sort. He'll keep throwing them until you wave." Mary sat up, then came to the window, wrapping a blanket around her shoulders. "You should close the window. You don't want a rock to hit one of us."

"He wouldn't throw anything that large." Kate glanced at Georgina's unmoving form. The child could sleep through any conversation right now. She must be growing.

"He'll probably be drunk," Mary said. "His judgment won't be the best. All that celebrating his entry into the Lightning Club."

"What do you know about it?" Kate asked with a laugh.

"Men like their drinking parties. And Charles is very keen on knowing everyone. He won't leave until the last hand is shook and the last back is clapped."

"You may be right."

"He'll probably appear for breakfast," Mary said. "In yesterday's clothing, and take the carriage to the newspaper with Father, so he can share his triumph all the way to the Strand."

"Surely the Lightning Club is full of sober men of business."

"Scientists, artists?" Mary gave a shrug. One corner of her blanket shrugged off her shoulder. "Likely not anyone who has to be up to unlock a bank."

"I said I'd wait up," Kate insisted.

Mary pushed the window sash down. The cold air vanished, along with the sound of the wind rustling through the few leaves left on the orchard trees. "You've waited up long enough. Blame me if he appears and you take an extra minute to appear at the window."

"It's so close to the wedding," Kate fretted. "And you know how particular he is."

"It's at least a month until you call the banns," Mary soothed.

"He wants his book out first, or he won't be able to pay adequate attention to it."

"We planned our honeymoon for the spring," Kate said. "In Kent, a little cottage where I can sew and he can take walks."

"Exactly. You wouldn't enjoy that in February, or even March."

"I don't want to wait any longer. A full year engagement? It's unheard of."

Mary sighed and pulled the blanket off her shoulders, then tucked it around Kate. "He's a busy man. He's going to be important."

"His priority is building a future for us," Kate agreed, pulling the blanket over her lap. The wool held her sister's body warmth. "But I do look forward to our life together."

"He's a perfect darling." Mary folded her arms across her chest. "I look forward to helping you set up your household."

She tucked her tongue into the side of her mouth, making Kate laugh. Kate reached out her arms and wrapped them around her younger sister's slim waist. "I do love you, Mary. Say you'll never leave me."

"I'll stay as long as I can," Mary promised. "You'll need help. The Hogarth and Dickens clans are large and healthy. There will be babies soon."

Kate's cheeks grew hot. "God willing." She turned back to the window. Her breath made frosty circles as she peered into the dark, waiting for Charles.

"What's your name?" asked one of the constables.

"Charles Dickens, of the *Morning Chronicle*," Charles snapped. "I was invited to be initiated into the Lightning Club this evening. When I solved the initiation puzzle and entered the center of the basement maze, I discovered the body of the club's president on the dirt floor."

"Are you acquainted with the man?"

"No," Charles said. "Here, I have the invitation." He reached into his overcoat pocket. The invitation didn't seem to be inside. He quested through the rest of his pockets, searching for the letter.

The man on the floor groaned. One of the other constables, none of whom Charles was familiar with, helped him into a seating position.

It was indeed Mr. Yupman.

"Tell them I was invited," Charles snapped at the man. His pockets did not seem to hold the invitation. It had probably fallen out when he was going up or down the rope.

Mr. Yupman pointed a quivering finger at Charles. "I've never seen this man in my life." His large head wavered on his neck and his head rolled back.

Charles turned to the first constable. "Surely you can see how ridiculous this is. How did you come to be summoned? And when? I haven't been here long."

"Now see here," the constable interjected.

Charles continued, overriding the constable's indignant words. "Why did this man, the club's vice president, call me a murderer when no one but me has even seen the body? Where are all the attendees of the party?"

"What party?" asked the constable.

"Why, the initiation party. To celebrate me joining the club."

"Which you can't prove you were invited to," the man said.

"Please send for Sir Silas Laurie, the coroner," Charles asked. "He'll vouch for me. I'm well-known. You can apply to 332 Strand. My employers will vouch for me as well. Both John Black and William Aga at the newspaper saw my invitation and remarked on it."

The constables all glanced at one another. "You'll have to come to the police station," said the first one. "While we sort this out."

"I think we can take care of this right now," Charles insisted.

He didn't want to be seen entering a police station under these circumstances. "I know some members of the police." He wracked his brain, trying to recall the names of people who'd been involved in the Harley matter last month. The constables here probably wouldn't know people from the Chelsea police station, where he was more familiar.

"Why don't you take us to the body?" said the constable who wasn't attending to the delirious Mr. Yupman. "You say it's in a maze."

"Yes, but I had to shimmy down a rope to get to it," Charles said. "There must be a different entrance, though it is very well hidden. I couldn't figure out how to leave, other than by climbing up the rope again. The trapdoor is in the room I just exited."

"Mr. Yupman?" asked the constable who crouched over the vice president. "How do we find this maze?"

"Secret staircase. Peephole. Saw him." Mr. Yupman swallowed convulsively, his eyes shifting in their sockets. "Saw my dear colleague die."

"His throat is slit," Charles said caustically. "Search me, please. I don't have a knife. Nor did I see the knife around his body. Investigate the room I just left. You'll see the story can't be as he says."

"We'll search you at the station," said the first constable. "Come now, man, you must see you can't stay here."

"It's his word against mine," Charles insisted. "If I slit a man's throat, I'd have blood all over me, not just on my hand. I'm dressed just as I was when I entered. I was at a dinner party tonight in Queen Square. A member of Parliament can vouch for me. And other important people."

"I'm sure we can sort it all out," said the constable soothingly, taking Charles's arm in an iron grip.

Charles hoped the desk sergeant could be made to see reason. If not, he'd explain himself at the coroner's inquest. Tomorrow was Friday, or perhaps it was already Friday. Surely enough jurors could be found on a Friday, and the inquest would be held right away. He'd give his information and not lose more than a day's work to this nonsense.

As the constable led Charles out to the street, he glanced back at the façade of the private museum. It seemed forbidding now, a charnel house for both animals and man.

Would it also be the scene of the death of his dreams?

Chapter 5

On Friday morning, Kate slid her feet into pattens, ready to brave the mud outside, though her head swum dizzily with exhaustion. She'd fallen asleep in the chair, waiting for Charles, then slid into bed next to Mary when the cold near the window woke her just before dawn.

Still, between the lowering dark of the clouds, so full of moisture that she could taste it, and the few hours of sleep, she couldn't lift her feeling of dread. Why had Charles never come?

She would have gone into London with her father so she could see him at the *Chronicle*, but her father said Charles wasn't scheduled to be in that morning because he was attending a demonstration of a train in Southwark. Charles wouldn't have missed that, since the first steam railway in London was scheduled to open next month.

"He was more sensible than I and went home to sleep instead of walking all the way here," she told her sister.

"Exactly. Charles is usually very sensible," Mary agreed, as she tied her warmest winter bonnet ribbon under her chin. "Are you well enough to pay calls? You look pale."

"I will manage. I promised Lady Lugoson we'd bring her a bottle of Mother's special chilblain lotion."

"I can bring it," Mary said.

"I'll be fine," Kate said firmly. Admittedly, she'd forgotten the lotion until that moment. She slid off the pattens and went into the kitchen to root through her mother's remedy box until she found it. Her mother had already left to visit the vicarage of St. Luke's. She hadn't insisted Kate and Mary attend, since George Small, the curate and her mother's particular friend, had been very upset over Kate's long engagement. His mournful expressions and occasional moans in Kate's presence had made visiting the vicarage most trying.

Mary raised her eyebrows when Kate returned. "You are upset."

"I am not," Kate rejoined as she finished protecting herself against the elements. "It's just that we've been through so much over the past month, and it makes me nervous when Charles doesn't do what I expect."

"Father put you through quite a test of loyalty," Mary agreed. "But everything is going to be fine. Charles had no idea how long the initiation would take. It might have gone all night."

"I know. Thank you for being so rational." Kate took the small bottle and tucked it into her muff.

Mary opened the door and instantly shivered. "It's dreadful. Should we brave the apple orchard?"

"It's too muddy," Kate decided. "Let's keep to the street. It will take longer, but at least we won't be covered with mud at the end."

Mary tucked her arm around Kate's, then shut the door behind them. They darted down the walkway and through the gate, then went up the street to Lugoson House.

Lady Lugoson's butler directed them into a warm parlor in the back of the house. The lady was seated in a comfortable armchair, one of a set of four around a small table. Next to her sat a handsome man Kate recognized as her fiancé, Sir Silas Laurie.

Mrs. Decker sat in the third chair. Kate had first met the middle-aged lady at Epiphany the previous year. She wore blue velvet with banded sleeves and a lace collar. Lady Lugoson's gown was lighter, a Naples yellow silk with red flowers, but then she hadn't needed to brave the outdoors.

Kate greeted them all while a maid moved a spare chair closer to the table for Mary.

"We are very intimate today," Lady Lugoson said.

"Your 'at homes' are usually in your long drawing room, I believe," Kate said.

The baroness rose. "Yes, *ma chérie*, and I do need to return to the rest of my guests. I have brought Mrs. Decker here for you."

Mary frowned. "For us? I don't understand."

Spots danced through Kate's vision. She clutched the table for support, attempting to draw in more oxygen. How she wished she hadn't eaten so many sweets the night before.

She felt a strong arm circle her waist, then pull her to the wall where a settee waited. Mrs. Decker came forward and waved a vial in front of her nose.

The shock of the ammonia revived her somewhat, though Kate's fears were undiminished. Why did Lady Lugoson think she needed Mrs. Decker to be here? Kate blinked and glanced at Sir Silas, who had seated himself next to her on the settee.

He wore an expression at once stern, distressed, and sad. "I am so sorry, my dear."

Mary jumped up from her chair like a marionette and ran to them. "Charles! Is Charles—" She stopped, putting her hand to her mouth.

"You're a coroner," Kate said, proud that her voice trembled only a little. "And acquainted with our Mr. Dickens. Is the news very bad?"

"He is in good health," the coroner said gravely.

Mary sank to her knees, setting her arms across Kate.

"Thank you," Kate whispered. Mrs. Decker patted her shoulder. "Then what has happened?"

"He has been arrested on a charge of murder," Sir Silas said in deliberate tones.

Mrs. Decker tucked away her salts. Her black ringlets, delicately threaded with white, bobbed as she shook her head. "A dreadful mistake, I'm sure," she said soothingly. "Bless him, a man on the rise will have enemies."

"That is very true," Sir Silas intoned. "Unfortunately, it will be difficult for me to investigate properly as a result."

"It's like when our friend Mr. Jones was arrested," Kate said, pulling out her handkerchief. "You can't order someone in police custody to your inquest."

"Exactly," Sir Silas agreed. "Mr. Dickens has taught you well."

"She's ever so interested in murder," Mary added.

"As am I." Sir Silas lowered his voice. "My contacts tell me that Mr. Dickens is insisting he is falsely accused, that the man was dead before he found the body."

Kate squeezed her handkerchief and took a deep breath, willing strength into her frame. "I know what I must do."

"What is that, my dear?" Mrs. Decker inquired.

Kate nodded at her sister. "We have to rescue Charles."

"How?" Mary asked.

"We have to solve the murder." Kate wiped away a tear. This was no time to be womanish. She needed to arm herself for battle. "When we find the killer, Charles will go free."

"Why Mr. Dickens?" Mrs. Decker asked. "Why would someone choose him for such a deadly game?"

"The inquest has not been scheduled until Monday," Sir Silas said. "But we will hear the particulars then."

"We will send Father," Kate said.

"Can we attend as well?" Mary asked.

Kate shook her head. "We do not want to see a body four days dead. You are too tender, Mary. But please explain, my lord, why not until Monday?"

"I have a very bad feeling about it," Sir Silas admitted. "I think the forces against Mr. Dickens reach high."

"Sir Augustus Smirke?" Kate whispered, seeing the spots again. She clutched Mary's hand. "Has he punished Charles so quickly? The critical article only came out two days ago."

"Was it the kidnapped girl?" Mary asked. "The one Sir Augustus supposedly took?"

"No," Sir Silas said with a frown. "The victim was Samuel Pickwick, an elderly man, the president of the Lightning Club."

"I don't understand," Kate said, pushing past her sleepless night and fear to try to understand this surprising information. "How does this Mr. Pickwick tie in to Sir Augustus?"

"He may not. One thing I can tell you," Sir Silas said. "The inquest will not puzzle that out."

"No, it is a subtler matter," Kate insisted. "But if Sir Augustus's revenge has fallen upon my dear Mr. Dickens this quickly, we have to assume his ire has not been subtle. Deviousness takes time and craft."

"Whatever happened was set in motion in just the past two days, if you are correct," Mrs. Decker agreed.

"Mr. Dickens is still at the police station. He hasn't been taken to Newgate quite yet," Sir Silas said. "I will be able to see him, I believe. If you would like to write a note of encouragement, I can take it to him."

"Both of us shall," Mary agreed. "Is there a writing desk here?"

"Across the room, my dear," Mrs. Decker said. "That little desk to the side of the fireplace. Write something to bolster the poor man's spirits, then return to your mother."

Kate had rather take a cab into London and see the Lightning Club for herself. It had been the source of such hope to

Charles, with the notion that he had finally arrived, been noticed by important people. He certainly had been noticed, but only to be knocked off his pillar of moral righteousness.

Mary had already hurried to the desk. She rolled up the top and pulled out a piece of writing paper, then prepared a quill.

"She is very fond of him," Mrs. Decker observed.

"They are good friends," Kate said simply. "While she writes, please, my lord, tell me everything you know about last night's events."

Sir Silas paced back and forth in front of the door, his coattails fanning around him. "Very well. Let us review the facts."

After being booked by the desk sergeant and led to a charge room for a very brief interview with a magistrate's clerk and removal of the contents of his pockets, Charles's chains had been threaded through an iron circle on the floor of a plain cell in the police station early that morning. He'd been told to sit on the bench placed against the wall. Forced into inactivity all day with limited food and water, he'd had only a chamber pot for company. The thought of having his name in the sergeant's book appalled him, no matter how spurious the charges were. His father had experienced much trouble with his debts, but Charles had resolved to do better than his father, as he felt the shame his father never seemed to possess for the damage to the family name.

While he'd been delighted to see a familiar face, Sir Silas's agitated manner and downturned mouth had ceased to give him much hope of returning home this day. "I know what anyone might. The Lightning Club's members are prominent in the sciences, poetics, sportsmanship, art."

Sir Silas paced in front of him. "Have you ever met any of them?"

"Not that I'm aware of. In truth, I only heard the name of one specifically just before I went into the museum. Snodgrass.

I met a friend on the street and he mentioned the man. A songwriter who had developed an opium addiction."

"Could this friend of yours be the key to this drama?"

"Certainly not. He's Jewish. Unlikely to be allowed to be a member. Besides," Charles insisted, "surely my troubles go back to Sir Augustus Smirke. He must be behind the club."

"You cannot fixate on any one possibility at this juncture," Sir Silas chided.

"The timing makes my theory likely."

"I do not disagree, Charles, but appealing to Sir Augustus will get us nowhere. We need to come up with some other plan. Have you never heard of any of them?" Sir Silas stopped in front of the door.

Charles thought hard. "You remember poor Pettingill, the nephew of my former employer Mr. Screws? I did see some monographs regarding the Hampstead Ponds in his rooms. They had the nautilus emblem of the Lightning Club."

"Very well. Anything at the *Chronicle*?"

Charles nodded. "Indeed. John Black, the editor, is a collector of books and I have seen Greek translations on his desk with that same emblem."

Sir Silas exhaled loudly through his nose. "All we can say is that they are a real organization with a publishing arm. For myself, I have not come across the name."

The sergeant opened the door. "Sir Silas, we have orders to remove the prisoner."

Charles stood quickly, his chains rattling. Instinctively, his back went to the wall. "Where are you taking me?"

The sergeant shrugged. The scent of onions bloomed in Charles's direction. "To Newgate. You're charged with murder."

"Can't you keep him here until the inquest?" Sir Silas asked.

"Until Monday?" The sergeant snorted. "You must be joking, my lord."

A constable, burly and with dirt streaked into the crow's-feet around his eyes, pushed through the door, a key in his hand. He bent and unlocked the chains, until Charles was left with manacles keeping his feet and hands in check. "Come along, you. Ve'll add you to the cart."

The chain between Charles's hands shook as he stared at Sir Silas, mute for once.

Sir Silas's lips compressed. "Did you ever meet Samuel Pickwick?"

"No, nor even heard of," Charles whispered. "I have no motive. I had no weapon. I did not kill him. Please, remember me to Miss Hogarth and Mr. Aga."

The coroner nodded as Charles was directed out. His very bones were stiff after so many hours in the January cold room. He fared even worse in the cart. Someone had taken his overcoat and his hat, probably for their own purpose, though possibly for evidence. He had no doubt that Pickwick's blood had ended up on his coat somehow. Shaking with cold, he told himself that he'd been blessed by the Fates that among the trio of prisoners, no one of note had been included. No crowd surrounded the cart in the wintery afternoon fog to see him be trundled to Newgate, a place he never thought to see as an inmate.

Charles saw the forbiddingly rough building appear out of the mist. He'd been here before as a reporter. For that matter, he'd often walked past it as a shiftless boy. One of his first sketches for the *Morning Chronicle* had been written about this very façade. The sketch he'd written about the interior would appear in his book, due out next month. What would happen to all his efforts now? Could Sir Silas find another suspect before the inquest commenced on Monday? All of a sudden Monday seemed much too close, instead of too far away.

Never, in his most fearsome imaginings, had he considered that he, Charles Dickens, rather than one of his characters, might have a reason to enter through the wicket, be forced into the realms behind the iron-plated, spiked doors, pushed through one gate after another, a very labyrinth of misery.

He knew well enough that the apartments weren't so terribly bad, as long as you weren't a poorly behaved prisoner or condemned to death. But they gave the men nothing to do. He'd go mad here if he had to stay for long.

He felt numb with shock as the constable unlocked the chains that had been fastened to keep the prisoners chained together on the cart, and turned their mortal bodies over to a greasy and drunken turnkey for processing.

Notes were taken, a surgeon had a look, pockets were checked. Charles had nothing beyond a few halfpence left to him, nor did anyone else after their time at the police station. They were taken up staircases, through more gates and doors, then Charles found himself separated from his fellow prisoners, none of whom had spoken to him.

Now, with some pitiful burst of self-confidence, he discovered he'd been taken into one of the rooms where the more respectably dressed prisoners were held. But he wasn't directed to sit at the long table where prisoners took their meals.

Instead, the latest turnkey to have charge of him, a massive, ill-formed fellow, pulled him toward the stump-bed of the wardsman. The jailer bent his face toward Charles's ear. He was so close that Charles could have counted each individual bit of grizzled stubble on the man's chin.

"Not to worry, Mr. Dickens. It will all be over in a month." The guard stepped away, and gave him a smile full of wolfish, crooked teeth.

Charles girded what dignity he had left. "Meaning you expect me to be hanged by then?"

The man gave a little giggle. Was he drunk? Was this a general sort of prisoner harassment or something more specific?

"I can pay for pen and paper," Charles said coldly. "How may I purchase these items?"

The man produced a graying, spotted handkerchief and blew into it loudly. Through some sleight of hand his action hid his movements and before Charles knew it, the turnkey was several feet away from him. He didn't follow and within seconds, was reprimanded by the wardsman, a well-behaved fellow prisoner, for being too close to the man's bed. His own ragged mat and bedding were pointed out; then he was sent to a chair until it was their time to go into the yard.

If anyone knew he was there, they could come to a series of gratings to see him, but without any ability to get the word out, no one would come right away. William and his other friends would be able to guess where he'd been taken soon enough. Sir Silas knew. Surely it would only be a day or two before someone arrived with money and hope.

He consoled himself with the thought that very few people were actually executed quickly these days. No doubt the turnkey enjoyed preying on lesser minds. Charles, inimitable and indomitable, was not one of those. He would figure out what had happened and be out of Newgate long before his birthday, just over a month away. Losing faith was not an option.

The next afternoon, Charles stood in the dismal Newgate yard with other men from his room, shivering without his overcoat and hat. He walked briskly back and forth between the forbidding stone walls, knowing this was likely to be the highlight of his day. At least it smelled a little better out here, narrow as the space was. The sky, despite the lowering gray clouds and scent of rain in the air, had never been such a delightful sight, and he kept his face upturned as much as he dared, knowing he couldn't risk ignoring his fellow prisoners completely. Even with the more respectable batch of men he'd been joined with, he could not trust a soul. Most were likely to be guilty of the crimes for which they had been arrested.

A couple of the men had visitors in the iron cage at the end of the yard. He remembered from his tour that the women prisoners could stand much closer to their visitors. Here, a full yard's distance kept men away from their visitors, even their wives, who had a separate cage from other varieties of visitors. A few coins were thrown toward the grateful prisoners, the distance not being enough to prevent that.

He had no one to lighten his burden. William would come as soon as he knew, but the story wouldn't probably make the rounds until tomorrow. For all intents and purposes he had disappeared, unless Sir Silas spread the news. But he'd almost rather the coroner be intent on proving the case against him false.

A small man, almost miniature really, sidled up to him. "Wot you in 'ere fer?"

Reluctantly, Charles's gaze left the clouds. He recognized the speaker from their room. He'd cataloged each of the men, grateful they'd left him alone. The man kept a stained length of cloth over his lower face and his hat down low at all times. He wouldn't know him if he took off these covering garments. "Murder," Charles said blandly, hoping to scare the man off.

He shrugged, nonplussed. "Did 'e try to kill you first?"

Charles shook his head. He had a feeling that declaring his innocence would not endear him to any of these reprobates.

"Expect we'll be seein' a lot o' each ofer, then, right?"

Charles detected a movement behind the cloth. A smile, maybe. "Charles Dickens."

"Bob Sawyer," the other man said promptly.

"Are you awaiting trial?"

"Yes, like eferyone is." Chewing motions showed behind the cloth. "They say I was passing billys between a certain gentleman and Petticoat Lane."

Charles was glad to hear his new friend was a mere fence rather than a man of violence, despite his attempt to hide his appearance.

Bob poked at him. "That turnkey, John Curdle, is tryin' to get your attention."

Charles looked over Bob's diminutive shoulder and saw the gaoler, the same man who had threatened him earlier, gesturing to him from the shadow cast by one of the tall walls. He, ignoring his sense of foreboding, nodded and walked to the side of the yard, hoping against hope that the news was good. Did he have a distinguished visitor? Or even better, would he be told this entire circumstance was a terrible mistake and he could go?

He hunched into his clothing as a gust of wind played flirtatiously with his hair. The turnkey stood about double Bob's height and Charles would have wished he hid his fearsome visage. Stubble did not hide the lantern jaw, and his nose had been pummeled so many times that it was a mushroomlike lump in the center of his face.

He looked a worse villain than many of the prisoners.

"You Dickens?" the guard asked.

"Yes." The man must remember him.

"I 'eard you vere a pretty thing," Curdle said.

Charles felt sweat bead along his spine, despite the nearly freezing temperatures. Curdle had seen him before. What was this game? He put up his fists in warning.

The turnkey snorted and spit. The next thing Charles knew, the man had him up against the wall. His big hand pressed hard against Charles's chest, making it hard to take a breath.

He leaned in. Charles turned his head with revulsion. But instead of going for the kiss he feared, the guard spoke in his ear instead.

"You vas wrong to attack Sir Augustus. A distinguished man like that, wersus a little turd like you?"

Charles's breath had caught somewhere between his lungs and his throat. Instinctively, he wriggled, like an insect caught by a pin on a naturalist's board. The man sneered and pushed harder. His other hand went to Charles's throat and squeezed.

This situation made no sense. Had the newly elected member of Parliament punished him for his article by killing or having Pickwick killed?

What connection existed between Sir Augustus and the Lightning Club? It didn't matter in this moment, because regardless, the turnkey was in Sir Augustus's pay.

He struggled to draw breath, but the act could not be managed. His chest burned. Survival became his only focus. Black spots danced devilishly before him. He squeezed his eyes shut, not wanting his last sight to be of this blackguard's face.

With his final clear thought, he ordered his body to go limp like a rag doll, hoping the guard would release him as his weight shifted.

His ploy worked.

He felt the pressure on his chest and throat ease as the man stepped back. Charles didn't have the oxygen to stop his descent and he collapsed on his knees. His first breath burned from his throat to his chest. He exploded into ragged coughs, hating that he had sagged into this subservient position.

John Curdle said nothing, did nothing, for long moments as Charles gasped, a fish out of water. His vision slowly returned. A couple of curious prisoners looked in his direction.

The guard must have noticed that his invisibility had diminished. While the prisoners must know not to be involved in such moments of casual brutality, it didn't mean they were incurious about the outcome.

Curdle kicked Charles's thigh and strode away. Charles gasped at the pain. He put one hand to his chest and another to his equally aching leg and tried to will his senses back into order. How had he so quickly gone from the heights of recognition on Thursday to this, an attempt on his life?

A pair of old shoes, newsprint sticking out from the damaged sides, arrived at the edge of his vision.

"Wot did you do to make an enemy of 'im?" Bob Sawyer asked.

Charles looked up, the movement hurting his aching throat,

and saw the small man's face just above him. "I don't know him. He's in the pay of an enemy."

Bob clucked. "You'll 'ave to sleep wi' one eye open. 'e's assigned to our floor."

"Brilliant." Charles moved just enough for the wall to take some of his weight. Saliva pooled in his mouth as the gravity of the situation sent his stomach into fits. The attack on his throat had stirred the old pain in his side, but he ignored this malevolent old friend. At least he wasn't noticing the cold anymore.

He needed to survive for forty-eight hours somehow. The newspaper would come to his rescue eventually since he was doing his job when he reported. Would it be soon enough?

Chapter 6

On Monday evening, Kate's father returned home from the appallingly delayed inquest into Mr. Pickwick's murder. When she heard the latch on the door open, she raced as decorously as possible to the small entryway and stood by the boot bench, desperate for news. A surprise visitor trailed her father, Charles's younger brother Fred, whose curly dark hair had caught some moisture and hung lankly over his eyes.

"How good to see you," she said, helping the youth unwind his damp muffler with maternal concern. "Do you bring news?"

"None of it g-g-good." Fred's teeth chattered. Worry cast his normally cheerful face with gray undertones.

"Let us hold our account for after dinner." Kate's father rubbed his pale hands together. "Mrs. Hogarth will be holding the meal."

"I'll tell her to set another plate," Mary said, coming down the passage. She peered at Fred, then dashed back the way she'd come.

"Will Mr. Dickens be released?" Kate asked, twisting her hands in her apron. "Please, Father, tell me that much at least."

"I have no news of that sort." Her father pulled off his boots and replaced them with slippers. "Now, Kate, lead the way to the table, please. We cannot keep our young visitor in his cold and hungry state."

Kate understood her father still resented Charles for the secrets he'd kept in December, but how could he be so cruel as to deny her news of her beloved? Could he truly have no details to offer? But she knew better than to argue. "Yes, Father. This way please, Fred. You know where we dine. Are you going to stay here tonight?"

Fred, still unsmiling, nodded. "I will, yes. Mr. Hogarth has promised to hire a cab for us in the morning to return to London."

"No need for wet feet," her father said. "We have misery enough in these difficult times."

Kate, full of misery herself, had to wait patiently for her mother and the kitchen girl to serve dinner to the entire family. Without being conscious of it, she tapped her toes on the floor underneath the table until Mary stopped her with a hand on Kate's knee. She hadn't realized her patience displayed itself so volubly.

"Could you at least tell me if you've been to see Mr. Dickens?" Kate begged, but her father merely fixed her with a stern gaze and forked stew into his mouth. "Where is he being held? Was he at the inquest?"

"We've had no word since Lady Lugoson's note that Sir Silas had seen Charles," Mary added.

"The coroner's role is to assess evidence collected by others, not run about like some sort of Bow Street Runner with the unlimited purse of the high and mighty," their father snapped.

Kate took those words as a bad sign. "But he saw Charles," she protested.

"As a friend," her father said, pushing back his plate. "Ye've put me off my chop, girl."

"I'll take it," her brother Robert said quickly, holding out his hand.

His father grunted and waved him away, then busied himself with his tobacco and pipe.

"It would be lovely to have a wee bit o' music..." their mother opined, her words trailing off at the ire in Mary's eye.

Kate could not believe her mother would be so uncaring, but at least Mary was as concerned as she was.

"Aye," their father said. "But ye'd best take the bairns upstairs so I can talk with Kate and young Fred."

"And me, please, Father," Mary begged.

"Very well." Their father forced a smile. "James, William, you may continue setting up the Battle of the Boyne with your toy soldiers in my study."

"Can I give Helen her new doll?" Georgina asked as soon as the boys had run out of the room

Kate smiled indulgently at her young sister, who'd spent the afternoon diligently turning scraps into a rag doll for their youngest sister, still recovering from a bad cough.

"Yes," their mother said. "Take Edward upstairs as well."

Smoke wreathed her father's head as Kate poured her father a cup of tea in the quiet after the children's departure. Even with the hardships of the holiday season, she had never so acutely desired to leave this house until now. But if Charles didn't free himself from this disaster, they would never have their own sweet home.

She clenched her fists under the table when she returned to her chair, doing her best to keep her expression placid. Mary's leg pressed against hers, giving her a bit of warm comfort against the January chill.

Her father took a sip of tea, then brought his pipe back to his mouth. Finally, he spoke. "The verdict today was, not unexpectedly, sudden wrongful death by the hand of another where the offender is not known."

"Oh, but that is wonderful news," Mary exclaimed, nudging Kate.

Kate exhaled shakily. "Sir Silas is still our friend."

Her father nodded. "Unfortunately, the police already have Charles. As you know, Sir Silas did manage to see him before he was taken to Newgate, and whatever transpired there, he must not have thought the evidence compelled his inquest to point its finger."

Newgate. It did not look good for Charles. He had regaled Kate with the story of his recent visit there, to write his wonderful sketch that would be in his upcoming book. At the time, Kate had assumed he'd embellished in order to tease her into a horror that required a cuddle to soothe. Now, she must discover the truth for herself. With a shudder, she asked, "What can we do?"

"We will visit," her father promised.

"He must be cold," Mary said, shaking her shoulders.

"We'll bring him money," Fred said.

"A shawl," Kate added. "And clean socks."

"I've assigned William Aga to investigate," her father added. "If anyone can uncover the truth behind Mr. Pickwick's murder, it is he."

"I will call on Lady Lugoson," Kate told them in turn. "Surely she, after a year's friendship with Charles, can persuade Sir Silas that my dear boy is innocent."

Kate lay in bed that night, quite unable to sleep. Mary's soft breaths made it clear that her sister had succumbed to exhaustion. However, it wasn't for a lack of feeling. Mary had cried herself into slumber.

Knowing she would wake Mary if she continued to fidget, Kate slid out of her side of the bed and pulled her dressing gown from the foot of the bed. She pushed her feet into the slippers she'd recently embroidered.

Her fingers felt along their shared chest of drawers until she found the candleholder. She went out of the room and down the stairs, hugging the wall.

When she went into the dining room, she found her father still there in his chair.

"Not abed?" she asked, setting her unlit candle on the table.

"That boy brings us one trouble after another," he said, pouring wine into a teacup.

"He has a grand personality. It leads him into living a grand life." She smiled. "He told me recently he is inimitable. I had to look up the word. It means unique."

"Oh?"

"William Aga calls him indomitable." She smacked her lips together. "That means impossible to defeat. And he is. I know it."

"He's a young man with enemies," her father said.

"He's a parliamentary reporter," she pointed out. "He writes things not everyone wants to hear. It's possible there is jealousy in the literary community. Not everyone gets to have their own book at just twenty-three."

"How do any of them tie into the Lightning Club?" asked her father.

Kate took a sip of her father's wine, struggling to come up with an answer. "The obvious villain behind this is Sir Augustus, but how he ties in I couldn't say."

Her father pushed a stack of newspapers toward her. "I've been looking through Charles's latest articles, but I do agree Sir Augustus is the obvious choice. I've been considering how to approach him, for all the good it would do."

"What connection might there be between such a man and a scientist like Mr. Pickwick?"

Before her father could form a reply, a knock resounded on the front door. Kate started to rise but her father lifted his hand, lowered it again, and rose himself.

As soon as he went down the passage, Kate thrust her candle into the fire, and when the wick caught, she lifted it and crept behind him, her pulse jumping in her wrists. Surely at this time of night, it must be news of Charles. Had the real villain been apprehended? Had her fiancé been released? Perhaps even now, he waited for her behind her father's front door, shivering in the frigid January air?

Instead, when she raised the candle, she saw an urchin, so layered in shawls and mufflers that she could not have said the color of his skin or indeed, if he was even a lad. The urchin handed her father a letter, then held out a mittened paw for a payment. Her father reached into his pocket and drew out what small coin he had.

"The likes of ye should be long abed," he said gruffly. "Who would send ye out at this hour of the night?"

The candle flame glinted in the boy's eyes, but he turned and dashed down the garden path and onto the street, quite heedless of ice.

"Young enough that his bones won't break if he takes a tumble," her father said, echoing her thoughts. "Didn't I tell ye to stay seated, daughter?"

"Not explicitly," Kate said urgently. "I hoped it was Charles."

"Now, Kate, we canna hope for a miracle." The part of his face not in shadow looked deeply serious. "I have great faith in William to find something we can take to Sir Silas."

"The coroner has kept the door open by not naming him," Kate agreed. "But who sent that letter?"

"Some kind of *Chronicle* business, I expect." Her father glanced down, then frowned and held the folded page to the candlelight.

Kate saw a red wax seal. "What is the design?"

"I'm more concerned about the name on it," her father said grimly. He flipped over the missive.

In elegant script, Kate read her own name. "How very odd."

Her father walked down the passage back to the dining room and its cozy fire.

Kate suddenly realized how chilly it was by the door and followed him with alacrity. "We need to prevent icy drafts coming in. Perhaps I can make a cushion to block the bottom of the door."

"Very industrious of you." Her father took his chair again, and a drink of wine. After that, he turned the wick in his oil lamp to make the flame brighter, and studied the seal.

"What is the design? Is it a signet ring?"

"It might be, but it has a design, not initials." Her father turned the letter this way and that. "It's a five-pointed star, perhaps."

Kate went to her father's shoulder and peered down, careful not to block the light. "I rather think it is meant to be a starfish. The center is a little thick, then the arms are quite thin."

"You may be right." Her father reached for his pipe. "It means nothing to me. I can ask Thomas Pillar tomorrow. He has a good mind for these things."

"May I open it?" Kate asked. "The answer may be contained inside."

Her father chuckled. "So practical. Have a seat, my dear."

Kate took the proffered letter and pulled a chair close to the lamp, then slid her finger under the seal. "There doesn't appear to be anything underneath it."

She unfolded the letter and read it aloud, growing increasingly confused. "It is addressed to me. It says, 'Miss Hogarth: A London man is never tired. A knowing man is ever a searcher. A measuring man is always hoping. Not every man can succeed. Meet our associate within twenty-four hours or your fiancé will pay the price.'" Kate paused. "It is signed, 'A friend.'"

"Crivens," her father exclaimed. "It's a puzzle."

"And one aimed right at Charles." Her face felt numb despite the heat of the lamp. "'Your fiancé will pay the price'? I don't like the sound of that."

Her father lit his pipe. Smoke drifted up from it, an alarming demonstration of the current trajectory of her hopes and dreams. What would happen to Charles if she couldn't solve this fiendish riddle? The paper visibly shook as she set it down.

Her father removed his pipe stem from his mouth and worked his jaw. "Kate, ye must remain calm."

She breathed in shakily through her nose. "I cannot. Who is behind this torment?"

The clock on the mantelpiece began to sonorously chime out the late hour.

"It is midnight, daughter. Off wi' ye. Take some rest."

"I cannot."

"This is a battle for morning." His hand slid over hers and squeezed.

The kindness brought tears to her eyes. "I will try, Father, but I am so afraid."

"It is a rational response." Her father put his pipe between his lips again and picked up the letter.

"Aren't you going to bed, too?"

"In a moment. I wish to commit these phrases to memory so that my sleeping brain can work upon them."

"An excellent notion." She stood at her father's shoulder and read over the letter five times, until her brain was full of the words.

"They begin to sound familiar to me." Her father sighed and set down his pipe. "But whether it is because I have read them so many times now, or at some point in the past, I cannot say. The brain has a way of sorting these things out while we sleep."

"Yes, Father." She kissed the top of his head, then picked up her candle and went into the passage, taking the letter with her so that one of her brothers wouldn't discard it if he came down earlier than she did. The draft immediately blew out the candle, and so she made her way up the steps and into her Mary-warmed bed by touch.

Though her brain churned the rest of the night, even in fitful dreams, she could not remember hearing those phrases in the letter before. Her father, so much better educated, might have more luck. As the clock downstairs chimed the fourth hour, she finally let go enough to lose consciousness.

Kate blinked hard when she felt someone rotating her shoulder. "What?"

"Sleepyhead," Mary said in her ear. "I'm already dressed and you aren't even awake. I can smell the bacon downstairs. Make haste or it will be nothing but porridge for you."

Kate groaned as the events of the night before returned to her. "Charles is in danger," she whispered.

"I know, dear. Newgate Prison is a terrible place." Mary smoothed her side of the coverlet.

"I didn't mean that."

Mary's sweet face went slack. "What? Has something new happened?"

Kate sat up and rubbed her eyes. She felt thirty, not twenty. "Yes, a letter came. Some fiendish puzzle."

"Are you sure it isn't some vicious trick?"

"I don't know, but I doubt it."

Mary frowned. "I don't understand."

"I couldn't sleep so I went downstairs after you began to slumber." She explained the boy, and the strange seal, then recited the letter from memory.

"Upon my soul," Mary said, pressing her hand to her heart. "Charles has found himself in something very dreadful indeed. Let me help you dress so you can go into London with Father."

Kate slid off her nightgown and took the proffered shift and stockings. "Do you think I should go to Newgate?"

As Kate dressed, Mary said, "I'm not sure Father will allow

it, but you must use the resources of the newspaper to uncover the plot against Charles."

"What can I do to aid William?" Kate sighed and pulled on her stays, then turned so that Mary could adjust the laces.

"I'm sure there is something. After all, no one cares about Charles more than you do." Mary pulled the laces.

Black dots swam before her eyes as her breathing adjusted to the tight lacing. "That makes me desperate, not intelligent."

"You're always intelligent."

Kate blinked. "Did you pull the laces just a bit tighter than usual?"

Mary regarded her. "You're simply exhausted. It's the stress. Let's get you into your petticoats."

Kate fixed her cap while Mary helped her with petticoats and pockets, then buttoned her camisole over her stays while her sister selected a dress.

"Very serviceable," Kate said, when her toilette was complete.

"I'm sure Charles would want you to look pretty for him," Mary fretted, "but you don't want to attract other eyes. I thought the gray was best."

Kate nodded. "And no ribbons that some miscreant might grab. This is an excellent choice."

The sisters went down together, ignoring the sounds of trunks moving across the floor and grunting noises in the boys' room.

"Must be wrestling again," Mary whispered.

Kate didn't have the strength to intervene. If they scraped the floorboards, they would pay for it later. At the top of the stairs, she put a hand to her cheek. "I cannot believe I forgot it. I am so fatigued."

"What?"

"The letter." Kate went back to their room and snatched the letter from the table next to their bed. She maneuvered around

Georgina's trundle bed, neatly made up but not quite tucked under the larger four-poster the older girls slept in.

Kate had delayed the start of their day long enough that her mother, Georgina, and Hannah, their kitchen girl, already had breakfast on the table.

Her mother frowned at her, but when her father came in from his study just behind them, he gave his wife a warning look and she returned to the kitchen without saying a word.

He patted the chair next to his armchair. "Come."

Kate took the chair, which was usually Robert's, and placed the letter next to the bowl. The seal gleamed like old blood in the firelight, for the sky outside held little of day in it presently.

"I have contemplated the letter," he said.

"Didn't you take any rest, Father?" Mary inquired.

"Some small amount."

Kate would have been surprised if her father had been able to sleep. "I could sleep little for thinking about it," she confessed.

"I believe the strange phrases are related to Dr. Johnson," her father revealed.

"The poet?" Robert asked, coming into the room with Fred, who had slept with the boys.

"Yes. Robbie, could you fetch my edition of Boswell's *Life of Samuel Johnson* for me?"

"Which volume, Father?"

"The third, I believe."

"Yes, sir." Robert cast his gaze narrowly on Kate for having taken his chair, then swept out of the room.

The rest of the boys tumbled in. The twins would be fed in the nursery later. Georgina came out of the kitchen, proudly carrying a tray of bacon. She set it in front of her father, then took her seat toward the opposite end of the table.

By the time their mother had taken her seat, Robert had returned with the volume in his hands. Their father took the book and set it next to him, then bowed his head for the morning prayer.

Kate knew she would get nothing more out of him until he ate. She took agonized glances at the book while she spooned a small portion of porridge into her mouth. Her extratight stays and miserable thoughts permitted nothing more than a few sips of restorative tea.

After what seemed like an epoch, her father pushed his empty plate aside and took up the volume. For some minutes he perused it while Kate and Mary cleared the table. Their mother followed them into the kitchen to give Hannah instructions, then went upstairs to supervise the nursery maid, Polly. Georgina settled at the end of the kitchen table with fabric scraps she was making into a rug.

"Ah," Kate's father said, while she scrubbed down the table. "This is what I was looking for. Do ye have the letter, my dear?"

Kate dried her fingers, then took it from her pocket and placed it in front of him.

Her father put his finger on a line of text in the book. "'When a man is tired of London, he is tired of life; for there is in London all that life can afford.'"

Kate nodded eagerly. "And the letter said, 'A London man is never tired.' It is very similar."

"'Tis," their father agreed. "What was the next line?"

"A knowing man is ever a searcher."

He nodded. "Bring me the second volume of the life, will you?"

"I'll get it, Father," Georgina said.

"No, ye won't be able to reach it," he said. "Kate?"

She rushed down the passage into his study, which had not been warmed for the day. Her fingers were icy by the time she dragged it from a bookcase shelf at the level of her forehead.

Her father took it with an absent smile, then flipped through the pages. His finger settled in the middle of a page. "Have a keek at this. 'Knowledge is of two kinds. We know a subject ourselves or we know where we can find information upon it.'"

"That's excellent."

"I expect it's all Dr. Johnson," he said, shutting the book. "What is the significance?"

"Clues," Kate guessed. "How many times have I told Charles that I love a mystery? But this one leaves me cold."

"It hits too close to home, with Charles in that dreadful place." He pushed back his chair. "I will take this research to William and let him deal with it."

"No," Kate said. "The letter was addressed to me. I have to find the associate before midnight tonight."

Her father stated his refusal, as she knew he would. "I cannot allow that."

"Father, I am good at seeing the next step in an investigation. Please, take me to the newspaper offices this morning so that I may consult with William. I may not like this, but I will focus on the puzzle at hand."

"What about tonight?"

"I promised Charles I would stand by him and I must. We are destined to be wed." She smiled at Fred's firm nod.

Her father ran his tongue over his teeth. "You won't go alone?"

"The missive did not require it."

He grunted. "Very well, then. I will trust your safety to William in this search. Georgina, run into the kitchen and tell Hannah to acquire a cab. We shall leave as soon as one can be procured."

Chapter 7

Kate stared anxiously out of the hackney as it bowled through the streets of London. Wind blew through the open sides, gritting her eyes, making her feel like she was caught in a squall. Yellowish fog obscured all but the tallest buildings. Though morning, it felt more like a bad dream had captured her.

The hackney wheels thumped over something on the street. The legs of a dead horse, perhaps. She hoped a child hadn't darted into the street and been hurt, but she didn't hear any cries.

Fred had fallen asleep. Her father continued to pore over his Bosworth volumes, muttering bitterly at the swinging lantern that made it hard to read. "'A measuring man is always hoping,'" he said.

"What is that from?" she asked.

"I'm not sure exactly, but Dr. Johnson wrote often on the subject of hope."

"'Not every man can succeed' was the last part."

"Indeed," her father murmured. "How about this one? 'Disappointment, when it involves neither shame nor loss, is as good as success; for it supplies as many images to the mind, and as many topics to the tongue.' It is one of his sayings."

"It's certainly on the topic of success. It does seem like it all relates to Dr. Johnson," she replied.

"What do we make of that?" he asked.

The hackney jerked to a stop before she could answer. She peered through the window, but the distance from the street to the building, presumably the *Chronicle*'s offices, was obscured by the fog.

"332 Strand," called out the driver.

Her father shut his books and swung his way out of the carriage, then helped her out. They said their good-byes to Fred, who strode off in the direction of his office.

They walked into the front room of the offices, greeted the secretary, then went down the passage to his private chamber. Her father had a bookcase here as well. He slotted his *Life* volumes carefully into a free spot on the bottom shelf, then took off his coat and hat with a sigh and went to light his pipe.

"Shall I go into the newsroom to fetch William?"

"No. Call one of the boys. Usually one is passing by," her father said, tamping tobacco into his pipe.

Kate went to the open door, still unbuttoning her cape. She waved at a lounging youth a couple of doors away. "Fetch William Aga, please," she instructed.

Another boy brought in a pot of tea and a cup on a tray while they waited. By the time it was steeped to Mr. Hogarth's satisfaction, William had swept into the room.

He wore a black tailcoat, checked trousers, and a cerulean blue waistcoat. The ensemble showed wonderfully on his tall, broad-shouldered frame, but Kate thought Charles would look just as dashing in that color.

"Hello, Miss Hogarth," William said soberly. "What is the latest? I'm going to try to see Charles tomorrow."

"Mr. Aga, it's quite a desperate situation," she said, feeling tears spring into her eyes where she had been calm before. He bestowed such a look of keen understanding as to make her lose her good sense.

"Not yet, I assure you," he said. "Charles knows his way around Newgate. He's tougher than you know."

"It's not that, troubling though it is," she explained. "This came at midnight."

She took the letter from her father's desk and thrust it into his hand. Frowning, he took a seat in a guest chair and opened the broken seal. While he read, she paced back and forth across the small room. Her father drank tea, smoked, and flipped through one of the articles on his desk that he needed to edit, though he didn't pick up his quill.

"Dreadful business," William fretted, folding the letter.

"Quite fiendish," her father agreed. "We've been through every sentence, and our theory is that they all relate somehow to Dr. Johnson."

"But he's dead," William said. "In when, seventeen-eighty-something?"

"Eighty-four," her father agreed. "He has no part in this, and all these disconnected sentences are nothing more than a waste of time."

William referred to the letter again. "But you have to meet with this person's associate by midnight."

"I do," Kate pointed out. "The letter is addressed to me."

William rubbed his eyes. "I do know that the house he wrote his *Dictionary of the English Language* in is still standing."

Her father rubbed his chin. "Where is that?"

"Not far at all. East of here. Less than a mile away."

"Who owns it?"

"It's a hotel now," William asserted. "I've known a news-paperman or two from the provinces who've stayed there when in town."

"Anyone connected to the Lightning Club?" Kate asked.

William ran his hand through his hair. "Charles and I couldn't think of anyone in the newspaper trade who'd been asked to join until he was. So no, I can't think of anyone. If Dr. Johnson had been alive at the same time as the Lightning Club, I'm sure he'd have been asked to join."

"Why don't you go over there with the letter?" Her father leaned over and tapped the seal. "See if anyone recognizes this star, or starfish, whatever it is?"

William held the seal up to the light. "A starfish, I believe. Perhaps there is a connection."

"What?" Kate asked.

"I did some research on the Lightning Club. Their symbol is the nautilus shell," William explained, handing her the letter.

"Maybe there is some kind of aquatic creature theme. Father, I would like to go with Mr. Aga. Perhaps we will be lucky and this associate will be there waiting for us."

"Ye should stay here," her father said

"Please, Father," she begged. "I must do everything I can to rescue Charles. He would do the same for me. Mr. Aga will keep me safe."

He sighed and puffed on his pipe. "William, will ye accept the charge of my daughter?"

"Yes, sir." William offered up his ready smile. "It's hardly a dangerous time of day, despite the poor conditions."

Her father opened his desk and pulled out small change. "For the cab."

Kate took the coins and gave the tea a longing look before she turned and plucked up her cape again, then followed William out of the door.

When they reached the street, she asked, "Do you know anything my father does not?"

"I think you have the most knowledge of all, with that letter being delivered last night. May I see it again?" She passed it to him and he perused it as they walked east.

"A letter started all of this," Kate mused. "The letter inviting Charles to the Lightning Club."

"It wasn't written in the same hand," William said. "I thought of that, but Charles showed me that original letter."

"Very well," she replied. "I didn't see it."

"Then Charles was warned that his article about Eatanswill was dangerous."

"About Sir Augustus Smirke and the lost girl, specifically," Kate said.

"Yes, and we know the newspaper wouldn't touch the kidnapping story."

"Charles didn't file it anywhere else?"

"No, I don't believe so." William took Kate's elbow and steered her across the street.

The fog had lifted slightly, enough for them to be able to see their hands in front of their faces, at least. William stopped at a seller of hot tea, gallantly wiping off two cups before passing a steaming one to her.

Kate sipped, her eyes closing blissfully.

"I thought you had rather walk and drink than take a hackney and be cold," William said.

"Yes. I was suddenly so thirsty," she agreed.

"I wonder why anyone would frame someone for murder, then send their fiancée off on an elaborate literary puzzle. Does your family have any connection to Dr. Johnson?"

"He's been dead over fifty years," Kate pointed out.

"Not helpful," William agreed, finishing his tea, then smacking his lips. He handed the cup back and the seller wiped it with a towel, then promptly poured it full again for another customer.

"With this fog, we could be followed and we'd never know," Kate said. "I can't help but think of when Charles was shoved into the road last month."

"As far as we know, he has an enemy."

"His enemies are ours. We are both mixed up in the business," Kate argued.

"Finished?"

Reluctantly, Kate took her last drink, then handed back the cup. They strolled down the street, for it was unsafe to move faster. William used the rest of the coin to purchase sausages. Kate thoroughly enjoyed the greasy treat, since she didn't know when she'd be able to eat again that day.

They went past Temple Bar, then turned north on Fetter Lane just before they met Fleet Street.

"A gibbet stood on this corner long ago," William remarked. "It was used at the end of old Queen Bess's reign."

"Let us hope our trip does not end as badly," Kate said, hoping her tone sounded glib.

When they reached their northmost point, William took her elbow again and directed her into a narrow maze of ancient streets, until at last they arrived at a small *L*-shaped court of late-seventeenth-century buildings.

Dr. Johnson's former home on one end was brick, four bays wide and five stories tall, not surprising, given that it had moved into the lodging business. Large windows would let in plentiful light, though the once-white paint looked gray and pitted. At least the building remained straight and sturdy despite its age.

They went up the steps to a less-than-imposing door. William tried the handle, which turned easily in his hand.

There was no real entryway to the house. They looked right on staircases ahead of them. To the left, they could see a fire burning in a marble fireplace with a darkened wood mantelpiece.

Kate nodded to the right, seeing a table with a ledger on it, which was probably where the hotel owner or manager checked in denizens. But William stiffened instead of moving in that direction.

Kate blinked and realized she'd heard a cough, too. Her heart racing, she turned to the left. A stool scraped against the floor, adding to the sound of habitation in the space.

William stepped in front of her and peered into the room. Kate huffed a little and angled around him. This was her mystery, after all.

A quick glance told her the coughing man on the stool was the only resident. A hulking fellow about William's age, he wore stained broadcloth trousers, and a black coat patched in the elbows.

He gave her a most insolent look. William moved to step in front of her again, but she put her hand on his arm to stop him.

"I am Catherine Hogarth," she announced. "William, will you please give me my letter?"

William's jaw worked, but he pulled the page with its mysterious seal from his coat and handed it over.

The man's left upper lip moved into a sneer. He stood abruptly, then stalked toward them.

Kate stood her ground, despite her hand trembling involuntarily against William's sleeve.

The man stopped, staring down at her. He licked his front teeth at leisure, then pulled off his grimy top hat, decorated jauntily with a dyed purple feather in the band, and pulled something from the lining. He held it out to her.

"What is it?" Kate asked in her coldest tone.

He said nothing, his arm as still as a marble statue.

William growled and attempted to snatch the letter, but the man's grip held it firm.

"Such games," Kate said dismissively, and held out her hand.

The stranger licked his front teeth again, gave her another sneer, then set the letter in her hand.

While she glanced down at the seal, the same starfish as before, he stepped around her, careful not to come too close.

"What is this about?" William said, turning as he made the demand. "What is the intent of this puzzle?"

The man kept walking. William trotted after him, then broke into a run as the man opened the front door and stepped out.

Kate went to the doorway, then followed them down the stairs.

"Stop there," William shouted, stretching his arms in front of him as if to tag the other man.

The stranger's legs, even longer than they had seemed at the stool, broke into a shambling run.

"Stop!" William commanded, but the man's pace only increased. His top hat slid sideways, then fell to the ground.

Both men disappeared into the narrow street beyond the square. Kate trotted into the square to touch the dirty old hat, hoping it might lend them some clue. If it wasn't secondhand, or third, the maker's mark might allow them to learn his identity. She didn't hold out much hope for identifying the maker of the ridiculous feather.

Before she could bend to snatch it, a boy came from behind the fence on the side of the house and dived. Her involuntary cry of outrage got her nothing but a cheeky grin.

"I'll pay for it," she called to his back, quickly disappearing around the fence, thinking that would stop him.

But it didn't. He was gone. Was he an underling under the command of the stranger?

She stood in the square, no longer the respectable place it had been fifty years ago, and realized she was quite alone. Did she even know how to make her way through the maze of passages back to the main street? Where was William? What was he going to do if he caught the stranger? Though she doubted he could.

"You can't leave me," she called into the fog.

Her father would be furious if William disappeared. He might lose his position.

Her fingers started to clench, but paper rustled between them. *The letter.* She had forgotten it.

She stared down, but the fog-obscured sky would not allow

her to read handwriting reliably. From what she could tell, her name looked the same, but it was largely her imagination telling her so. When she flipped it over, she felt the same starfish emblem on the seal.

"There will be some kind of deadline on this as well," she said aloud. Seeking some level of safety between four walls, she went back up the steps to the hotel.

But when she put her hand to the doorknob, it didn't turn. The man's accomplice, or maybe the hotel owner, had locked them out. She carefully tucked both letters into her muff, not sure what to do next.

Two ghostly figures turned into the square. She tensed and slid deeper into the shadows around the door, not knowing if they were friend or foe. But they walked past the hotel, revealing themselves as ordinary clerks, and opened a door in the next building.

The scent of hot seafood drifted past her nostrils a second later. It must hold a restaurant. Now that she thought of it, she had heard bells striking the noon hour.

She pulled one hand from her muff to tighten her bonnet strings. She could manage alone. How many times had Charles told her that he stayed safe all over London by a certain sort of walk, self-confidence in his gaze, that prevented anyone from seeing him as a victim?

She simply had to look like she belonged there. They had met confidence men the previous year. She had studied them, had she not? Wondered how they convinced others that their game was real? She merely had to apply some of that education.

Taking a deep breath, she raised her head. Walking down the stairs, she added a little confidence to her walk, like Julie Aga, William's actress wife, displayed. It was just a role. She was a boardinghouse owner, walking out to do the morning's shopping.

No, no. She didn't have a basket. She had banking to do, that was it. A woman of the world, with her own business, in her own neighborhood.

If only she could go into a public house like a man, order a brandy and water, and read her letter.

She muttered a little prayer aloud as she moved from one passage to another. Her sense of direction told her she was doing well enough, but in the fog she had no landmarks to discern.

Wait, no. She recognized that smell, a souring vegetal mess. Yes, they had walked this way!

Just a dozen steps later and she had rediscovered Fetter Lane. Her chest contracted under her stays as relief overcame her. But an instant later she thrust her chin into the air again. She still had half a mile to walk, though it would be easier now.

Pulling her assumed identity over her like a cloak, she confidently strode south.

All was well until a hand wrapped around her arm. She jerked back. "Not today!" she screeched.

"Miss Hogarth, it's me!" panted a familiar voice.

She pushed her bonnet out of the way and saw William's handsome face, covered with a sheen of exertion.

"How did you get here?" He put his hands on his thighs and bent over to catch his breath.

She could smell his sweat. "I wasn't sure you would return and someone locked the hotel door behind us."

"He lost his hat."

"Yes, but a boy snatched it. A henchman, no doubt, because I offered him money for it but he ran anyway."

"At least you tried." He straightened again. "Do you still have the letter?"

"Yes, but I couldn't read it."

"We'll take it back to the *Chronicle*." He flashed a grin at her. "Quite an adventure, eh?"

She nodded, still a little inside her role. "Where did you lose the man you chased?"

"He went in the opposite direction to the way we came. I might have been able to guess his moves if he'd gone the way we knew, but he lost me quickly enough. I think he darted into another building. I kept walking and wound up just east of here."

"A merry chase, but let's get you indoors before the cold catches up with you."

They walked alongside each other. The fog seemed more menacing now. She felt enemies around them in a way she never had before. Charles's enemies, who now saw that he had friends who would enter the fray for him.

"What is the purpose of all this?" Kate asked.

"I don't know," William said soberly, still with a hitch in his voice.

"I am afraid it is to keep us busy," she said with sudden clarity. "So that we don't have time to solve the actual mystery, that of Mr. Pickwick's death. If we can't bring Sir Silas a better murderer, Charles could go to the gallows."

"It's unlikely," William said, stopping her at the tea seller again. "Very few people are hanged, despite the execution order hanging over their heads. Still, Newgate is a dreadful place. It changes a man, that hotbed of vice and dissolution. The prisoners have nothing to do there."

"I'm well aware of that," Kate said sharply. "I've read Charles's sketch on the topic, same as you." She refused his offer of tea, resolving to drink a cup of her father's tea this time, then inclined her head west, eager to read the letter.

William followed her lead and breathed an audible sigh of relief as they reached the safety of the newspaper office. "I must say, my wife would never forgive me if any harm came to you."

Kate smiled at that pleasant declaration. "How is Mrs. Aga?"

"Tired all the time."

Kate pulled one gloved hand from her muff and unbuttoned her cloak as they navigated the passage behind the front office to her father's chamber. "I believe it is to be likely in her condition." Julie Aga was expecting a child, though her condition did not seem very far advanced yet.

"Yes, I am glad we have Lucy Fair to take care of her." They had taken the leader of a mud lark gang into their home to train her as a maid of all work after the Thames foreshore became too dangerous for a budding young woman.

Kate knocked on her father's door. "Is she still settled, now that your foster child has returned to his mother?"

"It is lucky for all of us that she has decided she likes to knit. Keeps her fingers warm, she says."

"Good. I'm glad she isn't restless."

When she heard her father say, "Come," they entered the room.

"Is there any tea left, Father?" she asked.

He touched the pot. "A spot for ye, my dear."

"Excellent." She poured it into his empty cup and drained it.

William cleared his throat. "My report, sir?"

When Mr. Hogarth nodded, William gave his editor the story. Kate enjoyed a professional storyteller's rendition of their adventure, but by the time he had finished, she had started flipping the new letter back and forth between her hands. Her name had been inscribed on the front in the same script as before, and the starfish seal was the same.

"Kate, what are your thoughts?" her father asked.

Her hands stilled. "I expect there were at least three people involved. The stranger with the letter, the lad who grabbed his hat, maybe a lookout, and someone in the hotel, who locked the door."

Her father nodded thoughtfully. "A group then, arrayed against our Charles."

"I'd like to read my letter now," Kate said.

"By all means." Her father waved his pipe. "Both of you, take a seat."

Kate perched on the edge of the chair. Her father handed her a letter opener and dislodged the seal. She unfolded the missive and read aloud. "It says, 'Miss Hogarth. Choose one of three. Love will find a way through paths where wolves fear to prey. The great art of life is sensation, to feel that we exist, even though in pain. Be thou the rainbow in the storms of life. The evening beam that smiles the clouds away, and tints tomorrow with a prophetic ray. I prophesize disaster if you don't meet our associate within twenty-four hours. A friend.'"

They all sat in silence for a good minute.

William folded his arms over his chest and dropped his chin. "These clues mean nothing."

Her father tilted his head and soundlessly mouthed something.

Kate sighed. She recognized a quotation from Lord Byron's poem "The Giaour" and assumed the rest was Byron as well. "First Dr. Johnson in poetic form and now Lord Byron quotations."

"What does it mean?" her father asked.

Disappointment clawed at her breastbone. William put her fears into words. "Someone is teasing Miss Hogarth."

"Who would do such a thing when Charles is in Newgate? Surely no one here at the newspaper," her father said.

"Charles travels in wider circles now," William pointed out. "Maybe one of Charles's literary friends like Ainsworth."

"Surely not. He's about to have his first book released. Mr. Ainsworth recommended him to his publisher. His reputation is on the line as much as anyone's," her father insisted.

"Novelists aren't the most conventional people," William said, then silenced himself with a grunt.

Kate lifted her voice. "I cannot stop playing the game, even if it is one. There is too much at stake."

William turned to her. "Then what?"

"What address in London is most associated with Byron? Maybe we could bring a couple of the office boys to keep our own lookout and catch someone involved."

"You're going to interrogate them?"

"Why not?" Kate retorted. "If you think it is a game, we shall play it like one. With the rules of play, not fear of villainy."

William gnawed at his lower lip, giving away his disquiet. Normally such an easygoing fellow, Kate could see a different side to him now. "Lord Byron lived briefly at number 139 Piccadilly before his marriage ended in separation."

"Very well," Kate said. "We shall go there. Father, can we borrow a couple of the office lads?"

"I suppose so, but I am not convinced," her father admitted. "Who would play games at a time like this?"

"Not everyone is serious," Kate admitted. "Why, Charles himself enjoys a good impersonation." She remembered the time last summer when he had arrived at her family home during a party, dressed up like a sailor to do a hornpipe, then reappeared like nothing had ever happened. "Such japes. We're all young yet."

William nodded. "That's the spirit. Even if the idea is wrong, it will allow us to face the situation with more aplomb."

Kate went somber. "Meanwhile, Charles is alone in Newgate."

Her father set down his pipe. "I'll check on him, lass. When I am done with my meetings. I don't know what luck I shall have, what with the fog, but I will try to find his exercise yard and see him."

Kate stood and trotted around her father's desk. She hugged his neck and set her face against his hair, smelling his comforting scents of tobacco and tea. "Thank you, darling."

When she released him, he gave her a nod. "Be off with ye, then."

"I'll round up the lads," William said. "I will meet you at the door."

Kate gathered her things. Her father opened a desk drawer and pulled out a small bag. Kate picked out a peppermint humbug candy. "Thank you."

He nodded, then picked up his quill. "I shall finish this edit, take my meeting, then depart for Newgate."

She put the candy in her mouth, then walked out of his office with her things. When she seated herself in the outer office to wait, her mind went to happier days. Charles bringing her and Mr. Screws hot potatoes so they could keep warm while they waited for their elderly acquaintance's carriage to arrive. Only a few weeks ago, it seemed like another age. Would she ever see him again, safe and comfortable in familiar lodgings?

Chapter 8

"Keep calm," Kate ordered.

She smiled at one of Charles's fellow reporters as he walked into the front office, hoping he hadn't heard her instruction to herself. It wouldn't do to lose her mind now. She rather wished Julie Aga weren't in an interesting condition at the moment. Outrageous and not entirely trustworthy, Julie would nonetheless have some unusual method of solving the case. A gifted actress, she could have pulled a ruse on anyone who might want to trick them.

"I was right sorry to hear the news, Miss Hogarth," the man said. He appeared to be a couple of years older than Charles, with unruly black hair and a hirsute face that likely never looked freshly shaven. "That Dickens can't settle into a quiet life."

"No. My father is hoping to see him today."

The man bit down on his lower lip. "He'd better do it in a hurry, if you know what I mean."

"I don't."

His bushy eyebrows drew together. "If he's got some toff

angry enough with him to frame him for murder, is that person really going to wait around to see the charges dropped? It's Newgate, after all, a bigger den of vice and crime than you've ever seen."

"Is there any way to protect him?" Kate asked.

"Find out who is behind all this, fast as you can," the man said.

"Are you going to help?"

The man shrugged and pulled a cigar out of his pocket. "I've got his job to do as well as mine, don't I?" He stalked off without saying good-bye, whistling a merry tune.

Kate stared at the man, aghast.

William arrived in the doorway just after the other reporter exited. The boy who'd brought her father the tea earlier ran past him and out the front door, followed by another gawky adolescent. "I've sent them to fetch a coach. The house is across from The Green Park in Mayfair. It would be a long walk in this weather."

She said nothing. William peered at her. "What's wrong? Or, at least, what is newly wrong?"

"Who was that reporter?" she asked.

"Alexander Goddard. Why?"

She frowned, feeling the weight of her sudden realization. "He reminded me that Sir Augustus is not likely to be Charles's only enemy."

William's lips tightened. He sat down next to Kate. "What did he say?"

"That Charles wasn't meant to survive long in Newgate, given that a toff put him there."

William patted her arm. "They've silenced him, Miss Hogarth. We have to hope they are satisfied with that."

"I think we should check this Mr. Goddard's relationship with the Lightning Club."

"I think he was merely stating the unpleasantly obvious,"

William said. "Although I must admit that Charles quite out-shines him at the newspaper."

"And he isn't engaged to the editor's daughter, either," Kate said.

The first boy ran back in.

"How far do we need to go?" she asked.

"A couple of miles?" William guessed. "Let's depart."

They went outside. William helped Kate into the coach, then the boys clambered in.

One of them stared out of the window. "The fog is rolling in."

"I told the driver not to rush," William said as he sat down. "We still have most of the twenty-four hours. There's no need for dangerous bowling about."

"Father will have a difficult time seeing Charles," Kate fretted.

William smiled sympathetically, then adjusted his hat as the coach jerked into movement. "He'll do his best. Charles is clever and doesn't need much sleep. I think he'll do well enough."

"In Newgate?" the younger boy piped. He shivered theatrically. "Can you imagine being inside wi' the likes of Captain Kidd? Now those were the days."

Kate regarded him with horror as he began to regale the coach with the tale, apparently picked up from some penny pamphlet, of the old pirate, who'd been executed more than a hundred years before.

She imagined the scenes outside, from the initial river view, to the city, to the increasing green landscape of the park until they arrived at Lord Byron's former home, knowing her dreams would be lurid tonight.

When William helped her down, she found they were in front of a neoclassical town house from the last century.

"Who lives here now?" she asked. "I can't imagine it is a hotel."

"No, I don't think so, but Lord Byron only rented it. He lived here with his wife, then with his half sister."

Kate shuddered at the implied relationship between the scandalous baron and Augusta Leigh, who was still alive. Her third daughter was reputed to be Lord Byron's as well.

She walked up to the stone balustrades. No light shone from any of the windows in the long three stories. She couldn't see the basement or the shorter two stories above.

"It has a deserted feeling," William said, joining her.

"The boys will have trouble keeping a lookout in the fog." When Kate turned around, she saw the coach horses but couldn't see past them to the park.

"I'll go up the steps," William said.

She watched him recede into the doorway and heard his knock. He waited half a minute then, having no response, knocked again.

Despair clogged at her insides as no one answered. Was this really just a dastardly trick? Maybe by that rival reporter? Where were the servants who should be answering the door of this palatial mansion?

As William came down the steps shaking his head, she shook her own in anger. "We need to take control of this situation."

"How?" he asked. "Mighty forces are arrayed against Charles."

"What has happened?" She named off the facts, holding up a finger each time until her hand lay open. "A prominent man was stabbed in a secret maze. Then they send Charles in to find the body. Someone claimed he must have done the murder. The police take him to prison. Can't they examine the body? Prove that Mr. Pickwick had been dead long before Charles found him?"

William tapped his shoe against the pavement. "That would have been discussed in the inquest."

"Right, and Charles wasn't named as the killer. Won't the courts sort all that out?" Kate coughed.

"I believe Goddard was saying he feared Charles wouldn't live that long."

"Meanwhile, what are we doing, out in this filthy weather? Someone is playing a game with me. Where is the man with the clue?" She stamped her foot.

"Maybe we came too fast? Maybe this is the wrong address?"

"No, this is it. I'm sure of that. The infamy of Lord Byron's behavior when he lived in this town house is too well-known. We easily managed the first clue." She stamped her feet. "There is no reason to believe we'd be wrong with the second."

"Then what?" William asked, as the older lad coughed repeatedly from his lookout by the horses.

Kate pulled the letter from her muff and, keeping William's gaze locked to her own, walked to the edge of the pavement and dropped it into the gutter. "That's what I'm going to do. Please help me into the coach."

"Cor, Miss Hogarth," William said in a tone of admiration when they were back inside, returning to the office through busy streets. "I begin to see why you are a match for Charles. But I hope you are right to dismiss it."

"Whoever is tormenting me is not in Newgate Prison," she pointed out.

Mr. Hogarth invited Kate into his study after everyone retired that night. She hid a yawn as she walked behind him into the small room.

"The fire is still lit," she said with surprise.

"I wanted to recreate that second note," he told her as he seated himself behind his desk. He took out a piece of paper and picked up his quill.

"You think I made a mistake?"

"I cannot say, but we have until tomorrow morning to sort it out, correct?"

"I expect so."

She found that she remembered every word, or at least thought she did.

"Rainbows," her father mused. "Wolves."

"Clouds, rays," Kate added. "It's been on my mind all day. They cannot have expected me to journey to Newstead Abbey, which had been the Byron family estate."

"I suppose ye could get to Nottinghamshire in a day, if the roads were acceptable."

"But it's January. Just leaving London in this fog would be a trial."

"No, ye were right to go to Piccadilly," her father agreed. "Perhaps this act of defiance will smoke out the devil behind the letters."

"Father," Kate said hesitantly, "you didn't share anything about your trip to Newgate at dinner."

"I wasnae able to see Charles," he admitted. "As I'm sure ye guessed."

"Why not?" Kate took a handkerchief from her pocket and twisted it between her fingers.

"They said he was temporarily in another ward but I could see him at the yard tomorrow."

"Why?"

Her father sighed. His pipe had gone out and he'd acquired a fresh ink stain on one finger. "He'd been attacked."

Kate had been standing, but she sank into a chair at the news.

"Not today," her father said hastily. "It wasn't on account of the Byron matter."

"When?" she asked in a fainting tone she didn't recognize.

"Sunday."

She shook her head. "And we had no idea. Can I go with you tomorrow, Father?"

"I should not expose ye to such a scene. And the letter I sent did not request access for both of us."

"I have to be brave for him. We sit in comfort while he is in prison."

"Still," her father temporized.

"They won't care if I join you." She warmed up another argument. "Anyone could be framed for murder. He works for me, Father, for me and our future children, and that article he wrote brought money to support us."

"I suppose one visit will not hurt ye," he said with a sigh. "Ignore everything but Charles. It's a dry night tonight. I hope visibility will be better tomorrow."

"Thank you." She stood and went around the desk to kiss him on the cheek, then made her way upstairs.

After waking Mary just long enough to have help with her garments, Kate climbed into bed next to her in a fresh nightgown. Tears rolled down her cheeks as she thought that Charles would still be wearing the now-filthy garments he'd been arrested in.

Her brain felt heavy when she woke sometime later. It was the dead of night. The heavily curtained windows let in not a speck of light.

She rolled over, not knowing what had woken her. Probably a bad dream. She coughed and something acrid hit the back of her throat. But they didn't have a fire still going at this time of night.

Then she heard a popping sound, like a stick had broken in the grate. She pushed back the covers, coming to full wakefulness.

Why did she smell a fire when there wasn't one in the room? She slid out of bed, pushing her feet into her slippers. When she heard another pop, she thought it came from over by the curtains. Had an animal entered the room and shut the door without waking the sisters?

She pushed aside one of the heavy curtains, shivering as the colder air trapped behind hit her. Grabbing a dressing gown, she rubbed frost away from the window and saw flames.

Her heart skipped a beat. Someone had lit a bonfire in the garden! It had been a dry night, no rain. What if it had been laid against the house?

"Mary," she called urgently. "Georgina, wake up."

"What? Stays?" Mary said drowsily.

"Wake up," Kate said louder. "Fire."

The small figure of Georgina sat bolt upright. "What?"

"Down below. We must rouse the house."

"I'll go upstairs for the twins," Mary said, climbing out of bed. "I'll bang on the boys' door on the way."

"Mother," Georgina choked out, and dashed for their door without even reaching for another layer of clothing.

Kate pulled the blanket from Georgina's little bed and followed her out. Mary was close behind.

She banged on the door to their brothers' chamber, then ran up the steps to the attic, where the nursery and the servants' rooms were. Kate opened the boys' door and shouted at them to get downstairs and fight the fire.

She heard her father's voice, then her mother's. Georgina started to cry. Her father came through just as Robert climbed out of bed, his sandy brown hair standing up in tufts. A fire still lit his room.

"What is it?"

"Fire," their father said. "I can smell it, too."

Robert made sure his brothers were up. Kate heard footsteps over their heads.

"Go to the fire," their father instructed. "I'll make sure the bairns get downstairs."

Robert shepherded the younger boys out of the room, then escorted their mother downstairs, her arm around the sobbing Georgina.

Kate wrapped the blanket she had around Georgina, then

went to grab her cloak. The boys had already gone outside before she shoved her feet into pattens and followed them. She went out the front door, smelling the fire more clearly, then walked around the side of the house.

The night had indeed cleared and she could see stars over the herb garden, except where smoke tunneled into the night sky. Crumpled leaves and shreds of newsprint dotted the edges of the fire. The villain had brought some kind of fire starter, then tossed whatever he could find nearby into it. She could smell applewood.

"Give me your cloak," Robert ordered. The younger boys were stamping the edges of the fire.

Kate pulled it off and Robert used it to beat the flames back.

"I think we can smother it," he said. "The water barrel is iced over."

"Can we kick it over anyway?" George asked.

"Do it," Robert said. "Kate, go! Get blankets."

Spurred into action despite the freezing cold, she ran toward the house, meeting her father at the door.

"It isn't too big," she said, panting. "Robert said he can smother it."

Her father piled three heavy waterproof capes into her arms, then found his boots while she went out the front door again. She heard her mother yelling to Hannah to take the washing-up water from the kitchen out the door to the boys.

When she reached the fire again, it had already diminished in strength. They laid the capes over the remaining area of it, then stomped it out. When Hannah unlocked the kitchen door and brought out the washbasin, James went for the kitchen jug.

They soaked the edges of the mess, then went back for more, until the danger passed.

The smoking remains diminished visibility, but before long, Kate could see no red remaining.

"What do you think?" she asked Robert. "Is it safe?"

Their father, lantern in his hand, walked around the smoke. Robert poked at her cape with a stick. She realized with dismay that in the dark, she'd reached for the beautiful white velvet cape she'd inherited from the late Christiana Lugoson next door, instead of the everyday wool one that she'd also been gifted.

She turned away with a sigh and quoted, " 'You speak as one of the foolish women speaks. Shall we indeed accept good from God and not accept adversity?' "

"Job feels apt right now," her father said approvingly.

Robert used his stick to pick up the edges of the capes. One ripped under his ministrations. "This was set purposefully. It's too round to be anything else."

"I don't think it would have caught the house," their father said, swinging the lantern around. "What could the purpose have been?"

Mary came out, dressed more warmly than the others, and carrying a blanket. She tugged George toward Kate and draped it over both of their shoulders. "Is it safe now?"

"I think the wind could have sent it in our direction." Robert licked a finger and put it toward the wind. "Just a few degrees of change and it would have blown the flames against the rosemary bushes."

"Thankfully it did not," their father said, pressing his palms against each other.

They circled the fire for a few more minutes. Robert, the most agitated of the boys, stayed on watch while the others went to clean up. Mr. Hogarth calmed his wife and the maids, then they took the children back to bed.

Kate and Mary went into the kitchen. They found it was early enough in the evening that the fire in the kitchen range had not yet gone out, so they warmed quickly, whispering over what had happened.

"It's my fault," Kate despaired. "No one came up to me in Piccadilly, yet they obviously saw me discarding the letter."

"It's a foul game meant to torment you. This sequence of events makes it obvious," Mary whispered fiercely. "You went to the house. They know it."

"Exactly," Kate agreed, adding water to the boiler that was part of the range. "Otherwise, I still had half a day to solve the puzzle. How I wish I had not behaved so."

Mary squeezed Kate's hand. "At least the fire was not so very bad."

"It could have been much worse," Kate agreed. "It was not set for immediate disaster."

They made a pot of tea for Robert, with a few sips for themselves to fortify against the cold, then washed their faces and hands in the last of the hot water that came from the tap. Regretfully, they left the warm kitchen behind.

Robert had rebuilt the fire in the dining room. He bade them to prop the kitchen door open so he could hear better if anyone crept around that side of the house again.

"What will you do now?" Mary asked as they went into the passage toward the staircase.

"I'm sure I'll get another letter," Kate said. "I hope they will reword the clue so we can better guess what it is they want. Perhaps I shall have to go to Newstead Abbey."

"Aren't you and Father going to see Charles tomorrow?"

Kate leaned against the wall, too weary to prop herself up. "Maybe they want to keep us apart."

"Isolate him?" Mary guessed. "It's possible, given what we've heard about doings at the prison. I'll go into London with you and Father tomorrow. I'll stay with him if you have to chase Byron."

"Mother will never let you. There is too much to do here," Kate said. "I'll be lucky if I'm allowed to go again."

Mary shrugged. "You and I are both leaving in a few months, once you and Charles are married. Georgina has become so useful and the twins aren't quite babies anymore."

At the end of her speech, she yawned widely. Kate pointed to the stairs. "Let us find what repose we can."

Mary nodded and climbed the stairs. Kate found her eyelids drooping even as they climbed the stairs.

Mary set the candle on her side of the bed, then pulled off her cloak and dropped it on a peg. Kate smelled smoke, thinking it was from the outerwear, then realized it was on her nightgown. She'd left the blanket with Robert.

Suddenly repulsed, she pulled it off and dropped it into a corner, then pulled on a clean shift. Luckily it was early enough in the week that she had plenty of clean clothing. She paced to her side of the bed and pulled back the quilts.

"What is it?" Mary asked sleepily when Kate went motionless.

Kate pointed. When Mary didn't react, she leaned over and shook Mary's shoulder.

"What?"

Kate pointed at her pillow. Mary looked blank, then blinked her eyes and stared.

A grimy piece of paper marred the white pillow.

Kate picked it up with shaking fingers. Mary lifted the candle up so she could see the words.

"'Miss Hogarth. Choose one of three. Love will find a way through paths where wolves fear to prey. The great art of life is sensation, to feel that we exist even in pain. Be thou the rainbow in the storms of life. The evening beam that smiles the clouds away, and tints tomorrow with a prophetic ray. I prophesize disaster if you don't meet our associate within twenty-four hours. A friend.'"

"Is it the same as before?" Mary asked.

"Exactly the same," Kate said dolefully, wiping dirt off her fingers. "It's the letter I tossed into the road."

"It can't be. A horse would have tread upon it, or a wheel." Mary lifted her face, displaying frightened eyes.

Kate turned the paper over and over in her hands. "I think it is exactly that. They fetched the paper as soon as we drove away. Maybe they never planned to give me another riddle at all, just to torment me."

"As they are tormenting Charles," Mary added.

Kate nodded. "Someone hates us both. Someone entered Father's house and knew where my bed was. Oh," she breathed. "What a violation. What if they are still inside?"

"They've gone to the trouble to learn all this. How could they know your bedroom?"

"A careless word from someone? I don't know. We have a large family, the two servants. Charles knows my room, so do the Agas. The Lugosons might know as well." Kate sank onto the bed.

"You can't stay here," Mary said. "It isn't safe."

"What about the rest of our family?"

"At least there is really nowhere to hide with such a large household. I'm sure the miscreant has departed." Mary climbed out of bed, her energy seemingly somewhat restored. "Still, I'm getting Father."

Kate pulled on her dressing gown, then returned to the letter. She lifted the candle and paced the floor, looking for footprints or any sign. The window was locked from inside. Someone had come into the house while everyone was either outside or huddled in the dining room. The kitchen door had been unlocked, with people moving in and out of the house in low light.

Mary led their parents into the chamber. Mutely, Kate held out the stained page to her father.

"Such evil doings," their mother muttered.

Their father read over the letter using his own candle, then handed it back to Kate. She explained her theory that she had gone to the right place with William, and a dastardlier game was afoot.

"I cannot disagree with ye, at least not at this time of night," he said. "We shall have to decide what to do in the morning."

"Is there nothing we can do now, Mr. Hogarth?" their mother asked.

"I will check all the rooms and doors, then instruct Robert on what has occurred," he told them.

"We could leave lamps burning," their mother said tentatively.

"Certainly, with Robert," he agreed. "Kate, you must think very hard about how Charles has dragged us all into this mess. Why would someone attack ye?"

"And the family," their mother added. "Charles has been imprisoned. What do they want to do to the rest of us?"

Chapter 9

Kate did not feel equal to arguing with her father as they bowled into London the next morning, so she stayed huddled in the corner of the carriage. If she and Charles didn't marry soon, she felt like she would break apart, torn by warring loyalties. She understood her father's concern. He had young children put at risk by whatever forces Charles had tripped into gear.

But then again, he'd been on assignment for the *Morning Chronicle*. Her father had edited the damning article regarding Sir Augustus's evil ways. How could he consider himself innocent of this mess? He'd approved the words Charles had written.

None of these thoughts would ever be said, however. No one spoke so to their fathers. She suspected it might not even be how wives spoke to their husbands. After all, how much misery could be prevented, if only a woman could set her erring husband on the correct path?

Kate kept her eyes closed as they drove up Old Bailey, where the executions occurred. Her father had lifted a glass at the old

Magpie and Stump public house once, in the upstairs rooms people could rent to watch people die.

They drove alongside the prison's stone walls, a busy road, especially at this time of day. Kate fancied she could sense the misery emanating from the area, despite the sea of humanity that surged along the dark place in complete indifference. Now her own Charles's despair had been added to the mix, where once he had been a mere tourist to the darkness here.

When the hackney stopped, her father helped her down, then he knocked on the door of the governor's house. This part of the prison looked like an ordinary place, not unlike a counting house as Charles had described to her. After a short wait, a turnkey came to fetch them. He would lead them into the bowels of the prison. They had to sign in. Her father had made arrangements in his capacity as a newspaperman so that he didn't have to take Kate to the common yards and expose her to the prisoners.

The turnkey walked them through the lodge, very close to where they had been in the hackney less than an hour before. They went by the collection of shackles that Charles had described in his sketch about his visit here.

Through gates and dismal passages, past railings and cages, smelling of unwashed humanity, they trod, until finding themselves in a large, nearly empty room, with a fire dying down in the fireplace. Kate shivered, sensing the despair that lodged here.

"The men have gone to the yard, but this is where Mr. Dickens resides," the turnkey said.

"I didn't write to ask for a tour," Mr. Hogarth said. "We want to see Charles Dickens."

"He isn't here," Kate said tentatively, glancing at the table pushed against the walls, the crates the men must sit on, and a bed in the corner. The walls held mats on pegs, but no place existed where a man might be concealed. "Are we going to go to the yard?"

A man entered the room, another turnkey with keys swinging off his waistcoat, and whispered in the first man's ear.

"He's in the chapel," the turnkey said.

"Why?" asked her father. "I expected to see him in the press-yard."

"His guard is feeling exceptionally unwell this morning," said the first turnkey with a shrug.

Mr. Hogarth frowned, but said, "Lead on."

They followed the turnkey back in the general direction of the governor's house. The prison chapel was behind it. When Kate walked in, the last of the trio, she found it as meanly decorated as the prisoners' chamber. An empty, shortened pulpit, one curtained gallery and another without a curtain, to keep the sexes apart. The Ten Commandments painted on the wall behind the altar, so regularly broken as they must have been by the prison population, could scarcely provide any much-needed education given how damaged the lettering was.

One forbidding, black-painted pew was centered in a rectangular pen, also painted in that hue. In it, Charles, without an overcoat or hat, sat on one end, and a very pale-looking man sat on the opposite side, his eyes rimmed with red.

"What are you doing in the condemned pew, Keefe?" snarled their turnkey guide.

The red-eyed man looked listlessly at the guide, but another guard, large as a statue on Charles's other side, said, "Giving Dickens a taste of what his last church service will be like. Personally, I regret leaving behind the days when they brought the coffins back here for services after the hangings." He slid sideways on the pew and elbowed Charles in the side.

Charles flinched. He often had pains there. His joy at seeing clean, fresh Kate, and her father, gave him respite from his considerable aches and pains. If only he could reach out to her and take her hand.

"Go have a smoke, Curdle," ordered the turnkey they were with. "I'll return Dickens to the yard when we're done with him."

Curdle rose slowly. "As you wish." He slid around Charles, making sure to rub his body against him as much as possible, then opened the door to the rectangle and stepped out, noticing Charles's fiancée for the first time.

Charles stiffened, not knowing what liberties the disgusting Curdle would take. But in front of his superior, he held his tongue.

Curdle held out the sides of his tailcoat and curtsied. "My apologies. I didn't realize we had a lady present." After an exaggerated leer, he sauntered out of the chapel, whistling. The sound bounced off the painted pillars, mocking them all with its resonance. His fellow turnkey, pale and ill, followed.

The look in their guide's gaze was not without sympathy as he glanced at the Hogarths. "I can't leave you alone with him, but I'll give you as much privacy as I can." He nodded at Charles, then went to sit in the ordinary's chair while Charles stepped out of the box.

"Returned to life," he said with a sigh as he closed the door behind him. Had ever a man not employed by the prison stepped out of the condemned box of his own free will?

"No manacles at least," Kate's father said, reviewing his person somberly.

Kate smiled tentatively at him. He wanted to run to her, to take her in his arms, but between the presence of her father and his unwashed state, he didn't dare. His hands went to his loosely tied neckerchief.

Kate frowned at the gesture. She often tidied his neckerchief if it had gone awry, well aware of how particular he was about his appearance.

He watched her face, mobile as it went through the emotions

of fear, disgust, then went to dutiful fiancée. Ignoring his stench, she went to him, ready to fix the bow, but as her fingers nudged the fabric apart, her gaze fell on the dark chain of marks.

"Oh, Charles," she sobbed. "What has happened to your poor neck?"

"There are men here," he rasped, "in Sir Augustus's pay. It doesn't hurt too much, but I'm afraid I can't tie my neckerchief quite as tight as usual."

Kate put her hand to her mouth. "Charles, you silly thing. What does it matter? Did they mean to kill you or merely frighten you?"

"If they wanted me dead, I would be." His voice went to a whisper. Ignoring Mr. Hogarth, he held out his hand to her, hoping to at least feel the slide of her fingers against his.

"You were only doing your job," she said, reinforcing his own thoughts. But before she could press her glove against his bare flesh, her father intervened.

"The situation is out of hand, Charles," he said, stepping too close for Charles to hide any gesture of affection for Kate. "They came for Kate. For my family."

Charles frowned. "Why would Sir Augustus send villains against Kate? Perhaps against you, since you are my editor."

"It began with my daughter," Mr. Hogarth said firmly. "She had a letter."

"A riddle," Kate interjected. "Father recognized the Dr. Johnson quotations, so Mr. Aga and I went to his former London residence."

Charles passed his hand over his eyes. "You were attacked?"

"No, they gave me another letter, then escaped. There were at least three people working together."

"And that letter?"

"Byron quotations, so we went to his rented house in Piccadilly, but the house was locked up. No one approached us."

She pressed her lips together tightly and let her head hang for a moment. "I threw the letter in the gutter, Charles. I thought someone was playing a game."

"Was there some sort of deadline? Did you miss it?" He knew Kate had little free time away from her family responsibilities.

"She was well within the deadline," Mr. Hogarth asserted.

Charles touched his bruises gently, then rested his hand on his throat. "You refused to continue the game, then."

"Did you receive anything similar?"

"No letters. Just a turnkey who attacked and threatened me in person," Charles asserted.

"Who would torment my family so?" Mr. Hogarth asked.

"Unless you are not telling me something, I don't understand," Charles admitted. Feeling dizzy, he went to an open pew on the men's side and sat down.

Kate followed, crowding very close, and Mr. Hogarth took the opposite side.

"There is more," she said. "Late last night, someone set a fire in the herb patch outside the kitchen door. I smelled smoke and raised the house. We were able to subdue the fire, but when I returned upstairs, I found the letter I'd thrown in the gutter back on my pillow."

Charles's eyes went wide. "Someone was in your house? In Brompton?"

"Exactly," Mr. Hogarth said with a dry cough.

"It must be Sir Augustus. I have no friend who would operate like an enemy."

Mr. Hogarth nodded slowly. "I knew of none. We would not keep anyone like that on at the paper."

"We've asked ourselves how Sir Augustus has influenced the Lightning Club," Kate said. "He must have orchestrated the murder somehow."

Charles started to nod, but it hurt his throat. "I suspect

Mr. Yupman is involved. His behavior was that of an actor in a play that night. He knew Mr. Pickwick was dead. Someone had the police in place."

"You must not drop your vigilance for a moment," Kate warned. "Please be careful because twenty-four hours has now passed since I received the Byron note and I don't know where I am supposed to go." She pulled the letter from under her cape and handed it to him.

Charles read the contents, noting the threat to him. "I hope you have until the middle of the night to figure it out. Is this twenty-four-hour timer reset because they returned it to you?"

"We don't know who these villains are or who is watching," Kate said.

"It is obvious that they had a spy on you in Piccadilly, even if they didn't approach. They set you up to fail, in effect, then punished you for it."

"But nothing bad happened to you this morning, right?" Kate asked anxiously, nodding at his words.

"Just the bad joke of putting me in the condemned box." Charles flipped the letter over again, trying to focus on the puzzle instead of his aches and pains. "You went to the house where Byron lived with his wife?"

She nodded.

He read over the letter again. "I think the first quotation is from work done after Byron left England, so that won't do. I don't recognize the second quotation." He paused. "I do recognize the third quotation. It's from *The Bride of Abydos*."

"That was an earlier work," Mr. Hogarth said. "I remember it well now."

"Lord Byron didn't live in Piccadilly then?" Kate asked tremulously. "Do you think I need to go to Newgate Abbey?"

"No, it would be somewhere in London. Ask Thomas Pillar. He is good with addresses."

The turnkey came toward them. "I'm sorry, but it is time for you to leave the prisoner."

Charles clutched Kate's hand for a moment, staring into her eyes. She smiled at him, the look of love in her sweet face undiminished by the circumstances they faced. "I feel renewed," he whispered to her. "Thank you for coming."

Mr. Hogarth coughed again, then handed him a purse and a bundle. "For expenses, and a clean shirt."

"Thank you, sir. This is very helpful." He hoped it was enough for a hat.

"I wish I'd thought to bring a salve. I should have known you'd have injuries," Kate fretted.

He smiled at her. "Just seeing you is a balm for all my sorrows." Knowing he had supporters outside, that his friends had not lost faith in him, mattered deeply. Especially since he knew his own family, his parents in particular, would provide him no support. No, that help went only in one direction. If his father had been imprisoned, Charles would have been burning shoe leather gathering help, as he had a little more than a year before. But in this situation, John Dickens would do no more than sit in a wine shop somewhere with his cronies bemoaning the foolishness of the young. Blackening his reputation further, no doubt. His father didn't seem to be able to help himself. As difficult as George Hogarth could be at times, the man was an improvement over his own flesh and blood.

The turnkey took Charles's arm and he let the man march him away. It was best not to treat any of the guards like enemies. He couldn't know who was in Sir Augustus's pay.

At the newspaper office, Kate's father called for tea. Kate felt her head hanging very low as she sat in one of his chairs, waiting for the essential beverage to warm her. But it would have no effect on the burning anger in her heart. That her Charles should be treated so! Or any of them, for that matter. Evil held the upper hand in this most unfortunate of circumstances.

"We must get ahead of them in the chase somehow," she told her father. "As long as we are followers, we will never win."

Her father screwed up his mouth, then stuck in his pipe stem. "We canna risk your mother and the bairns, Kate. This puzzle must be yer first priority. When ye are a mother, ye will understand."

Kate ignored his words. "Do we know where Sir Augustus is? Could you, or Mr. Black, go speak to him, persuade him to stand down? Maybe swallow your pride and print a retraction to Charles's article, or write something that would make the villain feel less threatened?"

An office boy arrived with tea and set the tray on the corner of the desk. He shifted from side to side, not yet departing.

Her father glanced up. "What is it?"

"Did you really go to Newgate, sir? Was it very dreadful?"

He grunted instead of responding.

Kate smiled at the boy. "It was very dreadful indeed. They took us to the chapel where the condemned men sit in an enormous black enclosure before they are hanged. Be good so you never end up in a place like that."

The boy bit down hard on his lower lip and nodded fiercely.

"Fetch Aga, son," her father instructed. The boy ran out.

Kate checked the pot, then took off her gloves and poured the tea. The comforting scents of brewed leaves and pipe smoke filled the room, giving her a warming sensation. "I'm very worried about Charles. A guard attempted to strangle him? And they are creating a great deal of emotional distress for him as well. I think he's lost weight, and where was his coat?"

"You cannot expect Newgate Prison to be a picnic on Hampstead Heath," he muttered.

"Charles is incredibly resourceful, but he needs us to help him, or he's not going to survive this," Kate said pointedly.

"We will attack the problem a different way," her father said. "You need to focus on solving the Byron puzzle. There are more people at risk than Charles."

Kate thought about Mary, Georgina, and Helen, along with the boy herd of her brothers. Her father made a good point. She stared into her tea. "Can you send a boy to fetch Thomas Pillar so I can get more addresses from him?"

Before her father could respond, William Aga arrived at the door, accompanied by John Black, her father's coeditor. William appeared sprightly and rested next to the older man, not to mention freshly shaved with sparkling clean linen, a greater opposite to Charles than could be imagined.

"How did your visit go?" he asked with a nod at Kate.

"They are tormenting him physically and mentally," Kate said.

Mr. Black shook his head in disgust. "I had hoped he'd come to less harm in the gentlemanly part of the prison."

"It doesn't do any good if turnkeys are being paid to cause problems. He's been physically attacked, John," her father said.

"Isn't there something you can do?" Kate begged.

"A machine set in motion is difficult to stop," Mr. Black opined. "Charles has created an enemy and that is not resolved easily."

Mr. Hogarth set down his pipe. "Here is what we shall do. William, I want ye to drop the Sir Augustus investigation for now and investigate Mr. Yupman instead."

"Why?" the reporter asked.

"Charles said Yupman wasnae surprised by the Pickwick death. He said the man behaved like an actor. He might be easier to track and influence."

"The Lightning Club is for the best minds," Kate said. "Do we even know what Mr. Yupman is famed for?"

"Marriage," John Black said after a long moment when all three men visibly struggled to reach for the answer.

"What do you mean?" she asked.

John Black slid a finger under the knot of his neckerchief. "He marries well. The daughter of an earl. Good fortune from her grandmother. Then his first wife died, and he married a wealthy famed wit, also in society, though not quite so highborn. She died in due course, and he married a lady painter, who's in the portraiture line. You know the sort of thing, royal ladies with dogs."

"How would that gain someone entrance to a club?" Kate asked, confused.

"Money, contacts," Mr. Black explained. "He knows everyone important."

"Like Sir Augustus, most likely," Mr. Hogarth said. "Let me explain what happened overnight." He told the editor and the reporter about the fire.

William blanched at the news. "We must take these letters more seriously, Miss Hogarth."

"I agree," Mr. Black said. "You must uncover who is behind them, now that they have moved into property destruction."

William put his hands on his hips. "I don't think you Hogarths should stay in your house until we've settled the matter. Why don't you move next door for now?"

"What do ye mean?" Kate's father asked.

"Lugoson House," William explained. "I'll write a note for you to take to Lady Lugoson. She has a full complement of servants to air out a few rooms for you."

"That is highly irregular," Kate's father said.

William fixed him with a steely glare. "I know my wife is not a favorite of yours, but you have a good relationship with her aunt. Lady Lugoson will take you in for your children's safety."

Kate wondered if this situation might actually do some good. Some of the conflict Charles had with her father stemmed from his friendship with Julie Aga. Maybe if he finally realized the positive aspects of cordiality with her, the old specter of her life as an actress could be put to rest.

"Do it, George," Mr. Black urged. "For the children."

"We shouldnae leave the house unprotected," her father protested.

"Then leave a couple of your sons downstairs. Even better, solve the mystery."

"As to the mystery," Kate spoke up, "where was Lord Byron living when he wrote *The Bride of Abydos*? Charles suggested we ask your under-editor."

"I actually know the answer," Mr. Black said. "That was written in 1813, when Byron lived at 4 Bennet Street, Saint James."

"You are a font of all knowledge," William said. "May I have a scrap of paper?"

When Kate's father pushed paper and inkwell toward William, the reporter penned a quick note. "Here. You can send it to the baroness with one of the boys or just take it home with you."

"Thank you," her father said.

Kate stood. "Let's go to Bennet Street. Maybe we can reduce the threat right now."

"And move that closer to the villain's end game," William said with an uncustomary air of severity that reminded Kate he was a crime reporter.

She nodded soberly and buttoned herself into the navy cape that had once belonged to Lady Lugoson's murdered daughter.

The Bennet Street house was more modest than Dr. Johnson's one-time abode, but not far from the Piccadilly house that Lord Byron had resided in with his wife.

William sighed heavily as they exited their hired carriage with two of the office boys, just up the street from the address.

"What's wrong?" she asked.

"I just feel I could be doing something more important rather than playing bodyguard," he confided. "I am not sure what, but we need to get ahead of the situation, which takes thought and planning."

"It wasn't your house nearly on fire," she said shortly. "Or Julie at risk."

"Miss Hogarth," William said with a frown, "I care deeply about the safety of your family. But strategic thinking is important in a situation like this."

"Charles has all the time in the world to think," she said. "We do not. We have to act."

She sent one office boy ahead and told the other to follow behind, making sure to keep enough distance between them to keep them from looking part of a group.

She had no sooner passed from the railing of the house next to Byron's than the same man they had met in Gough Square came out from the recessed entryway of Lord Byron's former abode. She recognized his large body and the patched coat. He even wore the same top hat the boy had rescued. The villain had warmer clothing than her Charles did at Newgate.

Glancing around, she noticed a few people in the street but none watched them. She didn't know which of the passersby were part of this unsavory game.

"It is one thing to torment me," she said crisply. "I am promised to Mr. Dickens. But I have young siblings, little more than babies. If the fire had spread to the house they could have perished."

He came quite close to her.

"Back away," William said, putting up his hand.

The man stopped. He ignored William and stared at her, licking his front teeth. She felt like a bug who had stepped into a spider's web. Drawing up her strength, she held up her hand. "Another letter from the starfish, I presume?"

He sneered and took off his hat, displaying hair so dirty, it might have been any shade of brown when washed. His hand disappeared into the hat, then he thrust the letter toward her.

She checked the seal. "How long will this continue?" she asked.

He took a step alongside the railing. William stepped around Kate, giving the miscreant an evil stare. The stranger popped his hat back onto his head and leaned forward. When he straightened, he had a knife in his hand. He whistled.

Kate heard a horse gallop up the street behind her. She didn't want to take her gaze from the knife, but then the horse came alongside her. The stranger took a step back. Before William could react, he'd sidestepped into the street and flung himself into the saddle with the ease of a circus rider.

In another moment, they could see nothing but the diminishing shape of horse and rider. Around them, street traffic continued undisturbed.

William's jaw had dropped open, but he closed his mouth when he turned to her. "If I had not seen it myself, I wouldn't have believed it."

"Insanity," Kate murmured, looking up at the three-bay house. "I expect he has no connection to this house."

"No." William went between the gates. The house was quite flush against the street. "He probably was paid to skulk in the doorway. I have no idea who lives here now."

"I'm going to open the letter," Kate said, waving in each direction to gather the office boys to them. She had no time to spare for theatrics.

"What does it say?" William asked.

She lifted the seal and unfolded the missive. "It says, 'Miss Hogarth. The labouring hind, who on his bed of straw Beneath his home-made coverings, coarse but warm, Locked in the kindle arms of her who spun them, Dreams of the gain that next year's crop should bring; Or at some fair disposing of his wool, Or by some lucky and unlooked-for bargain, Fills his skin purse with store of tempting gold, Now wakes from sleep at the unwelcome call, and finds himself but just the same poor man As when he went to rest. Such a poor man, your fiancé. Keep him safe by meeting our associate within twenty-four hours. A friend.'"

"A mouthful," William offered.

"More than," Kate agreed. "This is the third letter. How many more will there be?"

Chapter 10

"I want to know how long this game of literary quotations will continue. It's ridiculous," William muttered. He leaned against the railing of Lord Byron's one-time home and watched a vegetable seller trundle his cart up the street.

Kate found William's mercurial moods frustrating. She had too much on her mind to soothe him. "I agree, but we know Sir Augustus has Newgate guards in his pay. They've already hurt Charles once. I don't want him permanently injured."

William's brow instantly creased. "Of course not. We must play along and figure out to whom the letter refers."

"It does sound familiar," Kate said thoughtfully, tugging her bonnet down over her cheeks. "Where is the nearest cab stand? I will let the quotations spin around in my brain until the author comes to me."

Charles did his best to keep his senses alert and his thoughts on Kate's sweet face as he paced along the wall in the frigid prison yard that afternoon. He'd layered the clean shirt that Mr. Hogarth had brought him over the dirty one closest to his body for another layer of warmth, and knotted the coins into the fabric.

Unwittingly, his thoughts went to Kate's treacle tart. Such a luxury. He wished the Hogarths had brought him more clothing as well, but Kate knew nothing of prison life and Mr. Hogarth had thought only of the gentlemanly version. He hadn't considered that the guards might be enemies, and if Charles gave one his money, he was more likely to see it vanish than produce any goods. For now, it was best that he watch his fellow prisoners and see who might be active on the prison's black market.

As if in answer to his thoughts, Bob Sawyer sidled in his direction, a diminutive form swathed in cloth. "'Eard you 'ad a visitor."

Charles nodded. "Two of them."

"They give you anything you could sell?"

"Why? Do you want to steal from me?"

Bob held up his mittened hands. "Just thought you might need help disposing of the personal property. I only require a small commission, like."

"I'll keep that in mind." He wanted to be careful, but the cold had him speaking despite his better judgment. "Does anyone assigned to our chamber specialize in hats?"

Bob's eyes, the only part of his face clearly visible, took on a crafty narrowness. "No. Rotter can get knives, but we've a pretty dull bunch. I have connections down the passage. Tell me what you need."

Charles heard his name shouted. The visibility remained good enough that he could see shapes at the cages. "Excuse me." He walked in the direction of the iron bars, peering for the familiar voice.

His father wasn't a mirror of himself, yet the resemblance between them could not be mistaken. Charles smiled at the sight of the tumbled hair, gray now, yet full of the same curls and cowlicks as his, and the familiar nose.

His father, though, did not smile. "I thought you lowered, sir, when you lost your position last month over a bastard child."

"Who was not mine," Charles retorted. "More an excellent opportunity for lesser minds to gossip."

His father straightened his collar with thick furred gloves that Charles would have loved to possess at that moment. He tried hard not to catalog his parents' every purchase, for the exercise would drive him mad, given all that he had suffered for their profligacy. It did him no good to be seen as a man from a troubled family. Rather, he took pride in being a gentleman's son and ignored the rest except in the privacy of his own thoughts.

"And now, murder?" his father queried.

"I was framed, Father, pure and simple. And just like the business with baby Timothy, the truth shall prevail," Charles snapped.

His father sighed. "'From the body of one guilty deed a thousand ghostly fears and haunting thoughts proceed.'"

"And what guilty deed is that?" Charles demanded. "Don't quote the poets at me. Who do you know who has ever been a part of the Lightning Club?"

"Just you, son," his father said.

"You've been in London more than a decade," Charles said. "Surely you've run across some distinguished man. I must have someone to investigate, some thread to pull."

His father looked over his head. "'And homeless near a thousand homes I stood, And near a thousand tables pined and wanted food.'"

"Really?" Charles demanded. "Another Wordsworth quotation. That is of no use to me, sir. I might think you in the pay of my tormentors, to offer me nothing but that."

"I know it can be hungry times in prison," his father said. "It's no diet for a grown man."

As well his father ought to know, having been an inmate of Marshalsea Prison and various sponging houses over the years, because of his debts.

Still, Charles couldn't deny the way his eyes followed the small bundle his father pulled from his pocket. He tossed it over the wall and it dropped neatly into Charles's hand.

"A pie," his father said.

Charles rather thought the handkerchief it was wrapped in might be just as valuable, so desperate was he for goods to trade. He mumbled his thanks and inhaled the pie, hoping good reason would come back to him when it reached his belly.

For his sweet Kate had been placed in harm's way, and when any of his friends returned, he had to be ready to provide counsel to aid them. The Hogarths could not suffer for their association with him.

"Thank you," Charles said, after he had swallowed the last morsel. He slid the handkerchief into his sleeve. "I don't suppose you hid a bottle of wine somewhere on your person?"

"I am afraid not." His father sniffed and reached into his pocket. "These are from Fanny."

Charles took the freshly knitted mittens with a grateful heart.

As he pushed the filthy remains of the gloves he had been wearing into his pocket and slid the new warm ones on, his father said, "I did have a thought."

"What is that?" Charles flexed his fingers, hoping his joints would be able to warm up now.

"You've run afoul of Eatanswill," his father said. "That article you wrote must have led to this mess if you really didn't knife that scientist."

"I would agree," Charles said.

His father poked a finger into the frosty air. "I recall a novel that Tracy Yupman's second wife wrote. One of those vaguely veiled society meanderings, where it is clear that old gossip is being rehashed."

"Yes?" Charles leaned forward, until his nose almost touched the iron.

"She's thought to have eviscerated her husband. He was supposed to have been the basis for her character Sir Percival Dumper." His father winced and moved from side to side.

"Go on," Charles encouraged.

"I recall that Sir Percival had a country seat in Eatanswill." He shrugged. "It may mean nothing, or there may be some old tie there."

"That could be useful," Charles said. "Thank you for remembering that." He looked hopefully at his father's greatcoat, hoping that something else would appear out of it, like a magician's conjuring.

A cry went up in the back of the yard. A turnkey, telling them it was time to return to their ward.

His father shook his head sadly. "I am sorry for your troubles, Charles. Perhaps you reached too far."

"I don't regret my story," Charles said. "Men like Sir Augustus don't belong in government."

"My son doesn't belong in Newgate." His father nodded sharply, as if hiding some emotion, and turned away.

Charles sighed and returned to Bob Sawyer, his belly fuller but his head equally as heavy. Unsatisfactory as it was, at least his father had troubled himself to visit.

"Who was that?" the little man asked, as they formed a line in front of the turnkey.

"My father," Charles explained.

"Nice mittens," Bob Sawyer commented.

"They aren't for sale," Charles said. "The beaver gloves I had before were rubbish."

"Sell them," he suggested.

"Someone will want the old ones? Stained with blood and muck? With holes in the index fingers?"

Bob Sawyer shrugged. "There are people here who are a lot poorer than you."

Charles was taken aback. How had his natural sensibilities been so destroyed by hardship? "Indeed. I should not think only of myself."

When they were back by the fire in their ward, seated on barrels against the wall, he passed his gloves to Sawyer. "Sell them for a fair price or trade for a hat. I had rather give them to some unfortunate, but I need more clothing."

Sawyer pocketed them with a nod. "Wery vell."

Charles watched as one eye blinked, then the diminutive man hopped off his barrel and wandered off, leaving him with his thoughts.

William and Kate walked toward Charing Cross, with the office boys fluttering around them like a pair of tall birds.

"There's a stand in front of that bank," one of the boys said.

William passed him coins to hold a cab. Kate's attention went to the costermongers hovering under the equestrian statue of Charles I.

"Hungry?" William asked.

Kate nodded as the cry of "hot green peas" reached her ears. He smiled as he heard. "I could do with a spot of something warm, too."

They had the quartet of treats purchased in a moment and sprinkled their little cups with vinegar and pepper. After Kate refreshed herself, she pulled the letter from her muff and read it over, careful to keep it under the overhang of the stall.

As she had thought, she knew this quotation well enough. It had swum up from the depths of her memory. It belonged to a poem about farm life called "A Winter's Day" by their family friend, the famed poetess and playwright Joanna Baillie.

"May I?" William asked.

She passed the letter to him. "This is the first letter that includes lines by someone living."

"Oh?"

She nodded. "It's the work of Joanna Baillie, who lives at Bolton House in Hampstead."

"Could she be a part of this muddle?"

"Definitely not," Kate said. "You've heard of her?"

"Indeed. She's a famous playwright, if not one who pleases the masses with their love of spectacle."

"I'm certain she doesn't know Charles," Kate said pensively. "Read the letter again."

William lifted it and read the words. "Yes?"

"Charles is being mocked in these letters, don't you think?"

William read, " 'Such a poor man, your fiancé.' What sorts of things did the other two letters say?"

She quoted both of them, since they were committed to memory. "I guess not. They prophesize disaster, which was about our house, not him, and the first one said he'd pay the price."

"I'm not certain you are incorrect, from the wording of this new letter."

"And it doesn't matter. We can't stop chasing the answers, now that someone set a fire outside my family home. Even if we do leave for Lugoson House, it's Charles who is being threatened now."

"Your house may not be safe either, to be honest," William said. "Losing it would be a dreadful trial on your family."

Kate nodded. "Let's go see Father."

When William and Kate reentered the front office of the newspaper, she sent the boys ahead, then sat down on the bench near the door and opened the letter again. There hadn't been enough light in the carriage to read it.

"What has struck you now?" William asked.

"I just realized that they attacked my home. What about his?"

William considered. "You think they will try to rob him?"

"And Fred is there alone."

William nodded. "You aren't wrong. We should tell him to gather up what he can and go to his parents in Bloomsbury."

"He won't want to, and they may not even welcome him."

"Still, it's the right thing to do. His office isn't too far from my rooms, and I am supposed to attend a meeting this afternoon."

"Go ahead," Kate invited. "One of my parents will have to go along with me to see Miss Baillie, after all. It makes no sense to bring a stranger when they are acquainted with her."

William flashed her his ready smile. "Julie is so jealous that you get to have an adventure while she spends her time training a maid and learning how to make infant clothing."

"I would trade her all this running around for that. She is blessed."

William's sunny expression faded. "I just hope this outcome is better than the last."

She patted his arm. "It will be. I have a good feeling about it. Off you go. I'm sure my father will tell you all about what transpired tomorrow."

"Copy out the letter for me if there is any question," he urged. "Have one of the Lugoson House servants deliver it to me in Cheapside. We don't want disaster to strike again."

"Thank you." She smiled and rose. "Until next time."

He sketched her a bow, then returned to the street. She straightened her shoulders and went to confront her father with the latest development.

"Did you have the correct location this time?" her father asked, setting a page of splotched writing on his untidy desk. He leaned back in his chair to look Kate fully in the face.

"Yes. Leave it to Charles to come up with the correct answer, even from Newgate." She shook her head in admiration of his mental powers.

"There is nothing wrong with that boy's intellect." He held out his hand for the letter.

She handed it over.

It only took a glance for him to discern what she had. "Miss Baillie?"

She nodded. "It's the first time we've been given a quotation by someone who is still alive. I'm assuming I'm meant to go to Hampstead."

"They can hardly be wanting to send ye to Scotland," he agreed. "At least we can be sure of the text. It is all from the same poem. However, ye can't visit such a famous personage without sending a note first or planning to attend her scheduled 'At Home.'"

"But Father, she's an old friend of the family, and far enough away from London that anyone might drop by without knowing her plans."

"I think not."

"It is unlikely I would need to go inside. This person is probably lurking in the lane to give me another letter. In fact, he needs time to get there."

Her father pulled a fresh piece of notepaper toward him. "I will send a note. Ye have until tomorrow. What is this miscreant going to do, camp out in the lane all night outside her house?"

"I think we should proceed with speed," Kate insisted. "My fit of temper already risked having our house being burned down."

That gave her father pause. He set down his pen and rubbed the stem of his cold pipe. "Miss Baillie couldn't possibly be involved," he said in a fretful voice.

"She won't even have to know."

"It would be just our luck to have her out walking when we wander by, looking like a couple of cutthroats. Perhaps they even want that, to make the situation as uncomfortable as could be."

"They've threatened Charles's safety. My comfort doesn't matter. We know what they are capable of. Charles had the marks around his neck to prove it." She touched her throat, remembering.

Her father rubbed his muttonchops. "I don't like this."

"I don't, either. Why don't you send the note?" she encouraged. "Through the post. We can make the excuse that we arrived before it if we do come across Miss Baillie."

"Very well. We will go tomorrow morning, very early, and get there before the deadline."

"No, we should go now."

"I canna take ye," he said. "I have a newspaper to get out. And William?"

"He didn't return with me. He had a meeting to report on."

"It's best this way. I need to beg Lady Lugoson's indulgence myself, ye ken. I dinna like to leave the boys without my support if anything happens at the house."

Kate worried at her lower lip. "At least they know I didn't toss the letter in the street. They have no reason to attack tonight." She didn't like the sense that there were strange eyes on her.

"Very good. I'll just send this letter to Bolton House and announce that they might expect yer mother in the morning. It might even arrive before the pair of ye do." Her father scribbled away on the page.

Kate waited while he penned it, then offered to hand it to an office boy herself. She felt too restless to sit, and her father hadn't suggested she find a cab herself to return home. Her mother would expect it, her hands full with the children, but she could argue against the expense of two cabs in one day.

She took the letter to one of the boys, then wandered into the newsroom. Everyone greeted her politely. Though some of these men didn't lead the most regular of lives, they dressed and spoke well, and they didn't bother her as she seated herself at Charles's desk.

Thinking to find some clue as to what happened, she looked through his drawers. The contents were surprisingly sparse, but he had been sent home from work for a couple of weeks the month before, so she supposed he'd taken everything home very recently. She did find a bundle of notes and, assuming they were recent, pulled them out.

The dates were indeed new, but when she flipped through the pages, hoping to find his notes from Eatanswill, she discovered they were written in completely indecipherable shorthand. She could learn nothing.

When she looked up in frustration, a familiar face appeared through the open door into the passage behind the newsroom. What was Charles's father doing at the paper?

She rose abruptly, the movement of her skirts knocking Charles's chair into the one behind it. Apologizing for the loud noise to anyone listening, she fled in the direction of Mr. Dickens.

She reached her father's office just after he did and watched from the doorway as he pulled off his hat and held it between two hands.

Knowing Charles often complained of his father's poor spending habits, while admiring the gentlemanly charm that allowed him to get away with it, she cataloged his wardrobe and found it quite fine, if not so fine as Charles's. His hair had something of the style of Charles's, though thinned, graying, and without vibrance.

Her father rose from his desk as Charles's father announced, "John Dickens, Esquire, at your service, sir."

"Of course, of course, happy to see ye again." Her father stepped around his desk, his newly lit pipe in one hand. He shook with the other. "What brings you to the *Chronicle* today?"

"A sad business," Mr. Dickens said as Kate came into the room. His mouth pulled to one side. "Very tragic."

"Ye remember my daughter."

"My soul mate in tragedy," he said, taking her hand with great feeling. "My poor dear."

Before she could respond, he dropped her hand and turned back to her father. "I do not regret my son, and I may have been deprived of him for a specific purpose. I cannot say. But the truth is, I will need to cover his expenses while he is away, and I find myself without sufficient funds to do so. I have six living children, you know, a large brood, and must not sacrifice them all for the sake of one."

Her father glanced between her and Mr. Dickens. "I am well aware of the sacrifices of a large family, sir. We have been to see Charles this very day and brought him money and clothing."

Mr. Dickens's head drew back on his neck. "Excellent news. But only"—he tapped his chin—"I was at the prison just now and he didn't even mention it. He gobbled up the pie I brought him as if he hadn't dined for a week. Very troubling, sir."

"I agree," Mr. Hogarth said. "A young, active man out in cold weather with insufficient clothing will be hungry."

"Perhaps you could spare a few more coins?" Mr. Dickens suggested. "I could buy more food for the boy and bring it to him. You would not need to stir from your chair, sir."

"I do not think ye would be allowed in, not once they've taken the prisoners indoors," her father said equably.

"Oh, I should think, anytime, sir, anytime, as long as there is money involved." Mr. Dickens rubbed his thumb and forefinger together.

"I think not," her father said gently.

"What about the rent, sir? On his chambers? If you can spare something, I may be able to reason with his landlord."

"I expect that Fred knows where Charles keeps his money and they will have some arrangement between them that will not fall apart in the course of a few days."

"He must have savings somewhere, given that he's about to take on the responsibility of a wife. Perhaps Miss Hogarth knows where it can be accessed?"

Kate froze. She understood that Charles didn't trust his father, and for the first time she began to see why. It gave her an uncomfortable feeling in her chest to even consider that Mr. Dickens might access Charles's savings and keep some portion of it for himself. Surely, he would not be so unnatural? And yet, she knew Charles had covered the expenses of Fred's final months of education. He'd been very poor when she'd met him, and not ready to set up a household.

Looking at her father, she said, "Please do not trouble yourself, Mr. Dickens. We will handle things directly." She couldn't even suggest he speak to Fred, for fear that Fred really did know where Charles's money was kept.

Her father frowned at her.

"You must know where the lad's strongbox is?" Mr. Dickens ventured directly.

"I do not," she returned.

"His salary?" Mr. Dickens returned his attention to her father. "When is that due? I shall collect the funds and keep them safe."

"I shall have to research that, but ye must understand, Charles has not worked for us this week."

Mr. Dickens pressed his full lips together. But instead of flashing irritation, he gave a quick little bow. "Very good, sir. I see you have everything under control. My regards to the delightful Mrs. Hogarth. My wife was just saying the other day that we haven't seen her in an age."

After a few more pleasantries, he bowed out of the room. Kate shut the door.

"That was a begging letter in person, was it not, Father?"

"Don't be disrespectful." Mr. Hogarth stuck his pipe stem into his mouth. "He is Charles's father."

"I know, and of course I love him, but Charles would want it this way. If you gave Mr. Dickens Charles's salary, I don't think it would make it to his rent."

Chapter 11

"We have quite a trip before us," Mrs. Hogarth fretted early the next morning as they made their way down the steps.

"The sooner we begin, the sooner it will end." Kate heard the rattle of the horses' fittings at the base of the Lugosons' front staircase. At least she had the Lugosons' butler, Panch, on her side, and he'd ordered the tilbury with its large wheels and excellent suspension. "Are you ready, Mother?"

"How can I leave the children here all day?" She stopped in the middle of buttoning her glove. Her mother was not a woman to be hurried, house endangered or not.

They must. Otherwise, the consequences might be dreadful. But Kate didn't want to send her mother into a fit of fluttering and worry. "There are plenty of servants here, and Polly is in charge of the younger ones, same as at home."

Her mother pursed her lips, aging her face a decade. "We haven't checked on Robert."

"If there had been a fire at our house again, we'd smell it," Kate said. "I opened the window this morning in our room. It looks out to the orchard, and I saw no sign of smoke, nor smelled anything wrong." She'd shared a chamber with Mary and Georgina, like at home, but the four-poster bed had been so wide that all three had comfortably fit inside. They also could have sat comfortably in the enormous wardrobe. Mary had suggested the room suited giants more than Scotswomen.

"We should check on them before we go," her mother fretted.

"Mother, the carriage awaits. We'll drive by our house and make sure it still stands."

"Very well." The final button inserted, her mother drew on her cape, fur-lined and borrowed from Lady Lugoson for the journey.

Kate's navy cape already had fine, warm finishings. She knew plush carriage blankets waited for them outside. Panch had personally supervised hot bricks for their feet. Their drive had been equipped well.

A footman ushered them out of the front door and down the stairs. Kate made sure to keep her skirts from trailing as she did not want to begin with dampness around her feet.

Her mother entered the carriage first, then Kate followed behind, careful not to sit on her mother's skirts. Since neither of the ladies could drive such a sporty vehicle for so long, Panch had selected the smallest coachman, saying the three of them would fit comfortably in the seat. The driver, a man a decade older than her mother, pressed in beside them, and a box was tucked just behind Kate's feet full of victuals in case it was needed.

"Quite luxurious, is it not?" Kate asked her mother, as she attempted to spread her skirts under her cape. They'd slowly been working on her trousseau, and she wore skirts made over from old dresses, topped with a new bodice of red wool.

"It might take as much as three hours to reach Miss Baillie in the worst conditions," her mother fussed. She wore her Sunday best, a paisley print in soft twill, with an extra petticoat underneath to bell out the skirt and keep her warm.

"I hope the rain will hold off. We could make it in less than two," Kate ventured.

Lady Lugoson had assured them the night before that they would make the journey as fast as possible in this particular vehicle and soothed all of Mrs. Hogarth's worries about tipping over and spilling them into the road.

As the coachman snapped the reins and they lurched into the road, Kate looked around as much as she could, given the wide brim of her most fashionable bonnet.

"I think our house must have survived," her mother said tremulously as they passed their gate. "There is no sign of destruction."

"We are doing as instructed." Kate felt for the paper tucked into her muff. "Unless there is trouble on the road, we will arrive at Bolton House in time."

"What if you have misunderstood the clue?"

Kate could not look her mother in the face because of their bonnets, or touch her arm or hand because then she would lose the comfort of her muff. But she made her voice as warm as possible and said, "I know we are right. The text was all from Miss Baillie's poem. It was more straightforward than the other clues."

"I wonder why these miscreants want ye so far out of town?"

"I wonder that myself, but we can't risk not going. I hope Father can send someone to Newgate this morning to keep an eye on the yard when Charles is outside."

"It seems necessary," her mother agreed. "Under the circumstances. I did hope that Sir Silas would be at dinner last night, so that we could ask him if he's uncovered anything else about the murder."

"Yes, this business with the letters has kept us entirely unable to focus on poor Mr. Pickwick," Kate agreed. "When we've dealt with murders before, it is Charles who has done so much of the investigating. I've done little more than consult. I'm not spending my energies properly."

"It's not your place to investigate such unseemly business."

"It is when our family is in danger," Kate argued. "I am doing the best I can and can only pray that following the letter is the best hope for Charles's safety."

Her mother groused on about the house and her children for a good twenty minutes as they drove east. Kate hoped the coachman's ears were well covered so that he missed the complaints.

"Have you known Miss Baillie all your life?" Kate asked, hoping to change the subject.

"We've always been on the outer ends of the same circles, ye ken, because of her friendship with the late Sir Walter Scott. She was a friend of my father, being of that generation. I met her some twenty years ago."

"After you had reached the age of being sensible enough to be around a genius?" Kate asked.

"Any of the geniuses," her mother agreed. "Such a circle we had in Scotland."

"There are plenty of interesting people here in London," Kate asserted.

"Yes. Miss Baillie herself has been here since 1802 with her sister and mother. Her mother has long since passed. Goodness, but Miss Baillie is in her mid-seventies."

"She will no doubt be a source of wisdom for us."

"Absolutely. She has a mind like Shakespeare's, after all."

As they drove out of London into the countryside, her mother shared details of each meeting she remembered with Sir Walter Scott and Miss Baillie. Kate keenly felt Charles's loss, because she knew how he would have enjoyed the stories, and how much it would have cleaved him to her, the passage between him and these famed writers.

Someday, she knew, he would be as great as them, if only he could be freed from his present troubles.

Some two hours later, judging by the movement of the fickle sun and the stiffness in Kate's legs, the carriage horses trotted down a narrow lane, edged by evergreen bushes leaning over short brick walls, behind which soared bare winter branches.

The coachman called to the horses and pulled on the reins as they came alongside a row of four houses. Three windows wide and made from red brick, the houses were handsome examples of the previous century. The contrasting woodwork of windows and doors gave the buildings a friendly appearance. Kate could imagine hot cups of tea and oatcakes waiting within, with fresh butter and tangy jam. Just as excitingly, a chat full of her native brogue.

But that was not why she was here. Her heart rate increased despite the sluggish cold, as she looked carefully behind each bush and tree, and into the doorways, for some prowling interloper.

Bad news. No one waited behind the walls, no one waited on the staircases, not a soul hovered around the bushes.

Her mother yawned, giving movement to the sleepy winter appearance of the street. "It is nice here, isn't it, ducks?"

Kate nodded. "Yes, but where is my letter keeper?"

Her mother bit her lip. Kate saw a spot of blood where the wind had worn a dry crack. "Yes, where?"

"I do hope Father's letter arrived," Kate said, knowing she needed to get her mother out of the elements. If they hadn't been in such a rush, they might have stopped at a coaching inn to warm up, but as it was, they had made very good time for January.

She bent forward slightly to address the driver. "I will do my best to get you into a stable for a rest. We were unable to trade correspondence."

"It isn't far to an inn I know," he said in a gravelly voice, "if there's no place to warm the horses here."

"Excellent," she said.

He looped the reins over an iron railing at the front of the box and leapt down, then made sure the step was in place before he helped Kate out.

"I shall have to come, too," her mother said. "I am the familiar face."

The coachman helped Mrs. Hogarth to the road as well. When they stepped up to the brick wall, the front door of the literary lioness's house opened.

"It's Agnes Baillie," her mother whispered.

Kate's heart sank into her stomach as an elderly woman in a gauzy turban peered out through the doorway. Where was the dirty man she'd expected? She'd hoped to avoid the time of a social call. They had a deadline. Failure would have dreadful consequences.

"Mrs. Hogarth, what a pleasure," the elderly woman declared in a Lanarkshire accent.

"I do hope ye received my husband's letter," Mrs. Hogarth said, rushing up to the gentle lady.

Kate followed behind, still watching for lurkers. If they were not present, that meant she was in the wrong place again. Dread stopped her feet next to a bush as she realized that meant Charles was in terrible danger at any moment. Not only was she powerless to help him, now she had to make a polite social call on these genteel elderly ladies and then sit in a carriage for hours on the return with her complaining mother.

At least they were welcoming. Agnes Baillie gestured Kate to follow them inside.

"This is so kind of you," Kate said. "We have a carriage waiting outside."

"I'll bring ye in, then let the housekeeper know to make arrangements," the aged lady said. "Please, follow me."

"Hello, my dears," called an elderly Scottish voice when the Hogarths stepped behind Agnes Baillie into a cozy wood-paneled parlor.

A maid had helped them remove their heavy outer clothing, but Kate knew she'd be very warm quickly, for the room had been heated for the comfort of old bones. A fire crackled merrily away, burning much too hot for the safety of little ones.

Two women were seated at a round table. Kate recognized Miss Baillie. The graying curls wreathed around her face were the same as ever and her deep-set eyes as penetrating. Her cheeks shone very red in the heat. Across from her sat a literary lioness of the younger generation, Lucy Aikin, some few years elder to Kate's mother.

"Please, sit," Agnes Baillie urged.

"Oh, we couldn't take yer chair," Mrs. Hogarth said in her sweetest voice.

"I'll just bring another. Don't ye fret." Agnes gave her a close-lipped smile and went to the wall to fetch a matching rosewood lyre-backed chair.

Kate sank onto the down-filled cushion of the free chair after her mother seated herself. It felt like heaven after the hours in the jolting carriage. When the five of them had arranged themselves around the table, Miss Baillie rang a bell at her elbow to summon a maid to bring more refreshments.

While she made her requirements known, thrilling Kate with the treats to follow, she looked around the room, cataloging it for Charles. The contents would have pleased a lending library, though once again she thought the fire a bit too enthusiastic for a room filled with paper. In front of some of the books dangled bits of lace, or small miniatures. Kate fancied they must be of all the famed literary people who'd come to call. In fact, wasn't that Byron in front of a volume of Hume? Miss Baillie had a fine collection of Scottish philosophers and poets.

A bust of Shakespeare was inserted like a bookend next to a collection of his plays. Kate was gratified to see a bookcase filled with bound sermons, since the Baillies' father had been a minister and divinity professor.

How she felt Charles's absence now, in a room so designed for his comfort. A fully equipped writing desk with a slanted board waited under a curtained window. Creamy paper waited for the pen to scratch over it, ink bottles at the ready. She noted a volume of Maria Edgeworth's novel *Helen* at the end of the closest bookshelf to the writing desk, and imagined herself sitting on a stool next to Charles, reading while he wrote.

The tidiness of the room and the cozy smell despite all the books told her Miss Baillie knew how to keep her staff in line.

When she returned her attention to the table, their hostess was explaining the mound of papers heaped on the table in front of them as documents pertaining to the volumes of her *Miscellaneous Plays* that were being released later this year.

"You must be revising," Kate exclaimed. "My fiancé has his first book coming out next month and he's always huddled over pages."

"Too right," Miss Baillie agreed. "I have continued my *Plays on the Passions* with nine new plays, and there is a great deal to do."

"My goodness," Kate breathed. "It's a wonder you had time to see us. I wouldn't take away your precious time for the world."

"Oh, it is fine," Miss Baillie said, gesturing for her sister to clear the table. "Our dear Lucy was just telling me about the latest edition of her *Memoirs of the Court of Queen Elizabeth*, and all the errors she found when she checked the galleys."

"I do love that book," Kate said. "How much research you must have done, to uncover the fates of all those courtiers."

Miss Aikin smiled warmly. "I am afraid finishing my King Charles quite emptied my brain of the earlier generation."

"Who are you working on now? Charles the second?"

Miss Aikin shuddered. "What a dreadful man. Certainly not."

Kate giggled as the lady smiled again. The maid entered with a tray that nearly covered the table. But no sooner than a plate of tempting little cakes had been settled directly in front of her, that she remembered where Charles was, and what he faced, and her appetite fled.

"Why, ye've gone quite pale," Miss Baillie exclaimed. "What is wrong?"

"We are in terrible danger," Mrs. Hogarth explained.

"We came here in chase of a riddle," Kate managed after Miss Aikin gasped. "Honestly, it would have been better if we'd had no reason to see you. I inquire against hope to ask if you might have a letter for me?"

"A letter from your father, only," Miss Baillie said. "Was he meant to have enclosed something for you in it? I did think it was posted in London."

Kate shook her head miserably. "May I share the history of my woes with you?"

"You must," said the lady briskly. "We are at full attention."

Kate had been holding the latest letter the entire time. She passed it around to the ladies so they could read it over, then explained the progression of the letters. "And now, I have erred again, dear ladies. I must have chosen the wrong address."

Miss Baillie's cheeks had become even more flushed, though the fire had not built up again. "To think some villain used my work for this purpose."

"Fiendish," her sister agreed.

Miss Baillie had a firmness to her lips now. "I have no insight, my poor Miss Hogarth, other than to say the villain must be ruled by their passion."

"Which passion?" piped her sister.

"How dreadful," murmured Miss Aikin. "I quite despair."

Miss Baillie finished her tea. "I have written plays on passions such as love, hatred, ambition, fear, hope, remorse, jealousy, pride, envy, revenge, anger, joy, and grief."

"Joy must be out of the question," Mrs. Hogarth said uncertainly. "But any of the others?"

"Yes," Miss Baillie said decisively. "For love can be the most dangerous of all."

"We know Sir Augustus Smirke is ambitious," Kate ventured. "Many people have said he would take revenge on Charles for his unflattering portrayal in the newspaper."

"Very good," Miss Baillie praised. "Who else? Have you investigated the members of this Lightning Club?"

"No," Kate admitted.

"It sounds like the type of organization that Lady Byron would be aware of," said the Scottish playwright. "I shall write her and see what she has to offer us."

"That would be very kind," Kate said. "When I had the Byron clue, we went to her former abode."

Miss Baillie clucked her tongue. "Such doings all those years ago. That dastardly man."

"Brilliant poet, though," Miss Aikin demurred.

Kate kept herself still, desperate to return to her own woes, rather than those of nearly twenty years before, but the elderly would dwell on the exciting events of their past, and nothing better existed than ancient scandal. People would probably whisper about this someday. Maybe she would sit near an overlarge fire in forty years in lace gloves and cap and share old secrets about these bad days.

"What do ye know about Samuel Pickwick?" Agnes Baillie ventured to ask after the literary ladies had subsided.

"I'm ashamed to say, very little," Kate confessed. "In truth, I have encouraged Charles to look at the victim before, when he has solved murders, but in this case, I've done nothing but chase after clues."

"Why?" Miss Baillie inquired.

"There's been no time for anything else." Kate set the Dr. Johnson and much grimier Byron clues on the table next to the latest letter. Each of the ladies took one.

"Please, have another cake," Miss Baillie invited.

The Hogarth ladies munched while the others muttered over the letters.

"The letters come forward in time in the literary sense," Miss Baillie muttered.

"All are towering literary figures around London, but what does it mean?" Miss Aikin said.

Kate stared at the remaining cakes on the tray, with eyes that felt heavy from the strong application of heat. How she wanted to indulge. She wished a bakery in Brompton had such skill with lighter-than-air sponge batter. Such icing, delicate decoration, and the fillings were divine. She licked the taste of sugar off her lips.

Her eyes flew open. "Envy!"

"What's that, my dear?" her mother asked, equally somnolescent.

"The passion," Kate explained. "Envy. What if it is the key?"

Miss Baillie set down the letter she was perusing, dark eyes keen. "Why?"

"My Mr. Dickens is a literary figure, as are the others." Kate blushed. "He writes sketches, well regarded enough to have his own book on the way. Could it be that a failed writer is behind this?"

"What sort of writers belong to the Lightning Club?" Miss Aikin asked.

"Poets," Kate said. "A songwriter, from what Charles said at the prison."

Miss Baillie nodded and rose. "I will write Lady Byron at once. I suggest you look at failed writers among the Lightning

Club members, because the murderer has to have access to the private museum where these dastardly deeds transpired."

"Very good point," Kate said. "They must be someone who was once prominent, to have entry to the membership."

"Or merely work for the museum," Agnes ventured. "Ye canna rule that out."

"Is Sir Augustus a failed writer?" Miss Aikin asked.

Kate put her hands to her temples. "So many possibilities."

Behind her, out in the hall, a clock began to chime the hour. When she realized it had struck eleven, her hands dropped numbly to her sides. "We still have to find the letter. Ladies, Mr. Dickens is in mortal danger."

Miss Baillie nodded. "You had better go, my dear. I will ask Lady Byron to send word to your home."

After an interminable time of saying good-bye, Kate found herself back at the brick wall with her mother. Agnes Baillie had gone to ensure the carriage had returned with fresh horses.

Kate looked up and down the street, anxious for sight of the dirty man, but saw nothing other than a cart trundling down the street at a distance. How badly had they failed Charles?

Charles's ward was allowed into the yard just as the rain stopped. He had used the full powers of his imagination to cloak himself in luxurious winter raiment, persuading his body with the power of his mind that he was warm. After all, did he not tramp through the streets through all hours of the night in comfort?

But it wasn't like this, trapped between stone walls without an overcoat. He could duck into a tavern or a friend's house at will. Or return to his chambers. And he didn't have to be at the same knifepoint of vigilance, already bruised and battered from one attack.

He'd thought about what to do with the coins the Hogarths

had brought him. The black market in the prison thrived. He could get any sort of food or tobacco. The turnkeys either turned a blind eye or were part of the operations. He had dreamed of another meat pie, or warm smoke between his lips. A hat.

The most important currency, though, was information, and he needed it.

He leaned against a wall and watched Bob Sawyer in intense conversation with another of the men in their ward. Something wrapped in cloth passed from one hand to another. He didn't know or care what, unless it was a trade for his old gloves. Out of the corner of his eye, he watched the turnkey who had attacked him watch the other two men.

When the transaction had completed, the turnkey looked around, cataloging the other men in the yard. When his gaze went past Charles, he inclined his chin.

The man sneered but moved toward him. "Wot? Want another taste of me fists?"

"I want information," Charles said.

"Nuffin is free," retorted the guard.

Charles pulled the coins from his pocket and held them out.

"That will buy you one answer," Curdle said.

"Just one?" Charles tried not to sound desperate.

The man sneered, exposing a missing eye tooth. "Nuffin comes cheap 'ere."

Charles passed over the coins. "It is evident that you are in Sir Augustus's pay."

"Is that your question?"

"No," Charles said quickly. Everything he wanted to say seemed to form into a question. He thought hard, until the turnkey shifted from one foot to the other. "I have it. What is the connection between Sir Augustus Smirke and the Lightning Club?"

The man rubbed his stubbled chin and flicked away whatever he'd found there. Then he exposed his top teeth and picked casually at them. After a moment, he swiped the coins from Charles's hand and turned away. But before he walked, he said, " 'E's a member."

On the pavement outside of her house, Agnes Baillie pulled her shawl around herself and looked at the overcast sky doubtfully. "I wonder what has happened to that carriage?"

Kate looked up and down the street again, but the residential area had gone silent. "The coachman said there was a public house nearby. Did he go there?"

"It's possible. I'll have to ask the housekeeper if that was what she intended. I'm sorry, dears. Come back inside."

Kate considered standing there, stubbornly, offering herself up for sacrifice as it were, like some ancient heroine waiting for the beast to claim her. Then the thought struck her that a roomful of exceedingly learned women still waited for her at the house.

Her mother gave her an inquiring look.

"No one here to give us another clue," Kate muttered, and gestured her mother back toward the house.

They had to disassemble their cold-weather attire, for the room was hot enough to make a lady so clothed swoon.

"Ye must be so anxious, my dear," Miss Baillie said, patting Mrs. Hogarth's hand.

"It has been twenty-four hours. How could you possibly have gone to the wrong place since Miss Baillie certainly wrote the lines of that poem?" Miss Aikin said, echoing Kate's thought.

They all stared at each other. Kate drained her new cup of tea. Feeling desperate, Kate asked, "Do you have an original copy of the poem?"

"More than one," Miss Baillie agreed. "Agnes, dear, I think the first edition is in the corner case on the middle shelf."

While skirts swished into another part of the room, Kate closed her eyes and tried to compose herself with a prayer for Charles's safety. It was one thing to send someone to an herb garden in Brompton to light a fire. Surely sending word to someone in a prison to attack their victim out of sight of anyone doing their honest work as a guard would be a more complicated matter.

Agnes Baillie returned with the volume and set it in Kate's hands. She opened to the title page and perused it, then read aloud, something sparking connections deep in the back of her thoughts.

POEMS;

WHEREIN IT IS ATTEMPTED TO DESCRIBE

CERTAIN VIEWS OF NATURE

AND OF

RUSTIC MANNERS;

AND ALSO,

TO POINT OUT, IN SOME INSTANCES, THE DIFFERENT INFLUENCE WHICH THE SAME CIRCUMSTANCES PRODUCE ON DIFFERENT CHARACTERS.

LONDON:

PRINTED FOR J. JOHNSON, SAINT PAUL'S CHURCH-YARD.

MDCCXC.

Kate finished reading, translating the Roman year into 1790, then turned and began to read the poem, hyperconscious that she read in front of its lady author.

A WINTER DAY.

The cock, warm roosting 'midst his feather'd dames,
Now lifts his beak and snuffs the morning air,
Stretches his neck and claps his heavy wings,
Gives three hoarse crows, and glad his talk is done;
Low, chuckling, turns himself upon the roost,
Then nestles down again amongst his mates.

She licked her dry lips. Miss Baillie gave her an encouraging nod. Those tickles in the back of Kate's brain intensified. She frowned and turned back to the title page, then read it again.

"The publisher was J. JOHNSON, SAINT PAUL'S CHURCH-YARD," she said.

"Correct," said Miss Aikin. "Though Joseph Johnson, the famed publisher, is long dead."

"It's a London address," Kate said, her confused thoughts sparking into fire.

"The address was No. 72 St. Paul's Churchyard," Miss Aikin agreed.

"They sent us to London for the first clues," Kate pointed out. "And Mr. Pickwick was attacked in London."

"It's much more anonymous there," Miss Baillie agreed. "This dirty man ye speak of would not be noticed in the city, no matter how long he must wait."

Kate felt the urge to jump to her feet, in Charles's exuberant manner. Though she did not.

The maid came into the room. "Miss Baillie, there is a carriage in the street."

Miss Baillie rose and, following her as if she were royalty, the others all stood as well. "I think ye have a good idea. Ye must go to my publisher's former address and see if ye find him there."

Kate nodded. "It's the only intelligent course of action now."

"I do hope Mr. Dickens can survive for another few hours," her mother fretted.

Chapter 12

By the time they arrived at the *Chronicle* offices, it needed only an hour until dinnertime. Kate had argued with her mother in favor of going to the address directly, but as the fog rolled in and the afternoon became dark, she lost her courage.

"I am sorry for it, my dear, but it is hours past the deadline." Kate saw the outline of her mother's head shake as she responded to the latest plea.

"We must try," Kate insisted.

Mrs. Hogarth pointed into the darkness surrounding the carriage. "The man would be invisible at this time of day even if he was there. It's far more likely he has gone to do something dreadful, many hours ago now." Mrs. Hogarth attempted to pat Kate's hand, but Kate pulled it away and shoved it back into her muff.

She hunched deeper under Lady Lugoson's blanket as a gust of wind blew through. How could she have failed Charles so, when he needed her most? Instead of having the pleasure of berating herself, she spent the remaining half hour of the drive south into London planning a verbal assault on her father.

When they arrived at 332 Strand, Mrs. Hogarth sent Kate in to fetch her father so they could return home. An office boy, recognizing her, helped her down from the carriage and escorted her into the office.

Kate found it difficult to keep a sedate pace as she moved down the passage to her father's office. She smelled his pipe tobacco before she reached the door, but for once it didn't comfort her. How could everything around her seem to trundle along like normal when a catastrophe was in the making?

She knocked on the door and entered as soon as she heard her father's "Come."

"Are ye the master of the mystery?" he asked, absent-minded, as he scribbled something on a sheet.

"No, Father. No one was waiting in Hampstead. But we think we figured out the puzzle, and I need to go to St. Paul's Churchyard. Mother wouldn't take me because it is dark now."

"And foggy," he agreed. "No place for a young lady."

"But Charles!" she protested.

"The deadline would have been a good five hours ago," he said, as implacable as her mother. "I won't put you at risk."

"Send someone," Kate urged, wringing her hands inside her muff. "Please, to look for the man. I can describe him very fully."

"Fetch me a lad," he said. "And tell your mother to go straight home. We shall follow."

Kate took a long look at him. He had ink on his fingers and on the side of his cheek above his whiskers. "Yes, Father." She went back to the street and told her mother what her father had said. After the coachman drove off, she went back in, shivering, into the passage leading to her father's chamber, and walked toward John Black's office, then found herself in a little room where the errand boys must wait. It had a fireplace with a kettle, and a shelf with tea things. This must be where her father's ever-present genial beverage was renewed. She even saw some wine bottles in a crate on the floor.

Unfortunately, no one was there, and the hour drew late. She went through a doorway and found herself in another passage, then recognized the newsroom through a door.

"You there," she called, seeing one of the boys who'd gone on their Byron adventure.

The boy looked up. He was smoking a small cigar, mimicking his elders.

"I need you to run an errand for my father."

The boy stuck out his tongue and wiped a fleck of tobacco off, then wiped it on his waistcoat. He gave a long sigh, then followed her to the office, not quite old enough to dare to argue with her.

Mr. Hogarth glanced at the boy when he appeared in the doorway. "I want ye to go to the address my daughter has and look for the man she describes. If he is there, ask him for the letter he holds for Miss Hogarth."

"He won't give it to the boy," Kate protested.

"If he won't give it to you," Mr. Hogarth continued, "tell him Miss Hogarth will be along in the morning."

"But," Kate protested.

Mr. Hogarth shook his head. "I won't risk my daughter's safety on this nonsense."

"If they wanted to hurt me," she emphasized, "I'm sure it could have been accomplished over these past few days."

"They set a fire," her father said succinctly. "Now instruct the lad."

Kate told him the publisher's former address and described the man. "You saw him, right? When you came with Mr. Aga and me?"

The boy nodded. "Yes, miss."

"Go now," her father said. "There's a bonus in it for ye if ye are back quickly."

The boy, more motivated by coins than benevolence, sped out the door.

Kate unbuttoned her cloak, set it on a peg, then sank into a chair.

"Why don't ye fetch a pot of tea?" her father suggested. "It will be a wait and I might as well continue with my work."

"Yes, Father." Kate rose, feeling the anchors of depression weighting down her legs. "Did everyone stay at Lugoson House today?"

"No. Yer mother insisted on the children returning home until we came back from the newspaper. The longer we tarry here, the more at risk the children are."

"Why would she want that?" Kate asked, shocked. She hadn't been aware of the arrangement. "Lady Lugoson would have allowed them to stay."

"She has the work of the house to be done and doesn't want the maids idle," her father said.

"At least there is no open threat against our house right now," Kate returned. "Would a day have made such a difference?"

"Who knows what they might do next if they canna reach Charles?" he asked.

Kate returned to the room with the tea things. Her hands trembled as she scooped tea into a pot she recognized from its frequent appearances on her father's desk. Her thoughts swung between fear for her family home and fear for Charles. Was her house easier for the villains to access? At least they had more defenses than Charles did, and a place to shelter if they needed it. She feared for him, but what could she do to protect him but pray? If only this matter could be solved with an application of money. She could have begged Lady Lugoson next door for a loan and made Charles's entire problem go away.

Charles huddled as close to the fire in his ward as he dared, given that other men had been there longer, and he was at the bottom of the pecking order. The guard had been on watch as they shared out barrels for seats, so at least he had something under him better than the hard, dirty floor. Seven men each had a place in front of the fire. He wanted to be one of them, and wracked his brain for ways he could secure a higher status. After all, he was probably more intelligent than all these desperate wretches put together. But in a situation like this, what did he have to offer them?

"C-cold night," Bob Sawyer said, approaching him. He had a barrel in his arms.

"I need to cover my face like you do," Charles said, reaching out to help him with the barrel. "It must keep you warm."

The diminutive man shrugged as Charles set the barrel next to him. "Doesn't hurt. I saw you talking to that guard who attacked you. Did you make friends?"

"I hope so. It's not a good night to die," Charles said gloomily. "How did that man get the newspaper?" He nodded at a man on a stool very close to the fire, reading a grimy copy of the *Morning Chronicle* aided by the flames.

"Money," said Bob, hopping onto his seat. He handed over a brown lump. "Best I could trade for. Knit cap for gloves, made by a female prisoner."

Charles glanced at it and saw nothing moving in the yarn, so he pulled it over his head. "Thank you. How do people earn money here?"

"They know 'ow to bring in goods, and sell," Bob said. "You 'ave to 'ave a network inside and out."

"If they are industrious enough to do that, why weren't they intelligent enough to stay out of here in the first place?"

"Why weren't you?" retorted Bob.

Charles crossed his arms over his chest. "An excellent point. These are men with enemies, just like me. We must all have some character defect." He reflected on an acquaintance, who not so long ago had told him he was dishonest. For all he knew, the man resided here at Newgate somewhere himself. His immediate reaction had been to deny the accusation, but he'd been living a lie at the time, no matter what the reason. There was much to improve on in his character.

The troubling thought was, he might have several enemies, and not just Sir Augustus. He had caught a few murderers and confidence men over the past year, and some of them still lived, were at large, or possibly had a network like Bob suggested. No, he couldn't assume Sir Augustus was the only threat.

"How much would you charge to be my guard?" Charles asked, not really joking. "For I'm afraid I need one if I'm going to stay alive here."

Bob's cheeks flexed under the coverings. "Wot makes you think you have more value than any other man? Take your chances as they come." Bob didn't leave him, but turned his body away and stared moodily at the fire.

Charles wished for a knife in his hand and a thick steak in his belly. The food they served here was more plentiful than expected but uninspiring. He stood and pushed his barrel firmly against the wall and set his back against it. Staying here until they called for the sleeping hour meant he could claim the spot for the night. At least having the wall meant he had one side of him that didn't need defending. "Come now," he teased. "It was a joke. I expect you are far richer than I am."

Bob's eyes crinkled at that. "Aye, I could tell you stories."

"Tell them, please," Charles urged, adjusting his cap. "Let us have a tale to pass the hours."

Bob Sawyer's Tale

Some years ago, there lived a man, very badly, in a garret in London. He was young and old at the same time, and spent his days with his head in his hand, longing for proof of the fine inheritance his mother said would once be his, due to the great-grandson of a border lord she'd been married to long ago, the man she claimed was his real father, though he'd died before the young-old man had ever been born.

This man did not have much in the way of portable property, his mother having married down with each of her four husbands, until it was a wonder he didn't grow up with a gutter as his bed. He took such education as he could, as a charity boy in a school or two, and learned maps and roads and such, without coming across much training in the way of common sense.

Finally, one night, he resolved to take some action, having, for the third night, nothing more to eat than a crust of moldy bread. He ventured out to a low tavern, where some friends of his habitually spent their evenings, hoping he could find someone he didn't already owe coins to. One former companion took pity on his ragged appearance and bought him a gin and water, then invited him to sit at his table.

"Well now, Robert," said the old friend, "didn't you have an ancient obsession with Clyde Castle when we were boys?"

"My great-grandfather held the castle," Robert admitted, "but I was descended from a second son of a second son, so it's nothing to do with me."

His friend rattled a newspaper at him. "It appears they cannot find an heir for the old pile. And a title is going into abeyance."

Robert felt numb with shock, and probably not from the gin, though it was very bad. "What if I'm the heir?"

His friend laughed, pointing at Robert's ancient, tattered, worn-to-gray surtout. "Who would take you for an earl? Do you have the papers to prove it?"

"If my mother did, she burned them to stay warm," Robert admitted. "Cursed woman."

The friend laughed at his pretensions, and after he declined to stand another round of the nearly intolerable gin, Robert slunk home. The night had a finer air than he recalled, however, than when he had entered the tavern, and he found an apple dropped on the pavement by an unlucky seller. The full moon had glinted off it just so. After he polished that off, core and all, he found a carrot just inside the door of his building. He chewed it up, leaves and all, as he ascended to his garret.

All night, he paced back and forth in his room, despite several bangs of shoes against the ceiling, helpfully tossed by the inhabitant of the fourth floor, to mark each hour of the night. He clutched his front hair and back hair in turn, wracking his brain for any old friend of his childhood who might stand as witness as to his redoubtable identity.

Could he find the church where he was baptized? Though he had no idea where it might have been.

"What a wretch I am!" he moaned. "Can no one help me?"

"Excuse me, sir," said a very ancient, crabbed voice.

Robert turned to the curtainless window at his back, its cracks stuffed with rags, and saw a small, wide man, in green trousers and pointed boots. His nose echoed the boots in protuberance and his hat, which smelled faintly, was a brownish red that did not set off the collection of warts on his face to any good degree. "Who are you and how did you come here?"

"I am Redcap, bound to serve Clyde Castle."

Robert frowned. "Who bound you, sir?"

"Some eon ago, too far back to remember, your ancestors used to bless their foundation stones with the blood of their enemies. I might have been human once," the strange creature admitted.

"My ancestors?" Robert retorted, with a creak in his voice and hope blossoming in his heart. "You know who I am?"

"Oh yes, you are Robert, son of Robert, son of Robert, son of Roibeart, son of Ruaridh, lairds of Clyde."

Robert stepped forward and grabbed the little ancient creature by the lapels. "How do I prove it?"

Redcap growled, and in an instant, he was an arm's length away.

"Why, bless me," Robert said, astonished. "I think you are a goblin, and not a ghost at all."

The creature grinned, exposing pointed teeth. "They made us so, back then, but I was once a man. Small and dark I was, and still am." He pulled up a tiny, grimy sleeve and exposed a band of curious blue markings painted into his flesh.

Robert felt the stir of ancient kinship in his veins. "What do you want with me, Redcap?"

"The castle will fall if a true son of the blood is not in residence," the goblin said.

"What do I have to do?" Robert asked. "Do you have a family Bible with my name? Do you know the church where I was baptized?"

"We follow the old ways, Your Worship," said the loathsome thing, holding out its tails and giving him a little bow. "You need only to wish to return to the castle and you shall."

"I haven't the money to venture north." Robert tipped off his hat and let it fall, so he could better tear at his hair.

"Take my hand," the goblin commanded.

Robert let his hands drop to his sides and swallowed hard. He closed his eyes and held out his hand. Scaly cold skin touched his, then he was whirling through space, wind in his mouth and eyes and ears, spinning through his body, tossing and turning and fluttering one part of his body into another, until hard earth met his flying form and abruptly ended the operation.

Blinking, he opened his eyes and found himself seated on a patch of grass on the ground. When he swiveled his head, he saw a tall crenellated curtain wall, very old and mossy, behind him, and a tower in front of him, well constructed of stone but narrow and with only arrow slits for windows, in the style of some six hundred years before.

"Is this Clyde Castle?" he croaked, the experience having had the better of his voice.

But he was alone. No sign of the loathsome goblin.

"Dear creature," he muttered to himself. "Dearest Redcap, my own savior."

He climbed to his feet and set his hands to his hips, feeling like a warden of the borders, a real king's man. "Greetings!" he roared in his loudest voice, waiting for some followers, or at least the staff manning the place, to report to him.

No response but the wind. He began to suspect the castle was at the top of a hill. Wiping tears out of his eyes, he circled inside the wall, then found a staircase and climbed it.

Instantly, the sense of smallness underneath God's creation overwhelmed him as massive rain-filled clouds moved overhead. He stood on top of a stone wall, on top of a hill, overlooking a valley. It might have been England, or Scotland, or the land of Fairy.

Turning, he stared at the tower. A vague memory of poring over a book of castles at the British Museum, in those days when he could afford a reader's card, came to mind. He didn't remember this wall being a part of Clyde Castle. What he recalled did include a tower, but it was on one end, with a manor house in two parts attached to it.

That must be where the inhabitants were, not on this far end with the old tower. Feeling a desperate need for human contact, he ran clockwise on the castle wall. But when he'd circumnavigated halfway, he found the end of the tower and no attached manor house.

"Hellooo, the castle," he cried, the wind stealing his voice before it could reach past the wall.

No response came to his ears.

"Redcap?" he screamed at the clouds. But the goblin didn't come.

A surge of terror filled him. Was there no one in this forsaken place? His knees twitched and he was on the move again, racing around the wall. He found the stairs again and descended pell-mell, until he tripped and tumbled to the bottom.

He hit his head on the final, hard old wood step and lost consciousness.

Sometime later, he blinked back into awareness. Moaning, he lifted a hand to his head. It came back bloody. He heard a strange noise, a sort of cackle, then the sound of bodies coming round.

Joy surged through him. The servants had returned! They would have the papers and he would finally be the lord of the castle in truth.

A brand lifted over him, and through the flames Redcap grinned at him with those pointed teeth. "Welcome home, my lord."

Behind Redcap, Robert saw a multitude of goblins. They stretched out in two lines and circled him, dancing a macabre dance. One had a pipe and he began to play it. Robert put his hand to his head again. Instead of the stickiness of a drying wound, he pulled back his shaking hand to find it covered in fresh blood.

"Have you murdered me, Redcap?" he asked, feeling the weariness of his long, poverty-filled days, his failure to live as a gentleman.

"Did I chase you down those steps?" cackled the villain. "Did I cause your boot heel to catch on the stairs?"

"It doesn't matter," Robert said, feeling his body go cold. "At least I'm home."

Chapter 13

Kate hadn't seen any sign of William Aga at the newspaper office, but after she and her father ate the cold plate of meat Mrs. Hogarth had saved for them and helped bundle the children across the frigid apple orchard to Lugoson House, they found William and his wife, Julie, in the drawing room, seated near one of the two fireplaces with Lady Lugoson and Sir Silas Laurie.

The cozy adult gathering, with everyone in proper evening attire, looked about as far away from a wandering large family group with young children as could be imagined. Helen was sobbing, exhausted. Her twin had a runny nose. Georgina was inexplicably doing a little dance around her mother, who was trying to soothe Helen with a lullaby.

William saw Kate and gestured her over to an empty place next to him on the sofa. Her father looked annoyed and she knew he expected her to lessen her mother's burden.

Mary whispered in her ear, "Charles is your focus." She took Helen from her mother as the housekeeper arrived to remove the noisy Hogarths into guest chambers for another night.

After a minute, the crowd had vanished. Kate stepped onto the carpet that defined the cozy nook and curtsied to the baron and baroness, as well matched as carved bookends of Greek deities on their sofa.

"You look very well, considering the stress you must be under," Lady Lugoson observed.

"My mother and I drove out to Hampstead today to see Miss Joanna Baillie," Kate explained. "I wore my new dress."

Lady Lugoson frowned at that. Likely, she recognized some of the fabric as made over from her late daughter's vast collection of dresses. But one made do as part of a large family. New garments cost a king's ransom.

"How did Hampstead go?" William asked as Panch brought a chair into the seating area for Kate.

"Badly," Kate admitted. "Oh, the ladies were lovely. Lucy Aikin was there as well, and Agnes Baillie was most attentive, but we had chosen the wrong address for the clue and the dirty man was not there."

"Charles is in danger?" Julie inquired, her hand resting on her abdomen, displaying her consciousness of her pregnancy even though it wasn't yet visible.

"He could be," Kate admitted with a catch in her throat. "We had another idea, that perhaps I was supposed to go to the site of Miss Baillie's London publisher. My father sent a boy there, I think Ralph? But he didn't see the dirty man."

"He wouldn't though," William opined. "The dirty man would stay out of sight unless he saw you."

"It was too dark and foggy for my father to allow me to go."

"I know your father takes issue with just about everyone, including Charles," Julie said, "but really, to risk his life like this? It's appalling. Why don't we return to London and attempt to find this man?"

William smiled at his wife, while Kate thought about how

Julie called her fiancé Charles so familiarly, displaying, as she so often did, her rough past rather than her genteel present.

"I don't think the dirty man could see Kate in this foul weather and the fog is likely worse in town," William said. "However, I do have another idea about tonight."

"What is it?" Kate twisted her hands in her lap.

"Tracy Yupman," William started, but then a footman entered with a tea tray and placed it at Kate's elbow.

She had to stop William and ask if she should pour, then offered refreshments. Sir Silas did want a cup, and, chilled through, she quickly filled a cup for herself as well. Finally, she blushed and said, "Do go on, Mr. Aga."

"I called on a few parliamentary chambers and had a word with my various contacts. I found someone who used to work for a former M.P. in Eatanswill. This aged factotum revealed to me that Mr. Yupman is Sir Augustus's nephew. He remembered the story of excesses at Sir Augustus's wedding, and the drunken fight he had with his sister's husband."

"That must have been a very long time ago."

"Yes. The man I spoke to must be past his three score and ten."

"This family connection is very telling," Sir Silas said, his perpetually disappointed face looking more disconsolate than ever, while still remaining very handsome indeed. His darkness contrasted with Lady Lugoson's angelic lightness would make very interesting children.

"He must be the murderer, don't you think?" Julie asked her husband.

"He told a good story at the inquest," Sir Silas muttered.

"Can you have him arrested?" Lady Lugoson asked.

"What I need are witnesses to break his alibi," Sir Silas explained. "He insisted he spent the earlier part of the evening at a dinner. I called on a Mr. Jingle and a Mr. Trotter who also claimed to be at the same dinner and verified the alibi."

"I don't think I'd trust anyone named Jingle," Julie said. "Sounds like something out of a play."

Sir Silas nodded. "I'll have a word with the magistrate's clerk. He can assign constables to learn more about this dinner."

"Find out who was supposed to have cooked it," Kate suggested. "Was food really prepared for three? What did the serving staff see?"

"I don't know if servants could break the word of a gentleman," Sir Silas said.

"If they contradict the gentleman, you might not be able to arrest Mr. Yupman, but perhaps Charles could be freed?" Kate suggested hopefully.

"I didn't have him arrested," Sir Silas said irritably. "He is in the hands of the police."

"Still, sir, you are on the right path," William soothed. "What I suggest, Miss Hogarth, is that we drop in on Breese Gadfly. He is still at Selwood Terrace."

"Why?" Lady Lugoson asked.

"He can give us more information about the songwriter in the Lightning Club. Charles met Mr. Gadfly that night, on the way to his fateful meeting at the museum. Mr. Gadfly might be able to offer insight into other people who could break the alibis."

"It is true that I had no membership roster for this club," Sir Silas mused. "We know little about the dynamics of the situation."

"Exactly. Or the museum," William added. "But I think it is clear to us all that Mr. Yupman would be the instrument of his uncle's wrath against Charles. Whether or not he did the killing. Mr. Gadfly's contacts might lead us to information about who does the club's dirty work, for instance."

"What about Charles's other enemies?" Kate asked. "I expect you are correct, Mr. Aga. The familiar relationship you have discovered is very telling. But Charles has been a part of solving murders a few times. I am sure there are other people who hate him and would like him brought low."

"Ooh, revenge," Julie said in a low voice. "I like that."

Sir Silas's eyelids fluttered closed. "Ladies, this is not a stage play. A man was stabbed to death. The most likely answer is usually the true solution."

Kate's parents didn't object to the walk to Selwood Terrace. They were familiar with the property from the summer before when Charles stayed there. Kate and Mary had often ventured over together.

Her father's mouth had opened over his pipe when Julie rose as well, but he couldn't object to a wife accompanying her husband, whatever he thought of her.

The cold night air didn't sting Kate's skin quite as badly after being thoroughly warmed for a few minutes. Even her shoes seemed to have dried after resting on the hearth.

Plus, she had Julie on one side and William on the other.

"Quite like old times, isn't it?" Julie said happily.

Kate didn't remember ever being here with the Agas, at least, not without Charles, but she assented readily enough. "This path is well trod, during happier days."

"Though Miss Haverstock would not have agreed with you."

"No," Kate agreed with a shiver as they passed the Hebrew burying ground, though the lady was not buried there. "Poor lady. Do your current chambers suit for the long term, do you think? Or will you move again?"

"We managed well enough with a baby there," William said. "It was a blessing to have Mrs. Herring nearby."

"And now we have Lucy Fair," Julie added. "I don't think we'll move this year, at least. Someday it would be nice to have a little house of our own."

"Oh yes." Kate sighed. "A houseful of furnishings to carefully arrange, and servants to help with the heavy work. Room for proper dinner parties."

Julie grinned at her. "It's all about food with you and Charles."

"I think you feed him more than I do," Kate returned.

"I did last month," Julie agreed.

Then they were standing on the walk leading up to dear old Selwood Terrace. On the left were the rooms Charles had inhabited, with Miss Haverstock above. Across the hall, Breese Gadfly still held the best rooms, and the chambers above had briefly housed the Agas.

Kate stared at the bricks, illuminated lightly by the lamp glow of the interior rooms. "I wonder who lives in these chambers now, and what stories have been added to these walls?"

Julie shrugged carelessly. "Mr. Gadfly will know."

William leaned over a bush and rapped on Breese's window. Then Julie opened the front door into the tiny passage that Kate remembered so well, and knocked on his door.

Kate heard a clink behind the door as she followed Julie inside; then it opened. The well-lit rooms made their songwriter friend visible immediately.

"The Agas," he cried with evident pleasure. "And Miss Hogarth! No Charles? Is he to meet you here?" He looked past Kate as if hopeful of Charles's sudden appearance.

Kate glanced at William. Didn't Mr. Gadfly know?

"Let us in, Gadfly, and we'll share all the news."

"Gladly." He frowned and stepped aside.

Kate remembered the cheerful, luxurious room with its piano very well. The senior Gadflys were deceased and Breese had some kind of inheritance that allowed him to live rather well, along with a job of writing songs for theatrical productions. He'd kindly allowed Charles into the business, which had helped Charles through a difficult summer. They had written again in December, and Kate knew another of their songs was supposed to be sung on stage in February at a theater in Southwark.

Breese bustled around, plumping pillows on his armchairs and feeding fuel to his already-dancing fire. He poured wine for all of them.

Kate noticed a new piece of art on the wall after she'd hung up her cape. "It's been a long time since I've been here, Mr. Gadfly. This piece is very fine." She lifted a candlestick from the mantel and held it closer so she could see the painting.

Breese came next to her. "It's a Parisian fashion illustration. Used to design costumes for a friend's new play."

Kate considered the Frenchman centered in the frame, dressed for the outdoors in a sumptuous brocaded jacket with matching buff trousers. He carried a shiny cane, wore shiny shoes, and was crowned by the perfect beaver top hat. Behind him at some distance, another man watched, probably admiring the fine garments. He was not dressed for the outdoors, but his blue tailcoat added a pop of color to the pen-and-ink work. The element of desire in the receding figure's eyes, and the preening of the young man in the center, created a definite mood that reminded Kate of Charles's unstated concern for Mr. Gadfly's lifestyle.

He handed her the wineglass as she set the candlestick down.

"Do you have songs in the play?" she asked.

Breese nodded. "I do. Three of them, in fact."

Kate tossed her head gaily. "Then you could treat yourself to new art."

"Yes." Breese glanced between her and the piece. "Now, tell me why Charles is not with you tonight. Is he off on newspaper business? Killing horses underneath him as he dashes to Edinburgh? Rowing himself to Dublin, perhaps?"

"He's in Newgate," William said, not seeming to have caught the light mood.

Breese's face went pale underneath his whiskers. "No, not Charles. It must be some mistake."

"You saw him the night he was arrested," William said. "When I saw him, I asked him to walk me through every detail."

"That was a week ago," Breese exclaimed. "Surely he hasn't been there for a week." He clutched at his whiskers, then turned to the fire to hide his emotion.

"Most of it," William said.

"Samuel Pickwick was murdered in the museum," Kate told Breese. "They blamed it on Charles. If you know about the article Charles wrote about Sir Augustus Smirke, and that Tracy Yupman, the vice president of the Lightning Club, is his nephew, well, you can assume the same sort of things that we do."

"Charles was framed," Breese said hoarsely.

"I'm certain of it," William said. He drained his glass. "Charles said you knew a member of the club."

"Former," Breese said. "Peter Snodgrass. I asked about him earlier this week, since Charles and I had that conversation."

"I don't like the sound of that," Kate said, staring into her glass. She took a sip, hoping it would warm her, but she was too cold.

Breese gave her a sympathetic smile. "Discovered the goy was dead now, so I didn't think to write Charles. I've been busy with the new play." He gestured vaguely at the illustration on the wall, then put his hand over his eyes.

"Unfortunate," William muttered. "We were hoping to meet with the fellow, get some kind of insight. The coroner has been informed of the relationship of Yupman to Smirke, but we need a great deal more than that."

"Yes, but Charles also needs support. I'll visit him." Breese shuddered.

Julie set down her glass and squeezed his hand. "That is very kind of you. I'm sure he would appreciate it. Charles is a social creature."

"And he's in danger," Kate interrupted. "The more visitors he has, the more his enemies will understand he's being watched."

"Tell me everything," Breese implored.

William held out his glass. "You'd better refill this first, for there is quite a tale to tell."

Kate sat mutely as William shared everything that had happened. Julie had settled next to her, blazing warmth her body did not seem to share. "I'm sorry," she interrupted. "When did Mr. Snodgrass die?"

"He was found in November," Breese said.

"Good question," William praised. "And in what condition?"

Breese's mouth dropped open. "Knifed. In Limehouse, near known opium dens."

Kate shuddered. Limehouse had been the site of the cholera epidemic just a few years before. A vile, crooked area near the river, she'd never been anywhere near it.

"Limehouse, eh," William mused. "It would be assumed his death had something to do with his opium habit, not the Lightning Club."

"It could have been a rehearsal though," Julie added. "For the upcoming murder of the club's president."

"We should share this information with Sir Silas. He can access the coroner's notes for Snodgrass's inquest." He turned to Breese. "I thought you were going to tell me he'd died of the drug."

"People rarely do, from what I've been told." Breese smiled. "Do you know, I owe Charles a few coins? I'll bring them to him, so he can buy some comforts."

"That's very good of you," Kate praised. "He looked cold when I saw him. Maybe use the money for a new muffler and bring it to him instead of the coins? Meanwhile, I will go to St. Paul's Churchyard in the morning and continue to pursue my tormentor."

Breese's mouth turned down as if he'd just sucked on a sour fruit. "I don't like to consider what you are going to find at the end of that particular *regnboygn*."

Chapter 14

Kate woke early and shuffled around in the blanket until Mary stirred.

"What's wrong?" her sister asked sleepily.

She rubbed sleep from her eyes. "I'm worried about our house, I suppose."

"And Charles," Mary added.

"Yes." Kate put her hands to her temples. "I had the most terrible dreams all night. I don't think I had a minute of restful sleep."

"Take better care," Mary advised. "Charles will expect a rosy-cheeked bride, not a hollowed-out creature of despair."

"He cannot expect me to be in perfect form under the circumstances."

Mary winced. "I disagree. Charles is very concerned about appearance. He'll want you to offer hope for the future."

Kate cast the thought aside. "Help me dress. We can sneak out through the drawing room and walk through the gardens into the orchard. Let's go far enough to make sure the house is all right."

"Not Robert and George?"

"Of course," Kate said, remembering the fate of Peter Snodgrass in a rush. "You are an angel. We must check on them."

"They will want a hot breakfast."

Kate considered the hour. "I don't think there will be anything here yet."

Just then the door opened, and a maid crept in with a tea tray.

"Oh, you're awake," the girl said, the tray rattling.

Mary crawled out of bed to help her. "We didn't get a tray yesterday. I thought the privilege was for married ladies."

"This is the Hogarths' room, is it not?" the servant asked, her cheeks darkening.

"It's probably for our parents." Kate went to the curtain and opened it. She investigated the tray. "Two cups, not three."

"Sad," Mary said. "We could have taken something for the boys."

Kate pulled back a towel and found fresh bread rolls. She snatched two of them. "They will never know. For charity," she told the girl. "Not for us."

"Where is the right 'un?" the servant asked, her gaze dancing over the girls' faces.

"Just across the hall," Mary said, crossing her arms over her chest. "Can we make a fire?"

"It's the tweenie as does that. I'm in the kitchen," the girl said.

She had left the door open and slipped through. Despite the openings and closings, Georgina had slept on.

Kate glanced at the huddled shape still in the bed. "Come, get me dressed. At least we have some poor offering for the boys."

In twenty minutes, they were in the drawing room. The tea tray of the night before and the tray with liquors were all back in their places. Kate unlocked the door and they slipped out.

"Careful not to ruin your shoes," she told Mary.

"The ground is frozen. We'll be fine as long as we avoid patches of leaves that might be hiding a puddle."

The girls' breath flew through the air behind them like ghosts as they traversed the formal gardens. The orchard had muddy spots under the trees, but their shoes were still intact by the time they reached their vegetable and herb garden.

"No sign of another fire," Mary observed, interrupting Kate's discourse upon the previous night's discussion with Breese Gadfly.

The kitchen door opened before they reached it. Robert glanced out, unshaven, his brown hair standing in a nimbus around his narrow face.

"Eight bells and all is well," he announced.

Kate laughed and reached into her pocket and handed him the rolls. "All we can provide at this hour," she said.

"I don't suppose you are here to blacken the stove and get the fire going for the day," her brother said hopefully.

"No, but I'm sure Mother will send Hannah over soon enough," Mary said. "Nothing strange overnight?"

"Nothing at all. We took turns on watch, though I did find George asleep when I woke." Robert tossed one roll in the air and bit into the other one. "Delicious."

"Save the other one for George," Kate warned. "I'll ask him about it later."

Robert screwed up his nose. "Fine. Send Hannah soon."

Mary slid around him and reappeared momentarily with their pattens, which made it easier to return to Lugoson House. The French door had not been locked after them, so they made it back inside with no one the wiser, grateful that Robert had no greater concern than a cold stove.

At Lugoson House, they heard the rattle of a carriage in the street. When they came into the front hall from the drawing room, they found Sir Silas freshly arrived as well.

"Early morning walk?" he asked, sliding his greatcoat into Panch's waiting arms.

"Yes, our house is fine today," Kate said, "but we have new information for you."

He held up his hands in mock-pugilist fashion. "I thought your Mr. Dickens was persistent. I will question Mr. Yupman, though I am convinced Charles's article is enough to make Sir Augustus's nephew want Charles hanged for murder."

"Nonetheless," Kate said. "Someone did kill Samuel Pickwick."

"Indeed," Sir Silas said, with a rare little smile.

"And someone else," Mary piped up, less confident than usual in the presence of the baron.

His very fine eyes narrowed. "Pardon me?"

Mary cleared her throat. "Peter Snodgrass, sir."

"Knifed in Limehouse a couple of months ago," Kate added. Sir Silas's dark gaze transferred to her. "Who is this?"

"A member of the club. Early promise destroyed by opium. But what if his murder was practice for Mr. Pickwick's?" Kate asked.

"Do you know anything about the wounds?" Sir Silas's head turned, and Kate's gaze followed his to a pair of ancient crossed swords over the arch leading to the dining room.

"No, sir," Kate admitted.

"Very well." Sir Silas nodded. "I will have my clerk pull the coroner's report. Let me escort you to breakfast and no more talk of murder. It upsets Lady Lugoson."

Kate and Mary went into the dining room with him. A toothsome array of breakfast meats and breads was displayed cunningly on the sideboard. When Sir Silas held out chairs for them, a maid was there instantly to pour tea and ask if they would like eggs or porridge.

The baronet returned to the table momentarily with a plate

of ham and buns for each of them. Lady Lugoson arrived, giving him a welcoming smile, and sat across from Kate.

Kate watched Sir Silas hesitate as he sat across from Mary. She thought he wanted to be done with the pair of them. For herself, she'd rather have eaten out of sight, so she could have pocketed the rest of the largesse for her brothers.

Mary shook her head, shocked at the variety. "To think Mother threw a fit when Charles arrived with one bun for each of us!"

Kate smiled at her as her parents arrived.

"Did ye sleep well, girls?" her father asked.

"Well enough. We woke early and checked on the boys."

Her mother's hands fluttered and she stopped short of the chair next to Mary. "How is the house?"

"Nothing happened all night," Kate said.

"That's a comfort," she said.

"What do you think of this news about another knife death in the Lightning Club, Mr. Hogarth?" Sir Silas asked.

"I'm not aware," he replied.

"Breese Gadfly informed us last night," William said, coming in with Julie.

"It may or may not be important." Julie stopped to kiss her aunt's cheek, then sat next to her. "However, we've mostly forgotten the girl who went missing in Eatanswill."

"Good point," Kate said, ignoring her father's raised eyebrows. "Charles did say Sir Augustus is supposed to be mad. Maybe there isn't any good reason for what happened to poor Mr. Pickwick? Mr. Yupman could be mad as well."

Sir Silas sighed. "What I can say, is that I am inquiring into the life of Samuel Pickwick. Often, the reason for a murder lies in the victim's life, but he appears to have been beloved and blameless."

"Then Sir Augustus must continue to be investigated," Lady

Lugoson said with a shudder. "You know how I feel about young girls in the clutches of old men."

Kate knew she spoke from the heart, from the pain of her own experience with her late husband, a dreadful sort.

Her father nodded. "William, I think it is time ye followed in Charles's footsteps and went to Eatanswill yourself."

"A general investigation?" William smiled at the footman who had poured his tea.

"Interview Mr. Poor. Let's get to the bottom of this kidnapping allegation. See what the father has learned in the past week. I've seen nothing in the papers about the situation."

"No, it's been kept quiet, even though it could have been announced without mentioning Sir Augustus."

"The girl isn't important enough?" Mary suggested.

"Oɩ she's home in her bed and we simply aren't aware of that fact," her father offered.

After breakfast, Mrs. Hogarth asked Kate and Mary to make sure Polly had the younger children dressed for their return to their own home. Julie offered to go upstairs with them.

"Will you return to Cheapside or stay here while Mr. Aga goes to Eatanswill?" Kate asked the redhead.

"Stay here," Julie said. "The painting master is coming today. We've been doing watercolor, but my aunt wants to try oils next."

"That sounds delightful," Mary said wistfully.

"Join us," Julie suggested. "My aunt would love an additional pupil. She has indicated that my poor work makes hers look better."

Kate chuckled, but Mary shook her head. "Kate has to return to London to see about her letter and find the dirty man, not to mention Charles, so I have to help Polly with the children."

Julie nodded soberly. "I know I am in my last months of freedom. Having the baby to foster for a few weeks last month kept me confined to home. Everything will change soon."

"At least William can afford to keep a servant. That will help," Kate said, rather jealous if she was being honest.

"Charles can afford it, too," Julie said. "He is as prosperous as William. Don't let him blind you to that. You deserve help."

"He is very generous," Kate said timidly. "His family."

Julie rolled her eyes. "You will marry them, too, my dear. Are you sure you want them?"

"They've been kind to me. Really, they are a mere distraction to my life with him," Kate insisted.

"Speaking of distractions," Julie said, stopping on the landing just short of the nursery and turning to the sisters, "have you noticed how these poison pen letters have distracted you from the real and obvious connection of Sir Augustus to the situation?"

Kate nodded. "They have wasted time that should have been used to free Charles."

"Are you well?" Mary asked, seeing the way Julie held her stomach.

"I'm fine. Things are simply rearranging themselves here." Julie rubbed her abdomen indelicately. "I have started to loosen stays and let out seams. I won't be able to go out much longer."

"Does it hurt?" Mary asked tentatively.

"The answer is rather complicated, Mary, and I've no wish to frighten you," Julie said. "It is a woman's lot and I think it's best just to deal with it."

"Do you miss the stage?" Kate asked. She'd seen the girl's large personality and charisma struggle to confine itself to the domestic sphere. Charles had indicated that health problems had sidelined her somewhat. Not everyone bore children easily, and Julie had already lost one child.

"I have not yet given up on it, but it's nothing to be spoken of when one is trying to be respectable." Julie winked at Mary. She laughed as expected.

"Speaking of artists," Julie added, "I think we should look at failed writers who are connected to the Lightning Club."

"Meaning that they might be jealous of Charles?" Kate asked. "Like this could all be about someone being angry that Charles was being given a spot in the club? Miss Baillie had the same idea."

"Possibly while they lost theirs," Julie agreed. "I mean, we can't assume all the failed writers get murdered. You know, Charles was probably given the late Snodgrass's position in the club. His death is why there was an opening."

"We need a history of the club," Kate said. "I should have thought of that. Do we know if Mr. Yupman is a writer?"

"There is sure to be a history, if writers are involved," Julie mused.

"Do we know who the secretary is?" Mary asked.

They looked amongst themselves. "It's not Mr. Yupman. We know that," Kate said.

"Ask Charles when you see him again. See if he has any notion of who else might be in the club, who the officers were." Julie stamped her foot suddenly. "Now I wish I didn't have to paint today, so I could go with you into London."

"I am still a little nervous that something bad is going to happen," Kate admitted. "Or already has, at the prison. The villain behind the letters will surely know I did try to solve the puzzle in time, but I can't trust their good graces."

"Do you have any other leads?" Julie asked.

"I hope to hear from Lady Byron," Kate admitted, shocked that she could be in contact with such an infamous lady. "Miss Baillie said she might have information that would be of use."

Julie lifted her eyes to the ceiling. "Lady Byron. What circles Charles is entering into."

*   *   *

"I looked in some old books in the Lugoson library last night," Mr. Hogarth said as the carriage took them down Warwick Lane to the north end of St. Paul's. "Mr. Johnson's business was at 72 St. Paul's Churchyard. I know there have been bookshops and music shops, too, in the area for hundreds of years."

"Sir Walter Scott's publisher is just above, in Paternoster Square, I believe," Kate said, peering out of the window into the gray morning sky, not much different to view than the soot-blackened old buildings.

"Yes, all this nonsense is acquainting you well with literary London," her father said. "But the north churchyard has a fascinating history. Did you know a cross stood here in centuries past? It was called St. Paul's Cross, probably torn down two centuries ago, and the publishing businesses put up."

"What happened at the cross?" Kate asked, as the carriage rattled past Paternoster Square and into the churchyard.

"It was a public pulpit, but even before that, it was an area where they burned sorcerers and books. Later, sermons were preached here all year long, some quite controversial and engaging in the issues of the day."

They stopped in front of number seventy-two. "And now the preaching is done through books. Mr. Johnson was famous for his religious tracts."

"Exactly. The purpose of this area lives on."

Kate peered through the mist that seemed to cling to the bottoms of the buildings. Behind them, St. Paul's north transept loomed, feeling impossibly tall, with the dome behind hidden in the bad air.

"Do you see your dirty man?" her father asked.

"No, but then he cannot see me, either. I shall have to go into the street."

"Very well, but let me go first." Mr. Hogarth exited the carriage, then helped her down.

They walked toward the shop that had once been Mr. Johnson's. Out of the shadowed doorway appeared a large man, mist swirling around his boots as they moved toward him.

"That's the patched coat," Kate said, her pulse leaping.

"And the dirty hat," Mr. Hogarth said with disfavor. "I do not like this, Kate. He could overpower you before you took a breath."

"I must be brave for Charles." Kate whispered this, then stepped forward, facing the man.

He sneered at her, then licked his teeth, revealing his identity even if she hadn't recognized him by his clothing alone.

"I'd like my letter, please," Kate said, holding out her hand. "You led me on a merry chase to Miss Baillie's, but I did my best."

The man muttered something, but she couldn't hear him.

"I beg your pardon?" she inquired in her iciest tone, which was reserved for cheating tradesmen.

"You failed," he said.

He had a sore on the side of his mouth. It probably made it painful to open his lips very far. "I did my best," she repeated, and thrust her hand out farther.

"Look here," her father said, standing shoulder to shoulder with her.

The dirty man held up his hands, wrapped in tattered, yellowing cloth rather than clad in sensible gloves or mittens. "No clue for you. It's time to pay."

Behind Kate, a horse whinnied. She felt a sharp push from behind. When she cried out, her father turned to her and grabbed her arm.

Footsteps moved rapidly behind them. She looked to the right, and when she turned, the dirty man's coattail flapped on its way past a building.

"Do we go?" her father asked.

"No," Kate said. "He's good at not being found when he desires it."

"What do we do now?" He lifted his hand to the coachman, who nodded.

Kate turned and opened the carriage door. "We go to Newgate to warn Charles."

"I'm happy to say that it sounded as if the threat was coming, rather than something that is already transpired," her father said.

"You don't think they've hurt him?"

"Not yet." He helped her up the step and into the carriage, then followed behind. "This particular set of circumstances seems planned to hurt ye."

Kate considered this. "What did I do to Sir Augustus?"

"It's probably more likely that they want to hurt ye to wound Charles, since he cares about ye."

Kate knew that her father, being a man, would think of this as men's business only, but the situation felt very personal to her. Who in Charles's circle had she slighted? A couple of reporters had tried to pay addresses to her, but her father had never invited them to dinner more than once. The family had ignored invitations that came, unlike Charles's birthday party, which had been where she realized she'd come to care for him.

Her father had certainly been less than kind to Julie Aga, but Julie was mischievous, not cruel. Julie's mother, on the other hand, had been deprived of a slave last year when Julie had left the theater.

"Are the Chalke Company of Players back in London?" Kate asked.

"You are thinking of Miss Acton and Percy Chalke?" he inquired.

"Yes, I am cataloging our shared enemies."

"Last I heard, they were touring Scotland. I had a letter from a cousin who said he had seen a very fine performance of *Richard III.*"

"Let's hope they stay there," Kate said.

They could have easily walked the few minutes to the prison, but the streets were crowded with people out and about, going to their daily work, or hawking food and goods in the street. A group of several religious people formed a choir party just behind where the carriage parked, and Kate exited to the words, "When the woes of life o'ertake me, hopes deceive, and fears annoy, never shall the cross forsake me."

"Ah, 'In the Cross of Christ I Glory,'" her father said. "Did you know the author, John Bowring, was elected to Parliament last year?"

"I wonder how he'll get along with Sir Augustus Smirke," Kate said.

"Not well, I expect," her father said with relish. "Chalk and cheese."

Charles heard his name from one of the iron cages at the far end of the yard. The Scottish inflection told him Mr. Hogarth had come to visit. A wave of dizziness made the packed dirt whoosh around him for a moment when he stood up from the wall. He hadn't slept much on his rug, nor had he eaten much after weevils came out of the bread.

While he knew intellectually that the prisons had better food than the workhouses, when faced with the actual meals, his stomach had protested. Now he paid for it though, with weakness and sore eyes. He had to overcome his stomach to keep the rest of him whole.

Someone glanced off his arm. He turned instinctively with a ready smile and an apology but got nothing but incredulous abuse from a fellow inmate. Lowering his head, he went grimly forward, reaching the cage without any more interactions.

"Darling," he heard a female voice fuss. "Oh, Charles, you don't look well."

He frowned, expecting his editor's voice, but as his eyes dissected the gloom, he did see the man, but next to him was Kate. "Kate, my dear," he exclaimed, forcing merriment into his raspy voice. "I did not see you there. Come in for a Friday shopping mission? You will note I still know what day it is." His chuckle sounded false even to his ears.

"No, I came to warn you." She pulled her hand from her muff and stretched her fingers through the bars so he could clasp them. "I have terrible news."

Chapter 15

"What?" Charles felt the warmth of Kate's fingers despite the gloves. If only enough space existed between the bars for him to hold her entire hand. A bit of humanity was very welcome. But he didn't like the sentiment coming from her lips. "Have I not enough terrible news simply being locked in here, away from you?"

She bit her rosy lip. "I had a letter from our tormentors that used a Joanna Baillie quotation. My mother went with me to her home yesterday. A long trip, and no dirty man with a letter at the end of it."

"You failed?" His voice rasped as his heart dropped into his stomach.

Her lips curved up a little but her eyes remained bleak. "I thought I understood it by the end of the visit, and we sent a boy from the newspaper to the location."

"It was after dark," her father interjected.

Kate glanced at her father. "Yes, but the boy didn't see the dirty man. This morning we went to St. Paul's Churchyard ourselves."

"The dirty man was there, but he refused to hand over any further communication," her father said. "Blackguard."

"Did he say anything at all?" Charles asked. Kate's expression held too much seriousness for this to be the end of the update.

"He threatened you, Charles." Kate's fingers wound their way closer to his palm. "I know you are already being careful, and I see how tired you are, but you must keep watch."

She put her muff against the iron and reached her other hand through. Charles understood and put his other hand into the muff. Glorious heat, and a small purse.

"From Lady Lugoson," she whispered.

He pulled it out and, after checking to make sure no one was looking directly at him, tucked it into his pocket. "Thank you. Tell her to write Sir Silas and tell him that Sir Augustus is a member of the Lightning Club."

"Who told you that?" Kate asked, her eyes wide.

"The turnkey who is in his pay. I paid to have one question answered." Charles smiled merrily, feeling quite clever for being able to uncover anything while imprisoned.

"Spend your money on better food, my lad," Mr. Hogarth said, leaning in close.

"Yes, Charles, please," Kate added. "We can find out more outside. In fact, we've learned that Mr. Yupman is Sir Augustus's nephew."

His pleasure turned to shock as he realized he'd spent a good meal's worth of money on useless information. "Focus on following the letters properly, please, Kate," he growled. "I can do without a meal, but another beating would be very unwelcome indeed."

Her lips trembled. "I did my best. How could I, a woman who must obey her father, have gone to St. Paul's after dark without permission?"

"Julie would have found a way," Charles snapped.

Kate went pale with hurt. He reached out his hand to stroke her cheek and his mitten hit black iron.

"That is an unacceptable statement, Charles," Mr. Hogarth said coldly. "Do not let prison coarsen you." He pulled a wrapped package from his pocket, tossed it over the wall, then took Kate's arm.

"Wait," Charles called, but they had already walked away. He watched them disappear, then took the package back to his shadowed spot along the wall, keeping careful watch on his fellow inmates, but even Bob Sawyer was busy with other friends.

When Charles opened the handkerchief, a welcome bit of cloth, he found six shillings, slices of ham and cheese, and a slim book of poetry by Joanna Baillie. He opened the pages, thinking to find some secret communication, but found only printed words. His gaze stopped on one passage and he muttered the words to himself. "'I've loved thee long, and loved thee true. The prospects of my youth are crost, My health is flown, my vigour lost; My soothing friends augment my pain, And cheerless is my native plain; Dark o'er my spirits hangs the gloom . . .'" He shut the book, feeling too much kinship with the sentiment.

He needed to be careful. Kate had been true to him through so much and he couldn't drive her away now. Or even worse, slip out of Mr. Hogarth's good graces as he'd done before and lose Kate through the intercession of her parents.

When would he ever learn?

Kate heard voices in the hallway as she came down Lady Lugoson's staircase that evening to comply with the summons for dinner. She wore one of her new dresses at Mary's urging tonight, made from a blue fabric that matched her eyes. Charles would have loved it, and she'd wanted to wear it for the first time in his presence.

She twisted her fingers together behind her back.

"Thinking about Charles?" Mary asked. When Kate nodded, she said, "You have to keep your mind clear, or you won't be ready for what happens next."

"I expect you are right. I've never been in the thick of things before, not like this, with danger chasing me."

"It must be very uncomfortable," Mary offered. "To know eyes are upon you."

"Yes, usually all eyes are on Charles." She sighed and fluffed out her skirt.

When they arrived in the drawing room where the family and guests had gathered, they saw a welcome face. William had returned from Eatanswill and had picked up Charles's brother Fred on the way through town.

"Fred," Kate exclaimed, rushing forward to take Fred's hands, very cold from the ride. "Any news?"

"I was at the prison yard to see Charles," he said, "and William was there. Charles has a coat now and a Bible, and hasn't been attacked again."

"Did you have news to share from Eatanswill, Mr. Aga?" Kate asked.

He sneezed, then applied his handkerchief until his nose was red. His wife frowned from a sofa and would have risen, but William waved her down. "Amy Poor is still missing. I was able to obtain her description. Very dark brown hair, like polished wood, they told me at the news agent's. Light blue eyes. Tall."

Kate meant to simply shake her head, but in her heightened state of misery, the sad news made her moan a little, and Julie came toward them both. The former actress held out her arms theatrically. "What is the matter?"

"We can't take the time to find Amy Poor," William added. "I think one of us needs to stand guard at the prison yard as much as possible, since we know there is an open threat against Charles. I'll talk to all of our fellow reporters tomorrow. This could have happened to any of us and we need to stand together."

"A valiant idea, but Charles would want us to find the girl," Julie said, pulling William toward a sofa. "She could be the answer to all of this. If she can tell the authorities who kidnapped her, and that person was arrested, we might free Charles because of that alone."

Kate, Mary, and Fred followed them and took the opposite sofa. Lady Lugoson was seated in her favorite chair in front of the fire. The cushion and armrests were upholstered in a pale apple green silk that matched the walls.

"We need to sneak into Sir Augustus's homes and look for Amy Poor," Fred said, knocking his fist into his open palm.

William winced. "Miss Poor is probably his mistress by now."

Lady Lugoson made a rather French noise in her throat. The others turned to her expectantly. "If he made someone his mistress, he would have set her up in rooms since he has a wife."

They considered the logic of that. Kate couldn't hide her blush.

Julie was very brazen. "It will be easy to find the rooms. All we have to do is follow Sir Augustus. Lucy Fair and I can take the task. A mistress and her maid, market baskets at the ready, might be anywhere."

"Your expectations must prevent you from doing anything so foolish," William said. "Don't take any risks."

"What risk is it to go shopping with my maid?" Julie asked, her voice carrying a bit.

"I can help watch, too, along with my three younger brothers when they are out of school," Mary offered.

"Mother will never agree to that," Kate said, astonished.

"She will if I have the boys with me. As long as I keep them entertained. That's half her children out of the house on a fruitful occupation."

"I hardly think training the boys to be some sort of Bow Street Runners is what she would have in mind," Kate said.

"I should like to find Amy Poor," Mary said. "Really, any of us could be kidnapped if we became the target of some villain's desire. Who knows what dreadful thing might happen then?"

Kate thought her sister looked a little too dreamy-eyed at the prospect. "Has Charles been telling you the story of Scheherazade again?" she said acidly. "Not all such Banbury tales end with the heroine safe from beheading."

The Hogarths walked into the room, accompanied by Sir Silas. William quickly changed the subject to political matters and they passed an exquisitely dull evening, with Kate worrying all the while that dreadful things were happening at Newgate Prison.

Kate and Mary met the others in the dining room the next morning just as the food had been set out. They had already discovered that Lady Lugoson never dined so early, unless it was in her room. Fred had been allowed to stay as well, so he entered behind William and Julie, his eyes widening at the array on the sideboard.

"Have I gone to heaven?" he asked, his gaze fixed on the selection of bacon, sausage, and cold meats.

"Just Lugoson House," William said, clapping him on the shoulder.

While they were busy tucking into their plates, Kate heard Panch speaking to someone outside of the door, then the butler entered, followed by her brother Robert. She rotated her chair so she could see him stare at a plate of sausages.

"May I?" Robert asked, his fingers hovering.

"Of course," Julie said gaily, as the closest person to the family in the room.

"What's the news from home?" Kate asked.

Robert took the plate that a footman offered, then reached for the serving utensils near the meat selection. "Everything is quiet. Kate had a letter. From Ealing." He had an exchange with a maid about tea, then put his heaped plate in front of the empty spot opposite Kate and sat.

She held out her hand for the letter.

"Impatient?" he teased.

"It will be from Lady Byron," Kate said confidently. She scanned the letter, right down to the signature "A. I. Noel Byron," which was how the lady styled herself, even though she was Baroness Wentworth in her own right due to the unusual inheritance of a title. The world knew of the lady who worked so hard to open underprivileged schools, but the young woman had been the wild poet Byron's wife.

"How exciting," Mary said. "Does she invite you to visit?"

"She does." Kate grinned. "I admit I cannot imagine my good luck and I hope to make a good impression. Maybe Charles and I will be asked back for some evening if I succeed."

"You'll be fine." Julie yawned. Her skin had a greenish cast.

"I don't think you should be wandering London with us today," Kate told her. "I think you are feeling the effects of your condition."

"I always feel much better by ten or so," Julie insisted. "It's a passing problem."

"Where do the plans stand this morning?" William asked.

"You were going to check on Charles at the prison," Kate said. "Julie and Lucy Fair along with Mary and the boys are going to watch Sir Augustus's London home."

"We don't know where it is yet," Julie said. "But Panch will probably know. Ring the bell, will you, Fred?"

He applied his napkin, then went to pull the bell rope. A footman waited upon them within seconds and Julie asked to have Panch returned to them.

Kate had finished her food by then, and Julie had perked up enough for a piece of toast with a little marmalade.

"Yes?" Panch asked, inclining his head in Julie's direction.

"Where is Sir Augustus Smirke's London residence?" she asked.

"He rents a three-story house in Charles Street."

"That's expensive real estate," William commented. "Just off Berkeley Square."

"Oh my," Kate breathed. "You can't loiter in the street there all day."

"There are mews behind the houses," William added. "Lots of space to stash kidnapped girls, though I'm sure she would be in rooms with a guard, like Lady Lugoson said. If you go with Lucy, and Mary goes with the boys, to watch either side for a few minutes, at least you'll be able to discern if the family is in residence."

"What mischief are all of you making today?" Lady Lugoson asked, walking in, followed by the Hogarths.

"Just making plans to return home," Julie said innocently.

"I was hoping to take the boys into London for a treat," Mary added in the direction of their parents.

"Oh, I don't think so," Mrs. Hogarth demurred.

"Why not?" Mr. Hogarth said. "There is a glimmer of sunlight in the sky. No rain in the clouds. They could do with an outing."

Kate smiled, at least until she started counting in her head. There were far too many of them for one carriage.

"If you are ready, Miss Mary, I'll send someone for a cab."

Mary stood. "I'll just dash up to the nursery to collect the boys."

"I'll go with you to make it faster," Kate said, following suit. "That will give Julie a little longer to relax."

"How are we going to do this?" Mary whispered in the passage after they'd left the dining room.

"We can go right to Charles Street while Julie collects Lucy Fair. I have no doubt that she has some scheme involving a costume in mind. We can be gentry folk from the country taking in the sights of the wealthy and aristocratic. She and Lucy can be watercress girls or something."

"They are both too old."

Kate shrugged. "She'll know better than I. It's not like she'd actually go up to the baronet's door."

Mary laughed as they climbed the stairs. "She would if she had reason enough."

Half an hour later the considerable party had said good-bye to Mrs. Hogarth.

"Mind that yer home before dark with the boys, Mary," their mother cautioned.

"Before dark?" Kate inquired. "But Mother, it's winter."

"James is only eleven," her mother said. "He can't be staying out into the evening."

"We'll give him dinner," Julie said with a winning smile. "Have him home long before bedtime."

"In London?" Mrs. Hogarth said, aghast.

"In my home," Julie said. "We'll be indoors by five, I promise."

"Very well." Mrs. Hogarth sighed and pulled James to her. He squirmed away, very indignant at being treated as younger than his two older brothers. "Before seven," she said firmly.

James, Robert, and Fred piled into the hired cab along with the others, while Julie, William, and Mr. Hogarth took the Lugoson carriage.

"We'll see you later, in the street," Julie whispered in Kate's ear.

"Will we recognize you?" Kate whispered back.

William put his hand on his wife's back. She winked at Kate and stepped into the carriage.

"Do you think you'll ever live on a street like this?" Mary asked, awed, as they stared down the fine row of houses later that morning.

They could see the spiky, naked branches of plane trees dotted here and there. Every house they passed had neatly swept steps. Fewer tradesmen filled the streets than was usual in London, probably because they went into the mews to knock on servants' entrances.

"I don't know that this is what Charles would want," Kate said. "I think he would value garden space over a prestigious address."

"I think the address is more important than anything," Robert said.

"She's not marrying you," Mary said, nudging her brother.

"I have to get to the office," he said. "Are you going to be safe?"

Mary spread her arms. "Do you see anything to fear?"

"Danger lurks everywhere in London," he warned. "Remember what you are here to do."

"Amy Poor." Kate's voice sounded sober even to her ears. "If we find the kidnapped girl, she may be the answer to all our woes."

"What do we do now?" George asked, tugging Kate's arm.

"Walk the neighborhood, maybe in two groups?" she suggested. "There are enough of us. Fred, are you going to work, too?"

"Not today," he said. "I'm not as important as Robert."

Their brother touched his hat to them and strode off. He didn't work far from here.

"Let us stick with the original plan," Kate said. "Fred and I will stroll around, while Mary and the boys focus on the mews."

"We didn't need Julie and Lucy after all," Fred said, "but I suppose she craves amusement."

"One thing to figure out is which house is Sir Augustus's from the back," Kate said.

Mary nodded. "And what kind of buildings in the mews belong to it."

"Exactly," Kate agreed. "Let's rendezvous at the corner of Charles and Queen Streets when we hear church bells ring."

"Is this what we're going to do all day?" Mary asked.

Kate put her hand over her mouth for a few seconds to warm her lips. They felt like they would split open from the cold. "Eventually I should return to the churchyard to see if my tormentor has returned."

"The dirty man?" Fred asked. He made a fist. "I'd like to give 'im a piece of my mind."

"He moves too fast for that," Kate said. "Besides, he's our only link to whatever is going on."

"It would be nice if we could see Sir Augustus and get an idea about Amy Poor before you leave," Mary added.

"I agree," Kate said.

Mary blew her a kiss and walked away. Kate shooed off her younger siblings, then walked with Fred toward Berkeley Square.

"Which house is Sir Augustus's?" he asked.

"It has to be that smaller one on the left," she said. "Panch said it was only a three-story building."

To her surprise, he walked up to the mottled stone building, the red brick above each simple window giving it the look of eyes and brows. It did not have the decorative charm of many of the other houses, though it did have an attractive iron railing above the ground floor that matched its neighbors.

Fred lurked in the doorway for a moment, then moved back toward her. He took her arm and pulled her down the street. "It's definitely his."

"Why do you say that?"

"He has a custom door knocker." Fred paused. "It has a nautilus shell motif."

Chapter 16

Charles felt the kick that woke him through a sleepy haze. At the top of the night he'd been overly alert, afraid of attacks, but when the candles had been snuffed out and the other men settled down, his exhausted body had worked against his desire for wakefulness. Still, he lay on his rug. The kick didn't come again and he didn't hear anyone else stirring.

A guard came in and made a fire. The flames danced across the whitewashed walls, illuminating more than warming the stone. Charles blinked despite himself. There seemed no point in starting a new day. He knew it to be Saturday and like the last Saturday to Sunday, he expected little to happen on his behalf.

Tomorrow, all his friends would be tucked up in their churches, praying for him, to be sure, but unlikely to visit. He pulled his fingers into a fist and knocked it against his forehead.

If his friends could not aid him, he needed to solve all the puzzles himself. He was the inimitable one after all. What leverage did he have over Sir Augustus? What could be threatened against such a man?

Maybe the loose knot in the coil was Mr. Yupman. A vice president, not a president. A nephew, not an uncle. He'd dealt with a problem by fainting, not the most masculine of responses. Charles had thought he'd heard creaking when the man moved. He might have been wearing stays.

Charles's eyes opened more fully at that amusing thought. At least he had himself for companionship.

He grimaced when he saw he had company almost as close as himself. His nearest fellow prisoner, a stranger of around forty with dirt caked into the wrinkles radiating from his eyes, was only inches away from him, and stared directly at Charles.

That was when Charles's nose, irritated by the cold and damp and nearly impenetrable, stirred to life. He could discount the human offal smells of many men together, but the coppery hint of blood was new.

He rubbed sleep out of his eyes. "What are you staring at?" he asked the other prisoner. He didn't even know the man's name.

When Charles sat up, he discovered why the man stared. He looked at eternity, not this room. From Charles's new vantage point, rusty stains appeared on the prisoner's filthy, faded neckcloth.

The staring eyes of death had been watching Charles. No kind regard here, but another murder victim.

Charles turned away with a shudder. The realization that a dead body lay next to him hit him in pieces. A man was dead. A man was murdered. The man had been murdered next to him. The blood was not quite fresh. Charles himself had been kicked recently. Surely more recently than the murder. He'd slept through a murder? His body jerked in shock. How loud was a throat cutting?

Remembering who he was, a reporter who had seen death before many times, he forced himself to look again, to think rationally. The last dregs of sleep left him as he contemplated the scene.

Who had kicked him? He glanced around quickly as light began to enter the apartment from the windows that looked out over the interior of the prison.

No one glanced in his direction. No Redcap goblins fancifully danced their macabre glee at another death. He put a hand to his side, rubbed the ghost of old pain away, and told himself to think.

The door was heavy and he would have heard it open and close even in his sleep. Therefore, the killer was in here with them, unless there was a secret passage in the walls. Generally, he would not put it past prisoners to attempt to tunnel, but Newgate was notoriously difficult to escape.

He posited that this death had something to do with him. A deliberate attempt to frighten him. Or even an accidental murder. Could he have been the intended victim?

He untied his neckerchief and pulled it over his nose, then leaned in for a closer look. Now that he was more awake and the light had improved, he noted that the wound was similar to that found on Samuel Pickwick. But if the killer was the same man, he'd have had to be planted here, whether by arrest or design.

He didn't know enough about cutting throats to know if all such wounds were the same. William might know, but he could hardly drag the body into the yard for inspection.

This could be the payment for Kate not finding another clue. But if her fiancé had been the target, that meant Kate was the focus of all this ill will. That the Lightning Club adventure and Samuel Pickwick's murder were tied to her life, not Charles's.

He sat back on his rug. Kate, the center of all this? A twenty-year-old girl who lived with her parents and siblings? His brain refused to search for any connections to villainy that he knew weren't there. She loved a mystery, but she didn't go looking

for them. He knew everything about his Kate. She had no enemies. He was the man of the world, a man in the middle of
things. He had enemies. A strange sort of pride filled his veins
at that. Only twenty-three and he had a member of Parliament
as an enemy.

A low-pitched cackle assaulted his ears. He glanced up.
Ralph Rotter, another of the prisoners, a large, shambling fel-
low with a flat-backed head and a wandering eye, pointed at
Charles and made that strange laugh again.

"Pissed yerself, Dickens?" he said, his upper lip wrinkling
and flexing in a sneer.

Charles glanced down at his leg. He'd knelt in a blood pool
in his half-awake state and it had soaked up his leg. Attempting
to hide his revulsion, he put a tough expression on his face. "I
expect you know it's blood, Rotter. You know anything about
this?"

He pointed at the body

Rotter frowned, not seeming to notice that the man was
dead. "Jenkens. In fer killin' his ma."

"He killed his mother?" Charles asked, aghast.

Rotter shrugged. "No trial yet. What's the werd?"

"Alleged?"

The other man nodded and kicked at Jenkens's leg. When
there was no response, he kicked again, with a note of casual irritation.

"Err, Rotter?" Charles pointed at Jenkens's neck.

"Wot?" Rotter demanded. "I don't see too good."

"He's dead," Charles explained.

"Natural causes?"

"No, there's blood everywhere," Charles said casually.

Rotter took a step back and wiped at his nose.

"Next time you tell someone they've got a mess down their
leg, you might want to take a sniff first," Charles said, enjoying
getting one over a bully.

"You kill 'im?" Rotter said.

"No," Charles said, horrified. "You'd need a knife for that kind of work." The thought struck him. Why hadn't he thought of that? Who would have a knife in Newgate Prison? The wardsman was a prisoner as well, chosen for good conduct. He wouldn't have a weapon. None of the turnkeys slept in here.

The thought of one of these men locked in here with him having a weapon made his stomach turn.

"Oy!" Rotter shrieked into the room. "Dickens 'as killed Jenkens!"

The room, so quiet before, stirred instantly to life. Charles watched as the mound of covers on the bedstead wriggled and frothed, then the wardsman's head popped out of filthy blankets. He stumbled to his feet, then sat down again to put his shoes on.

Coming forward, wiping his mouth and eyes with his fingers, he stared wildly at Rotter. Three or four men had rolled off their rugs by then and crowded behind the wardsman.

"What did you say?" he asked, wiping more white crust from his eyes.

Rotter pointed. "Look at that."

The wardsman stepped around Charles, his eyes still bleary, then slowly bent forward.

"Mind the blood," Charles said helpfully. "I've ruined my trousers."

The man jerked back as soon as his gaze reached the neck. "Who's done this?"

"I said, Dickens," Rotter called again.

Charles shook his head, doing his best to indicate that the bully was utterly insane. "I didn't even know his name."

"Who did it then?" the wardsman asked.

"Someone with a knife?" Charles suggested.

The wardsman sped into motion, knocking the men behind him about as he went to the door and banged on it. "Raise the alarm! Search the room!"

Charles pushed himself into a standing position and folded up his rug with his foot. He suspected they had frequent acquaintance with death in the prison. The life here was not cozy enough for an extension. Men would die of natural causes or hanging. Fights broke out as well. But this kind of injury could not be common. Unless, of course, it was. Which would mean they were all trapped with a serial killer of men, who would take any life in a kind of mania.

Charles didn't really believe that, however. Coincidences aside, the death of Jenkens had something to do with Samuel Pickwick, and his life depended on sorting out why.

The heavy door opened, disrupting the noxious scents of many men sleeping together. Two turnkeys came in. The wardsman directed them straight toward the back-corner wall where Charles had slept, having no seniority to be closer to the fire.

He leaned against the cold whitewash, hands at his sides, keeping very still, uncomfortably conscious of his small stature and state of exhaustion.

Rotter pointed at the corpse. "Neck slit from ear to ear," he said. Charles doubted he'd seen anything at all. Rotter seemed to be enjoying this drama, a chance to be the center of attention from more important men.

"Who did this?"

Charles recognized Keefe from his earlier interactions with the turnkey. The man still looked ill and ready for a seat just about anywhere.

Rotter pointed at Charles. The other turnkey grabbed his arm, hauling him away from the wall. Charles felt exposed, as a ring of men stared at him.

"I woke when someone kicked me," Charles said, choosing

his words for maximum persuasion. "I'm new here, and I've had no means to get whatever blade killed this man."

"He's had plenty of visitors in the yard," sneered one of his fellow prisoners.

Charles marked the man carefully, as an enemy. Taller than average, very black hair and prominent cheekbones. Smelled like wet dog. Coat sleeves too short. "Come, Keefe," he pleaded, "you know we're all searched when we leave the yard. I'm no villain."

"You're in here for murder, same as most of these men," Keefe said. He coughed, then covered his mouth with a handkerchief. Charles saw a spot of blood when he tucked it away again.

"I was framed," Charles insisted.

"So were I," said his new enemy. "It were someone else stabbed my sister fourteen times."

The crowd of men laughed. "Where did you sleep?" Keefe asked the tall prisoner. "It's Darbandi, right?"

"In the corner." Darbandi pointed to a spot on the far end of the wall south of the corpse.

Charles felt uneasy, being the new man in the room. Maybe he really would be the scapegoat.

Keefe stared hard at him, then went back to the body. "This is Jenkens, right?"

The wardsman stepped over to check again. "Yes."

Keefe turned, gnawing at his lip. "Where's Gronk?"

"Gronk?" asked the other turnkey.

"Double murder," Keefe said. "Round belly, red hair, slovenly. Jenkens's mother was married to Gronk's father. They're awaiting trial. It's assumed they conspired to kill them both."

Charles heard a scramble near the fire, a clang as metal hit stone. The door of the ward opened. Two more turnkeys arrived, one of them better turned out than the other, probably the head man of the area.

"Secure the knife," Keefe shouted.

"Grab Gronk!" cried the other turnkey, as a short, thickset prisoner made a break for the door.

Charles returned to his spot against the wall as a melee ensued. Prisoners, forgetting docility, rushed in Gronk's direction, whether to help him or reach the door for themselves, Charles couldn't say.

He regretted all the time he'd spent thinking about his own situation and not assessing the power structure and relationships among his fellow men. He had no idea what the prisoners whispered about in their small groups. He hadn't cared, a bad habit for a reporter.

Another turnkey came into the doorway and blocked it as men flailed about.

Gronk, with more dexterity than the average man despite the protuberant belly, twisted and turned and even did a tumble headfirst at one point, until he was brought down by a yank at his coattails from the lead guard.

Charles watched with concern as Keefe doubled over. Had he been attacked? No, just another coughing fit.

As more turnkeys poured into the room, a knot of fighting gathered near the doorway. Charles suspected a loose plan for some of the men to break free and get out, though they wouldn't get far. Still, it would be a fine adventure, even if it landed them in a solitary cell for a while.

In another minute or two, he saw Rotter standing casually along the wall perpendicular to him, surrounded by a few of his cronies. He smirked in Charles's direction. Charles wondered why they had left the fight.

No one minded the body or paid the alleged mother-killer any respect.

But Gronk put up quite a match, kicking and screaming as three of the turnkeys hoisted him up.

Where was the knife? Charles hadn't seen anyone secure it.

It must have gone into the fireplace. "Where's the knife?" he called at Keefe as he tucked his handkerchief away again.

The man jerked his head up. "Where's the knife?" the turnkey repeated.

His voice had much more authority than Charles's. One of the other turnkeys kicked and punched a space around the door, then slammed it shut.

"Everyone against the wall," he shouted, brandishing his billy club.

Most men went to the walls along the fireplace, it being the warmest place in the room.

"Spread out," the turnkey demanded, hitting the floor with his club.

Slowly, the men complied. Rotter gave Charles a dirty look and he knew he'd made an enemy, though he assumed no one had come to stand near him because of the body, which stunk slightly more now than it had in life.

Keefe walked slowly to the fire and peered around the stones. Then he conferred with the other turnkeys.

"Silence!" the most aggressive of them shouted, when a few of the men began to murmur to each other.

Charles watched the room carefully. Rotter was the biggest bully and he had followers who might have brought the knife to him. Was the man smart enough to ensure that he didn't have it on him?

"Keep an arm's distance apart," Keefe warned. When the trio of guards returned, having offloaded Gronk to others, the lead turnkey gave the order to search each of the men.

Charles saw Darbandi lick his lips and glance in the direction of a pile of scattered rugs in the center of the room, just after he was searched. He knew then that the knife was hidden there, or at least contraband. Had he ever seen Darbandi conferring with Gronk? Was there some alliance there?

"We need to deal with that," the lead turnkey said with disfavor when they passed the body.

"The knife first, I think, sir," Keefe said. "Now, Dickens, turn around."

Hands, none too gentle, poked and prodded at his body. When he heard labored breathing near his ear, he whispered, "Check the rugs in the middle of the floor."

"Why?" rasped Keefe.

"I saw Darbandi staring at them," Charles whispered.

Keefe grunted and released him. "You stink of the grave, Dickens."

Charles turned around. "It's Jenkens's blood. It's all over my trousers."

"Ask your friends for new clothing." Keefe narrowed his weary eyes at Charles, then moved on.

The turnkeys went over each prisoner methodically, while Charles wracked his brain for any connection between Darbandi and Gronk. But then, he didn't even remember noticing Gronk and Jenkens were particularly chummy. He'd paid no attention to anyone, nor asked for fellowship with any man except Bob Sawyer. This was no way to get along in Newgate. If circumstances forced him to remain here for much longer, his visits from the outside world would begin to drop off, and his main earthly companionship would be inside these walls. Surely there were men here as innocent as he? He remembered those two men he'd written about in his Newgate sketch. Pratt and Smith had been hanged in November on flimsy evidence and for an even sillier crime. Yes, he probably would find men like himself here.

He leaned his head against the cold wall. At least his book would be a bestseller. Everyone would want to read his Newgate sketch now. He'd be famous.

The guards finished their search, calling to each other, "Nothing," "Nothing," "Nothing."

Charles watched as Keefe inclined his head toward one of the guards and whispered in his ear. The man nodded and whispered in another ear. The guards moved toward the center of the room, flanking Keefe in the middle.

Charles turned his attention to Darbandi. When he scanned the man, he saw his hands closed into fists. No wonder Keefe had wanted protection from the others when he found the knife. The guard kicked at the frayed, grayish rugs, turning each one over methodically.

Darbandi winced when a clink resounded as the middle rug was flipped. Keefe bent down, coughing as his stomach pressed against his knee, and came up with a sharpened piece of metal, far from clean.

"Who does this belong to?" one of his companions called. The three scanned the room.

"Dickens," muttered one of the men next to Darbandi.

Charles cataloged him. Pockmarked left cheek, lank brown hair that brushed the back of his collar, lazy eye, crooked thumb that made it hard for him to grasp things.

"Dickens has been here a week," the guard retorted. "This is the work of some longer effort."

"Coulda been smuggled in 'ere like that," Darbandi's supporter insisted.

The guard stepped forward, ignoring the suggestion. Charles tried to imagine upright Mr. Hogarth sliding him a handmade knife, or merry William. He rather thought either of the girls might be willing. Julie might even know someone who could make one. Kate, on the other hand, would not. She'd be more likely to offer an embroidery needle.

The guard stared at Darbandi and his two closest companions for several seconds, then raised his hand and gestured forward. "Let's take these three for questioning."

The men protested loudly as they were grabbed. Darbandi spit in the direction of the body, or Charles; he wasn't sure. Then the room went silent again; just two guards remained, along with the prisoners, the wardsmen, and the corpse.

One of the remaining prisoners did mutter something about that. Rotter laughed. He and his friends had survived the situation without questioning so far. Charles figured Darbandi had done it, because he knew where the knife was hiding, but it wasn't very sophisticated logic. For all he knew, the knife had been passed to him in a chain of hidden movement, and Darbandi had merely been stuck with it at an inopportune moment.

To think, it was only morning. What would the rest of the day be like?

Kate and Fred were casually strolling past Sir Augustus's mansion when they spotted an ethereal blond girl with a basket of watercress, a bit too early in the day. Usually, these girls came around at teatime.

"I think that's Lucy Fair, Julie's maid," Kate whispered to Fred. "Can you spot Julie?"

"Should be easy with that hair," he said, scanning the street. "Maybe she decided to stay home, with the baby and all."

Kate didn't find it likely, so she perused the general circle around Lucy Fair. She didn't see Julie, but then noticed a man leaning against a railing across the street, an unlit cigar in his hand. His coat looked familiar, plus it nearly enveloped his thin frame.

"I can't believe it," she muttered. "She dressed as William!"

When Fred frowned at her, she put her finger and thumb along his chin and turned his head toward the "man."

"No, that can't be," he said. He grabbed Kate's arm and pulled her into the street, ducking behind a trap driven by a rosy-cheeked elder statesman in thirty-year-old breeches.

The "man" chewed on his cigar as they approached. Kate gestured at "him" and the cigar wobbled.

A carriage came around the corner, slowed by a cart of boxes being pushed down the middle of the street.

"Couldn't you have chosen a simpler disguise?" Kate asked, noting the mustache was nothing more than coal dust and greasepaint up close.

"Just a little fun," Julie said in her gruffest voice.

"I'm sure Amy Poor isn't having any fun," Kate snapped as the cart rolled by, propelled by a boy a little too small to have full control of it.

"Women can't loiter," Julie pointed out. "I could stand here for half an hour like this and not be noticed."

"I suppose," Kate huffed. "We'll walk past then and check on my sister and brothers. See you in a little while."

Fred grinned at Julie, who winked at him. Kate took his arm and they strolled on, pacing the carriage, which wasn't a hired conveyance, but didn't have any obvious markings, either. A horsemeat man came up from the servants' stairs as they passed one house, reeking of his product.

"Someone must not love their pets," Fred said, wincing.

Lucy the watercress seller turned left ahead of them. They followed as the mews swallowed her up.

"I don't see the other Hogarths," Fred said, craning his neck.

"They are probably somewhere else on their circuit," Kate answered.

They walked past the mouth of the mews and went down the next block before spotting the Hogarths. Lucy Fair walked just behind them.

"We're getting too bunched up," Fred said.

Kate pointed at her sister and gestured to the left, figuring she and Fred would keep walking straight.

Lucy Fair reached them and grabbed Kate's hand, soiling her glove with her watercress girl's grimy paw. "Look!"

Kate turned around and saw a new cabriolet coming toward them. They all moved to the side of the pavement.

"That's his carriage," Fred said, pointing at the green and blue shield on the body.

"There's a woman in it," Kate's brother George said, tall enough to peer in.

"Could it be Amy Poor?" Kate asked, shocked.

"She's a beauty. Golden hair. Looks a bit haughty," George reported. "Pink bonnet."

"Not her then," Kate said, frustrated that she couldn't see. "Amy Poor has dark hair, according to Mr. Aga."

Lucy slid around them and went left, probably going to warn Julie. The rest of them waited for the carriage to turn in the same direction, then spread out and sauntered in its wake.

When they reached Charles Street, the carriage had already paused in front of Sir Augustus's house. Kate put up her hand. "Mary, you and the boys walk past the carriage so you can keep an eye on it. I'm going to confer with Julie."

She and Fred waited on the corner until the group of Hogarths were half a block ahead of them. Lucy said something to Julie as she passed by, then went downstairs to a servants' door across the street to keep up her ruse as a seller.

"Is that him?" Kate asked, as an extremely tall man came out from the covered front entrance of Sir Augustus's house, followed by a smaller man in a much smaller hat.

"Charles described him as unusually tall, with a large belly," Fred said. "Looks the picture to me."

Kate walked to Julie, keeping up her pose. She had the cigar lit now. Smoke hung moodily in the air around her as she held it at her side and knocked ash into a bush.

"It looks like we've found him," Kate said, slowing to a turtle's pace so she could talk to Julie without being seen to have a conversation.

The two men climbed into the carriage. It rocked a little as the weight redistributed.

"I wonder who the haughty young lady is," Kate said.

"Could be anyone. Lucy and I will follow them," Julie said.

"Your sister and the boys will trail along for a while, and if it gets toward dinnertime, they are to meet us at my rooms."

"What will we do? Trail behind?" Fred asked.

Julie shook her head. "Your part in this is over. Take Kate to St. Paul's and try to get the next letter. I need to get a look at these three people for myself."

"I do so hope the dirty man is there," Kate said. "But you're right. There are enough of us to tackle more than one part of this mystery."

"Don't despair," Julie said, waving her cigar as she stepped into the street, closer to the carriage. "We'll have Charles home soon."

Chapter 17

"Do we really think we're going to have any luck at the churchyard?" Fred asked.

"We don't have any way to make contact with my tormentors," Kate admitted. "But it makes sense that they would expect us to return to the last place I was supposed to go."

"What about Newgate?" Fred asked. "That's another spot they know we would venture to, since Charles is there."

"We'll go there next, if we have no luck at St. Paul's." Kate considered what to do, then directed Fred to the west. "Let's go toward Green Park. Hopefully we can find a cab stand. St. Paul's is nearly an hour's walk from here."

She fretted as they walked, but they found a cab stand ten minutes later and were able to dash across London at a decent pace. She calmed down when the St. Paul's dome grew in the sky, at the highest point of the city on Ludgate Hill. Long ago, there had been a prison on the hill, in the times of the Tudor and Stuart kings. She wondered if it helped to survive incarceration if one had a nice view of the city life one couldn't join.

After she ordered the cab to stop in the same place as before, she turned to Fred.

"Should we have him wait? If the dirty man isn't here, the cab can get us to Newgate faster."

"It's only up the street and we aren't made of money," he pointed out.

Kate nodded and reached for the purse in her reticule. "I'll pay."

"I'll give Charles what blunt I have left," Fred said.

She handed the driver coins and they both climbed down. The courtyard had a hustle and bustle it had not the last time she had been there. Shops ringed the church's edifice, lending an air that Jesus himself might not have appreciated, but at least it was mostly publishing around here, rather than moneylending or something worse.

Like blackmail.

They walked to No. 72, nondescript except for its history. Before Kate could take stock of the current shop, the dirty man stepped out of the doorway, spinning a cane through his fingers. The feather in his old hat caught the breeze and waved at them.

She drew back, her gaze going to the cane, and clutched at Fred's arm. Was the dirty man going to attack them?

"You'd be better off watching the prison, stupid girl," the big man sneered.

"Better off?" Fred asked, a shaky tone to his words.

"Bad deeds there overnight." The man licked his teeth.

Kate's flesh crawled. "Charles? What has happened?"

"Stupid girl," the man mocked. "You're responsible for a death."

Kate's fingers went numb. "A death? Because I went to Miss Baillie's house instead of here?"

"How is that possible?" Fred demanded. "That's ridiculous! Anyone would have gone to the person's house. That's what the other clues wanted!"

A solitary man wandered by, looked at them but said nothing, and went into the next shop. Frantic, Kate scanned the area. Who was a henchman of the dirty man, and who had blood on their hands? Charles's blood.

A thought struck her. "A death" didn't sound like the death of someone she loved, who she was going to live with and have children with and very possibly bury someday very far into the future.

The dirty man screwed up his face, sucking audibly on his teeth. She could imagine what he would look like as an old man, his face all knotted together like a wrinkled apple. If he lived that long. He'd probably still have that ridiculous hat, might even be buried in it.

"Who did you kill?" she demanded.

"Not me, dearie, that's not my line."

"Is Charles well?" she ventured, more shakily.

He made a "heh, heh, heh" noise until she wanted to scream.

"You'd tell me, wouldn't you? I mean, you'd just let the words out, because there is nothing worse that could happen to me than that. I might even fall down dead at your feet if you said it," Kate cried, her voice rising. "What has happened to my Charles?"

Fred grabbed her around the waist just as she launched herself at her tormentor, blinded by tears.

"Oi, oi," said a gruff voice.

Kate felt herself being hauled back. She wiped her streaming eyes with her free arm and saw a constable, his helmet pitching low on his forehead. What if he arrested her for being a public nuisance? Her body began to shake in earnest. She glanced at the dirty man. He smirked. Fred's grip on her had broken but he stood with a boxer's stance, ready to attack on her behalf.

"Wot's this now?" said the constable, giving her a suspicious, narrow-eyed stare.

"Such a fierce wee sparrow, ain't she?" mocked the dirty man, before she could speak. "It's just a little tease. She wants this from me." He pulled a letter from between the fastenings of his waistcoat, made by a missing button.

"Does she owe you money?" the constable asked.

Kate could not believe, given the tidiness of her attire, and Fred's, and the disgusting nature of the other man's, that he was the one being given credence. Was this a ruse? Was the constable in the dirty man's pay? Or not even a constable at all?

"Nah," the dirty man said, with another suck at his teeth. He thrust the letter at Kate. "Here you go, pretty birdie. Don't be late when I request the pleasure of your company again."

She took the letter with trembling fingers. The dirty man doffed his hat in the direction of the constable and strode off.

The constable stared very hard at her. "Don't be making any more public disturbances in this 'ere house of God," he said, equating this commercial area with the cathedral behind.

"No, sir," Fred said, pushing himself in front of her. "She'll be fine now, I promise. He's a very rum sort, that man."

"Bit of a tease, but I've seen him around for years, and never any mischief in 'im," the constable said.

Kate's ears pricked despite her upset. "He lives in the neighborhood?"

The constable glanced into the sky, then returned his gaze to her. "I expect so. Seen 'im at the cookshops, the bakeshops, quite frequently at the Queen's Arms and the Horn."

"Taverns," Fred guessed.

"Nothing wrong with that, as long as he isn't creating a public disturbance." Before he could say more, they all heard a policeman's rattle at a distance. Saying not a word more, the constable strode off toward the summons.

"Possibly a real policeman after all," Kate said, turning in the direction of the street, her feet eager to move. "But we must get to the prison. What if Charles has been hurt?"

"I don't believe it for a second," Fred said, the expression on his face making him look so like Charles in one of his rants about politicians that she wanted to throw her arms around his neck. "Whatever is going on here, they've gone in for torture, not killing. Why destroy their plaything? If Charles is dead, they can't toy with him, or you, because you'd be shut up in your house in mourning."

Kate nodded. "An excellent analysis, if we can assume their behavior has anything of the rational in it. And that I would doubt. Setting their trap for me here and not in Hampstead, for instance. They set me up to fail on my quest. They knew it would happen like this." She put up her hand in protest. "You can't tell me otherwise."

"Oh, I'm not protesting," Fred said. "We need to get to the prison and find William. He'll know what's going on or I'll eat the dirty man's hat."

Kate let her feet move, leaving the churchyard behind at a speed greater than her usual sedate pace. Would she ever see the dome of St. Paul's in quite the same light again? Even the fleeting winter light seemed to cast more shadows than usual, highlighting the other people in the street in odd, macabre ways. Was that flower seller missing half her face? No, Kate saw she merely had a large birthmark when she turned. Or that gentleman leering at two well-dressed women heading in the direction of the cathedral, he seemed to have no hair or eyes at all, from the way his hat was tilted.

"You're shaking, Kate," Fred said, taking her arm. "You have to be in better cheer to see Charles."

"If indeed he is with us on this earth to be seen, rather than dead and gone to heaven," Kate rejoined.

"He's fine," Fred said. "Not to be, well, spiritual about it, but I think I'd know if he was gone. It's been nothing but Charles, Charles, Charles, since he went to prison. I've thought of little else, which doesn't serve me too well at the office, let me tell you."

They passed a tavern. Singing could be heard through the cracked door, one of the old ballads about lost love. Kate had a sudden fierce longing for the old Scottish ballads she'd grown up with, a comfort for the ears. "You've been alone at Furnival's Inn most nights," Kate said.

"I can't sleep for dreaming about him, cold and tossing about," Fred admitted. "Perhaps because I'm frozen, too, with him not there. I daren't outspend my means so I'm not using as much coal. The windows are coated with ice in the mornings. Even the pitcher is rimmed with it."

"I wish we didn't live in Brompton," Kate told him. "You could be warm and cozy with us if we were closer, and you would still arrive at work on time."

He pulled her out of the path of a mound of horse droppings that the street sweeper hadn't dealt with yet. "I wish you were married already, so we'd be there together through these long evenings."

Kate squeezed his hand and felt better. The rough granite walls of the prison came into view, embedded with small windows covered in grates well above the street, to prevent the smaller prisoners escaping through them.

They went around to the yard and stared through the visitors' box for a few moments but didn't recognize any of the prisoners presently there. Fred craned his neck, peering along the wall. No other egress existed for spotting prisoners, since the walls were stone, topped by deadly iron spikes. "I don't see William."

Kate forced her words to sound calm. "Let's go to the governor's house. He has the credentials to get inside the prison. If anything has happened, he wouldn't wait outside."

They walked around the building to the center of the longest part of the building and knocked on the governor's door.

A servant opened the door promptly, an ill-used man of middle years, dressed like any clerk in well-worn trousers, a little too short, and a black frock coat shiny in patches with long use. Kate wondered if this was the same man who had welcomed Charles last year when he'd been a journalist on a mission rather than an inmate.

"Good afternoon," Fred said, his voice squeaking a bit. "We are looking for William Aga, the journalist. Is he present within?"

"Who are you?" the servant inquired.

"Frederick Dickens and Miss Catherine Hogarth."

The servant nodded, muttering "is it my job?" under his breath, and closed the door in their faces.

Fred turned and stepped to the side to lean against the wall. "We don't have a great deal of time before it gets dark. I hope he returns soon."

"I know, we have to get to Julie's rooms. I wonder what they've learned."

"Likely nothing," Fred said. "Why haven't you looked at the letter yet?"

"I've been too worried about Charles's fate," Kate admitted. She pulled the sealed letter from her muff. "Shall I read it?"

Fred made a flourish with his hand. "Please do. In the shadow of Newgate seems an appropriate place for it."

Kate took off her glove so she could slide a fingernail under the seal, the same red one with the starfish, then read the missive just loud enough for Fred to hear. "It's addressed to me, as always. '*One Thing quite necessary to make any Instructions that come either from your Governors, or your Books, of any Use to you, is to attend with Desire of Learning, and not to be apt to fansy yourselves too wise to be taught. For this Spirit will keep you ignorant as long as you live . . . We hope you are more educatable than your fiancé. Find us again be-*

*fore twenty-four hours have passed or you will pay the conse-
quences. —A friend.'"*

"Couldn't we assume from the tone of the letter that Charles
is still alive?" Fred asked hopefully.

Two women passing by gave Fred a look of sympathy. Wag-
ons and carriages passed them in the road, going about their
daily business in all ignorance of the human souls incarcerated
nearby.

"The servant needs to tell us if it is true that a man has died,"
Kate said. "At least we need to learn that much."

"I agree." Fred shuffled his feet. "We have another quotation
to decipher, and I hope it's obvious that the answer sticks close
to London, so we don't have to go through the same nonsense
as you did in Hampstead."

"I have to go to Ealing tomorrow either way." Kate turned
the paper over and over in her hands. "To see Lady Byron."

"Is that wise?"

"She might know something about the source of all this
mystery. We need to be able to lop the villainous beast off at the
head."

"I know," Fred said. "I wish it wasn't you who had to do
everything."

She squeezed his hand, remembering how young he was.
"Charles needs us to be brave. Besides, I've had lots of help,
like from you."

He blinked at her. "I know. Does the letter mean anything
to you?"

"I feel sure I have heard the quotation before, but my brain is
a sad muddle right now. I need quiet and a good library."

The governor's house door opened again. The servant, looking disgruntled, gestured them in. They followed him into the
little office that Charles had described so well in his upcoming
sketch. Had he any presentiment of his future experience in this
place when he'd visited as a tourist?

The room only held a couple of clerks, working on stools at a desk. They paid no attention to the visitors as they transferred a stack of paper between them. Kate glanced at the clock and saw she and Fred needed to leave for Cheapside soon.

The far door opened and another man entered, a little older than the clerks, with the high color and emaciated stoop of a consumptive, followed by William.

Kate forgot the room and the other people and rushed to him. "No one was in the exercise yard. What is happening? Charles?"

William smiled his merry smile at her. His eyes even crinkled at the corners. Kate grabbed the edge of the table for support, suddenly feeling her stays were much too tight. She bumped one of the clerk's arms and his pen dotted ink across his page. He muttered something profane and attempted to blot it away.

Kate, though, had eyes for no one but William. His smile must mean nothing bad had happened. She tossed off an apology, then lifted her hands to William, begging for news.

"The men were in the yard at their usual time," he said.

Fred came next to Kate as the second clerk joined the first in trying to save the page, giving Kate black looks. "Just start over," he advised the clerks. "Tear out the page. You've only done three lines."

Both clerks' mouths turned down identically in a half moon. Fred began to laugh. "You must be related. Am I right?"

Kate pinched his arm. "Listen to William, Fred. It's important."

William tapped his foot. "Charles was fine when I saw him in the yard."

Black spots dotted Kate's vision. She needed to sit. The room was so hot all of a sudden.

"Hey now, stand up," she heard Fred say, then she was bodily plunked onto a stool.

"What's all this?" the older clerk asked.

Kate put her hands to her face as William spoke.

"This is Catherine Hogarth, Mr. Dickens's fiancée," he explained. "She'd thought he might have been murdered. Now that we know otherwise, I do want more information about the dead prisoner and who murdered him."

Kate squeezed her eyes shut. A hand came down on her shoulder and Fred asked in a squeaky voice, "Dead prisoner?"

"In Charles's ward," William confirmed. "A man named Jenkens had his throat slit like Samuel Pickwick."

"Did he look like Charles?" Kate asked, voice quavering.

"This is John Keefe, one of the turnkeys," William said. "He can explain."

"No," said the man who had come in with William, "but he slept next to him. We think instead of murdering him, the plan was to suggest Dickens had done Jenkens in."

"But you don't think that," William said in a leading tone.

"No. Dickens observed one of his fellow unfortunates staring fixedly at a pile of rugs in the middle of the room. He alerted me and we found the knife. Bit of a fight but we got the bad 'un." The man stopped to cough.

"Charles isn't under suspicion?" Kate asked, starting to feel better.

John Keefe shook his head, his mouth still covered by his handkerchief. "Family business between the other prisoners. Nothing to do with Dickens. In fact, he'll make a good snitch."

William went very still. "He's a reporter, a trained observer. Not a snitch."

The turnkey coughed one last time, then tucked away his stained handkerchief. "Most of them would claim they saw nothing, even if a man was robbed of his last breath in front of them."

"Charles doesn't belong here." Kate's voice came out in a wretched whisper.

William nodded. "At least we know the murder had nothing to do with Charles, and likely nothing to do with your letters."

"What letters?" the turnkey demanded.

"Someone has been sending me around town on quests, threatening Charles if I don't do as they demand," Kate explained.

The turnkey screwed up his mouth. "Have they been able to do anything bad?"

"There was a fire one night," William said. "Outside Kate's bedroom window. And Charles was attacked."

"Are you sure these incidents were related to these quests?" the turnkey asked.

"They must be," Kate said. "Besides, Charles was framed from the start. He found a murder victim and was blamed for killing him, but he'd never even met the man."

"He had a letter, too," Fred added. "It's all been letters. That's how it started."

"Ah," the turnkey said, losing interest as one of the clerks gave in to Fred's suggestion and tore the damaged page from the ledger. "I think you lot had better go before you cause more mischief."

"I am terribly sorry," Kate said.

"I understand," said the turnkey, pulling out his handkerchief again. "I'm sure it's very trying for a young lady who isn't used to this sort of thing."

Fred pulled Kate out of the office. Within a few moments they were back on the street, in full view of the passersby. Kate was sure she looked a crumpled, tearstained mess. William was a large, comforting presence next to her though, and he stepped into the road with his hand raised. An empty cab slowed, and he gestured them into it.

Kate hadn't realized how warm the office had been until they had the wind blowing in their faces. Her body shook with the chill, but she tried to focus on the news. "How did Charles seem?"

"Frustrated," William reported. "But he had that keen twinkle in his eyes. At least he had something to occupy his mind. I believe the so-called victim was a presumed matricide, so no great loss there."

"That's good to know," Kate said. "But I don't like Charles being locked up with those villains."

"We'll figure it out soon. How about you? Any luck with Sir Augustus?"

"We last saw Julie and company chasing after his carriage," Kate said, trying to make her voice sound normal again. "Fred and I went after the dirty man, and he was at the churchyard today."

"I hope my wife's enthusiasms do not overcome her abilities. What was the news?"

Kate smiled sympathetically. "A new letter. I feel I'll be able to sort it out if I have time to think. The quotation sounds familiar."

"I'll take a look at it." William grunted. "You see Lady Byron tomorrow?"

"Yes, but she asked me to visit at an early, unfashionable hour, so I'll be well within the twenty-four hours the letter gives me. I'm sure the answer is back in London."

"No doubt," William agreed. "Lady Lugoson will lend you her vehicle again. It will take about an hour to reach Fordhook, the lady's home."

"That should, I expect, still give me three or four hours when I return to London, no doubt with the answer."

The cab deposited them in front of the chophouse on the ground floor of the Agas' building, across from Mary-le-Bow Church. William helped Kate down, then Fred.

"I'll acquire food," he said.

"We don't have too long before we have to leave for Brompton again."

"Would you come back here in an hour to take a party out to York Place?" William asked the driver. "When the bells ring three of the clock?"

"I'll do me best, sir," the coachman said.

William tipped him well, then turned to Kate. "Run upstairs, and I'll be there soon with whatever food I can gather."

Chapter 18

Julie sent Lucy Fair to the bread box for a loaf. "Bring back the cheese and a knife, too. We'll toast it over the fire."

"That sounds cracking," James Hogarth said enthusiastically.

Kate settled Mary and the boys onto the sofa, then she and Julie took the armchairs that Lady Lugoson had handed down to the Agas.

When Lucy came into the room lugging the food, Mary jumped up to help her slice the cheese and bread and slide them securely onto the toasting forks.

"I have news," Julie said to Kate in a low voice. "After you left, I did get a look in the carriage, and you'll never guess who the young lady was."

"Who?" Kate asked.

Julie frowned. "I couldn't place her at first, but as soon as I arrived in my rooms, I realized who she was."

"Who?" Kate asked again, impatient.

Julie's dark golden eyebrows lifted, casting her face into amusement. "So impatient. It's unlike you, Kate."

"I am in a state," Kate admitted. "But the news?"

"It was Evelina Jaggers," Julie announced in a portentous whisper. "You remember. Miss Haverstock's ward, the one Charles asked your father to remove from his party?"

"Goodness," Kate exclaimed. "She is acquainted with Sir Augustus? I wonder what that means. She had said she would leave England."

"It means Charles has two enemies who know each other," Julie said.

Kate stared at her friend. "Of course. Two enemies. No wonder Charles is in trouble."

Julie nodded. "No wonder indeed."

"What do we do now?" Kate asked. "It's not as if we don't know that Charles was framed for murder. How does this knowledge help us?"

"We must wait for William's thoughts." Julie inclined her head and looked skyward for a moment, then a sly smile crossed her face. "To distract you, I'll tell you a family tale Lady Lugoson told me."

"Lords and ladies?" James asked, stretching out on the rug.

"The very same," Julie agreed. "The most exciting girls of the realm, some three hundred and more years ago."

"Girls," eleven-year-old William muttered, rolling his eyes.

Julie's Tale

"The Boleyn girls weren't those kind of nice girls that history is allowed to forget," Julie said, with a suggestive eyebrow raise at Kate's younger brothers. "In fact, they were rather naughty. My aunt says we are descended from one of them. Mary, to be exact, from a child she bore in France to her true love. Like me, that child wasn't raised by her mother." Julie frowned and paused.

"This doesn't sound very appropriate," Kate warned.

"She was a married lady by then, very respectable," Julie insisted. "But she died, and her child was forgotten by history. This is about Mary's love story. At least I always think of her life as a love story, but perhaps it was only one-sided. Because she wrote one of the most extraordinary letters, yet her husband didn't die of grief, wailing over her body, but went on, had more children, and everyone assumed Mary's children with her husband were dead." Julie held up a finger.

Lucy Fair settled the toasting forks over the grate, then scooted closer to Julie. "Do go on."

Julie grinned. "Mary and Anne had an ambitious father and the girls were born just high enough to be placed in royal courts in Europe. Can you imagine, Lucy, being your age and waiting on a queen?" She stood up and twirled her skirts, then gave a low, respectful curtsy as if to a crown.

Lucy giggled, a noise that Kate had never heard from the former mud lark.

She imagined this was how Julie appeared on stage. Her brothers were completely captivated by the graceful actress, back in female attire.

"Mary was older and beautiful. She captivated the French king, Francis, and then the English one, Henry." Julie shuddered. "Henry, that dreadful king with six wives."

George put his hand to his throat. She pointed at him. "Yes, you know that story. But Mary came first, and King Henry married her to his cousin, William Carey, to give her babies a father."

"Why?" William asked.

"I do not claim to know the minds of kings," Julie said in a lofty tone. "But marry her milord Carey did, until he died young."

Kate made a face. "And I thought my Mary, Queen of Scots, story was sad."

"Ah," Julie said, waggling her finger. "But as I said, my story is a romance.

"Mary's sister, Anne, was unhappily married to King Henry by then, having no power to stop him from all his mad deeds to have her."

"What happened to Mary?" Kate asked. She'd never heard of the woman before.

"She was in Anne's court. But she knew, better than most, how fickle King Henry was. She'd probably been his mistress longer than Anne had been his unlucky wife. Mary traveled with them to France and around England, no doubt seeing how badly the marriage was going, and a couple of years before Anne's head went on the block, she secretly married William Stafford, a young soldier of noble blood." She clasped her hands together. "My ancestor."

"I'm guessing it didn't end well," Kate said with a laugh.

Julie spread her hands wide. "She lived longer than her two better known siblings, but not without more trouble."

"What happened?" Lucy said.

"Like I said, the marriage was made in secret. Stafford wasn't a courtier and he had no money. Back then the king's rule was absolute, and he was furious. Mary and William were penniless and desperate." Julie leaned forward. "That was when she wrote the most beautiful letter to dastardly Lord Cromwell, making it clear how unhappy her life had been, since her earliest years."

"What did the letter say?" George asked.

In tones of great richness, Julie spoke the letter she'd memorized. "'This shall be to desire you to be good to my poor husband and to me. I am sure that it is not unknown to you the high displeasure that he and I both have, both of the King's Highness and the Queen's Grace, by reason of our marriage without their knowledge, wherein we do both yield ourselves faulty, and acknowledge that we did not well to be so hasty nor so bold, without their knowledge. But one thing, Good Master Secretary, consider: that he was young, and love overcame reason, and for my part, I saw so much honesty in him that I loved him as well as he loved me; and was in bondage, and glad I was to be at liberty.'"

The front door rattled. William came in with sliced beef. Julie cleared her throat and spoke normally. "William has heard all this before, so I'll skip around a bit."

She smiled and continued, back in her performing voice. "She wrote, 'So that for my part, I saw that all the world did set so little store by me, and him so much, that I thought I could take no better way but to take him and forsake all other ways, and live a poor, honest life with him.'" Julie coughed, then continued. "Later, she goes on to say, 'For well I might a had a greater man of birth, and a higher, but I ensure you I could never a had one that should a loved me so well, or been a more honest man.'"

As Julie smiled in triumph of having memorized the letter so well, Kate considered the words. What had she chosen by deciding to love Charles? Was a poor, honest life what she had in store? She'd never know, if he didn't leave Newgate Prison.

"That's so romantic," Lucy Fair gushed.

"The king should have cut off her head, like he did her sister's," James crowed, then rolled around on the rug pretending to slice himself in the neck.

"I'll do it for you," William cried, then pounced on his younger brother.

"Now now," the elder William said, putting his foot in between the two boys and forcing them to separate. "Surely our shared name conveys a certain level of dignity."

"Is something burning?" Julie asked.

"Oh, the bread." Lucy quickly pulled her skewer from the fire and used a cloth to push the cheesy bread onto a plate.

*   *   *

"You the one who is going into solitary tonight?"

Charles stared at the man who'd just plunked a stool in front of his, placed carefully in a corner so he only had to defend two sides. He didn't recognize the new prisoner. A turnkey had just brought a trio of new men in to await their time in front of the magistrates. This one had skin so fair that Charles could see the blue vein pulsing in his temple. His eyes were marked with the outdoors around the sides, but otherwise he looked very young.

Charles had chosen his position for solitude. The only problem was that at this distance from the fire, he could feel the chilblains forming. He just had to get himself chucked into Newgate in January. At least William had taken pity on him and supplied a change of trousers and socks, though it had been many hours before the turnkey on duty had brought them to him. Bob Sawyer had taken the bloodstained ones for trading purposes.

"No," he said. "Who would be spreading a rumor like that? I haven't been in any trouble." Unless the guards thought he'd be safer in solitary. More likely though, they'd be setting up an assassin for an easy kill where no one could hear his screams.

The unfamiliar man shrugged. "Wot I heard was, that you would have a room to yourself tonight."

Charles sneered. "Then there's no point in you trying to befriend me, is there?"

His expression must have been ferocious, for the new man jumped off his stool and took it to another place in the room.

Charles leaned very hard against the wall to quell the streak of fire that had just jumped up his spine. What if that room the man had mentioned was a coffin, in truth?

If someone was going to kill him in the same manner as Jenkens, how could he protect himself? Jenkens had died so quietly that he wouldn't have woken at all if it hadn't been for the kick. His hand went to his neckerchief, also part of William's largesse but not so fine as he normally wore. Undoing the present knot, he retied the fabric more tightly.

He rather suspected it had been a purposeful kick that woke him, probably in the hopes that Charles would manage to cover himself suspiciously in blood, perhaps in attempting to save the doomed prisoner.

The day's high emotions took their toll on him as he sat in the cold corner. He wished for a hot rum-and-water, for a warm cup of energizing tea, even the worst coffeehouse's brew to keep him going, either in more comfort or with more alertness, but his eyes were drooping and it couldn't be long before the turnkey's call for lights-off, denying them the comfort of the lamps.

Out of the darkness in the opposite corner of the room, he heard raised voices among the rather ghostly apparitions. In this light, he couldn't be certain whether the voices were contemporary prisoners, or the memories of past submissives to the law. Between these ancient stone walls, no one could escape fear of the supernatural. In this Charles could place himself no higher than any other man.

"I paid you." He heard the words break above lower mumblings. "For a service."

"Which was delivered," another voice said.

"Not to satisfaction," said the first voice. "They found it within minutes."

"That wasn't what was paid for," insisted the higher of the voices. "I delivered the item to the place requested."

"Not successfully."

"Very successfully," said the salesman. "It is nothing to do with me that it didn't last there long."

"Darbandi was hauled off like Gronk," growled the lower voice. "Now I'm going to be a target of his gang because of your failure."

"I didn't fail." The voices came closer to Charles. "Darbandi's fate has no bearing on our commerce. I did what I was paid for."

Charles craned his neck but didn't leave the relative safety of his stool. How complicated had this morning's operation been?

Someone adjusted a lantern at the wardsman's bed, offering a little more light. Charles recognized Rotter and Bob Sawyer as they crossed in and out of the little pool of radiance.

The knife must have been passed from Gronk to Darbandi's band of men to Rotter, and then to Bob Sawyer in a chain of evidence-hiding.

Charles felt cold chill his back like the fire had burned before. He'd been the one responsible for breaking the chain. Darbandi had sensed the truth, but he'd been hauled into solitary. Would Rotter come looking for him after he handled Bob Sawyer?

The two men were in the darkness now, just feet away from him in his corner. Charles keenly felt the dearth of allies in that moment. How he wished for his cane. His only weapon might be the few coins he had.

Rustling noises sent his animal senses into a high alert. A whoosh, a connection of one surface against a softer one, an exhalation of pain.

He couldn't imagine Bob would hit Rotter, which meant the large man had just attacked the small one.

Charles jumped off his stool as more scuffling noises whirled past him. He wasn't the only one who'd recognized the sounds. The wardsman's lamp flamed up again.

Charles drove his stool into the larger man, knocking him away from Sawyer. The legs of the stool caught around Rotter's meaty thigh and Charles couldn't disengage. He kept moving forward, an out-of-control carriage, until Rotter bounced off a wall much closer to the roaring fire.

"Fight, fight!" chanted one of the men.

Charles pulled the stool away. "Don't attack Sawyer. He's small," he panted.

"You," Rotter muttered, breathing hard. He seemed to be in poor condition for a man of his general shape, but then, they were all prisoners and Charles had no idea how long Rotter had been here awaiting trial.

"I don't care about your deal," Charles said. "But I do care about safety. You belong in solitary. We all have to exist in this ward together. Do you want someone to slit your throat?"

Rotter sneered, clutching his thighs. "I'd be more worried about yours."

Bob Sawyer reappeared, followed by the wardsman, his lantern illuminating the scene like a spotlight on a stage.

Charles and Rotter both blinked, then Charles realized they were indeed on a stage. Men ringed them, longing for bloodshed, or at least some diversion.

If they had been onstage, this would have been the moment for Charles's great speech, a summation of the events, a revelation that the conspiracy spread from Gronk to Darbandi to Rotter. He'd probably leave out Bob Sawyer, because he, in the play, would be his brother-in-law, or secret son, or some such. Or maybe, in some final, shocking twist, he would betray Bob Sawyer as well and show himself the villain.

This was no play, however, and mostly, Charles wanted safety and no trouble for himself.

Charles gently set the stool in front of himself. "I apologize. I didn't like to see the little man attacked by such a large beast as Rotter."

"It ain't none o' yer business," called one of Rotter's henchmen.

His voice cracked at the end. Charles peered into the darkness. How old was the henchman? Fifteen? Sixteen? How old were any of these little blighters, with their criminal attitudes and sunken ways? He might be one of the oldest men here, very possibly the best educated, and certainly the most gainfully employed.

Could any of these men be extricated from their life of vice
and crime? Or was he merely doing his best to survive this pit
until others could prove him innocent?

"I protected you from Rotter because you can't defend
yourself against him," Charles said to Bob Sawyer. "But you
are as guilty as he is, in the greater scheme of things. I don't
want to be a part of any of it, so leave me alone."

Sawyer dropped his gaze.

Charles turned to Rotter. "As for you, I have powerful friends
who have your name. If anything happens to me tonight, yours
will be the name that goes to the coroner, and you will be the
one to hang." He held up a hand as the other man smirked.
"They will mark you for darker things than just a killer, to make
sure of it. Do I make myself clear?"

Rotter's mouth worked, but he said nothing. Charles turned
away. He'd made himself as safe as he could for tonight. He
nodded to the wardsman and went to the wall to take down his
rug, which thankfully had avoided the blood spatter.

The door to the passage rattled. A turnkey came in to call
"Lights out!"

Everyone went to fetch their rugs. No one made eye contact
with Charles. At that moment, he desperately wanted to be a
bully himself, to take Sawyer's rug, and Rotter's, and maybe
the nasty little henchman's as well, to be warm for once in this
cursed place. That, however, would make him no better than
them, and he knew his sanity in this place would only be mea-
sured by how he kept himself above the moral tone of this pur-
gatory.

They ate beef and bread and cheese, next to the fire. It wasn't
a proper meal at a table at all, just a picnic on the hearthrug. The
Agas had a bohemian streak.

To get matters trundling along before they had to return to
Brompton, Kate showed Julie and William the new letter. Julie
snatched it from her and read it aloud. The younger Hogarths

and Lucy, freshly horrified, hadn't seen or read any of the earlier letters.

George slammed his fist into his palm. "I say. That isn't right."

Mary patted her brother's arm. "No, it's torment."

"I'm afraid I don't know that one," William admitted.

"I know I've heard it before," Kate said. "I just need a bit of quiet to tease it from my memory, or even better, time with books to find it."

"You don't have the time," William observed.

"I know." Kate swallowed down frustration. "It's an early day tomorrow, but if Lady Byron knows something useful, we can cut this snake of an organization off at the head."

"I'm afraid of the consequences of you taking time away from the letter quests to sort out the murder," Julie admitted.

"That is no doubt the point," William said. "To confuse Kate and keep her busy, along with her friends."

"It's the work of a feminine mind," Kate exclaimed. "I'll bet Evelina Jaggers is behind the letters. It's just the sort of thing a bored girl might do."

"Could be," Julie said. "But why would she kill an esteemed scientist?"

"I don't know, but we have to play the game for now. Maybe Lady Byron will know the quotation if I can't recall it by then," Kate said. "She is famous for her pursuit of learning and education for others."

"That's true," William considered. "She's very respectable despite the scandal of her youthful marriage. I don't suppose she wrote those words."

"Maybe," Kate said with a laugh. "But I would think I'd remember that."

"Byron," Julie said, going a little swoony-eyed.

William scowled at her. "The worst husband ever. Would you rather have him?"

"What a horrid thought." She blinked her eyes at him. "I

married my hero. It just goes to show you should never marry a man who wooed you with letters. Deeds are the thing."

Kate hoped that Charles saw all her efforts to free him as a sort of wooing, and fixed their wedding date properly. That had been one of Lord Byron's petty tricks, to play games with the wedding date. She remembered reading that the vicar who married them was a guest of Lady Byron's parents for three weeks before the groom condescended to arrive at their home.

She shuddered.

"What's wrong?" Mary touched her arm.

"Nothing more than a passing footstep on my grave," Kate said. "It's too easy to have melancholy thoughts right now. But Julie, what happened with Sir Augustus?"

"We didn't have much luck," Julie admitted.

"We watched the house for another hour after the carriage left," Mary said. "To see if anything else happened, but it stayed quiet."

"I don't think I want to be a Bow Street Runner if this is their job," young William said.

"Boring," James agreed, filching the last half slice of beef from the plate.

At Kate's warning glance, he asked William for permission and their host granted him the morsel.

"Just because nothing happened today doesn't mean anything won't. Think about all the excitement at Mr. Screws's house last month," Julie said. "The situation can develop."

"Where did the carriage go?" Kate asked.

"Sir Augustus went to a coffee 'ouse, but he told his carriage to wait," Lucy reported. "We waited, too. I sold all my watercress, which made it awkward."

"I sent her home. Since I was dressed as a man, I didn't stand out," Julie said proudly.

"She was there for your protection," her husband exclaimed. "Julie, your condition."

She shrugged. "I should have taken one of the Hogarth boys

with us. I hadn't thought of that, but if it happens again, I'll borrow George."

The adolescent blushed at being singled out. Julie continued. "After that, Sir Augustus's carriage went around the block to No. 10 Downing Street. I saw him go in and then returned here."

"He must have had government meetings," William said. "Just a day of work for him."

"Unfortunately. He wasn't stashing Amy Poor there," Julie agreed.

Kate put her head in her hands. "Where does that leave us?"

Julie patted her hand. "Did you really think a few hours' watch in Charles Street would answer all of our questions? Patience is the thing. Sir Silas is working on the murder, you are chasing the clues, and Lucy and I will continue to watch Sir Augustus. Any one of us could bring Charles's imprisonment to an swift end."

"Don't forget about me. I'm chasing the murder, too," her husband said.

Kate lifted her face. "Any insights?"

"I had the name of the doctor who examined Mr. Pickwick from one of the constables involved. He is of the opinion that Mr. Pickwick had been dead the better part of a day before Charles was arrested."

"That's fantastic," Julie exclaimed.

"All they have to do is pay another doctor to say differently," Kate said.

"It wouldn't be that doctor," William said. "I paid him to show me his original report and made a good copy of it. We know Charles has an alibi for the hours before he was arrested."

"He was with me at Edward Baines's dinner," Kate said, brightening. "Many distinguished guests. And busy with his duties before that."

William nodded. "It's very good evidence. Better if more than one doctor was involved."

"I don't suppose it's enough to get Charles released," Mary said.

"No, but it might change the verdict of a trial." William smiled. "I'll keep hunting, but it's hard to imagine I'd find anything so good as this, short of having a confession from someone else."

"What about Mr. Yupman's servants?" Julie asked. "Does he have an alibi?"

"He only keeps one man in a boardinghouse." William picked up a crust that had lost all its cheese and chewed on it. "Seems to be of temperance habits, and I haven't been able to reach him yet."

"If it wasn't for the Amy Poor matter, I'd help you," Julie fretted.

"No, you wouldn't," William said. "I can do my job, Mrs. Aga. You have plenty to occupy yourself."

"At least we can assure our families that Charles couldn't have done it, on the basis of science," Mary said, patting Kate's hand.

Kate squeezed her sister's hand in response, needing the comfort. "It will all depend on what forces are arrayed against him, I expect," she said sadly.

"He has the *Morning Chronicle* behind him," William said. "When the time is right, we will feature the autopsy evidence on page one."

Chapter 19

The next morning, Kate felt better than she had in more than a week, since Charles's arrest, in fact. Yesterday had seemed like such a frustrating day, but the truth was, William's evidence should save Charles. Surely the magistrates would see her dear boy was innocent, with a member of Parliament to give him an alibi to contest any drama caused by Sir Augustus.

She still had her letter to sort out though. With knowledge of the very real consequence of failure, she had spent the previous evening in Lady Lugoson's library, but the room was so over-whelming in comparison to her father's one bookcase that she was unable to find anything useful.

Her father had not been able to source the quotation from the capacious resources of his brain, either. But he'd been confident that the subject matter of the quotation was exactly the sort of thing Lady Byron would know.

Kate kissed Mary's cheek. "I need to wake Mother so we can leave."

"Good luck," her sister whispered, then turned over to protect her ears from Georgina's snoring.

Kate went down the hall to her parents' room. When she

knocked, her father opened the door, already dressed for the outdoors.

"Are you coming with us?" she asked, happy to have his support for such an important visit.

He shook his head gravely. "Bad news, I'm afraid. I have to go into London. I had a messenger from John Black that I'm needed at the *Chronicle* for an editing project. Some disaster has befallen the leading article for tomorrow's edition."

"Very well. Mother was coming with me," she said. "Are you taking the carriage Lady Lugoson offered me? Do I need to find another conveyance?"

"No, there's a cab waiting for me." He paused, then delivered the bad news. "Yer mother is ill, Kate."

Her mother had particularly wanted to chaperone the visit, since Lady Byron had known Sir Walter Scott and was a dear friend of the Baillies.

"Oh dear," Kate exclaimed.

"Yes, she has been stricken by a ghastly headache and canna bear any sort of light." Her father patted her arm. "I don't see what's to be done, at this time of day."

Kate knew she couldn't go alone. "Fred came back with us yesterday afternoon. He's at our house with the boys. I know we can't leave our house unattended and Mary will be needed for the children, but Fred would go with me."

Her father rubbed his hand down his muttonchops. "I expect it's fitting, since it is his brother who is in prison."

"I'll have the coachman take me to our house and pick him up?" Kate suggested.

"I'm going downstairs right now," her father said. "I'll ask if a footman is available to take a note across the orchard to order him to make ready."

"I'm surprised you were allowed to go on a Sunday morning," Fred said, munching on a sausage from the ample hamper she'd been provided along with Lady Lugoson's carriage.

"I know Lady Byron is a Unitarian," Kate said, looking out the window at the blur of passing buildings. "Both she and her daughter had small at-home weddings. Nothing in a church."

"Would you do that?"

"No. We're to marry at St. Luke's." Kate thought about it and spoke again. "I have nothing in common with these aristocrats. Lady King knew her husband less than six weeks before their wedding last year. Meanwhile, I have met Charles, been courted by him, been engaged these past nine months and no wedding."

"It's hard to comprehend what goes on when a fortune marries a fortune," Fred said wisely.

She poked him. "What do you know about it?"

He shifted. "I work for a lawyer now."

"Ah, right. I just hope the lady is as pleasant as the Baillies. They are very old friends, though Lady Byron is only in her forties."

"Byron died in 1824," Fred said, rather pompously. "That was ages ago."

"I'm sure he was much older than her. She was the aristocratic sacrifice to his monstrosity. I hope it is not the same for Lady King. She is just about my age."

"It sounds better when all the monstrosities are in the past," Fred agreed.

"Well, we're in the middle of our own version." Kate pulled a bun from the hamper. She hadn't taken the time to eat.

The scenery became increasingly rural as they headed into Ealing. Halfway between the city's bustle and the countryside, the town's gardens filled London's markets. Kate admired the parade of old inns and green trees as they drove to Fordhook. She wondered if she'd ever live anywhere so attractive with Charles. While he spoke lovingly of Kent, he seemed quite addicted to the bustle of London.

She cast herself into a reverie of presiding over a dinner

party. At first, she populated it with the likes of Lady Lugoson and Lady Byron, but her imagination quailed at the thought of serving such ladies. She replaced the faces at the table with William and Julie, Fred and her sister, and some of the as-yet faceless names she'd heard Charles mention, William Ainsworth and Charles's publisher, John Macrone. She'd serve a soup to start, and a nice chop, then move on to pudding. Charles loved her treacle tart. His friends would praise her cooking.

The carriage slowed, then stopped. Her dreams had taken her all the way. Fordhook was a long house with two main stories, featuring a bowed window in the front with covered walkways spreading along the walls on either side. Ivy clung to various parts of the building. Trees huddled against the house on either side, giving the place a cozy, wintery appearance. Kate noted two large chimney stacks and hoped the country abode would be warm.

"Better than Newgate, eh?" Fred said, looking over her shoulder.

"Anything is. The windows alone dwarf those tiny, desperate barred things at the prison."

Fred sighed. "Why aren't you moving?"

"I'm a bit frightened, I suppose. Lady Byron. She's a reformer, you know."

"You spent the night at Lugoson House, dining at a baroness's table. I admit this lady is very grand, and rather older, but you've met Lady Holland as well. This is your world, at least sometimes."

Kate smiled at Fred. "Do you want it to be yours as well?"

"No," he said quickly. "It takes such a lot of work to sparkle enough to be in the company of these people. Charles has the dash and flash and energy to carry it off. I'm a quieter sort."

"He is quite amazing," she admitted. "I wish he was here with us."

The carriage door opened for her, and she stepped down, holding the gloved hand of a footman who had come out of nowhere. Lady Byron was known to be extremely rich, so Kate couldn't be surprised by all the staff coming and going.

She and Fred were led into the interior. The parlor they were directed to had comfortable sofas surrounding a large country fireplace. A portrait of a young woman in contemporary dress filled the space above the fireplace. She suspected it to be Lady King.

A green curtain hung over another part of the wall and the large windows had filtered light coming in from the front of the house. A maid came in and quickly tended to the fire, then the footman announced Lady Noel Byron.

As she came forward, Kate bobbed a quick curtsy and Fred bowed his head. Perhaps not quite so old as Kate's mother, the lady had graying dark curls arrayed around her face, which still held vestiges of a girlish sweetness. Her high forehead and dark eyebrows spoke to a keen intellect.

As for her dress, this wealthy woman wore a wrapped-front, patterned wool gown with a pleated skirt. Her sleeves were significantly less voluminous than had been the fashion earlier in the decade and Kate thought it a nice change, not to mention the cost saving of using less fabric. The skirt was a bit shorter than Kate was used to seeing as well, and the tips of Lady Byron's shoes peeped out from the hem.

"It's a pleasure to meet you, Miss Hogarth," the lady said. "I've heard excellent reports of your mother from Agnes Baillie, but I understand you are under some difficulty now?"

"I am engaged to wed Charles Dickens, the writer known as Boz, my lady," Kate explained. "He has been framed for a heinous crime, and the Misses Baillie thought you might be able to provide some insight into the sort of men we are facing."

"And Miss Hogarth is being tormented by letters, my lady," Fred added. "The latest one has an education riddle in it."

"That is a field I am known to have expertise in," the lady

said. "Why don't I see what I can do to help you sort this muddle?" She directed them to the sofas and the maid brought a tray.

Over tea, Kate spilled out the entire story, from Sir Augustus to the Lightning Club to the dirty man with his threatening letters.

Lady Byron frowned. "I don't like this business about the fire in your garden. It's the work of a madman."

Kate nodded. "Even worse, the attacks in the prison. I worry about my Mr. Dickens every day."

"I believe you said you had one of these letters with you?" Lady Byron inquired.

"Yes." Kate handed over the latest missive.

Lady Byron bent over the seal and examined it, the gold in her earrings capturing the glow of the firelight. "Unusual," she murmured. Then she opened the letter and read.

After a minute, she said, "The quotation is no mystery. The author of these lines was Sarah Fielding, the sister of Sir John Fielding and Henry Fielding."

"The Fieldings?" Kate exclaimed.

"Fate has led you to the right spot," Lady Byron said with a nod. "Henry Fielding once lived in this house. He was a novelist, you know. And the Fieldings—"

"Founded the Bow Street Runners," Kate exhaled. "It's as if my tormentors knew I'd be coming here, even though they claimed I wasn't supposed to go to Miss Baillie's home at all. I'd have had no reason to be introduced to you otherwise."

"They might be watching your mail," Lady Byron suggested, the tip of her nose going pink. "Powerful, wealthy enemies might have few limits of decency."

Kate sighed and nodded. "I am only familiar with the appearance of the one man. I have no idea who might be watching. Mr. Dickens knows of the turnkey henchman only. I'm sure there are others."

Lady Byron patted her hand. "You remind me of my daughter, but she is carefree, enjoying her new marriage and expectations. We must put you on the path to the same happiness."

"They say your marriage was nothing but disaster," Fred said bluntly. "Who is chosen for happiness and who for misery?"

Kate froze in horror at his tactless words.

The baroness stared at him for a long moment. "I have never lived a public life, but I am the widow of a man who did. I am grateful that my daughter has chosen a different path."

"My Mr. Dickens will see his first book out next month," Kate said softly. "I dream that our trials will be done by then. We have been engaged since last spring already, and no wedding."

"Mine was much delayed as well," Lady Byron said. "Whereas my daughter's engagement was less than two months."

Kate and the baroness stared at each other for an almost impolite moment, but Kate thought she understood the warning. She felt that sensation of footsteps over her grave again. But she sat up even straighter, shaking it off.

"We"—she cleared her throat delicately—"are here to implore you for information on the Lightning Club, and any knowledge you might have of Sir Augustus. I don't know if you are aware, but Mr. Dickens heard a man accuse the baron of kidnapping his daughter when he was in Eatanswill. We know that the baron is both a member of the Lightning Club and the uncle of Tracy Yupman, who presided over Mr. Dickens's false initiation, and accused him of the murder of Samuel Pickwick."

"I never met a more congenial, kindhearted man than Mr. Pickwick," Lady Byron said, equanimity restored. "He toured my school here, Ealing Grove, and was very enthusiastic about our gardens."

"I usually look to a murder victim for the reason for his murder," Kate said. "But I admit, with this letter quest I've been sent on, I've had little opportunity to dig into Mr. Pickwick."

"None at all, rather," Fred interjected. "That is William Aga's job."

"Who is that?" Lady Byron inquired.

"He's the crime reporter at the newspaper," Kate explained.

"I see." The lady considered. "Mr. Pickwick, I believe, had an unencumbered and spotless personal life. He was of an age with my husband, but was a scientist, not a poet. Never married, had a professional rivalry or two, but no enemies. He was the least likely man to be murdered."

"Do you know Mr. Yupman?" Kate asked.

"He courted a friend of mine years ago, but she is a dedicated invalid." Lady Byron took a sip of tea. "I think him a coward, no great man of anything."

"Sir Augustus could probably influence someone like that," Fred suggested.

"Mr. Yupman has no money but an allowance from his uncle," Lady Byron added delicately.

"That makes the orchestration all the more likely," Kate said. "Mr. Dickens was warned that Sir Augustus was a powerful enemy, but he didn't even mention the kidnapping."

"I still think we have to follow him and find the girl," Fred said. "Charles can write one of his scathing commentaries and ruin Sir Augustus's reputation."

"Reputation doesn't matter for a man when money and position are involved," Lady Byron said. "The subject must be approached more scientifically, with facts and logic. Do you have any proof of this kidnapping? Any statements from witnesses, members of both families?"

"We have my fiancé in prison and me on yet another twenty-four-hour deadline to follow a letter," Kate said bitterly.

"Very well then. Where do you go next?"

"I'm going to head to Sir Augustus's club and follow him. I should be the one to follow at night since it's the most dangerous," Fred boasted.

Kate locked eyes with the baroness. "I believe I'm going to go to Bow Street first."

"Shouldn't you go to the home of Sarah Fielding herself?" Fred asked.

"It won't be quite that obvious. With the clues, first it was the author's house, then a more specific residence." Kate nodded to Lady Byron. "We went to your former matrimonial home, that is, but that wasn't the right one, then the authoress's publisher, and now it makes sense my tormentors are sending me even farther afield from a home."

"Sir Augustus, unlike Mr. Pickwick, was at Harrow with my husband," Lady Byron said. "Those schools create dreadful tendencies in boys. I've spent years educating myself on a healthier way to raise children."

Kate twisted her hands into each other. She was long since done with her tea and biscuit. "You can well believe Sir Augustus is at the heart of my predicament. We also know a young lady is involved, an enemy of Charles's who was spotted with Sir Augustus. Can you think of any way for me to stop these letters? I worry that Charles will go to trial and be convicted of murder and I will still be running around chasing after ghosts."

Lady Byron placed her tea saucer and cup on the table. She stared into the distance, not really seeming to focus on anything. "I believe I would consult a lawyer. I would also let yourself be seen with powerful friends. If Mr. Dickens's book is released, that may have a protective quality. If it is successful, that is. My husband's fame excused much."

"A lawyer?" Fred asked. "I work for lawyers. Could we have a letter drafted to Sir Augustus to call off his dirty man?"

"That could be considered slanderous," Lady Byron said. "Without proof. But you could reveal that you know of his involvement in the Lightning Club, and his relationship to Mr. Yupman, and how suspicious that would be to the readers of Mr. Dickens's newspaper. That might have some effect."

"And what of Amy Poor, the kidnapped girl?" Kate asked.

"Who is looking for her?" Lady Byron asked.

"I don't know, other than us," she admitted.

"Someone needs to speak to her relatives," Lady Byron said. "Here, I will write a letter for you." She rose and went to a writing desk underneath one of the windows.

Kate and Fred flanked her as she wrote a letter of inquiry to Wilfred Poor in Eatanswill. "There," she said, after blotting it. "I will have it sent today and write you when I have an answer."

"That is very kind of you," Kate said.

"You are most welcome." Lady Byron smiled, showing a hint of that girlish beauty that must have attracted Lord Byron to her so long ago. "I know it is intimidating to approach those of us who are high rank, but I wish to assist wherever I can. Do see your lawyer. They can work wonders."

Charles sat shoulder to shoulder with the men in his ward for Sunday services in the melancholy chapel. The men didn't seem to be in a religious mindset. Just being in the presence of women, even though they couldn't see them due to the construction of the space and the screen the women sat behind, threw them into paroxysms of bawdy speculation.

The chaplain droned on and on, one of those thin, spiritual fellows who thought prison an excellent time for a spiritual reclamation, rather than an opportunity for less successful villains to interact and plan future devilment. Charles had no idea how to improve prisons, but he also knew of no one who had any better ideas than this.

What did it say that he'd only become friendly with one prisoner and one prison guard? Nothing about his character flourished here. If he stayed here another week, he'd have to pay for paper, pen, and ink so that he could write something. It would be disastrous for him to let his shorthand skills weaken.

The services finally ended. They lined up to return to their ward. Charles, reluctant to go back, managed to be last in line behind the new man who'd either threatened or warned him, he wasn't sure.

One turnkey led them into the passage, a mother duck with his line of ducklings. Keefe slipped in behind Charles and whispered in his ear, "I'm hearing noise about you, Dickens. Do you want to go into solitary? It would be safer."

"What kind of noise?"

"A price being offered among the turnkeys to look the other way while you are injured."

Charles stopped when the line turned the corner, leaving him alone with Keefe for a minute. "Who is coming for me? Rotter? Darbandi?"

"I don't know. Could be anyone."

"I don't understand why I'm the focus of so much ire. I'm being toyed with. My fiancée is being toyed with. My brother is distraught, my friends powerless." Charles paused. "None of it makes sense. I have not injured Sir Augustus Smirke in sufficient fashion to acquire this much malice, this much force to be arrayed against us."

"Yet nothing has really happened," Keefe said. "To you."

"Exactly. The nearest to disaster was the fire at my fiancée's home, which amounted to nothing but a scare."

"You're being tortured?" the turnkey suggested.

"Does Sir Augustus toy with people?" Charles asked. "Have you heard any stories about him kidnapping women?"

Keefe coughed. He rubbed the side of his mouth. "He is related to the prison governor. I believe the baronet is the wealthiest and most senior member of a large family."

"I am not surprised."

"I have met a couple of women here over the years who claim to have been ruined by him, but it's not as if they were murdered."

"Then that might suggest I will not be, either?"

"Or that it isn't really Sir Augustus pulling your puppet strings," Keefe said, before he began to cough again.

Charles leaned against the stone wall and waited for the fit to pass. Not Sir Augustus? When the coughs paused, he said, "It makes no sense to be anyone else. The man who accused me of murder is his nephew."

"Who do you know who might have the power to influence Sir Augustus?"

Charles considered. "He was attempting to win an election when I met him. As a result, he needed the help of those who could sway the voters. And he did win the election."

"Maybe you have enemies within that group of men."

Charles thought. Something niggled in the back of his memory about that day in Eatanswill. He ran back through that day. The incidents with Wilfred Poor, the horsemen, losing his hat . . .

"I remember thinking I saw someone connected to the murder of my neighbor last summer," Charles said. "Not a murderer, but the lover of a woman who radiated unfeminine purpose. She hates me."

"I think you should ask your friends to discover where that woman is right now," Keefe said. "Could she be a relative of Sir Augustus?"

"Her family was Haverstock and Jaggers. Those are the names I know. Any relatives I heard of are deceased, except for a loathsome property manager on a bastard line."

"Where is he?"

"I have no idea." Charles blinked. "I know he was attempting to help Miss Jaggers to right wrongs done to her, but she was the coldest, most superior young female I've had the misfortune to come across. I rather hoped she and her swain had emigrated."

"It might be a forlorn hope."

"I thought I saw Prince Moss that very day." Charles considered. "I do not know how much money she might have raised by now, from what was left of her tangled affairs. Her property had been stolen from her, and she turned to dark deeds in order to right the wrong."

"She is the person who belongs in Newgate, rather than you?" Keefe suggested.

Charles smiled. "I'd rather have had her gone from England and started over again. She is young still, and in the absence of portable funds, perhaps she or Prince Moss might have had to retain employment in Eatanswill. I know where they resided in London. I will have my friends check into them."

"It does not sound as if they would presently have the resources for this devilment."

Charles moistened his dry lips. "Nor the education. Moss was a farmer. Miss Jaggers, well, I cannot say what she did with her time other than plot, but she's just a girl, younger than my Miss Hogarth by some years."

"And solitary?" the turnkey asked. "It will give you time to consider these matters. Are you sure that is not the correct path?"

"Solitary would be a waste of my time here." Charles smiled crookedly. "I want to write a novel someday, and this experience is fuel for a dozen of them."

"You can't write a novel if you are dead," Keefe warned.

"I have in mind something historical, from those years when Newgate was a more exciting place with better villains than this."

Keefe's cheeks creased with laughter. "No highwaymen these days."

"If I go into solitary, I will not be able to see my friends," Charles said on a more practical note. "And I must. I rely on them for information and for what they bring me, money and such."

"It won't matter if you are dead."

Charles nodded, huddling into his coats and neckerchiefs. At least the cold made everything smell less. Why would it come to that when Kate was being toyed with like a cat with a mouse? Surely the villains involved wanted more entertainment value than this. "Thank you for your concern. I appreciate knowing I have kind eyes looking out for me."

"My eyes won't do you any good, when the knife comes for you," Keefe cautioned.

Chapter 20

Fred helped Kate into the carriage outside of Lady Byron's Ealing home, ready to take her to the next stop on their day's adventure, Bow Street. Kate's brain still buzzed with excitement. She had met Lady Byron and the revered reformer had been kind. What a noble lady. While the Hogarth family might be higher socially than the Dickens clan, it could not be denied that Charles's exploits had brought her into very elevated company. Did his merits ensure that they would spend their married lives amongst such people? If he became as celebrated as a Lord Byron, where would that leave her? Great men did not often have happy home lives.

She clasped her hands together in the warm muff and stared at the fur, feeling a blank void open ahead of her. How many enemies would she and Charles have to fend off in future days?

"What's wrong?" Fred asked.

She forced a smile at him. "I wonder where your brother's talents will take us, over the years."

"It won't matter if we can't rid him of this murder charge," Fred said, with a complete lack of whimsy that shocked Kate back into reality. "Is there anything left in the picnic basket?"

The carriage jolted into movement as she pulled the basket toward her, using her boot. Fred bent forward, as she could not, and hoisted it into his lap. Kate waved away the remnants of their breakfast and pulled the carriage blanket over every inch she could cover.

"What are your thoughts about the latest letter?" Fred asked, munching on cold fowl.

"It's an insult. The letter is suggesting that Charles is not wise. It is such an Evelina Jaggers letter," Kate said bitterly.

"What does Miss Jaggers want Charles to learn?" he asked around the meat.

"Probably to stay out of Sir Augustus's business," she retorted. "Perhaps she has become his mistress to pay her bills."

"My, you can be shocking." Fred snickered and finished his cold leg, then tossed it back into the basket with a napkin after he'd wiped his lips and fingertips. "They won't let any of this go. We have to find Amy Poor. She can testify against Sir Augustus and properly ruin his life."

"Unlikely. But if we can trade her, and Sir Augustus's good name, for the real murderer, that will be good enough for me. Charles safe and back to his regular routine."

"Then he'll always have enemies," Fred pointed out.

Kate slid into him as the carriage hit a damaged spot in the road. Fred put out his arm to brace her. "One problem at a time," she said. "At least let him stay out of trouble long enough to have his book released into the world and us married."

"Why would you want to marry a man in such habitual trouble?" Fred asked. "I was about to have an apoplexy last month when your father sacked him."

"Look what happened. He had another job in days," Kate said. "He's resourceful. To focus on practicalities, could you acquire an appointment with a lawyer in your firm? Lady Byron is probably correct that the threat of exposure is the best remedy."

"Exposure of Sir Augustus's involvement with the Lightning Club? I do not think it will concern him in the least. I think we should consult Sir Silas first."

"I've had another idea. I could write Sir Augustus as an innocent, to ask for his help and counsel, as I know he is a member of the club and Mr. Yupman's uncle." Kate lifted her hands from under their blanket shelter for a moment. "Maybe he would be susceptible to a young woman's appeal, and I could learn something that might incriminate him or his nephew."

"Such audacity." Fred laughed. "The next thing I know, you will tell me you intend to apply to be a Bow Street Runner yourself."

"We will be in the right place," Kate joked. They continued the conversation in an equally light manner as the carriage returned them to London.

Gray clouds seemed to chase them into the city, then let their contents loose as they drove down the busy streets, now that the churches were emptying.

The carriage took them down Long Acre, past business after business concerned with the making of coaches. They could hear costermongers and their attending barra boys hawking in the open space of Covent Garden, just south, and then they drove into busy Bow Street, with all manner of people rushing about, in the business of law.

The street, despite the magistrate's court, was no different than many in London, with rows of buildings in various heights. Though they had made good progress, the carriage came to a halt three buildings down from No. 4, because of all the other traffic blocking the courts.

"Do you want to get down and walk?" Fred asked.

Kate pointed out the window. "We're better off staying in here. We'll be able to see better than from the street, and we won't become soaking wet."

"Very well," Fred said, amused. "When we're done, we'll have to return to Brompton."

"I can leave you at Furnival's Inn," Kate said, "so you don't have to walk back into town."

"I'm meant to escort you," Fred protested.

"I'm perfectly safe in Lady Lugoson's carriage," Kate demurred. "It will give me time to think about what I would want to say in a letter to Sir Augustus."

Fred's lips compressed. Kate could see that he did not want to comply with Lady Byron's suggestion. He much preferred only taking direction from a man, Sir Silas to be exact. But Lady Byron was older and knew much of the world. Kate trusted the reformer's advice.

The carriage lurched forward and didn't stop again until they'd driven two building lengths. Kate pressed her nose against the cold glass, looking for the dirty man.

The rain made it exceedingly difficult. She wiped away steam caused by her breath, which made her glove damp, the last thing she needed.

"Give me a napkin, will you?" she asked

Fred complied, and she used it to keep the circle around her face free of condensation while she watched. The carriage lurched again, half a house forward, then a quarter.

"I can't believe it!" Kate crowed. "There he is! The dirty man."

The carriage moved again, startling Kate. She bumped her head on the window, then fumbled with the latch.

"What's wrong?" Fred asked, sliding toward her on the seat to help.

"I can't get it open."

"You're proving yourself to be as clever as Charles," he said, as she gestured wildly in the direction of the dirty man.

He slid the window down, then opened the trapdoor to tell the driver to stop.

The carriage wasn't moving anyway. Kate leaned her head out of the hackney and shouted at the dirty man, "Sarah Fielding!"

The dirty man did a double take when he saw her hanging

out of the cab. She waved at him impatiently and held out her hand for the note that he must have in his possession.

Giving his teeth a long lick she could see even through the drizzle, he moved toward them, weaving through passersby.

The man smirked and held up a letter. She opened and closed her hand, hoping he would hand it to her, but he shook his head. Seeing raindrops splatter the letter, she growled in frustration.

"He's not coming any closer. What is the matter with him?"

"I'll handle it. We're right in front of the magistrate's court and the station house is right up the street. The place is crawling with peelers." Fred opened the carriage door and jumped down.

Kate watched, openmouthed, as the lad ran straight at the dirty man, barreling into him, his head ramming into the taller man's belly. "Go to a hackney stand nearby and water the horses," she told the driver. "We'll find you."

She jumped out after Fred as the dirty man doubled over. She ripped the letter out of his hand. Fred went wild, jumping on the man's back until he fell onto the pavement.

"I need the police!" Kate screamed at passersby. The police station was just up the street. Surely the constables came and went between the court and the station, but they were ignored, just another dirty, ill-bred sight in this neighborhood.

She shoved the letter into her muff, then helped Fred pull the dirty man to his feet. Keeping a firm grip on his arms, they hauled him toward the police station. When he wrenched his arm from her, she caught the whiff of strong spirits on his breath. She grabbed him again and held on for dear life.

"You should be worried," the dirty man slurred, attempting to wrest his arms away.

"Be quiet," Fred ordered.

"She hasn't read the letter yet," the dirty man said in a singsong voice.

"Don't let go," Fred said. "He wants to trick us."

"I know," Kate said. They only had precarious control over him as it was. Underneath her gloves, she felt little roundness of flesh, more the grinding of bones. Maybe the dirty man covered up for weakness and lack of strength with his leers and jeers.

"Your masters must not pay you well," she remarked. "You are skin and bones."

The dirty man grunted.

"Come now, Sir Augustus is a very rich man. Why do you allow yourself to be treated this way?" she asked.

"Never 'eard of 'im," the dirty man grunted.

"Well, one of his underlings then," Kate said. "There's a lot of money there, and you're obviously not getting any of it, despite being the one taking all the risks. Yours is the face we've seen. You're the man we can attach to the fire."

The police station door opened as they walked up and they stepped between the men exiting, dragging the dirty man right to the sergeant's desk.

Around them arrayed a selection of blue-coated policemen whom they would have been grateful to see on the street a few minutes before. Kate's arms hurt all the way to the shoulders from dragging.

"What's all this?" the sergeant demanded. His thick black brows came together like a caterpillar over his sunken eye sockets.

"He's a blackmailer and an arsonist," Fred declared.

"Who are you?" the sergeant asked.

"I'm Fred Dickens and this man has sent my brother's fiancée chasing all over London following orders based on threatening letters," Fred said.

"Do you have any proof?" the sergeant demanded.

"I don't want to let him go," Kate said.

The sergeant lifted his hand and two constables, neither looking much older than Fred, stepped forward. They gestured and Kate and Fred reluctantly let go of their prisoner.

Kate reached into her muff and pulled out all but the newest letter.

"What's all this then?" the sergeant asked, confused, as he perused each rather grimy missive.

"They are clues I had to follow," Kate said.

His lips turned down. "It's a game, then."

"Not at all," she told the sergeant. "Look at the threats both implicit and explicit in them. I refused to follow one of the clues and they set a fire outside my window in Brompton. We have more than a dozen people in our house, including young children."

"They could have died," Fred interjected. "And my brother is wrongfully accused and in prison because of these plots."

"My mother won't let us sleep there anymore. She's too afraid. We've had to take a berth at our neighbors," Kate added, conscious that she was holding the final letter, unopened, away from the police.

"Poor lady," muttered the sergeant, handing the letters back to her.

"They aren't all very easy to solve either," Kate answered. "The answers are easily chosen incorrectly."

"Are you working alone, tormenting this here respectable-like young lady?" demanded the sergeant to the dirty man.

"I want my lawyer," the dirty man said with a sneer.

"So you ain't denying it?" the sergeant asked.

The dirty man shrugged.

The sergeant picked up his pen and dipped it into his inkwell. "I'll just add him to the ward book, here, then a constable will take him to the magistrate's clerk."

"For what?" the dirty man sneered.

Kate sensed he was starting to realize he was going to be incarcerated, just like Charles.

"Arson," she said. "At the very least."

"I never," said the dirty man.

"Threat of harm," Fred added.

The dirty man shifted, but before he could spring into any sort of action, two constables appeared behind him.

"Name?" the sergeant asked.

The dirty man didn't answer. One of the constables, as tall as the dirty man, but with a sore on the side of his mouth that Kate sincerely hoped he didn't like to lick, boffed him on the back of the head.

Kate clutched Fred's arm as the dirty man answered, "Jem Smirke."

Fred's mouth dropped open. Kate shook her head. The dirty man had the same last name as Sir Augustus? This was not the place to reveal a conspiracy. They'd be the ones who sounded insane.

The sergeant took their names and addresses. Fred boasted about his legal employment, suggesting his masters would be keeping an eye on the case.

Kate felt light-headed by the time they departed the police station.

"You need something to drink," Fred said sympathetically. "The air is foul inside that place."

Kate nodded. "The back of my throat is a fug of cheap tobacco."

They walked down the street, looking for a beverage stall. To the right, they found a little court that held a number of street hawkers, ringed by the assembly who patronized the courts. Rather ragged people and farmers, in from the country for justice in their quiet season, to lawyers in their black frock coats and their apprentices, boys like Fred, in secondhand clothes and still young enough to bump against each other and talk in loud voices, all jostled around the stalls.

"Get your tomato pills," they heard someone calling loudly. "Cures jaundice, bilious disease, rheumatism, coughs, and headaches."

"Must be heading in the right direction," Fred said, tugging her arm into the court.

"Broxy," called a man pushing a wheelbarrow along the side of a stone building. "Meat available here."

"Stay far away," Kate said with a shudder. "Taking your life in your hands to eat that, Mother says."

"Eels," called another. Kate didn't hear the patter as he scooped a mound of jellied eel into a bowl.

"Sounds good," Fred said, hopefully.

"I'm just thirsty," Kate said, pulling him past the cart.

"Hot potatoes," called one vendor. Kate could see steam rising, but three policemen in their reinforced helmets and blue coats blocked that cart.

"Cottage soup," said another.

Kate almost stopped at the soup, but then saw what she wanted ahead, despite the delicious smell of meat broth wafting into the air as the man ladled soup into a bowl. She walked straight past a muffin man, too dirty to be patronized despite what was on his tray, and directly toward the glorious sight of "Hot pea soup! Pease porridge hot! Pease porridge cold! Pease porridge in the pot! Only nine days old!"

Kate smiled at the old nursery rhyme. She'd taught Helen and Edward the claps that went along with it only a few months ago.

"That's what you want?" Fred asked. "Ginger beer over there."

"Pea soup is perfect. You get what you like." She pulled coins from her little bag inside her muff and handed one to him.

After she paid for her soup, she stood close to a building to keep out of the still-steady rain and drank down the thick, hot pea mixture, flavored with ham. After she returned the bowl, she found the driest point of the wall and scanned the last of the dirty man's letters. Her brain could not quite yet comprehend that this man was some cadet member of Sir Augustus's family. Was he in disguise? In reality, some young gentleman engaged on a cruel lark?

Kate shuddered and read. "'Miss Hogarth. While others soaring on a lofty Wing, Of dire Bellona's cruel Triumphs sing; Sound the shrill Clarion, mount the rapid car, And rush delighted thro' the Ranks of War. Your fiancé lies rotting in prison. What shall be his end? A friend.'"

"There you are," Fred said, reaching her empty-handed. "That the letter?"

She tucked it away. "Yes, but I have no idea what the clue means. It does not appear to lead to anything, anyway. There is no deadline, merely a taunt."

Fred sighed. She could smell the beer on his breath. "Maybe this was the end of it, anyway. It wasn't smart to have a clue lead to Bow Street."

"You are right," Kate agreed.

"What shall we do now?"

"First, find Lady Lugoson's carriage, then I think we should head toward St. James's Street and have a look at Boodles."

"Do you think Julie and Lucy Fair are there?"

"Maybe. I believe they went to Sir Augustus's home first. Then they probably followed him to church. By now, you would think he would have escaped domesticity for his club."

"Unless he's visiting a mistress, or Amy Poor," Fred suggested.

They walked past one hackney stand and didn't see the carriage, but they found their driver at the next one, and directed him to No. 28 St. James's Street. Kate watched out of the streaked window for Julie and Lucy Fair in their surveillance disguises. Fred asked to read the letter and she handed it over for his perusal under the lantern that swung in the corner of the carriage.

"We should take this over to Newgate," Fred said.

"I want to see your brother," Kate agreed, "but I don't know if we should share this letter with him."

"It's very depressing, but you know he will insist on an update. He'll want to know what is going on."

"I just wish I knew if he was in mortal danger now, or if the point of this missive is to let us know that he is intended to rot in Newgate."

"What is your best guess?" Fred asked.

"We know two men are dead and Charles is in the unfortunate position of hanging for one of the deaths."

"At least it sounds like he won't be a scapegoat for that prisoner's murder."

"Who can say for sure?" Kate asked. "William's reporting on the murder gives me hope, however." She hoped that some other unfortunate was not the scapegoat for that death, like Charles had been for Mr. Pickwick's.

The carriage pulled up in front of the stucco-fronted brick of Boodles. The famed bow windows framed two men in chairs, one of whom might be about Kate's father's age, the other, a couple of decades younger, but no beau gallant to entice a lady's eye as they perambulated by.

"Over here!" came a coarse cry behind them and to the left as they stepped down from the carriage.

Fred glanced at the men in the window, then pulled Kate to the left. "I think that's Sir Augustus," he hissed. "The older one. Let's kidnap him and beat the truth out of him. We have the carriage."

"We can't get Lady Lugoson involved in something like that," Kate said. "Be reasonable, Fred."

"How can you think about anyone but Charles at a time like this?" he countered.

Julie, wearing a pair of her husband's shoes to give her some height and size, and her painted-on mustache, came up to them and tilted her head to the left. They walked past a set of houses, all in private use.

When they were a good number of feet away from Boodles, Julie spoke. "That is Sir Augustus in the window. He probably wants to be noticed, since he is new to Parliament."

"Are we absolutely certain?"

"I asked the doorman," Julie explained. "Yes, your average seated fifty-year-old gentleman looks just like any other, so I wanted to be sure. The younger man is the private secretary of Sir Francis Burdett."

"What should we do?" Fred asked. "Any sight of Amy Poor?"

"No, but William wrote up a good description of her after he spoke to her father in Eatanswill." Julie recited from memory. "Twenty years old, dark-haired, one front tooth longer than the other but a good smile nonetheless, slim figure, wearing an old dress with a striped black and white skirt and a black bodice."

"Other than the tooth that gives us little to work with," Kate groused. "What color eyes?"

Julie gave a manly shrug. "William didn't think to ask. I thought the tooth was a good detail."

"I don't mean to insult your husband," Kate said calmly. "I just was fishing for any bit of information."

"I think we should kidnap him," Julie said. "We can take Sir Augustus to the Thames foreshore and let the nasty mud larks who replaced Lucy Fair's gang work him over. I'm sure they would do it for money."

Kate shivered. "Charles said he's not going to go there anymore. He certainly wouldn't want me or Fred doing so."

"Did the new gang attack you and William like they did Charles?" Fred asked.

"There's been so much ice on the ground, and me, well, you understand"—Julie gestured to her stomach—"that we haven't tried. I don't think he expects any of the current bunch to be re-deemable, and he and Charles have their hands full with fundraising for school fees and helping out the mud lark families with young children."

"Kidnapping is out," Kate said firmly. "He's bound to have many supporters inside Boodles, not to mention the staff. The three of us cannot overpower and lift Sir Augustus into the carriage fast enough. We might end up in Newgate with Charles."

"I'd like to try," Fred said, a martial light in his eyes.

"Watercress?" said a familiar voice, as Lucy Fair sauntered up to them, a nearly empty basket on her arm.

"You're good at selling," Julie said. "If William ever finds himself out of work, I'm going to put you out on the streets to earn for us."

"I think my bunches are too big," Lucy said. "Not much profit in what I'm doing."

"Anything new to report?" Kate asked.

After Lucy shook her head, Kate recited the latest letter to the pair, and Fred recounted their successful capture of the Dirty Man, also known as Jem Smirke.

Julie shook her head admiringly. "My stars, you would kid-nap someone, wouldn't you? I'm very impressed. That should stop the letters at least, so you can concentrate on Charles, Kate."

"The last letter didn't send me on a quest anyway," Kate fretted. "There was no deadline. I'm very concerned. Charles could be attacked because we took Mr. Smirke to the police. Who is he? He can't be Sir Augustus's son. He's far too foul to be the son of a gentleman."

"A poor relation." Lucy shuddered. "They'll punish Mr. Dickens fer wot you've done, mark my words."

"Sir Augustus will have him released soon enough," Fred said in a comforting voice. "It won't do to have his relation go to trial. But at least we showed some power of our own. He de-served worse."

As Fred spoke, the doorman at Boodles disappeared into the stone portico.

Kate clutched at his arm. "Something is happening."

"People will be coming out," Julie said. "I wish I knew someone with a membership, but Sir Silas doesn't belong and I don't know any other gentlemen of fashion and means."

"I tried to sell watercress at the servants' door, but they laughed me off," Lucy said.

As they watched, Sir Augustus exited the club with two other distinguished-looking men. None of them seemed to have a care in the world. Sir Francis's private secretary twirled his cigar with a flourish. The man on the opposite side of the baronet took his arm and spoke into his ear confidentially.

"Would you look at that," Julie fretted. "And us without a plan."

Chapter 21

"Race back to the carriage," Kate told Fred. "Lady Lugoson's coachman needs to turn it around so we can follow Sir Augustus."

"Look." Julie pointed at a gleaming barouche pulling up directly in front of Boodles. "You don't need to turn around after all. Get back in and follow."

"You don't see too many of those, even in London." Fred gaped at the fancy carriage. "I wonder how much that cost."

Lucy muttered inarticulately before Fred could recover his senses. Face contorting and going red, the erstwhile watercress seller thrust her basket at Kate.

"What's wrong?" Kate asked, confused.

"Lucy?" Julie asked, in her gruff man's voice.

"He's—he's—evil!" Lucy gasped, then shook her head and ran down the street, right at the small group of men. Her hands pulled together, her fingers turning into claws.

She reached Sir Augustus, and raked her nails down his waistcoat, visible under his open greatcoat. "How dare you hurt Charles? He's good and kind!"

"Fred," Kate cried. "Get her!"

Julie sped after Lucy, followed by Fred. Kate, encumbered by the basket, moved more slowly. The girl's hands were fists now, pummeling ineffectually at the tall, robust man's midsection. Would they all be arrested? If Fred attacked, would he wind up in a Newgate ward alongside his brother?

Before any of them could reach Lucy, the doorman fastened his arms around her waist and lifted her into the air. Her legs kicked out and she snarled, reverting to the old, wild ways of the mud larks instead of the tidy young maid with the saintly, clean face she'd become over the past month.

"Please," Kate called without thinking. "She's just a child. She's worried about a man who's been kind to her, sir."

Sir Augustus noticed Kate then. As she trembled, he perused her face insolently, then continued down her cloak all the way to her shoes. Then his gaze moved up again, noting the basket with its couple bunches of watercress, now looking more like a market basket than one with items for sale. Kate clutched it to her chest, feeling exposed despite her many layers of fabric.

After one last daggerish look at her lips, the new member of Parliament's expression changed from irritation into a congenial wreath of smile. He chuckled loudly, turning to each of his companions as if signaling them to do the same.

When all the men were equal in merriment, he chuckled again and patted Lucy on the head while the other men continued to laugh. "Set the girl down," he told the doorman. "No harm done by the child."

Fred, too caught up in the drama to recognize the changed emotion of the moment, stepped right into the half circle of men. "Where is Amy Poor?"

Sir Augustus didn't pretend not to know who Fred referred to. He ran a hand down his stomach and played idly with his watch chain. "You have to ask my nephew, Yupman, who is engaged to wed her."

"Yupman?" Fred said in an outraged voice. "Engaged?"

The baronet inclined his head icily, a superior becoming irritated at his inferior.

Too many thoughts pummeled Kate's brain. The sure knowledge that Mr. Poor knew nothing of this mock engagement fired her frustration. "I am engaged to wed Charles Dickens, known best as Boz. Do you know who that is?" she snapped.

Sir Augustus opened his mouth slightly. His tongue ever so delicately rubbed at the bottom of his front teeth.

Kate gritted hers, then spoke again. "Do you know where he is?"

Sir Augustus's lips curved up. His mouth was thin, but longer than the average man's. Kate had a sense of everything moving in slow motion.

"Newgate Prison, I believe, and well he deserves it."

The private secretary, who had been in the bow window with the baronet, turned his expression into a frown. "I say," he said in an air of surprise. "I always found Boz to be amusing. It's a pity he is in prison."

"What is this all about?" asked the third man.

Kate took her chance. She didn't know who he was, but the man dressed well, like a banker, and she couldn't take the risk of not influencing someone important. "Boz is wrongfully accused of murdering Samuel Pickwick, the president of the Lightning Club."

"Blimey," the man exclaimed. "Surely someone should hang for killing that most distinguished scientist."

"No one would disagree," Kate said compliantly, "certainly not my Mr. Dickens, the man who merely discovered the corpse. The man who should hang is the one who slit Mr. Pickwick's throat."

"Who was that?" asked the third man.

"I am certain Boz is innocent," she proclaimed. "He'd never

even met Mr. Pickwick. I'm sure the architect of his woes is that very nephew of Sir Augustus, Tracy Yupman."

The third man blinked very slowly. "On what evidence?"

"He accused my fiancé of killing Mr. Pickwick," Kate said. "What reason could there be other than to scapegoat Boz for a murder he himself committed?"

The man turned slightly, lifting his brows at the private secretary. "That's for the magistrates to decide, don't you think?"

"Please help us," Kate begged. "I don't know who you are, but you must be very influential. My fiancé's life is being ruined over this. Newgate is no place for an innocent man."

"I well believe that." The man searched her face.

Kate stayed still, projecting all her belief in Charles into her features.

The man nodded after a moment and reached into his pocket. He placed five guineas into her hand. "For his care, my dear. Be brave."

While she'd interacted with the man, Sir Augustus and his younger companion had somehow accessed the carriage. The third man nodded at her, then climbed in himself.

Kate swayed, the coins seeming to weigh her down. She wished for sleep, some way to forget this nightmare.

"Engaged to Amy Poor?" Fred said, outraged, breaking the spell as the carriage drove away.

"You need to leave now, before I call the constables," the doorman said.

Julie turned to him. "Amy Poor was kidnapped from Eatanswill. She's not engaged to anyone. Can't you help us?"

The doorman ignored the words as if they hadn't been spoken by the actress. "Run along. A constable will be along on his beat any minute now."

Kate glanced at Julie. Lucy was openly crying, like a wronged and maligned child.

"Should I take her home?" Julie asked.

"No," Lucy wept. "We have to help them, Mr. Dickens and the poor girl."

With a glance at the doorman, Kate took Fred's arm and pulled him up the street toward the private residences. The carriage had already gone into the center of the street and was vanishing into the misty rain.

"Should we follow it?" Julie asked, trudging along with her heavier male walk.

"No," Kate said. "I don't think the man who gave me the money is involved at all."

"I agree," Julie said.

Kate stopped on the pavement once they were a few houses away and looked at her friends. Fred looked supremely frustrated, Lucy wiped her eyes with her sleeve, and Julie was starting to droop a little with fatigue. Kate had never been happier for the sight of any of them.

"I am grateful for all of you and I know we will rescue Charles," she said, in her best rally-the-troops manner.

Fred screwed up his rosy mouth. "Do you think we should believe that Tracy Yupman has Amy Poor?"

Julie lifted a finger to pause them and pulled Lucy with her across the street, then directed them for five minutes or so toward the Mall until they reached a street hawker. The woman had a cart with a metal tin in a bucket.

Kate instinctively raised her hands to the charcoal fire.

"Rice milk?" asked the hawker, exposing her mottled teeth.

Julie nodded and the woman dipped her ladle into the basin as Lucy fumbled for coins. Rice thinned considerably with milk, not so much as it would have been in a poorer area of town, drizzled into a small bowl. The woman poured a little allspice and sugar over it from a metal shaker. Julie had her portion finished before the others were even ladled out.

"Do we need to take you home?" Kate asked, thanking the

woman as the warmth of the bowl transferred to her cold fingers.

Julie leaned against the wall, just barely protecting her from the light rain. "No, this will do me. We need to sort out where Mr. Yupman lives. Sir Augustus implied that he has Amy Poor."

"We have to act on that assumption," Kate agreed. "I'm sure Sir Augustus is a liar, but perhaps the lie was the engagement."

"Mr. Aga will know," Lucy piped up, subdued now, her voice a bit hoarse. She lifted the hawker's spoon to her lips.

"Yes," Julie agreed. "He knows Mr. Poor wasn't asked for his daughter's hand in marriage, for one thing."

Kate finished the last drink of her milk. "We could check in at the newspaper and get the address."

"What if your father is there, or someone else in authority to send you home? It's getting late," Fred said.

"Then what should we do?" Kate asked him.

"Let's go to that private museum where Charles was arrested," Fred suggested. "It's also the Lightning Club, right? The only address we know? One of us can very politely ask one of the staff where Mr. Yupman lives. We're all respectable enough."

"I like that idea as much as anything," Julie said. "Let's head to the museum. Do you remember the address, Kate?"

"Like it was burned into my memory," she agreed, and handed her bowl and spoon back to the hawker with a smile of thanks.

"I'll find a cab," Lucy said, and ran up the street.

"Where is it?" Julie asked.

"Finsbury Square. A house with green railings outside and a labyrinth inside, Charles said."

"Maybe a minotaur stabbed the good Mr. Pickwick," Fred said with a nervous laugh.

"I remember Charles thought he heard noises in the maze,

but he wasn't sure if it was a trick of his ears or not," Kate said. "We have to assume it was Mr. Yupman, coming into the maze by some other means."

"Why would Mr. Pickwick have been there?" Julie asked.

"To greet Charles?" Kate suggested. "Because it was his initiation into the club?"

"I thought we had assumed all along that he was never meant to be a member of the club, and it had all been a ruse," Julie said.

Kate frowned. "That's an excellent point. But the body couldn't have been dragged there. There was no sign of disturbance that Charles noticed."

"He couldn't see much," Fred said practically. "He could have had someone breathing down his neck and he'd only have noticed if he smelled onions."

"Charles's letter was on official stationery," Kate recalled. "Whether it was real or fake, someone with access to their paper sent the letter."

"I like the idea that Charles really was being invited to be a member," said Julie, always loyal. "He does have a book coming out. He even could have been invited to take the place of that songwriter who was murdered, since he's written songs as well."

"Then they would have invited Breese Gadfly, not Charles," Fred said.

"He's Jewish," Kate said softly. "It might have ruined his chances."

"Then he's lucky," Fred insisted. "Because he wasn't put into this position."

Julie shifted from side to side, then spoke in her normal voice, instead of the gruff one. "I admit I cannot understand how Mr. Yupman committed the murder if he sent Charles into the maze. Was there another way into the center of it? A trapdoor or something?"

"There has to be. Mr. Pickwick was an older gentleman and rotund, I believe," Kate said.

"It's like something out of a play," Julie agreed. "How long was Charles in the maze?"

"He didn't know," Kate said. "He didn't hear any church bells, which either means the walls were too thick, or time went much faster than he realized."

"It's impossible to know, unless the police have a record of the original complaint."

"They have ward books," Kate said. "They wrote in one when they took custody of Mr. Smirke from Fred and me."

"I doubt they'd let us see it, but maybe Sir Silas can ask," Fred said.

Lucy ran toward them. Her hair had come loose, and the blond locks flowed behind her, making her look more like an angel than ever.

"Every time I see her, she's more beautiful," Kate commented.

"I know," Julie said with a sigh. "And around fourteen is such an awkward age. I don't know what to do with her, other than keep training her."

"The training for a maid of all work should be useful for any girl's future, including marriage," Kate said.

Julie nodded. "I agree. Someone will want her as a wife, and young, with a face like that. I just hope we can guide her to choose someone kind and well employed."

"Newspapermen are quite unconventional," Kate pointed out. "Maybe one of them in a few years. They have some education, and a good income."

"Yes, one of them ought to do. We've been happy enough." She smiled at Kate.

As Lucy arrived, a hackney came down the street behind her. "That's the one," she said, pointing at the driver, who wore a green velvet jacket and stained leather leggings.

When the open cab slowed, Fred helped Julie into the cab, which looked odd, given that she was dressed like a man, then Kate. There was no room for a fourth person.

"Run along home," Julie told the girl. "Get dinner started. William will expect a hot meal."

"What?" Lucy asked, a hint of anxiety in the word.

"Potato soup," Julie said. "It takes a bit of work to get the lumps out, but it will keep."

Kate waved at Lucy as the cab started moving, then tossed the watercress basket to her. The girl caught it and waved back.

"If the last of the bunches survives all the way home, we can lace the soup with it," Julie said. She put a hand indelicately to her stomach. "I'm hungry already."

"Are you always hungry?" Kate asked.

"Not in the mornings, so I have to make up for it later in the day." Julie's eyelids dropped. "I hope the baby comes early in the summer, so I do not have to be hot and cross in the stifling air."

"Your expectation of a day will become more obvious over time," Kate said. "My mother guessed the date almost perfectly with Georgina and the twins."

"Mrs. Herring across the hall said first babies are very often late. She said the first and the last are the most dangerous, because you don't know if you'll have the strength for the first, and by the last, no one does." Julie laughed.

"My mother survived it all, as did Charles's, and your mother and aunt," Kate soothed. "I'm sure you'll be fine."

"No doubt, if nothing goes wrong. I'm strong," Julie said. "I have had quite an adventurous life."

"As well we know," Kate said. "Do you think you'll ever return to the stage?"

Fred had been leaning away, attempting to avoid the woman-ish conversation, but he turned back at the mention of Julie's acting career.

"I like the amusement of days like these," Julie said, motioning to her dress. "But I can probably find enough fun in private theatricals, when Charles is rich and has his own house to stage such things."

Kate thought about the future. "You'll have a house, too, I'm sure. Between Mr. Aga's professional skills and Lady Lugoson's private income."

Julie lifted her hands in a Gallic shrug. "It's possible, but my aunt marrying Sir Silas will change things. They could have children, you know. She's not so very old. She could have five."

"She'd probably like to," Kate agreed. "With only one son living, and him already quite grown."

"It will change everything, but then you won't be next door to see it all," Julie reflected. "This year, a great deal will change for all of us."

They drove into Finsbury Square and found the four-story house with green railings across from the burial ground. A small brass rectangle bore the inscription MUSEUM.

Without consulting the others, Julie marched up the stairs and knocked. Fred and Kate arrayed themselves behind her just as she rapped the knocker a second time.

"I don't see any sign of light behind the windows," Kate ventured.

Fred stepped next to Julie and listened at the door. "It seems very silent."

Julie tried one more knock, then tried the door. "It's locked." She considered. "It isn't a complicated lock."

"It wasn't the night Charles came," Kate said. "I suppose that means no one is there. He didn't see enough of the property to know if anyone actually lives inside."

"Should we go into the alley?" Fred suggested. "Or try to find that door that Charles came out of?"

Julie reached under her hat. Her fingers came back with a couple of long pins. "Block me."

Kate's eyebrows rose, but she turned and surveyed the street, flanked by Fred, as Julie did something to the lock with pins. She didn't judge the illegal behavior. After all, they were trying to find a kidnapped girl.

A carriage rumbled onto the street, then turned into the burial ground before Kate could panic. Julie swore something under her breath, more gentlemanly than ladylike. Then a group of three men approached from the opposite street.

"You'd better stop," Fred said. "There are men who will pass right by."

Julie turned. Kate could feel her breath.

"Let's try the servants' entrance," Julie said. "Turn around and we'll pretend to knock again until the men pass."

They did as she suggested until the trio of men passed by, also heading to the burial ground.

"Popular place today," Fred commented.

"Downstairs," Julie said.

Kate led the way down the stairs, then inside the railing so they could reach the servants' entrance. "Charles never saw this door."

"Right," Fred said. "The maze level must be one level below this one."

"He had to drop into it from the ground floor," Kate remembered.

"Maybe it's a shared floor?" Fred said.

"Wait," Kate said. "I remember. Charles said the house was really two connected buildings. Maybe one set of servants' rooms is the maze."

"Great," Julie said impatiently. "Let me pass." She surveyed the door.

"What do you think?" Fred asked.

"It's an older lock," Julie reported, putting the pins between her fingers again.

The others turned again so she could work. This time, Kate heard a click, then a rush of air behind her as Julie opened the door.

"Success," Julie crowed. "Let's be careful."

"I hope there aren't any more dead bodies," Kate said.

"I doubt that." Julie sniffed. "I rather think you like finding them."

Chapter 22

The prisoners had been led back into the wards from the exercise yard some time ago and dined well on mutton and bread. Charles sat at the table in front of the fire next to Bob Sawyer, sharing a half-a-week old copy of the *Morning Chronicle* that another prisoner had finished reading the night before. On his other side sat an elderly man, quite deaf and confused, in the prison for stealing a tray of muffins from a street hawker. Among his moans, Charles had picked up on the assertions that he thought the tray was his, and guessed he had once been a hawker himself.

Across the table, with their backs to the fire, sat a trio of housebreakers who'd been caught red-handed inside a magistrate's home. Charles suspected they'd never see freedom again.

"What were you meant to be doing right now?" Bob asked him, lifting a finger from the page. The paper was too old to leave ink stains on his flesh.

"I often go to services in Bloomsbury with my family. My parents have rooms there with my younger siblings," Charles said. "Or I could go to Brompton, to St. Luke's with my fiancée."

"What else?" Bob asked, turning the page. He ignored a fellow inmate who leaned over him and asked to have a turn with the paper.

"Then I go to a public house to work with my papers. Dine with friends, walk the streets, puzzle out new ideas for sketches, or plan a novel." Charles smiled reflectively, enjoying Bob's behavior toward the inquirer, who belonged to the group who had whispered about him when Jenkens had died. "I haven't written a word yet. I worry over the notices for my upcoming book. Now I wonder if I will ever read them at all, unless they are pushed through the grate by one of my friends."

"They will fall away," Bob Sawyer predicted, "and forget about you."

Charles leaned back, stung by the assertion. "I haven't even had a trial yet."

"It is good to be arrested in Middlesex," Bob reflected. "The magistrates have sessions eight times a year, instead of just four."

"I don't know if my case will be heard before April," Charles fretted. "I expect to be here until then. How could the case be ready by next month? At any rate, it gives my friends time to uncover the real murderer."

"What is the case?" Bob asked. "Who did you kill?"

"I killed no one," Charles said.

"Very well then, who was killed?" Bob rejoined.

"Samuel Pickwick, a scientific man who was president of the Lightning Club."

"Who do you think killed him?" asked Bob promptly.

"My friend William Aga has researched him. As the late Mr. Pickwick was never married and quite alone in the world, beloved by all his friends and club members, I think the fault is mine. I think he was killed to have this effect on my life. Framing me for murder is a most prolonged torture." Charles gestured around the room, this movement serving to loosen his own grip on the newspaper.

The other inmate pounced, pulling the paper away from Charles. Bob snatched at it, losing his balance. The small man swayed backward. Charles grabbed for him, but he tumbled to the floor. The standing inmate, now with the paper, snickered and walked away, carrying the paper to his friends, who had stools to the side of the fireplace.

Bob came up windmilling his arms. "Point me at them," he roared. One of his scarves came loose, the coil sliding to his neck, showing a receding chin dotted with lumpy red spots.

The wardsman, who'd been smoking a cigar just in front of the fire, turned around and gestured at Bob. "None of that nonsense now, Sawyer."

Bob flashed his teeth at the functionary, then busied himself with rewinding his scarf. By the time he'd resettled his wounded dignity at the table, the door to the chamber had opened. Two turnkeys stepped in.

"Dickens," Keefe called, his voice hoarse. "You're wanted."

A couple of the other prisoners at the table catcalled. Charles kept his expression blank, though his entire body vibrated with hope. Was he being released? Or interrogated? Or murdered?

"Good luck," Bob said.

"What do you think is happening?" Charles whispered as he stood.

"Important visitor, I expect," Bob said. "Someone who is too fancy to come to the yard."

Charles nodded and walked to the turnkeys. The one he didn't know held out a pair of manacles.

"No," he protested, instinctively recoiling.

"It's policy," the man said with a repulsively eager grin.

Charles had the sense that the turnkey enjoyed his job.

"It's all right, Dickens," Keefe said.

Charles schooled his features into impassivity and allowed the insult. Keefe led them into the hall, one of his hands busy with a lantern, which swung gloomy patterns over the plain walls. Moans came under the doors of one of the cells, and faint chatter could be heard from another. Charles had never taken a scientific survey of the place, even when he'd visited for his sketch. He could only think that far too many men, and women too, were trapped inside.

The desperate hope struck him that he did wish his trial was next month. If he could be exonerated, then he'd be free; if it was Newgate for him, at least he'd know. He'd be established in a ward with a fellow set of resigned men, forced to create a society with the convicted. This group of unsettled souls he was with, none having undergone trial yet, gave such an air of desperation and unknowingness to daily life.

He heard another moan and realized it had come from his own lips.

"In pain?" Keefe asked.

"Only a little," Charles said.

A tiny smile played over the turnkey's lips as he swung the lantern over the entry into a new corridor and turned. "Your sentence will not be so hard as mine."

Charles knew the other man meant he did not have much longer to live. "If you have any money, you could quit this place and live on savings, have a more relaxed ending."

The other turnkey snorted. "And 'im with five kids and a grasping mother-in-law? She'd sooner see 'im hang than relax."

"I see," Charles said, smiling faintly. "Perhaps you are better off here then."

"More pleasant company, most days," Keefe said, still with that little smile.

"Who is my visitor? An important one? Sir Silas Laurie?" Charles guessed.

"No, a fine lady," said the second turnkey. "One that's much too nice for the yard. She's been put in the governor's house so that she might speak to you in comfort."

Charles frowned. "My fiancée? Or Sir Silas's? Is it Lady Lugoson? A beautiful blond lady, not in her first youth? My future spouse is a bit younger than me, light brown hair."

"This is a very young sort of lady," Keefe said. "Very beautiful. The lamps made her hair look like spun gold."

"Oh?" Charles said, very puzzled. "Go on."

"Has airs, like one with a title," Keefe said, warming to his theme. "I could see the silk of her dress under her coat, sun yellow, with ruffles going down. A pretty little pair of boots just peeking out from underneath."

"Pink silk bonnet, very impractical," added the other man. "And a red velvet coat over the dress."

"Embroidered," Keefe added. "Looks like royalty."

"Gentlemen, you have made me most confused," Charles admitted. "I don't know anyone who fits that description. Are you sure that the young lady does not have red hair? Is it possible that these fine garments are more costume than regular attire?"

"Golden," insisted Keefe. "Much too fine to be a wig."

"Such a nose," said the other turnkey. "A little tilt at the end, gives her the air of a queen."

"Ah," Charles said, the facts before him clicking together. He remembered such a nose. "Haughty?"

Both men nodded. They came to a T in the corridor and took the left, stopping in front of a door that Keefe unlocked. He led them out into a yard, very dark and cold. Charles immediately shivered, but soon they were inside the governor's house, coming through the back. Charles had been here before.

Light shone under doors, giving the place a less gloomy air than the wards. It felt warmer, too, better insulated. But Charles still shivered, thanks to his moments outdoors. The cold air had stimulated Keefe's cough. He leaned against a wood-paneled wall for a moment to hack.

"Will you remove these now?" Charles asked, lifting up his hands, the chain between the manacles clinking.

"No. The lady especially asked that they be kept on."

Charles tightened his mouth. "Did she? She ought to be afraid I'd strangle her with the chain. Is it a Mrs. Moss?"

"No, she is an unwed lady," said Keefe.

Charles snorted in the privacy of his thoughts. "Why is she being treated so carefully, a beauty or not?"

"She had a letter from a member of Parliament," Keefe said, wiping his mouth.

"Let me guess. Sir Augustus Smirke?" Charles asked.

The other turnkey nodded.

"I begin to see the architect of my despair," Charles muttered.

"What do you mean?" Keefe asked.

What Charles wanted to do was slam his fist into the walls, but he couldn't let the turnkeys see how close he was to snapping. Here, in these circumstances, control was the thing. He was an actor on a stage. "This girl is engaged to a young man I thought I saw in Eatanswill, the day of Sir Augustus's election. All this time I thought I'd made an enemy of the baronet because of a newspaper article I wrote, when it is likely all of this has happened because of an old enemy resurfacing."

"Why do you have an enemy?" asked the second turnkey suspiciously.

"This lady had been wronged. Undeniably. She is not fond of me, but she was supposed to have left England by now. I hoped to never see her again."

"Sir Augustus is far too powerful to have leading strings," Keefe said. "I know well who he is."

Charles shrugged, though the weight of the manacles dragged at his shoulders. "This young lady is a master of manipulation. I don't know a great deal about her family, but they weren't poor. She might have had connections to his family."

Keefe yawned, displaying his mortal exhaustion. Charles fretted, knowing the turnkey was the only friendly face in a position of authority inside these walls. Had he the strength to forge other relationships with turnkeys? He turned to the unshaven, greasy-haired, pork fat–smelling guard, who nonetheless had a ruddy good health about him.

"Do you like arrogant women?" Charles asked the other guard.

"'Course not, but it's rare to see a face so pretty," the guard said. "Like a picture."

"As I recall, she excels at sitting still," Charles mused. "A picture. That's very good."

"Expect we should open the door," Keefe said. "You seem reluctant to see her."

"The interview is unlikely to end well," Charles told them. "She hates me even though I never hurt her."

"Maybe she hates everyone," Keefe said. "You see a lot of that here, and a lot outside, too. People whose futures wait here inside the prison. Just one deed, leaching out of their brains and into fact, and here they are inside these old, cold walls, living out their fate. Society don't want them."

"No," Charles agreed. "Some people are born criminals. Well, gentlemen, feast your eyes on a beautiful specimen of that reality, before the years coarsen her."

The second guard opened the door to a small sitting room. The wood paneling in the hall also covered the walls here. A fire crackled in the grate of a properly large old fireplace. The furnishings, a sofa faded to gray and two armchairs, were old but serviceable. No ornaments decorated the room to give it character. It looked like what it probably was, a safe space for the more distinguished types of visitors to interview prisoners without anyone having the opportunity for mischief.

Evelina Jaggers sat in one of the rubbed-down blue damask patterned armchairs, as still as advertised. It had only been a bit more than six months since he'd seen her, not long enough to age her in any way. A decade or so wanted until lines of cunning began to appear on her face.

Charles wondered how long it might be until murder took her life. She begged for it, a future ending to her unholy career.

For now, though, she might be eighteen, her golden hair and high color worthy of admiring glances. A deep red pelisse draped over the sofa. The heat had been too much to keep it on. Her full skirts and full sleeves might have dwarfed an equally lithesome figure, if not for the personality, equal to any encompassing garment.

"I do not like that shade of yellow on you, Miss Jaggers," Charles said. "It makes you sallow."

Her expression remained impassive. "I like the metal accents on you, Mr. Dickens," she responded in a throaty voice with a hint of laugh underneath. "Manacles suit you. I understand they are quite in fashion here."

"They would suit you better," he snapped back. "For all that you could hide an entire arsenal of escape tools in those sleeves."

"I am sorry, I didn't bring any tonight. I do have a gift for you though." She perused him, her aristocratic nose wrinkling slightly. "Though a change of clothing might have been better. You do smell, Mr. Dickens."

"I have been here quite some time," he said stiffly. "Please forgive me."

She had a wooden box in her lap, he discovered when he allowed his eyes to leave her face momentarily. Too wily of an opponent not to notice, she held it out to him.

Charles glanced around, just then realizing the guards had not come in with him. He could strangle her. It would be his death in the end, too, but then, she may have already assured that in her manipulations with Sir Augustus. Had they locked the door? He blinked, horrified by the darkness of his thoughts.

"What are you thinking?" she said softly. "Nothing pleasant, I imagine. I see the future path of Mr. Moss's thoughts peering out from behind his eyes sometimes."

"Does he hate you now, too?" Charles asked, trying to keep his tone conversational.

"We are buried in Chancery. As you can imagine, sorting out my foster mother's estate."

Charles allowed himself to smirk. "You will grow old in the shadow of the court."

"Sir Augustus has promised to work on reform," she said. "He thinks they will be able to appoint more judges in the next five years or so."

"What do you live on until then?" Charles asked. "Delaying your marriage? And Mr. Moss's farm?"

"Sold." She held out the box again.

He sat on her pelisse, deliberately crushing the fine velvet. The chain between his hands caught on her silk skirt as he took the box in his linked hands.

The box, of some soft, unadorned wood, had a top fitted over the bottom. He pulled it off, finding a flat cracker. Poking down to the bottom, he found only crackers.

"How odd," he said. While he'd had no idea what she might have brought, he'd hoped it was an insulting gift nonetheless of some use. Given what she'd done to her old enemy, he'd never dare eat or drink anything that had been in her possession.

"Unleavened crackers." She lifted her face. The light from

the fire brightened one side of her features and cast the other into darkness. "Do you know their significance?"

"Something Biblical about leaving affliction behind. It doesn't matter," Charles said shortly. He closed the box and dropped it onto the pelisse. "Don't waste my time with dramatics. You have a taste for revenge and underhanded dealing. I am not surprised to find you in the midst of the likes of Sir Augustus. I'm sure you have the upper hand by now."

"I'll tell you," she said, smiling serenely. "I'm sure you know your Bible. Leavening is symbolic of sin, isn't it? The way it spreads through dough is a metaphor for the way sin spreads through a body, through a community. It brings everyone into bondage in the end."

He stared at the fire. How he disliked her. He had since the first time he'd seen her at Miss Haverstock's inquest the previous summer. Now he knew why he'd seen Prince Moss in Eatanswill. She'd manipulated the farmer into working for a politician. Could she somehow be involved in Mr. Pickwick's death? What was her connection to the revered scientist, or had he simply been in the wrong place at the wrong time?

"Can you start a life without sin?" Miss Jaggers asked. "That's what the matzo symbolizes, you understand, according to my once-Jewish foster mother. If it is not too late."

"'The wages of sin is death,'" Charles quoted.

"Indeed. Sadly, I suppose it is too late for you," she mused.

Before he could snap back, she dreamily asked, "How does it feel to have been in Newgate for so long?"

His jaw worked, his normally loquacious brain refusing to feed words to his mouth. What kind of game was she playing at?

It didn't seem as if she'd wanted any response. Her soft, fresh lips parted into a sweet smile. "Compare your experience to how I felt last year, a should-be rich young lady at the height of her beauty, confined to a bedroom in a retired servant's house. A young lady in an unfashionable district, when she should have had a nice living."

"You had a nice living," Charles retorted, hearing himself speak like a disgruntled middle-aged man. "You weren't old enough to be out in society yet, whatever society your birth afforded you." He warmed to his theme when she looked at him with those perfectly innocent robin's egg blue eyes. "An orphan whose closest relative was an eccentric and elderly aunt-by-marriage. I doubt there was any society to join. Whoever your parents were."

Her lips parted and she spoke again as if an actress who'd merely been biding her time to her next speech. "Finally, I reacquire some of my fortune. With sensible advice from Sir Augustus Smirke, a friend of my late father's, I buy property and a cotton mill in Eatanswill."

"That's the connection," Charles muttered. His fingers, without active thought, reached for a cracker. While his body wanted the comfort of food, his mind knew he couldn't trust them to be free of poison, or some hallucinatory product. He closed the lid and dropped the box on another part of the cape, then wiped his fingers on the sensuous fabric.

She ignored him in favor of continuing her pretty speech. "I make love to Sir Augustus, by then a candidate for Parliament, so that he'll keep child labor laws suppressed, an important factor in rebuilding my fortune."

Charles frowned. Child labor laws? They had been much in the news. The last set of new laws had been passed into law right about when he began his parliamentary reporting career. Inspectors were supposed to ensure that no one under the age of nine was employed, and all children worked no more than twelve hours. But many found even these rules oppressive and wanted them rolled back, or unenforced, while their opponents pled for no more than a ten-hour workday for the most vulnerable members of society.

"I have no guardian but Chancery to see to me, but keep dear Mr. Moss close with promises of our future together." She blinked her long-lashed eyes. "He does not have too much longer to wait. I turn eighteen soon. And whom does dear Mr. Moss see one day in town, but Charles Dickens interfering in my life again."

"I was in Eatanswill reporting on the election," Charles protested.

"Charles Dickens, with his over-the-top reporting on matters that have nothing to do with government," she said, as if he hadn't spoken. "Finally, I am done. I am tired of his pretensions and they have to end. Mr. Moss agrees.

"I will not be preyed on. Grave injury was done to me as a very young lady, but I will not be sported with from now on. I will live my life for myself and my own interests." Her voice had risen, the triumphant tones of a conquering general.

"You are the heroine of your own tale," he said. "I can see that." He turned so that their gazes met.

Her stance went rigid. She wasn't a born performer, not exactly. Not yet, at any rate.

"How dreadfully young you are," he continued. "Someone killed Mr. Pickwick and it wasn't me. I imagine, Miss Jaggers, that you know exactly who did." He raised his hand, though she didn't protest. "No, I don't think you killed that venerated scientist. But you know who should be punished for that dark deed. Sir Augustus's nephew, perhaps? Or some functionary? Give me a name. I have done nothing to injure you but refuse to be your friend."

Her nostrils flared and her lips turned down slightly. The sneering expression marred her fresh beauty little. "Sir Augustus has pulled his nephew out of many scrapes. He meets his every need, from employment to amusement to women, but it never seems enough. Not everyone can settle on one sweet little darling like you have. I hope that your sweet Kate," her voice acid on the word *sweet,* "enjoyed the little game I set out to mock both of your pretensions."

"You are the mistress of the literary puzzles?" Charles asked. "How droll, that you should amuse yourself this way. Perhaps someday, as your suit drags away endlessly in Chancery, stealing your youth, you might find yourself master of ceremonies in some provincial watering hole, amusing the genteel crowds."

She fixed him with her gaze. "Remove yourself from my pelisse, Mr. Dickens."

"Is that all?" he demanded, too angry to fall into her Medusa's pit of ocular perfection. "Who killed Mr. Pickwick? Give me the name."

She snapped her fingers. "The story I heard at Sir Augustus's fireside late that night was of no importance. Other than as a vessel to teach you not to interfere with me." She smiled and rose. "Such a lovely web I wove around you, thanks to Mr. Yupman's endless inability to function without his uncle's counsel."

He rose, too, automatically, out of politeness. She reached around and swept the bloodred fabric from underneath him. It arced around her, the fabric somehow settling perfectly on her shoulders.

The door opened ahead of her, as if on some sort of pre-arranged signal, then shut again behind her. She'd never stopped moving. The sound of the door's close receded into memory.

He dropped back onto the sofa, the cushions cold underneath him. Her pelisse had sucked up all the warmth of his body. The entire room seemed colder now, but they must be leading her to the street before returning for him.

After that curious interview, he remained unsure of how exactly she was involved. Mr. Yupman must have gone to Eatanswill, or sent someone, in the aftermath of the murder, to ask for help. Miss Jaggers had seen the opportunity to have him framed for Mr. Pickwick's death, then distracted his supporters by sending Kate on her pointless series of quests. A girl's mean trick, that was all, to pull him so dangerously into a murder investigation.

He put his hands to his face, where his nose was already growing cold. Miss Jaggers had probably sold the goods she could recover to buy her factory and domicile. Then she'd proceeded to assess the largest threat to her business. Textile mills employed mostly the young, people her age or younger. She'd found her way into her father's old friend's local society. Her ticket must have been her beauty. Did she lie about her age? Who was acting for her? That appalling cousin of hers who had been the architect of so much misery for himself last summer?

Charles blinked away the past. He'd be taken back to the ward soon. While he had a moment here in relative comfort, he needed to think, and think hard. When Sir Silas came to visit again, he needed a name, not just a new path for investigation.

He needed a killer. Had Evelina Jaggers given him the name? Prince Moss had seen him in Eatanswill. Prince Moss likely knew Sir Augustus.

Charles rubbed his eyes with the base of his palms. The edge of his vision caught on the box of crackers. Had she meant to shame or poison him? He stood abruptly, lifting it up, and went to the fire.

He opened the box and let the crackers fall over the coals, wishing he could put past memories of poverty and pain into the fire as well. When the crackers had turned black, he considered the plain wood box. It could be used in the prison for trade, but if nothing else, it was imbued with the ill will of a beautiful young lady.

As he tossed the lid over the coals and waited for it to catch, he called all his considerable powers of discernment into play. Young Moss wouldn't have any reason to access the Lightning Club. Miss Jaggers or her swain must have persuaded Sir Augustus that Charles Dickens was a threat to them all, one who must be stopped. Not just a reporter who had supported his opponent in the Eatanswill election and written a strongly-worded article, but a menace who must be eliminated. Sir Augustus had access to the Club, not these young devils.

He tossed the base of the box on top of the smoking lid. Charles now knew the why of his being framed for murder, but how had the murder been transacted? Who had cut Mr. Pickwick's throat?

Chapter 23

Julie pulled a stump of candle from a hidden pocket in her husband's coat and lit it from the stove in the museum's dark kitchen. Fred followed her lead and hunted around on open shelves until he found a couple of rushlights, then lit them from Julie's candle and handed one to Kate.

"We haven't seen any servants yet," she remarked.

"The club may not be used right now, because of President Pickwick's death," Julie suggested. "I wonder who is keeping the stove fueled?"

Fred circuited the kitchen again, then pointed at a green baize door. "That's the way out of here."

"We need to get into the other side of the double house," Kate said.

"What about searching storerooms?" Julie asked. "That's a good place to hide someone."

"These people have no shame. They're claiming Miss Poor is Mr. Yupman's fiancée. I think she's either being held for some kind of ritual, or she'll be locked into a bedroom," Kate thought out loud.

"Do you think Amy Poor could be held in the maze?" Fred asked with an air of shock.

"I think we should check it." Kate wanted to see it anyway. An indoor maze. What woman had a chance to have such adventures? Soon she'd be busy with her own home and children. Right now though, she could see things the way Charles had.

"What if there are more dead bodies?" Julie asked with a shiver. "I might have nightmares."

"Take my hand," Kate instructed. She held it out, and Julie squeezed her fingers through her gentleman's glove.

Fred opened the green baize door. All three of them glanced through, their lights illuminating T-shaped oak flooring branching in all three directions.

"Where are the stairs?" Kate asked after they stepped through.

"They must be at the end of one of the passages," Julie hypothesized. The door shut behind her. "Which way would the maze be from here?"

Fred turned in a circle, his eyes closed. "I'm sure it's down the long corridor."

"Let's each take one passage," Julie said, pulling her hand away from Kate. "We need to know how to escape if we hear anyone coming."

Kate frowned. "We just follow our way back to here again." She reached for the doorknob behind her and turned it. It didn't move, or even rattle. "Oh, it can't be."

"What?" Fred asked, joining her.

"Try the door."

Fred put his hand on the doorknob. When it didn't turn, he muttered something in Latin under his breath. "It locked behind us."

"That's ridiculous," Julie exclaimed. "Why would it do that?"

"Maybe someone knows we're here?" Kate asked tremulously. "Could someone have entered behind us?"

"I didn't hear anyone." Fred pursed his lips. "There's no way out of the kitchen except by going back up to the street."

"Or there is a secret passage," Julie suggested.

"Anything is possible"—Kate sighed—"in a place where there is a maze in a basement."

"We might have missed something," Julie said. "I'll take the left and Kate can take the right. Fred, you go straight ahead."

"I don't think it is safe to separate," Kate fretted.

"It's important to search quickly," Fred argued. "Before anyone comes."

"Don't go through any doors," Kate cautioned, giving in. "Meet back here as soon as you've reached the end."

The others nodded, then they separated in search of access to the maze. Kate walked slowly down her passage, the vague scent of cabbage receding in favor of mold. As she walked, she recalled what Charles had told her about his experience.

He'd been in a dining room. The trapdoor had been in the floor, with a rope into the maze. He'd been deposited at the mouth of a nautilus shape. There had been rough walls and a dirt floor, then he'd encountered plaster walls, an opening with a table. And a body.

He'd had to retrace his steps and reclimb the rope to reach an exit. But he'd been in darkness all the way through his initial pass of the maze and suffused with horror on the way out. Even Charles wouldn't have been quite his calm, assessing self after coming across a corpse and finding that he'd been trailing his hands through the victim's life blood.

Abruptly, her passage came to an end. The tip of her shoe bounced off the far wall. She turned around in a circle, rubbing her banged toes against the back of her skirt. Her rushlight hadn't uncovered anything other than plaster walls and planked floor. Careful to keep the rush vertical so that it wouldn't burn too quickly, she walked back, making sure to check the walls closely.

She'd found nothing by the time she reached the green baize door. Footsteps on the planks notified her that Julie was close.

"Any luck?" asked the actress.

Kate shook her head. "Nothing whatsoever. I walked even more slowly on my return, checking again."

"As did I." Julie pulled off William's top hat and fanned herself with it.

Kate tried the door again, just in case. It was still locked. "Let's set off after Fred. That passage must be longer."

Julie shrugged like a man but spoke in her normal voice. "There isn't anywhere else to go. I can pick the lock and get us back into the kitchen."

Kate was about to assent, when they heard running footsteps.

"I found a door," Fred reported. "The passage is wallpapered but I found it by running my hand on the wall."

"Well done," praised Kate.

"Let's go," Julie said, returning the hat to her mounded red curls.

"I wonder if there will still be a blood trail," Fred said. "From taking the body out. Why couldn't Charles find the door?"

"We don't know if it enters the maze," Julie pointed out.

"Where else would it go? The maze must be large," Fred said in a practical manner as he stopped in front of the wall.

Kate lifted her rush. "The wallpaper has shells hidden among the leaves," she reported, surveying the dizzying blue shapes.

"Look." Fred traced his fingers along a faint outline. "You can see how my finger pokes into the shape. And here." He moved his finger across. "It's a keyhole."

Julie handed her candle to Kate and pulled her discarded

hairpins from her pocket. "Here we go." She crouched down and fiddled with the lock.

Like the street entrance to the kitchen, it wasn't hard to manipulate, giving Kate hope that they might just as easily get through the baize door when it was time.

The door swung open, as if it was held in place only by the lock. The air was colder behind it, the warmth of the kitchen not reaching here.

"We must be in the second house," Fred said.

"Amy Poor?" Julie called experimentally. "We're here to save you."

No response came back, just dank air. Kate felt ringlets of her hair tingle damply against the back of her neck. "We should go in and explore a little bit. We can't be here forever. This is a good rushlight, but it can't possibly last much longer." Screwing up her courage, Kate stepped into the dark passage they had revealed.

"Was that the end of the passage?" Julie asked behind her. "Could there be more doors?"

"No. I went all the way to the end, then came back."

There could still be more doors behind them on the way to the kitchen, since Fred had probably stopped looking for anything more in his excitement in finding this one, but Kate knew he'd been right about finding the maze.

She held her rush out. In front of her hung a thick rope, smelling faintly of tar. She followed it up a good dozen feet until it snaked along the side of a trap door in the ceiling. "Look, there's the rope."

"Ah," Julie exclaimed. "This door was across from the trap-door. Charles must have been in such a hurry to escape that he didn't notice it."

"If they keep the kitchen door locked it wouldn't have done him any good to escape this way," Fred pointed out. "But how do they get the food upstairs?"

"They must go outside." Julie pointed to the open end of the room. "Come, let's go through the maze."

Kate called for Amy Poor, but it didn't feel like any other living being was in the maze with them. The air seemed devoid of breath, of heartbeats other than their own, too cold for warm bodies to be within. "We should probably go upstairs. I don't think anyone is here."

"You are going to climb the rope?" Fred asked.

"You'll have to go up first and open the trapdoor, then help me up."

"Let's hope it doesn't come to that," Julie said. "I sincerely doubt that Charles found everything, under the circumstances."

"It cannot take so very long to go through the maze," Kate said. "And it may give us more theories as to what happened that night."

"Agreed," Julie said. "We have three lights. Let's go fast."

She moved into the shadowy part of the open space. Kate followed her, holding her rushlight in front of her. Dark spots dotted the earth floor. Blood? Why hadn't anyone cleaned it up? Had Charles done his exploration literally over the blood of Samuel Pickwick? He'd mentioned a metallic smell as he walked. She couldn't smell that now though, just the dank odors of an underground space.

"We could be in a crypt," she said.

"Shh," Julie responded. "We're cracksmen now. Use your eyes and your ears, not your mouth."

Kate went silent after the order. Julie was used to adventures, unlike her.

Fred's rushlight danced over the walls. The texture of the light changed a few feet away.

"That must be the start of the plaster," she whispered.

In a few feet, she was proven right. She tapped the wall that began to curve inward. As they moved in, the wall developed a hollower sound. "Might be all plaster."

"Look," Julie said, holding up her candle. She stepped back and tilted a tall plaster screen into the passage. It had hidden the change in the wall from real to false.

Shocked, Kate stepped alongside her. "A second passage. Charles didn't notice this."

Julie moved toward the left. "It's very narrow. Only a chimney sweep's child would find the space comfortable."

"Probably not meant for anyone. They just made an artificial maze in the center of the room. It will take up less space as it narrows," Fred said.

"But that might be where the door is hiding," Kate suggested.

Fred tapped the wall dividing one passage from another. "Hollow."

Kate swept her rush over the compacted dirt. She thought she saw something and peered into the tiny passage. The earth had a few dark half circles on it. She touched one with her shoe. It didn't press the sole, or down into the earth like a pebble. "I think it's more blood drops."

"They couldn't have hauled a body through this opening," Julie argued. "It's too small."

"No, but the killer might have had blood on his shoes, and escaped this way." Kate pointed.

"How did the police miss all this?" Fred said. "We have a curved wall, which is artificial, and a straight wall, which is part of the house."

"They already had their murderer," Kate said, disgusted. "And a respectable man fainting and fluttering and pointing his finger. We have to tell Sir Silas, so he can get someone in here before they clean it up."

"Let's go through," Julie suggested. "Mind the blood if you can."

"Charles said he thought he heard someone else in the maze. They must have been here in this hidden part," Fred said. "You go first, Julie. You have the best light."

Kate's rush spluttered a bit, and Fred's was in the same shape. "We don't have much time," Kate urged.

Julie slid into the open space. "Careful not to burn yourself," she cautioned, holding her candle in front of her. "It's a good thing my belly isn't big yet."

Kate winced at the vulgarity but followed her in. Her slender body made it through, but she heard Fred's coat rubbing the plaster.

"It's already widening," Julie reported.

Kate ran her free hand along the plaster surface. She smelled coal. "There must be a chute here somewhere."

"Which means there is a way outside and a way upstairs," Julie said.

Fred's rushlight sputtered and went out. He bumped up against Kate. She stifled a scream.

"I'm sorry, it's just me," he said in her ear.

They could walk two abreast now. "No one seems to be here." The smell of coal intensified.

"Here it is," Julie said. "A door."

Kate held up her dying rushlight as Julie investigated the door.

"Locked," Julie reported. She handed her candle to Fred and they gave her as much light as they could while she fiddled with the lock. It gave way under her expert ministrations after a couple of minutes.

Fred shined the rapidly diminishing candle into the doorway. "Stairs. Must be the servant's staircase. Narrow, and the runner is thin and worn. I can't see the top with this light."

"Success!" Julie crowed. "Let's see if Amy Poor is here."

Fred went up the stairs first. "Another locked door."

"You'd think they were hiding something," Julie muttered. Fred stepped aside while Julie worked.

This one took longer. Kate's light went out, and they were left with only the candle stub. At least it was good beeswax, and smelled much better than the rushlight. She had lost track of time and had started to worry about how long they had been in the house when she heard a click.

Julie slowly opened the door. A wall greeted them a few feet away, but the darkness wasn't so absolute. The trio walked onto a wood floor again and found themselves in a passage.

"It's very quiet," Fred said.

"Charles said there were portraits," Kate remembered.

"I think we're still in the servant's area," Julie mused. "Let's go to the right. I think that is toward the street."

They trailed her, ears sensitive to any noise, but all Kate heard was their shoes on the floor. Julie turned unerringly and went through an unlocked door.

"Here we are," she whispered.

Kate saw an open foyer. A staircase curved upstairs.

"That must be the front door," Fred said.

"We want to go up," Julie told them. "That's where bed-rooms would be."

"Lead on," Kate said. "But stay low. What if someone comes to the front door?"

Julie blew out her candle stub before it could burn her fingers, and went up the steps. Kate and Fred followed.

"Left or right?" Julie asked.

Kate glanced around. She could smell ink and paper, a little reminiscent of the *Chronicle* offices. "Neither," she said. "Bed-rooms would be up."

"I thought this was a museum," Fred said. "Where are the taxidermy animals and collections of bones?"

"There are two more levels and an attic," Kate said.

Fred shook his head and followed her to the next level.

At the top of the stairs, Kate sniffed the air again. "It's grown mustier here."

"Storage," Julie said. "Smells like the basement of a theater."

"I suppose there was plenty of space on the ground floor for the exhibits," Fred groused.

"We're here for Amy Poor, not a museum viewing," Kate pointed out.

Julie turned left and opened the first door on the passage. She poked her head in, then turned back to report. "Boxes and bugs."

"Bugs?" Fred asked.

"Moths and beetles, mostly. Pinned in boxes. Set out on a table. Must be working on a new exhibit or something." Julie shrugged. "I wouldn't want to spend my time finding the best place for a pin to attach a dead bug to a box."

"Let's go upstairs," Kate said with a shudder, thinking of what might be done to them if they were caught. "Two more levels."

Fred took a step in the direction of the bug-filled room, but Kate pulled him back by the ear, as if he were one of her own little brothers, and set him into the path of the staircase. They crept up. This level didn't even have a runner of tired carpet up the middle. An air of sour disuse filled the narrow passage.

"This floor looked the same size as the ones below from the street," Julie said. "But it feels smaller from here."

"The rooms must be larger?" Kate guessed. "But with this house, who knows what they have done to it?"

"I don't think anyone is here," Fred guessed.

"I'm starting to lose hope," Julie agreed.

Kate opened the first door on the right. She found a musty bedroom with a large canopied bed taking up most of the room. The blankets were pulled back, as if someone had jumped out and no one had come to make it up again.

"Look, a tea tray," she pointed out. "Still next to the bed."

Fred walked over to it. "The toast has a spot of mold. It's at least a week old."

"Whoever resided here hasn't returned since Mr. Pickwick was killed," Julie guessed. "Do you think this was his room?"

"The entire floor might be like this," Kate said. "But I would be happy to know more about the man if we find his quarters."

Fred looked at the contents of a writing desk under the window. "Three books of poetry. Doesn't sound like the club's president."

"No, he'd have scientific tracts," Kate agreed. "Let's go to the next room."

They went out, shutting the door, and peered into the next two rooms. Of similar size, they didn't show signs of recent use. At the fourth door, they had more luck.

"It's more spacious," Julie said, surveying the room.

"It's the corner of the house." Kate pulled down her muff so she could tuck both her hands into it. Cold was creeping in.

"The window is open," Fred said.

Kate turned around in a circle on the rug in front of the fireplace. "This feels like a president's room."

Julie pointed over the fireplace. "Who do you suppose that is?"

Kate stepped closer to the painted image of an elderly, rosy-cheeked man in a wig characteristic of some fifty years ago. "Maybe a previous president of the Lightning Club?"

She heard a clunk and turned around, startled. Fred had pulled the window down.

"You shouldn't do that. What if someone hears and comes to investigate?"

"They might hear us talking if the window stayed open," he said.

Kate nodded and walked to the next window. They were looking over the back of the house. The small lawn would give the brilliant men of the club room to pace, smoke, and contemplate the mysteries of life. Then she turned to the bed. The embroidered green coverlet was pulled back messily.

Another tea tray had been discarded next to the bed. Only stale crumbs remained.

She heard a thump and whipped around to admonish Fred again, but he was at the writing desk, a match to the furniture in the other rooms. Julie, openmouthed, pointed up.

Slowly, Kate's gaze drifted from Julie's finger to the ceiling. "Who is up here with us?" she asked. "Not a maid, I'd expect."

"A club member?" Fred asked.

Julie shook her head. "Amy Poor."

Kate dropped her voice to a whisper. "Maybe she heard us moving around and is trying to get our attention."

Julie pointed to the door. The others followed her out. They returned to the servant's staircase, crowding into the narrow space. Kate's skirts dragged along the walls. The stairs weren't made for fashionable clothing.

"What room?" Julie asked.

The passage here was still narrow. The walls hadn't been painted in years, and dingy lines of black were rubbed along them. There were a third more doors here than on the floor below, evidence of smaller rooms, even though Kate remembered the attic floor was smaller from the street.

Fred pointed to the door across from them. "That's above Mr. Pickwick's room."

"We don't know it was his," Kate protested.

Fred pushed his finger into his open palm. "I found letters addressed to him just before we heard the noise."

Kate heard a muffled thump. She caught Julie's gaze and they nodded at each other.

Fred took a visible breath, then tried the door. "Locked."

"Miss Poor?" Kate said through the door. "Can you hear us?"

Another thump.

"She might have something in her mouth. Maybe she's attempting to communicate in some kind of code," Julie said, pulling out her reliable hairpins. "It's so dark in here."

"Give me what's left of your candle." Fred pulled out a small box of lucifers and struck one against the sandpaper in the box. It flared to life.

Julie handed him her candle, then returned to work. Kate held the candle near her to illuminate the lock.

"My hands are sweating," Julie muttered.

"All that banging doesn't help," Fred said. "Whoever is in there must be angry."

"Of course she is," Kate said, impatient with Julie's unusual slowness. "She's been imprisoned."

Julie dropped a pin. She swore like a sailor, bent lithely to retrieve it, then went back to work.

Kate's mouth rounded. Julie couldn't be wearing stays. How daring the former actress was.

After another long pause, she began to worry about the life of the candle. There wasn't much wick left. Finally, she heard a click and Julie grunted in satisfaction. She stepped back, wiping her hands on her trousers.

Fred cleared his throat. "Stay behind me, ladies." He opened the door.

The room was utterly dark. The thumps they had heard intensified.

Kate stepped around Fred, holding the candle, and kept moving toward where the windows ought to be. She held out her hand. "Just curtains," she reported, pulling one back. Then she turned around to see what the light had to show them.

Chapter 24

After Kate's eyes adjusted to the light coming in through the window, she saw Fred frozen with shock, Julie's candle still held high. She smelled unwashed body and old soup. A fire had been laid in here not too long ago, but the chimney must be partially blocked. Attempting to open the window to let out the stench, she discovered it was painted shut.

Julie rushed to a curtained bed, the only furniture other than a stool and low table by the fireplace. She pulled the faded blue velvet aside, casting dust motes into the air. They danced around her top hat as she cried, "'I am sick when I do look on thee.'"

Kate hurried to Julie. A girl no older than the actress was spread-eagled on the bed. Thick skeins of a silken rope were tied around her wrists and ankles, anchored to the bedposts. One rope had some slack, enough that she had probably been thumping her leg against the bed. A handkerchief covered her lower face. She had greasy curls of dark walnut hair spreading everywhere, and a forehead covered in spots. The nightdress had rusty stains, giving Kate a terrible sense of what the girl had suffered.

Kate couldn't have described her horror, now that the curtains had been opened. Julie, ash-pale, blinked back tears as she pulled off her coat and spread it over the girl's body.

"A knife," Kate called to Fred. "We need a knife."

"Don't come too close," Julie warned. "Guard the door."

Fred handed Kate a folding penknife, then went to the door and faced it.

Kate bustled to the bed and opened the knife. Not bothering to survey the knots, she started cutting one of the ankle ties. Julie gently pulled the soiled handkerchief over the girl's head.

Kate glanced up and saw another handkerchief was shoved into the girl's mouth. Julie slowly pulled it out. A cut on the girl's lip broke open and bled. She coughed convulsively, lifting her head.

Julie soothed her with a hand on the crown of her head. "We'll have you free soon."

Kate's arms ached by the time she had the ankle ropes cut. Knots still held fabric circles around the girl's limbs, but at least she could pull her legs together now.

The victim had the strength to move her body that much. Julie whispered, "Shh, there now," when the girl groaned.

Kate sawed at one of the arm ropes. Her legs had been allowed to lie flat, but her arms were up and over her head. After a while the position would be excruciating, but the girl had no tears left to shed.

"I wish we had something for her to drink," Kate fretted.

"I could go to the kitchen," Fred said, still with his back turned.

"I'd rather you stay on guard," Julie said. "And you'll need to carry her out of here."

Amy Poor's arm dropped to the mattress when Kate finished with the first arm rope. She rushed around the bed to attack the last one.

"I wish we had some way to preserve this, some way to show

how we found her here." The knife had dulled. She had more trouble making headway on this final rope.

"She'll tell the police what happened," Julie said, stroking the girl's brow.

"Thank you," Amy Poor managed, but even that attempt at speaking brought on a fit of desperate coughs.

Julie helped roll her to her side, supporting her since she still had one arm in an awkward position. Eventually, the coughs subsided.

"There we go!" Kate said brightly as the last bit of fabric severed. She closed the knife. "We'll have to wait to remove the rest, but at least we can take you somewhere warm and safe."

"Do you want me now?" Fred asked.

"Help me," Julie said to Kate.

Julie and Kate pulled Amy Poor into a sitting position and buttoned William's coat around Amy. The large coat enveloped the girl down to her small, naked feet.

"She's decent now," Kate called.

Fred came forward and had his first full look at the girl. A cry of shared pain escaped his mouth.

"Do you think you can get her down the stairs?" Julie asked.

"I'll go first," Kate said. "I'll unlock the front door and find us a cab."

"I'll do it," Julie said. "I'm still dressed like a man."

Kate shook her head. "It will be easier for you to help Fred since you are wearing trousers. We have to think of the staircase." She left the room and, forgetting caution, ran down the main flights of stairs to the entrance of the museum.

In the entryway, she ignored the frozen glare of a stuffed bear as she paused to catch her breath. After a moment, she unlocked the door and sped down to the street. Outside, life passed like usual. A muffin man hurried by, his tray empty. Across the street, two men strolled, one of them tapping his cane against the pavement. A trap rolled by, then a man on horse-back.

She ran around the side of the building, fretting since she didn't know where the cabs congregated in this part of town. Spotting a butcher's boy, his arms full of packages, she asked him where she might go. He directed her to a spot across from the burying ground.

Ten minutes later she had returned to the front of the museum. A cab would be arriving as soon as the horses were watered. She climbed the front steps into the museum.

Amy Poor sat on a staircase step. Someone had found a bottle of wine somewhere, and Fred was encouraging her to drink right from the bottle while Julie paced back and forth in front of them.

"The cab will be here soon," Kate said. "I expect we'd better wait to carry her down to the street."

"Don't let her drink too much," Julie cautioned. "She'll be sick from it."

Fred nodded and took the bottle away. Kate could see he was considering a fortifying sip of his own, but one look at the sorry state of the girl's broken mouth dissuaded him. He set the bottle aside with a grimace.

"Are you Amy Poor?" Kate queried.

The girl nodded.

"Mr. Yupman claims you are his fiancée. Is that true?" she asked.

The girl shook her head this time. "I worked for his uncle, as a parlor maid. One night he surprised me on the back stairs, said my father was downstairs waiting for me." She swallowed hard.

"Go on," Kate encouraged.

"When I went out the door there was a carriage. Sir Augustus lifted me in, but it wasn't my father there, it was Mr. Yupman." She stared down at her damaged wrists. "That was only the beginning."

"Did you try to escape?" Kate asked gently.

She nodded. "He brought me here and locked me into an unused bedroom. Kept me quiet with some kind of drink that made my head swim. I knew there were other people around. I thought if I could leave the room they might help me. I did get out one night. I'm not sure how."

"The club members were there," Kate encouraged.

Amy's mouth trembled. "Mr. Yupman. He said he would save me from the police, but not with marriage."

"Save you?" Julie asked with a frown. "Save himself, you mean?"

Amy Poor lifted her head weakly. "I killed a man. I am going to burn in hell."

Fred jumped to his feet, knocking the mostly-full bottle over. It rattled down the two steps to the floor, spilling out a rich purple-red liquid.

The scent made Kate's stomach growl, but she ignored it. "Killed a man? Who?"

"He was . . . an older man. Rotund. Mr. Yupman said it was Samuel Pickwick."

At the girl's words, Julie whirled around. "You cut that man's throat?"

"It was late one night. I don't know how long I've been here, but they didn't have me tied up at first, just locked into the room. I used a pin from my dress to open the lock when the drink had worn off. I opened the door and went into the hall. I was trying to find stairs." Amy Poor started coughing.

"There now." Fred attempted to soothe her. "Is that why there are bloodstains on your, err, garments?"

"Fred," Kate admonished.

"What?" Fred asked. "I'm just asking about the evidence. For Charles's sake."

The coughing subsided. Amy Poor stared at him with a deadened expression. "I didn't know what I was doing. I just wanted to run away and he kept asking questions."

Through the window by the door, Kate saw a cab pulling up. "How did you get a knife?"

"I'd stolen the penknife from Mr. Yupman's pocket the night before," Amy confessed. "It was dark. I thought Mr. Pickwick was Mr. Yupman and I still had the strength to fight then."

"It was more than a week ago now," Julie confirmed. "You've been through a lot of bad treatment since."

"What happened after you attacked him?" Kate asked.

Amy gestured up the stairs. "They tied me up. Mr. Yupman kept visiting me." She dropped her head into her hands and let out a low, animalistic moan. "I heard noises. Shouts, dragging. It smelled like blood. In my mouth, in my hair, in my eyes."

"She's becoming hysterical," Julie warned, settling her hand on Amy Poor's shoulder.

Kate verified that the cab had stopped in front of the door. "Fred, can you pick her up so we can take her down to the street?"

"Where are we going to go?" Fred asked, scooting closer to her on the stair.

"The police," Julie said. "We have to take her to a police station. The one on Bow Street will do."

"They aren't going to want her there." Fred gently settled one arm around the girl's shoulders. She gave a low moan but didn't shy away.

"We can take her right to the magistrates," Kate added. "Then we'll send for a doctor."

The museum's front door opened, startling all of them. "What is all this?" a tall, middle-aged man with a long, sheeplike face roared.

Kate and Julie turned and rose to their feet on the same

breath. Julie, moving swiftly in her male clothing, rushed at him, her head knocking into the man's chest. He fell backward out of the front door as Amy Poor screamed.

"Is that Yupman?" Fred asked.

Julie followed Yupman down the steps.

Kate heard a cry she assumed was agreement as she raced after Julie. "Pick her up. We don't want to lose that cab." She went to the door and stopped, stunned momentarily at the sight.

Tracy Yupman lay on the landing with his legs stretched down the stairs. Blood had started to pool around his head, though he still moved a little, as if trying to get up.

"Help me," Julie called. "He can't get away."

Kate did her best to help despite her stays, and they dragged the half-conscious man, who was surprisingly light given his sex and ability to torment Amy Poor, down the remaining steps to the cab. His head hit a step, but Kate was glad because it knocked the senses out of him again and made him easier to move.

"Bow Street," she said to the cabdriver. "We need the police."

"It's a tight fit," the driver said.

"It's going to be worse." Fred hefted Amy Poor into the small space.

She whimpered when she saw Yupman was in the cab with them, but he was secured under Julie, who sat on him, holding a handkerchief to his head wound. Fred kept Amy Poor in his lap. The driver muttered something under his breath about "all the tea in China" and whipped the horses into movement.

Kate was crushed in between the victim and the accused. Every time Yupman began to protest, Julie lifted herself a little bit, then sat down hard on him again, causing him to let out a gasp. Kate appreciated her quick thinking and bravery.

They drove into central London, on a straight line to the Covent Garden area. Caught in the middle, she could only look forward to the horses in their traces, to the other carriages weaving in and out between them, and think toward the future and Charles.

He hadn't killed Samuel Pickwick, and now they had the killer. The fact that they considered Mr. Yupman to be far worse than a murderess was a matter for the police.

"The police will take her into custody," she said to Julie. "Can we persuade a doctor to come and see her?"

"They will have a matron who will understand what has happened to her," Julie insisted. "We'll make sure she has the care she needs."

"Charles must testify to what he heard in Eatanswill," Kate added. "Then they will know she was kidnapped."

"Fiancée," Yupman squeaked before Julie knocked the air out of him again.

"We know better," Fred snarled as Amy let out a fresh sob. "It took forever to cut her off that bed, you demon from hell."

"I know you're uncomfortable," Kate soothed the girl, "but we only have another mile to go."

After the longest mile of Kate's life, the horses finally stopped in front of Bow Street. The humanity teeming around the police station and court seemed to still in disbelief as Fred struggled out of the carriage with Amy Poor, and a well-dressed woman and a woman dressed as a man hauled Tracy Yupman in between them through the door.

The sergeant stood up from his desk in shock at the absurd sight.

"We have the real killer of Samuel Pickwick," Julie announced in a ringing voice she'd perfected in the theater. Mr. Yupman struggled between her and Julie. "Take us to the magistrate."

"Send word to Newgate," Kate added. "My Mr. Dickens must go free this instant!"

Chapter 25

Evening had started its descent over the prison walls on Sunday night. Their ward had been in the yard minus a couple of prisoners who had been tasked with sweeping out their room and cleaning the fireplace.

Charles and Bob Sawyer had unfortunately been given the task of the cleaning.

"To think, at nearly twenty-four, at the height of my career, that I've been reduced to being a tweenie," Charles said, disgusted at the state of his cuffs and hands after raking out soot.

"Better than a maid of all work," Bob said with a giggle. "I've had a few lady friends in that capacity and it's a hard life."

"When would you have time to be friends with one of those busy girls?" Charles asked.

"Oh, there's allus time for a bit o' flirtin' at the kitchen door," Bob said, pouring ashes into a square of newsprint and forming it into a bundle. "They'll need to get a chimney sweep in here soon, with the smoke this is producing."

"Strange to think of creature comforts in a place like this," Charles mused. "I was surprised to discover the warmth of the fire and the good food, when so many people outside are cold and starving. It doesn't seem right."

"We would o' been better if we hadn't been cold an' starfin' outside," Bob said promptly. "Who can blame a man for going into the receifin' trade when it were their father's afore them and their grandfather's before that? The roof has to be paid for, as the old man used to say to the little birdie that made a nest just over the door."

"I have no intention of following my father's path through the world." Charles took the small bottle of vinegar he'd been given and poured some onto a brush to scrub the fireplace bricks. "Any more than is necessary." In fact, his father had learned shorthand first, but Charles had taken the opportunity to work hard and rise, unlike his father.

Bob Sawyer swept the last bit of ash through Charles's feet and surveyed the fireplace. "That's done, an' not a minnit too soon. Nearly dark."

"Here." Charles handed him the vinegar bottle. "Splash a bit of that around."

"Can't do sloppy work or no prifileges for you," Bob warned, but he did as Charles suggested, then scraped at the vinegar with the broom.

Charles shivered as he finished half of the bricks. "Start building up the fire so we can light it the second this is done. In a few minutes no one will be able to see the bricks anyway."

"Good point," Bob said.

They'd been provided with a bucket of coal and fire starters. Not enough, Charles had noticed, to be able to immolate themselves, but sufficient for a start to the evening that could be built on by a turnkey assigned to that purpose.

When the door to the ward opened a couple of minutes later, he still had a fourth of the bricks to go. Bob had finished laying the fire, rather inexpertly. He scrambled to his feet and picked up the broom to look like he was working. His coal-dusted fingers left streaks on the broom, damp with vinegar.

Charles set down his brush. "Light the fire, Bob. It won't burn so brightly that I can't finish."

"More coal?" Bob said hopefully in the direction of the door as he fired the single lucifer they'd been given.

Charles saw the boxer's face of John Curdle, his least favorite turnkey, in the light of the flame. After what had happened in the past, he always hoped to see Curdle solely in the company of others, but he was alone this evening. The other guards must have more important duties, like organizing the final meal of the day. Bob set the lucifer to the kindling.

"Should we stop?" Charles asked. "I'm nearly done."

"You are," Curdle sneered.

"Right," Charles agreed, nonplussed. "Just a bit more work on the bricks here. The light from the fire will help." He picked up his brush again.

The lucifer went out. The light from the fire was too low to illuminate anything much past the fireplace. Curdle held his lantern up to his face. Between that and the windows, Charles could see him quite well. He dipped the brush into the extremely soiled water bucket, hoping enough of the coal would dissipate so that he could finish the bricks without embarrassment. He liked being left nearly alone here in the ward and wanted to keep this duty.

As soon as he put the cleaner brush to the bricks again, the turnkey raised his voice. "You're done with Newgate."

"What?" Charles asked, running the brush along the top of the bricks. "Has my trial date been set? It's Sunday, isn't it?"

"Someone else said they killed that Pickwick fellow."

The brush dropped from Charles's fingers. It glanced off the bucket and fell in, splashing water on Charles's legs. He barely felt the cold though, so shocked was he by the news. No other emotion hit immediately.

His fingers prickled as he clenched his hands into fists. "Who? Who killed Samuel Pickwick?"

The turnkey sneered. "They say it wasn't you."

Charles stepped past the fire, pretending not to notice small Bob Sawyer, huddled just inside the enormous space. "And Sir Augustus? What does he say? I know you are in his employ."

The turnkey produced a knife in his free hand. He must have concealed it in his sleeve. "Sir Augustus says not being a murderer doesn't mean you're going to leave Newgate alive."

Charles took a step back, reaching for the bucket. Shock kept him clearheaded, instead of terrified. He thought hard. He hadn't heard Curdle close the door after it had opened. If he could escape into the passage there might be others around, especially at this time of night with a meal coming.

Just as his fingers grasped the metal handle of the bucket, Bob Sawyer rushed out from the fireplace and barreled straight at Curdle. His head hit the guard right in the belly. Curdle made an "oomph" and stepped backward. Bob rammed him again.

Charles grabbed the fire bucket with his other hand and ran at Curdle from the side. He raised the bucket over his head and hit Curdle's neck and head.

Curdle bent over. The knife clattered onto the deal table in front of the fireplace.

"Come," Charles called to Bob.

"Hold on."

Charles heard a rattle as Bob grabbed for something, then they ran out of the room while Curdle moaned somewhere behind them.

In the passage, Charles slammed the ward door shut. "Maybe I can hold him in long enough for you to bring help," he panted.

Bob laughed, the sound goblinlike in the darkness, and rattled something. "I have his keys."

Charles couldn't see a thing, but he heard the metal turn the lock. "That was quick thinking."

"We're going to be in a lot of trouble," Bob said. "Too bad that you nearly got out of here."

"What do you mean?" Charles asked.

"You may be free of one murder charge, but if Curdle dies you'll spend your life here just the same," Bob said.

"Run for the yard," Charles urged. "Curdle probably didn't see you. I'll say it was all me. I have powerful friends."

Bob patted his arm. "God bless you, Charles Dickens. But too many people know I was with you."

"I'll say I attacked him alone," Charles wheezed. "You saved my life."

Voices floated down the passage. Light shone on the bricks as men with lanterns approached. Bob left the key ring still hanging in the wardroom lock and pulled Charles against the wall.

"What are you doing out here?" demanded a well-dressed and well-fed man with an idiosyncratic receding hairline.

Charles recognized the prison's governor from his painting on the office wall. John Keefe was with him, along with another turnkey.

Bob straightened to his full diminutive height. "That Curdle, sir. He tried to kill Charles Dickens."

Charles opened his mouth but found a throat burned with coal dust. He coughed heavily, then said, "Sir Augustus Smirke paid him to do it, sir."

"Did you kill him?" Keefe asked, not without sympathy.

"I don't know, sir," Charles admitted. "Hit him with everything I had and then we ran for the door."

"Exactly what happened?" the governor asked suspiciously.

"He had a knife," Charles said. "It landed on the table. If he's unconscious, you'll still find it there. Otherwise, search him."

The governor nodded at Keefe. "You take the prisoners. You

others, see to Curdle. I've had enough with Sir Augustus meddling in Newgate affairs."

Keefe gestured to the prisoners. Charles sighed and followed him, accompanied by Bob. "Solitary?"

"We'll find you a place while everything is sorted out."

Instead of a solitary cell, Keefe locked them into some sort of meeting room. He did light a fire before he left, saying he needed to receive further orders.

The ward's fireplace had been much larger than this one, but the room itself was sufficiently smaller to make it acceptable. Comfortless though, with nothing on the walls and not a speck of warming upholstery anywhere.

Bob sat in one of the six chairs arrayed around a heavy oak table. "I think we were having mutton stew tonight."

It had been mutton stew every night Charles had been here. "I am sorry for your stomach," he returned.

"It's not the first meal I'fe had to miss," Bob said reflectively. "But the first I'fe been denied here in prison. Best eats I efer had."

Charles sighed and stared at the fire. He felt too full of nervous energy to sit. How did anyone think a man like Bob would stop committing crimes when prison life was superior to the life he had in the streets?

He reached into his innermost pocket, debating with himself, then closed his fingers around his entire fortune. "Take this," he said, setting every coin in his possession on the table in front of Bob.

The light of the flames danced off the small man's face as he looked at the shillings and smaller coins in surprise.

"Why?"

"You can buy a real meal once we're done here," Charles said. "Or whatever you need."

"You can't think they'll release you tonight, after what's happened," Bob said.

"Whatever my fate is," Charles said, "I think the governor

understands what happened. Our incident ought to be swept under the rug. I can go without my next meal. I'll dine on my future prospects."

Bob nodded and with a wave of his hand, the coins vanished under one of his wrappings. "Fery kind of you, Dickens. Remember me when you are outside again."

Charles took the chair next to him. "I do not think you are so badly off here," he reflected. "A habitual sinner with a nightly bowl of mutton stew."

"Don't worry about me," Bob said. "A man like me can do business just as well on the inside as the outside. Besides, there's allus a chance I'll go free after my trial."

"For your sake," Charles said, holding out his hand, "I hope you get one of the soft judges, but our system seems overly harsh on property offenses while occasionally being most lenient on offenses to people, which I cannot accept."

"It was better in the old days. Easier to work around a constable than one of these new police."

Charles saw a flash of teeth as Bob grinned just as the door opened.

"You're wanted, Dickens," Keefe announced. "You'll have to give a deposition on what happened."

"Yes, sir." Charles inclined his head to Bob before Keefe set manacles around his wrists and led him away.

After the door was shut and locked behind them, Charles said, "I might be a corpse instead of a man if Bob Sawyer hadn't been so brave."

"He would have been a corpse, too, Dickens. Curdle wouldn't have left him alive."

"I'd like to offer to be a character witness at his trial. Such things shouldn't matter, but they do, if the right judge is presiding," Charles said. "Sawyer isn't going to hurt anyone if he's set free. He's a middleman, a receiver. Only exists because of the sellers and buyers."

"You can't be suggesting we simply return him to his life of crime," Keefe said acerbically.

"He's had no education for anything better. A mind like his might have been turned to other things if his father had educated him for a better trade." Charles sighed, feeling the aches and pains of the scrubbing and fighting for his life descending on his muscles.

"I still hope a man can find religion and turn his mind to higher pursuits. It's often so loud in here though, that a man can't hear himself think. Well," Keefe said, opening a door, "here you go, Dickens. These men won't be my problem for much longer."

Inside the room, Charles found the prison governor assembled with Sir Silas Laurie and a number of lawyers, as well as a couple of uniformed policemen.

Sir Silas nodded. "Hullo, Mr. Dickens. We're going to take your deposition now. I'll reopen my inquest tomorrow with the testimony from Mr. Pickwick's murderess, and you should be walking out of Newgate sometime tomorrow afternoon. I will also have the inquest regarding the songwriter Peter Snodgrass's death reopened as well, in light of the facts."

"I'm sure his family will want to know the truth." Charles smiled down at his manacles almost fondly. Soon they would be gone, and he would happily say "never again" to them.

Charles still wore his filthy, coal-stained clothes as two turnkeys escorted him to the governor's house the next afternoon. He'd spent the night locked in a solitary room and hadn't slept a wink, for fear that Sir Augustus still had some sway over the proceedings.

"I don't think you have anything to worry about," Keefe said reassuringly. "Tracy Yupman was charged with kidnapping in front of a magistrate this morning. Our friend Sir Augustus will be too busy dealing with his nephew's disgrace to worry about you. The girl who was kidnapped was charged with manslaughter, but it is assumed she will go free someday due to being incapacitated at the time."

"Poor girl. I will follow her case with interest," Charles murmured, "and offer her what assistance I can. Of course, no crime will attach to Sir Augustus."

"It rarely does, to men of that rank," Keefe agreed, his mouth turned down.

Charles thought about Evelina Jaggers, and what part she had played in his being framed for murder, but then, before he could worry at length about what she intended for his future, the turnkey was opening the office door, and Kate's sweet face appeared, and Mary's, flanked by their father, along with William Aga.

Kate squeaked a happy cry and rushed toward him. Charles wanted to pull her into his arms, but it wouldn't be seemly. Instead, when she reached her hand out to his, he clasped it warmly.

"Marry me, Kate," he exclaimed. "Today I am a free man!"

She smiled weakly and said, "I hope you stay free, my darling."

"What do you mean?" His elation diminished at her tone.

She handed him a letter with her free hand. A red seal was affixed, the raised emblem like a starfish.

"What is this?" Charles asked, noticing his friends had crowded around, as if to protect him from the outside world.

"It was in our post this morning," she said tremulously. He could imagine how her heart fluttered at some terrible news, from her voice alone. "It's like all the other letters I received from that dreadful dirty man, the relation of Sir Augustus."

"You didn't break the seal," he observed.

"It's addressed to you," Mr. Hogarth said.

"It was the only thing that kept me going this morning," Kate confessed. "That it wasn't addressed to me with some wild claim of hurting you last night."

"I was locked in an office, already out of the wards," Charles said absently. He turned the folded and sealed paper over in his hands, then pulled it apart. "I'll read it aloud. It says, 'Mr. Dickens. We thought to play a jape on you, and torment you in the plaster maze. Instead a girl did a dreadful thing, in a terrible daze. You became the perfect foil, for our little game. To make you pay for the death of Pickwick, for this we gave you fame. The timing was so perfect, I'm sure you do agree, to repay you for past kindnesses, this you abundantly see. A friend.'"

"Who is the rhymer?" William asked.

Charles licked his wind-cracked lips. "Evelina Jaggers, I expect. She came to see me, and still wants me punished for my part in her tumultuous past."

"You have a network of enemies now, Charles." Kate frowned. "We must be careful."

"I don't think I'll be joining the Lightning Club and its powerful members, if it even survives this scandal, for protection. But other great friends will come along in time." He squeezed her hand. While he knew she'd made her point well, they had too many things to look forward to, and he had no intention of settling down into a quiet retirement at twenty-three. "I am happy for our steady and reciprocal attachment," he declared. "Which nothing but death will sever. Look forward, my darling Kate. We have such great larks ahead of us."

Acknowledgments

I want to thank you, dear reader, for picking up this fourth book in the A Dickens of a Crime series. If you haven't read the first book, *A Tale of Two Murders*, the second, *Grave Expectations*, or the third, *A Christmas Carol Murder*, yet, I hope you take the opportunity to enjoy more Dickensian adventures through 1830s London. I am so grateful for the book reviews you wrote, and please keep them coming.

Thank you to my beta readers Judy DiCanio, Dianne Freeman, Cheryl Schy, and Mary Keliikoa on this project. I also thank my writing group for their support, Delle Jacobs, Marilyn Hull, Peggy Laurance, and Melania Tolan. As always I appreciate the editorial support of Elizabeth Flynn. Also, thank you so much to my agent, Laurie McLean, at Fuse Literary, my editor, Elizabeth May, my copyeditor on this book, Pearl Saban, and my publicist, Larissa Ackerman, for your work on the series, along with many unsung heroes at Kensington.

If this isn't your first book in the series, you may note that I have included the point of view of Catherine "Kate" Hogarth for the first time. I thought it would be fun to see what she might be thinking in a disaster of this nature. With her fiancé locked up in prison for much of the book, it gave her a chance to shine as a sleuth. Her family, unlike the Dickens clan, was a literary one, and I enjoyed visiting some of the female book world figures of the time. This is the point in the series where I have left Dickens's real life quite far behind, for a couple of weeks, at least. I was curious to see what would happen if I put him in prison, given his opinions about crime and punishment, and see how the situation played out. My plot is entirely fictitious as is most everyone in the book.

I was inspired by that rambling masterpiece, *The Posthumous Papers of the Pickwick Club*, when planning this novel. The story of how the book came to be is a fascinating one, and has much to do with its structure, or lack thereof. I encourage you to read it if you never have. *Pickwick* is my favorite Dickens book. I hope I did my inspiration justice. One excellent way to tackle it is to listen to the audio version performed by Gerald Dickens, the author's great-great-grandson. It's such a wonderful version and will hopefully make you love the book as much as I do.

BOOK CLUB READING GUIDE for

The Pickwick Murders

1. Charles Dickens's novel *The Posthumous Papers of the Pickwick Club* inspired aspects of this novel. What themes did you recognize? Does reading this book make you want to read or reread Dickens's work?
2. How do you like to read classic fiction? In print, audio, ebook—or do you just watch the movie or miniseries? How does the medium affect the work?
3. We spent a lot of time in Newgate Prison in this book. The author stayed close to Dickens's own description of the prison from his 1835 visit there. What surprised you? Did it make you want to learn more? What has changed in prison culture in the many years since?
4. Did you enjoy the glimpses of historical figures? Had you ever heard of Joanna Baillie and Lucy Aikin before?
5. Lord Byron and his daughter, Augusta Ada King, Countess of Lovelace, are popular figures in Western culture even today. Have you ever thought about Lady Byron? Did it surprise you to know she became an education reformer? You can learn more about her and her daughter in both fiction and nonfiction titles.
6. Did you like seeing Kate's point of view in the book, or were you jarred to realize that the book wasn't from Charles Dickens's point of view only?
7. The author veered farther than usual from the true experiences of Charles Dickens's life in this book. Did you like how this made him a stakeholder in the murder, or did the author go too far afield of reality?
8. What do you think about Kate's relationship with her parents in this book?
9. What do you think about Julie Aga's experiences in this

book? What are your thoughts about the way actresses have broken or stood beyond the culturally appropriate behaviors of their times? For example, when thinking of Julie, the author's thoughts venture to the seventeenth-century actress Margaret Hughes (her supposed ancestress), considered the first professional public actress in London.

10. Dickens's novel *The Posthumous Papers of the Pickwick Club* includes a number of short stories within the text. To honor that tradition, the author included a couple of tales in this book as well. Did they add or detract from the main novel for you? Did the stories enhance the overall themes for you?